*In Flanders fields the poppies blow
Between the crosses, row on row,
That mark our place; and in the sky
The larks, still bravely singing, fly
Scarce heard amid the guns below.*

*We are the Dead. Short days ago
We lived, felt dawn, saw sunset glow,
Loved and were loved, and now we lie,
In Flanders fields.*

*Take up our quarrel with the foe:
To you from failing hands we throw
The torch; be yours to hold it high.
If ye break faith with us who die
We shall not sleep, though poppies grow
In Flanders fields.*

'In Flanders Fields'
John McCrae, 1915

Those who cannot remember the past are condemned to repeat it.

George Santayana

The Poppy Girls

The Poppy Girls

KIRSTY DOUGAL

PENGUIN BOOKS

PENGUIN BOOKS

UK | USA | Canada | Ireland | Australia
India | New Zealand | South Africa

Penguin Books, Penguin Random House UK,
One Embassy Gardens, 8 Viaduct Gardens, London SW11 7BW

penguin.co.uk
global.penguinrandomhouse.com

First published 2025
001
Copyright © Kirsten Hesketh, 2025

Set in 12.5/14.75pt Garamond MT
Typeset by Falcon Oast Graphic Art Ltd
Printed and bound in Great Britain by Clays Ltd, Elcograf S.p.A.

The authorized representative in the EEA is Penguin Random House Ireland,
Morrison Chambers, 32 Nassau Street, Dublin D02 YH68

A CIP catalogue record for this book is available from the British Library

ISBN: 978-1-405-95870-7

*In memory of Lucy Reddings, Gwendoline Reddings,
Pamela Reddings, John Reddings, Ethel Lomas, Ivy Lomas,
Alice Morey and Edith Stuckey.
All killed when a German bomb hit the Poppy Factory
air raid shelter in November 1940.*

Dear Reader,

Thank you for choosing to read *The Poppy Girls*. I've loved researching and writing this book and I'm so excited to share the adventures of Carrie, Sarah and Mabel with you all.

Whilst the main characters in this story are fictional, the Poppy Factory in Richmond upon Thames is not only real but is still operational today. The factory was set up by Major George Howson in the 1920s to provide employment opportunities for disabled war veterans and, whilst individual poppies are now manufactured elsewhere, the factory still handmakes Royal and regimental wreaths and is well worth a visit. Likewise, my descriptions of the Poppy Factory estate are based on fact, although I have taken a little liberty with the layout. The flats specially constructed for the Poppy Factory employees and their families – complete with their unusual washing lines – and the social club housed in Cardigan House all very much existed. There really was a Brownie Pack and a rowing race between employees who had one arm and those who had one leg. Whilst Cardigan House and some of the flats have since been demolished, much of the estate is still as it was. Even the old pet cemetery is still in situ although not quite where I have described it! Very sadly, the air raid on 29th

November 1940 is also based on truth. The Poppy Factory air raid shelter was struck by a German bomb, resulting in the deaths of the eight Poppy Factory women and children to whom this book is dedicated. So many bombs had fallen across Richmond that night that no external help arrived, and the residents of the Poppy Factory really were left to dig out their friends and neighbours themselves – a reminder of the true cost of war, with echoes that ring down to today.

On a somewhat lighter note, part of the Poppy Factory really was requisitioned during World War Two by the Ministry of Aircraft Production to assemble radios, although, in reality, this did not happen until 1942. There is no definitive information on whether women were or were not employed in this part of the factory – and Little Poppies is totally fictitious. However, as women generally formed such a vital part of the workforce during the war, it seems reasonable to suppose they played an active role.

The beautiful Richmond upon Thames provides the backdrop to this story and, whilst many of the settings are broadly accurate, I did take the liberty of inventing both St Mark's and St Andrew's Avenues to suit the story. The ARP – Air Raid Precautions – was active throughout Richmond – although a Packard ambulance might have been more common after the US entered the war.

I thoroughly enjoyed researching and writing this story, and I really hope that you will enjoy reading about the Poppy Girls.

With love,
Kirsty xxx

Chapter One

'Carolyn Harper?'

Carrie propped herself up on her elbows and squinted towards the voice. The girl was in shadow, blocking out the sun, and Carrie couldn't immediately work out who it was.

'Yes?' she replied, lazily.

It had been nice lying there, heavy-limbed, almost, but not quite, asleep. The thump of leather on willow, the drone of bees, the faraway rumble of traffic – one could almost forget that, after months of quiet in the 'Phoney War', the British Expeditionary Force had been forced to retreat across Europe and, even now, was being rescued by a flotilla of small ships from the coast at Dunkirk. Carrie should have been revising for her Highers, of course, but the beastly Sarah Turner had deliberately aimed a ball at her on the tennis courts that morning. She now had a bruise the size of her fist forming on her upper arm and she hadn't been able to concentrate on anything.

'Yes?' she repeated, grumpy now.

Why *was* she being so rudely interrupted?

It was the last period of the school day and her only free period. She wanted to savour every second.

'Miss Bateman wants to see us now,' said the voice.

Carrie struggled to a sitting position and brushed some

grass from her school skirt. The voice belonged to the new girl in their year; the pint-sized one who'd arrived out of the blue from the East End of London a couple of months before with her thick cockney accent, her cloud of curly dark hair and her face full of freckles. Carrie knew that the newcomer was jolly good at maths – her mental arithmetic leaving even Carrie's in the shade – and that she was lousy at both cricket and tennis, claiming never to have played either before. But Carrie couldn't actually remember her name.

Something beginning with an M . . .

Mary?

Maude?

'Miss Bateman . . . us . . . now?' she echoed, staggering to her feet.

The headmistress had announced at assembly that she was planning to talk to the Higher School Certificate candidates in small groups before their exams started the following week. She had added something about giving them individual advice for the future. Carrie had just assumed that the meetings would be during break or at lunchtime and that she would be called in with the hand- ful of other girls who were planning to take up places at prestigious universities that autumn. Girls she had some- thing in common with, like her best friend Daisy, who, until a couple of minutes ago, had been half-asleep next to her on the school field and who was now looking equally baffled at the unexpected turn of events. Why on earth was Carrie being called in with Miriam or May or whatever her name was?

Still, it wouldn't do to keep the head waiting.

Carrie ran her fingers through her thick honey-blonde hair – always liable to tangle – and waggled her fingers goodbye at Daisy. Then she followed Maria or Maggie across the grass and through the open door into the school hall. The temperature dropped sharply as the heady scent of roses and crisp aroma of recently mown grass gave way to chalk, ink and smelly old plimsolls.

Carrie hurried to catch up with Martha or Muriel – goodness, there were a lot of names beginning with M! – as they crossed the dusty hall. It wasn't difficult because Carrie was a good six inches taller and her stride, naturally, longer. The two girls turned to each other . . .

'I wonder why we've . . . ?' they started simultaneously – and then both burst into self-conscious laughter.

'Jinx,' said Carrie, automatically. 'You aren't going to university, are you?' she added. The new girl hadn't been at any of the lunchtime meetings, but that didn't necessarily mean anything.

'No,' the girl confirmed. 'And you ain't recently been evacuated from Bow?' she added.

'No, although I lived nearby until I was four.'

Carrie still retained the last vestiges of an East End accent to prove it, much to Pa's disgust.

'I'd suggest alphabetical order,' said the new girl. 'Green,' she pointed at herself, 'and Harper,' she pointed at Carrie. 'Only, there's a third girl coming and she wrecks me theory.'

'Who's that?' asked Carrie, as they headed down the corridor towards the – usually out of bounds – teachers' offices.

'Sarah Turner. Someone else went to fetch her from the cricket field. Look, there she is now.'

Sure enough, Sarah was already standing outside Miss Bateman's office with muddy knees, socks round her ankles and chestnut hair escaping a ponytail tied for practicality rather than style. She was chatting animatedly to her best friend Joanne – Sarah was *never* on her own – and looked equally surprised to see Carrie and Myrtle (or Minnie) approaching.

Why on earth *were* the three being called in together?

Sarah gave Carrie an insouciant smile, and Carrie ignored her – and her suddenly throbbing arm – with as much dignity as she could muster. The two knew each other well enough – indeed, they had lived in adjacent blocks of flats for years – but they were hardly what you would call friends. Sarah was popular and sporty, always in the thick of the gangs and the feuds and the ha-ha jokes. Carrie, by contrast, was quieter and more self-contained – some might even have said a little aloof. Carrie knew Sarah thought her a boring old stick-in-the-mud and pathetic at games to boot and Carrie, for her turn, thought Sarah thoughtless, slapdash and not very kind. It went further than that, however; Sarah was the hockey teacher's pet and Miss Virginia *always* let Sarah be one of the girls to pick teams, and Sarah *always* picked Carrie last. To be fair, Carrie knew that she was one of the worst at games – all gangly limbs and a fear of getting bashed – but still. She wasn't the very worst, and, either way, it wouldn't have hurt for Sarah to have rung the changes just occasionally. And, as for deliberately aiming a ball at her . . .

Joanne melted away and the three girls stood in silence, trying to avoid eye contact. Sarah scuffed her plimsolls on the light grey linoleum, not registering – or caring – that she was leaving black scuff marks. The new girl stared out of the window, impassively, not giving anything away. And, for her own part, Carrie just knew that her cheeks had flushed bright pink, the colour even now spreading down to her décolleté.

Then the door to Miss Bateman's office swung open, and there was the head herself, wreathed in smiles and rubbing her hands together briskly.

'Ah,' she said, holding the door open for them. 'The Poppy Girls.'

The Poppy Girls?

Carrie liked Miss Bateman. She was enthusiastic and brimming with energy, everything Ma was not, but she really seemed to have lost her marbles this time.

On the one hand, it was now abundantly clear why Miss Bateman had called the three of them in together. She had latched onto the fact that they all lived in the workers' flats attached to the Poppy Factory just down from Richmond Bridge; 'the estate', as it was rather grandly called by its residents.

The Poppy Factory had been set up in London in 1922, the year Carrie had been born, to create remembrance poppies and wreaths for the Royal Family and the Royal British Legion's Annual Poppy Appeal. The poppies and wreaths were all made by disabled veterans from the Great War for whom respectable employment opportunities were still few and far between. In 1926, the factory had outgrown its premises and had moved to Richmond upon Thames, and many of the workers and their families were now housed in the specially built blocks of flats that flanked it. Carrie and her parents lived on the top floor of one of the blocks – in a three-bedroomed apartment they laughingly referred to as 'the penthouse'. Sarah lived with her parents and umpteen younger brothers – Carrie wasn't sure how many siblings she actually had – in one of the flats opposite. And, as for the other girl . . . well, Carrie had no idea. Now she came to think about it, she had vaguely seen her walking up and down Richmond Hill over the past couple of weeks, but then so did lots of pupils at the Richmond County School for Girls. Carrie had had no idea that she also had a father who'd been wounded in the Great War and that she also lived on the estate.

It didn't matter, anyway.

Whatever Miss Bateman might say, she didn't like Sarah and she didn't even know the girl from London.

There might only be three girls their age living on the Poppy Factory estate, but that was certainly no reason to call them the Poppy Girls.

Miss Bateman gestured for the girls to sit down and they duly perched on the three wooden chairs arranged on one side of the desk. The head settled into her considerably more comfortable seat, folded her hands into her lap, and regarded them shrewdly one by one. The smiles and bon-homie had gone and there was silence. All Carrie could hear was the raucous caw of seagulls heading to the river, and a car backfiring on the London Road.

Then Miss Bateman swung ninety degrees in her seat so she could look out of the open window behind her desk. 'All of you sitting your Highers next week are leaving this school and starting your adult lives in the shadow of war; a war that twenty years ago we fervently hoped – indeed,

6

were repeatedly told – could never happen again. People's lives are being turned upside down; almost a hundred pupils enrolled at this school in September have already left Richmond for safer pastures . . .'

Carrie's attention threatened to drift away.

She had heard all this hundreds of times before. Both at home and at school, everything always came back to the war.

'That it *has* happened is, of course, a tragedy for the whole of Europe,' Miss Bateman continued. 'And I'm afraid it's only going to get worse. Even as we speak, our troops are being evacuated from Dunkirk. You will hear a lot about resilience, unity, the Dunkirk spirit – Anthony Eden spoke about it on the wireless a couple of days ago – but, mark my words, this is a major retreat. There's every chance Hitler will set his sights on Britain. Invasion is a real possibility.'

Carrie shifted in her seat.

Goodness, this was gloomy.

'It's particularly poignant for the three of you, of course,' Miss Bateman was saying. 'You've grown up surrounded by the legacy of the Great War; you've seen the terrible price your fathers have had to pay for serving King and Country. You've witnessed firsthand the appalling things war can ask of our young people, and the price that some survivors must go on paying. And, now you're leaving school, I wonder how you will face your own war, and the role you see yourselves playing. You've been in a unique position through living on the estate, my dears, and that's why I called you in together. I'm fascinated to know how the Poppy Girls will face the future.'

The silence stretched until it threatened to become awkward.

Carrie stared down at her ink-stained fingers.

Did she have a unique perspective on the war? Miss Bateman seemed to think she should, but Carrie didn't agree. She was just a seventeen-year-old girl – not even eighteen for another month – and her parents were just . . . her parents. She ventured a look at the others; Sarah and the London girl were both busy with their socks and their ponytails, clearly as embarrassed as she was.

'So, remind me,' Miss Bateman said brightly, 'what are you each planning to do next?'

There was another silence.

'Let's start with you, Carrie,' said Miss Bateman. 'Fabulous win in the History Cup, by the way. First in a long time.'

Carrie beamed. 'Thank you, Miss,' she said.

The Framlingham History Cup was hotly contested by the local schools every year and this year Carrie had been the Richmond County School captain, responsible both for choosing the team and for steering it through the competition.

'And you're still planning to go to university?' asked Miss Bateman.

'Ra*ther*,' said Carrie enthusiastically. 'Fingers crossed the war doesn't get in the way of *that*.'

University was, Carrie knew, when life would really begin. Richmond was all well and good – it was a pretty enough little town, but it was small and staid and familiarity could breed contempt. Carrie couldn't wait to escape and to reinvent herself. She wanted to meet new people.

To meet *men*.

'And it's London, isn't it?'

'It is,' said Carrie, proudly. 'Provided my Highers go to plan, I've been accepted to study history at Birkbeck.'

And her Highers *would* go to plan; there was no doubt about that. War or no war, Carrie had studied hard all year and she was on top of her revision. University was well within her grasp. She glanced around the room, almost expecting a little round of applause. No one in her family had been to university and it *was* a huge achievement.

But Sarah and the other girl didn't look in the faintest bit impressed.

'Birkbeck,' repeated Miss Bateman matter-of-factly. 'It's about the only university left *in* London, isn't it?'

Carrie nodded.

She *had* intended to study at the more prestigious University College, but that had relocated to Aberystwyth shortly after war had been declared. Most of the other London universities had promptly followed suit – LSE had gone to Cambridge, Imperial to Reading and King's to Bristol. To be honest, Carrie wouldn't have minded going to any of them, but Pa had put his foot down. Staying in Richmond – a neutral territory – was one thing, but it wouldn't look good for a Harper to be escaping to safer pastures, now, would it? Besides, Pa had been adamant that Carrie came home each evening. That stipulation was partly to do with the war, of course, because London proper was deemed more dangerous than sleepy Richmond. But Pa said it was mainly because no matter what dangerous ideas were pumped into her head during lectures, and regardless of what unsuitable people she might choose to fraternise with in her free time, he would know she was safely in her own bed every night.

Carrie had gone along with it all fairly happily. Being under twenty-one, she didn't have much choice. She might hate her father at the moment – and for very good reason – but she had to pick her battles.

'Good, good.' Miss Bateman gave her a perfunctory smile and turned to Sarah.

'And how about our cricketing star?' she asked.

Sarah smiled, none too modestly. '*My* plans have changed, Miss,' she said. 'I *was* going to do teacher training, but I've decided to train to be a physiotherapist instead because there are going to be so many soldiers needing rehabilitation.'

'Interesting,' said Miss Bateman, with a warm smile.

'*And* I want to do my bit for the war effort,' continued Sarah. 'My father was awarded the Distinguished Service Order in the Great War and, whilst I won't match that, of course, I can't just sit by and do nothing. I intend to get work in a factory or suchlike over the summer.'

Sarah smiled sweetly at Carrie, who glanced away.

Embarrassed.

Outmanoeuvred.

How proud she'd been to announce her university plans just seconds earlier – and how unpatriotic and naïve she now felt.

Gah, how she disliked Sarah!

'We might not be the most industrial of areas, but there's still plenty of war work around,' said Miss Bateman. 'Chrysler Motors just down the road in Kew have switched to military production for the duration; there's the Hawker Aircraft factory in Ham; and, of course, there's the

Richmond ARP where I volunteer. Everyone's desperate for manpower, or should I say *woman*-power – with so many men in uniform or moving away. You certainly won't find yourself short of opportunities.'

Carrie was still smarting. 'But should we do war work?' she burst out, without really thinking it through. 'I mean, surely things aren't as simple as all that. War's a terrible, terrible thing – you only have to look at what the last one did to our fathers. Aren't we better off staying out of this one? Besides, just look at what happened the last time women took over men's jobs. My mother says that as soon as the men came back from war, the women went back to keeping house. Aren't we better off getting qualifications that *can't* be taken away?'

There!

Let Sarah put *that* in her pipe and smoke it.

There was a charged silence and Carrie wondered if she had won.

But then Sarah gave her a patronising smile.

'I don't see it like that at all,' she said. 'After all, if we don't all pull together now, the universities might soon be teaching in German.'

'Too true,' muttered Miss Bateman.

Carrie sank back in her chair and rubbed her arm.

She might have lost the battle, but she hadn't lost the war . . . and she wouldn't change her mind.

She thought of the old Santayana quote, 'Those who cannot remember the past are condemned to repeat it.' It had stayed in Carrie's mind ever since she'd first heard it in a history lesson several years ago and after reading Santayana's works under the bedsheets at night, she'd vowed then and there to study history at university. After that, she'd use what she learnt to be a diplomat or a journalist or a teacher and help to make the world a better place. After all, if more people had taken Santayana's advice, maybe this war wouldn't have started at all. And surely war was never a good idea; win or lose, it was the ordinary people who suffered – paying with their lives or, like Pa, with their terrible injuries . . .

Meanwhile, Miss Bateman had turned to the new girl.

'And how about you, Mabel?' she asked.

Mabel.

Of course.

Mabel smiled politely. 'To be honest, I can see both their points of view, Miss,' she said. 'As for myself, I ain't really got any plans as of yet. What with me move out here and getting used to a new school, I'm just getting me feet under the table, so to speak. And, of course, me Ma and Pa have taken over running the Remembrance Club . . .'

'Remind me what that is?' interjected Miss Bateman.

'Sorry, Miss,' said Mabel. 'It's the Poppy Factory's social club – and there's ever such a lot to do now so many of the casual staff have moved away. Me folks will need help lugging crates and pulling pints. Once me time is me own again, I'll think about what comes next.'

Carrie couldn't help warming to Mabel.

She seemed so straightforward; not one to boast or score points or bring anyone else down. She just said it how it was. And fancy her family now running the Remembrance Club – the very heart of the Poppy Factory estate!

She tuned back into the conversation. Miss Bateman was winding things up with some well-worn phrases about leaving school and going out into the world . . . and then the bell rang to signal the end of the school day. The whole thing had seemed a little pointless as far as Carrie was concerned and she stood up with fairly indecent haste.

'Will you be walking home together?' asked Miss Bateman, as they all shook hands.

Despite it all, Carrie stifled a grin.

Honestly, you'd have thought Miss Bateman could have guessed *that* question would go down like a lead balloon.

The three girls glanced at each other, embarrassed all over again by the forced association. Then, one by one, they shook their heads.

'I've got cricket,' said Sarah, with evident relief at having such a cut-glass excuse. 'The last practice before the big match.'

'Of course,' said Miss Bateman, heartily. 'Tiffin will be hard to beat but never say never.'

'I'm meeting me friend Ruby,' said Mabel. 'She's moved out from The Big Smoke as well and she ain't allowed back to her boarding house until after five, so we'll wander around the shops together.'

Carrie didn't say anything.

She would be walking home alone – as she usually did – with a stop-off at Woollies to buy Ma some cotton.

Miss Bateman smiled from one to the other.

'Well, good luck in the examinations, girls, and good luck in the future, whatever that might hold. I shall keep a keen eye out for whatever the Poppy Girls get up to next.'

The girls glanced at each other as they went their separate ways.

The Poppy Girls indeed!

Chapter Two

Tuesday 4 June 1940

Carrie left school and started trudging home along Parkshot.

Signs that the country was at war had been everywhere in Richmond for almost a year, but Carrie was more aware of them than ever after Miss Bateman's comments about an imminent German invasion.

The public baths next to the school had been sandbagged and Carrie knew – because Pa had told her – that the building had been gas-proofed and designated a major decontamination centre in the event of a chemical attack. Men would be treated in the first-class dressing cubicles and clubroom, whilst women would be restricted to the second-class side of the baths. And, if the worst came to the worst, another part of the building had been turned into a mortuary . . .

So that was something to look forward to, then!

Still deep in thought, Carrie cut through to the main street where the queues of women in front of the food shops and the many men in military uniform were other reminders of the conflict. The meeting had unsettled her. There was the war stuff, of course, but there was more to it than that. It *would* sometimes have been nice to have had company on her daily walk to and from school; to have had a giggle and a chance to put the world to rights. It wasn't as if she didn't have pals, of course – she had Daisy and one or two others, although she didn't see them outside school very often. In an ideal world, it would have been nice to have been friends with the other girls her age on the estate. After leaving Miss Bateman's office, they might have clapped each other on the back and then, linking arms, turned to face the future, eyes shining with loyalty and resolve . . .

Carrie stopped in her tracks and gave a little snort of laughter.

That was the sort of thing that happened in the flicks – not in real life.

Anyway, it was too late now. They were all about to leave school and all she could do was make sure that the next phase of her life turned out exactly as she had planned.

Carrie duly popped into Woollies, picking up the last reel of Coats & Clark's navy-blue cotton for Ma. Ma believed it was only a matter of time until fabric and cotton were rationed along with bacon, butter and sugar, which had been restricted since the beginning of the year. Carrie didn't much care about that, but it would be a disaster if chocolate bars went the same way. It was already bad enough that the prices were sky-high and the choice was so restricted – imagine if she couldn't buy them at all! Maybe she should buy a bar of Fry's Chocolate Creme just in case it was her last chance . . .

Carrie headed on down George Street, nibbling her treat as slowly as she could, and mourning the fact that it definitely wasn't as creamy and delectable as it used to be. She decided to walk the long way home – up Richmond Hill rather than down the Petersham Road – so that she would have finished it by the time she got home and Ma wouldn't be able to have a dig. Really, the only mystery would be the nature of her mother's complaint. Would it be the wasted money or the lack of patriotism? The latter made no sense; that particular bar of Fry's Chocolate Creme was already in Woolworths, so the poor soldiers had already missed out. Then again, it could be the spoilt appetite, or the mucky fingers . . . the possibilities were endless. Far better that there was simply no evidence of the 'crime.'

Carrie savoured each mouthful as she trudged up the hill. Chocolate may be a little less unctuous nowadays, but it was still infinitely tastier than the carrot fudge and mock bananas made out of boiled parsnips Ma had recently taken to rustling up. Carrie wasn't sure whether these new culinary adventures were borne out of necessity or whether they were primarily to set a good example to the other housewives on the estate. Either way, they had both been something of a . . . challenge.

Carrie kept walking, further than she needed to, past the grand Georgian houses and hotels and up towards Richmond Park. Then, worn out, she slumped against the metal railings towards the top of the hill. Goodness, it was hot. Her plait was sticking to the back of her neck, her school blouse was glued to her back and, despite her best efforts, she had melted chocolate all over her hands. She licked her fingers as she admired the view. It was dominated by the deep-blue curve of the Thames as it flowed between Twickenham and Richmond, flanked by fields and meadows and the occasional, almost artistically arranged, copse of trees. Every shade of green was in evidence, from the darkest olive to the brightest emerald to the palest, most delicate pistachio. Pa was fond of telling her it was the only vista in England protected by an Act of Parliament and that the little island covered in trees plump in the middle of the river was also protected in perpetuity against development. The view had been immortalised in paintings by everyone from Constable to Turner – surely even Adolf Hitler wouldn't have the audacity to bomb it.

Fingers licked clean, Carrie debated whether to carry on up the hill and through the wrought-iron gates into Richmond Park. It was her own special place and, despite being huge, Carrie felt she knew every square inch of it. There was nobody to demand anything of her, no rules to follow – nothing but endless grass and scattered trees and herds of deer grazing happily in the shadows or running skittishly across the lawns. Like everything else, it was changing, of course – there were anti-aircraft and searchlight batteries over by Sheen Gate, something to do with explosives over by the Isabella Plantation and some very strange chicken wire structures right in the middle – but it was still lovely, and still somehow hers.

In the end, Carrie decided there was no time to go up to the park that afternoon because Ma would be waiting for the navy-blue cotton. With a sigh, she tore her gaze from the view and started retracing her steps back down the hill before peeling off left into the Poppy Factory estate.

It wasn't really an estate, of course.

At least, not in the sense that a stately home with grand buildings, manicured lawns and a fleet of servants could be called an estate.

The Poppy Factory 'estate' was really just a hotchpotch of buildings – the factory, the workers' flats and the social club – crammed onto a steeply sloping, triangular piece of land wedged between Richmond Hill and the Petersham Road. Firstly, Carrie skirted the social club, commonly known as the Remembrance Club, where Mabel's parents now worked. It was situated in Cardigan House – a sprawling, redbrick mansion once the home of both Lord Cardigan and King William IV. It had since seen better days – ivy sprawled unchecked up the walls and there was peeling paint on the window frames – but the three hundred or so residents of the estate certainly made good use of its bar and games rooms – to say nothing of the new air raid shelter in the cellar – and it was always a hive of activity. Carrie couldn't help peering through the windows in the hope of seeing Mabel as she walked past – she had warmed to the girl that afternoon – but there was no sign of her.

Glancing at her wristwatch and realising just how long she had dallied, Carrie broke into a run, schoolbag bumping uncomfortably against one hip, gas mask against the other. She ran across what remained of the Poppy Factory's smooth, green bowling green – recently dug up to construct a second air raid shelter beneath – and skirted the allotments, which nowadays eschewed cheerful chrysanthemums and delphiniums in favour of functional carrots and cabbages. There certainly wasn't a single poppy in sight. Heart catching in her throat, she bypassed the old pet cemetery where Marigold was buried and then dashed down the steps that ran as an alleyway between two blocks of flats and emerged onto the private road that ran through the heart of the estate.

Carrie slowed to a walk and, as ever, glanced right to the Poppy Factory itself. Even today, when she was hot and bothered and at odds with the world, the magnificent building couldn't fail to cheer her up. The factory had originally been housed in the old Lansdown Brewery – a redbrick Victorian building situated between Carrie's flat and the Petersham Road – and work on a new, state-of-the-art building had begun eight years previously. Built in the new Art Deco style, its three storeys of sleek lines and geometric shapes had become a real local landmark, visible even across the river in Twickenham. Today, its stark white flanks and sharp angles looked particularly impressive against the cornflower-blue sky, and the vertical red recessed lettering spelling out 'Remembrance' was especially vivid. Whatever Carrie might think about the sleepiness and claustrophobia of Richmond, there was little doubt that this building was one of the jewels in its crown.

But now, Carrie turned her back on the building and walked quickly up the road, between three-storey blocks of flats built especially for Poppy Factory workers and their families. Nothing much had changed here since the war had started, except for blackout blinds at every window and vegetables instead of poppies and roses in the wide flowerbeds outside each block. Unlike the factory itself, there was nothing architecturally significant about the flats; their tiled façades, bow windows and little balconies similar to a thousand suburban streets up and down the country. Carrie had often wondered why there hadn't been at least a nod to their disabled inhabitants when the flats were being planned. Did it really make sense for Pa and the others to have to clomp up and down several flights of steep stairs all the time . . . ?

The only slightly unusual thing about the street – and nothing to do with the disabled community – was the washing lines. Each flat had its own dedicated line, which started from its balcony and ran to a specially constructed pole about fifteen feet away from the building at the edge of the road. That way, every housewife – even those on the top floor – could dry their washing in the fresh air, giving the estate a distinctive look on washing day.

Over the past year, a popular song called 'We're Going to Hang out the Washing on the Siegfried Line' had played continuously on the radio, the song's catchy melody and light-hearted lyrics intended to boost morale. The Siegfried Line was a German defensive line along its western border, and the lyrics referred to the idea of British troops advancing and hanging their washing on it as a sign of victory. Nowadays, of course, everyone's washing line was referred to by their surname: the Harper Line, the Turner Line . . . and so on. It was silly, but it never failed to make Carrie smile, and she found she was humming the tune as she ran down the front path to her block of flats.

Carrie pushed open the heavy door, letting it clang shut behind her. She ran up the utilitarian, stone stairs to the second floor and unlocked the door to the penthouse, longing for a cuppa.

'Is that you, Carrie?'

Carrie suppressed a smile. 'Yes, Ma.'

Who else would it be? She didn't have Pa's distinctive clip-clop of a walk, and no one else had a key to the flat.

'You took your time. Did you remember the thread?'

'Of course.'

Carrie dumped her bag on the tile-effect linoleum in the

hallway, pulled out the cotton, and went into her mother's sewing room. It was the smallest of their three bedrooms and, like her parents' bedroom and the living room, faced south towards the river. In fact, if you looked beyond the old brewery building, the Harpers actually had their own private view of the famous vista protected by Parliament. Today, however, the thin, voile curtains were closed against the harsh sun and the room was hot and close. Ma, sitting at her Singer treadle sewing machine, glanced up as Carrie entered, looking thoroughly disgruntled with the world in general and with Carrie in particular. Her blonde hair – the same shade as Carrie's, but drier and thinner – was piled haphazardly into a messy bun on top of her head, and her mouth was pursed in her habitual expression of disappointment.

Carrie placed the cotton on the corner of the desk. 'Last one,' she said, lightly.

Her mother grunted. 'What happens when I can't get the right coloured cotton?'

Carrie shrugged. 'I suppose we just do the best we can,' she said. 'Anyway, it's only blackout curtains, so it hardly matters.'

'Hardly matters . . . ?'

'I'll pop the kettle on, shall I?' said Carrie, quickly.

'I need you to run an errand first,' said Ma. 'There's a letter here for your father. It's from the government or one of the ministries – I don't know why the postman delivered it here when it should clearly have gone straight to the factory. That's the trouble with all these new tradesmen; they simply don't know how things are done. The new postman is actually a woman, and I'm sure she's a nice enough girl, but . . .'

Ma trailed off, puffing out her cheeks and Carrie sighed. She badly wanted a cuppa and to talk to her mother, both about her meeting with Miss Bateman and the threat of impending invasion.

'Can't it wait a few minutes?' she asked.

'Not really. It needs to go across straight away, and you're late enough as it is. Spit spot.'

Carrie sighed again. Nowadays, the post arrived late morning, so the letter would already have been sitting on the table for five hours. Surely another few minutes wouldn't hurt? Besides, if it really was that important, why hadn't Ma taken it over to the factory herself? It was hardly a long way; Carrie had counted it more than once and knew that it was precisely two hundred and thirty-seven steps from their front door to Pa's office.

'And you can wipe *that* look off your face,' said Ma, tartly, cutting across her thoughts.

'What look?' replied Carrie innocently.

'That look that suggests I should have taken the letter across to your father myself. Have you any idea what I've had to do today?'

'Not really . . .'

'I had to take your father's spare leg to be mended. All the way to Ealing Broadway on the bus. You've no idea how cumbersome that thing is to lug around, nor the looks I get when the bus is busy. It takes a whole seat to itself!'

Almost despite herself, Carrie grinned and Ma allowed herself the ghost of a smile in reply. 'Meanwhile,' Ma added, the smile slipping away, 'judging by the look of *you*, despite your imminent exams, you've spent the day lying on the grass and eating chocolate. Be off with you!'

'Ma . . .' Carrie protested.

Ma plucked a blade of grass off Carrie's shoulder, pointed at a microscopic chocolate smear on her cuff, and handed Carrie the letter. 'Shoo!' she said, flapping her hand.

Carrie spun on her heel and shooed, resisting the temptation to slam the door behind her.

Gah!

Carrie walked back down the stairs, turned left out of the block of flats, and dawdled to the factory.

She hadn't reckoned on seeing Pa so early in the day, and she needed to steal herself for the encounter.

Deep down, Carrie was sure that she loved her father, but it was often very difficult to like him, and he certainly caused no end of angst in her life.

There was what he had done last year, of course . . . but she wouldn't allow herself to think about *that* . . .

But take even today, for example. She was sure part of the reason Sarah disliked her so much – had always picked her last in hockey – was because Pa was third in command of the whole Poppy Factory.

It was true; Pa reported only to Major Armstrong, primarily a figurehead who represented and promoted the organisation, and Major Spencer, who had overall control of strategic vision. That left her father effectively in charge of the day-to-day running of the entire operation, responsible for several hundred workers and the production of over thirty million remembrance poppies every year. As her father was fond of saying, 'That ain't too bad for a joiner's son from Bow.'

Much to his chagrin, Pa hadn't been one of 'The

Five' – the original team who'd launched the Poppy Factory under the leadership of Major George Howson back in the twenties – although he had joined the group very shortly afterwards. Tragically, Major Howson had died of cancer four years previously and Pa had been responsible for bringing his coffin into the factory and arranging a vigil right up to the funeral as had been his wish.

Whichever way you looked at it, Pa was a big cheese.

And didn't he know it!

He strutted up and down, running the Poppy Factory as if it were an army battalion, barking out orders and ruling everything with a rod of iron. In fact, military language was very much the order of the day. You didn't 'start work', you 'presented for duty'; you didn't 'go on holiday', you were 'granted leave'. Sergeant-Major Harper had very clear ideas on how things should and should not be done, and woe betide anyone who stepped out of line or tried to show a little initiative.

By contrast, Sarah's father – for all his fancy war medals, his popularity and his affability – was a mere middle manager.

It shouldn't have mattered.

It really shouldn't have mattered at all.

There should have been absolutely nothing stopping Carrie and Sarah from becoming fast friends, had they both so chosen.

The problem was that Carrie's father's very clear ideas on how things should and shouldn't be done also extended to his home life. This manifested itself in many ways, but one of Sergeant-Major Harper's chief diktats had been that Carrie shouldn't mix with the other children on the estate. That would have been unseemly. Pa was fond of saying – and he said it often – that it was all about setting yourself apart and setting a good example. If Carrie had received a farthing every time she had heard *that* . . .

Oh, Carrie was allowed to mix with the children of 'The Five' – or, at least, she would have been, if there had been any around. But Major Armstrong didn't have children and all the other children of 'The Five' were very much older – many having escaped the Poppy Factory completely.

That left Carrie effectively friendless. For the most part, she hadn't really minded. She'd had no particular yen to rush down the hill on a hot summer's day and to throw herself into the chilly waters of the Thames, let alone to play chicken jumping from Richmond Bridge where the currents and eddies could be unpredictable.

She'd had no wish to take part in the elaborate snow-ball fights that took place around the estate most winters. She'd hated the sensation of melting snow trickling down her back ever since Sarah had pushed a huge snowball into her neck from point-blank range. Hide-and-seek and blind man's buff, and all the skipping games might have been fun . . . but not being able to join in was hardly the end of the world. Ma had taken her to the library every week and there had been walks along the river and the occasional trip to museums in London. And, of course, Carrie had had her schoolwork and her novels and her cat, Marigold, and that had been enough. If occasionally, she had looked wist-fully out of the window and fancied that she was Rapunzel or the Lady of Shalott, waiting to be rescued . . . well, she was just being silly and sentimental.

But Carrie did have enough self-awareness to know that

the other children must see her as aloof and stand-offish and maybe a little cold. She knew that *Sarah* must see her like that, and that Carrie's higher social status at the factory may be at the root of her antipathy.

But it wasn't Carrie's fault that things were as they were.

And Sarah could very easily not have chosen to be such a cow.

Carrie picked her way through all the wheelchairs and bath-chairs parked outside the back door to the factory and smiled at Barney, the old doorman.

He grinned, gave her a mock salute in return, then opened the door. 'Urgent missive for your dad?' he said, gesturing at the letter in her hand.

Carrie nodded, puffing out her cheeks, and hesitated just a moment before she went inside. Then she pushed open the inside door onto the main factory floor and, for a moment, just stopped and drank it all in.

Rows and rows of gentlemen – smartly uniformed in white shirts, dark ties and dark aprons – were sitting in neat, serried ranks, each of them absorbed in a specific task. Some were cutting out fabric petals, others were ham-mering the flower centres, yet more were bent low over complicated pieces of machinery, twisting the stems. Then there were those – often the veterans with one arm – who were assembling the finished flowers, using a specially adapted wooden frame to hold the individual pieces steady and in place until they were ready to bind them together with the bitumen centre.

Once upon a time, there had been four different types of poppies, designed to suit different budgets, including a cardboard one specially for children. Carrie could remember Ma pinning one of those onto her coat each winter and how proud she had felt. More recently, however, the four designs had been consolidated into one and, nowadays, the poppies were made from two layers of different fabrics – an under layer of lawn cloth and an outer layer of silk. There was also a green fabric leaf, faux stamens and a black bitumen centre. There were rumours that the design might be about to change again due to the shortages in material; no one was exactly sure what was going to happen, but Carrie had heard Pa mumble about the metal centres and stems being replaced by cardboard.

The war affected *everything*.

But, for now, it was business as usual, and the noise of a hundred men at work – and their associated bangs and clangs and clatters – assaulted Carrie's eardrums. She was used to it, of course, but she had seen visitors clamp their hands over their ears in consternation when they first arrived. Carrie supposed that factories up and down the land sounded much the same and that, really, was the whole point.

This looked and felt and sounded just like a regular factory.

Each gentleman sat at a specially designed workstation and performed a task that had been tailormade for him and, as such, there was next to no sign that everybody was missing either a limb or an eye. Everything ran like a well-oiled machine with each worker carrying out his task efficiently and with the minimum of fuss.

Pa had told Carrie that the convention in most factories was to rotate workers between jobs. This helped to relieve boredom and kept productivity high, and it also helped to avoid the strains and sprains that could be caused by repeating the same task over and over again. This was something that the Poppy Factory couldn't do – at least to the same extent – but nobody looked like they very much minded. Everybody looked busy and focussed. Carrie knew that the quotas the Poppy Factory was given from the government were ambitious and that the war, if anything, had increased those targets. This was proving something of a problem as some workers had left Richmond for supposedly safer havens.

No wonder there was an air of busy enterprise, bordering on panic!

As Carrie walked through an arch at the far end of the factory floor, poppy production gave way to wreath making.

That large one with the poppies being arranged onto an arrangement of black leaves was, of course, for King George VI himself to lay at the Cenotaph in November; Carrie had grown up knowing that the black leaves were traditional for the sovereign and that the decorative ribbons were in the King's racing colours of scarlet, purple and gold.

That smaller one would be Queen Elizabeth's and was decorated in *her* racing colours of blue and gold.

Carrie knew all about the wreaths because Pa had drilled them into her ever since she could walk and talk and she certainly knew them better than she did the men who were making them. Every now and then, a gentleman would look up and nod at her and Carrie would smile back, but they were the signs of respect and courtesy rather than those of warmth or friendship. In fact, Carrie would have been hard-pressed to name more than a dozen of the men, even though she had lived alongside many of them for years.

The vast majority of the men were, of course, pretty old. They had all fought and been injured in the Great War, so they were at least forty – a generation older than Carrie. But, to her surprise, there was a man at the end of one of the rows who was barely older than she was. He was nice-looking, she noticed; handsome even, with dark hair – which held a slight curl even given his military cut – and a sharp jawline softened slightly by the mere suggestion of a five o'clock shadow. His sleeves were rolled up, the muscles in his forearm moving as he slowly cranked the heavy metal wheel in front of him.

At first, Carrie wondered if he was an external supplier who had come to mend or maintain the machine, but then she noticed the crutches neatly stacked to the side. At that moment, the man glanced up, saw her notice the crutches, and his cheeks flushed. Carrie, searched for something pleasant and neutral to say . . . but she couldn't find the words. Instead, she just kept walking, head held high, her cheeks flushing with mortification . . .

Oh, this was terrible.

The first of a new generation of young men at the Poppy Factory . . . his body and life shattered by the war.

She had jolly well better get used to it.

Carrie reached the end of the factory floor and – eschewing the lift – headed upstairs to the offices on the first floor.

Even though Pa's office was at the far end of the

hallway, she could hear him barking down the phone to some unfortunate long before she reached his door. She was sure he hadn't always been this aggressive; the war had definitely made him worse. She rapped tentatively on the glass partition and her father glanced up impatiently, the groove between his beetling brows softening slightly when he saw Carrie. He beckoned her inside without either stopping his conversation or lowering his voice, and Carrie duly entered, shutting the door behind her. Her father – as short and dark as Carrie and her mother were tall and fair – continued marching up and down the office as far as the telephone cord would allow. That moustache really was doing him no favours, Carrie thought uncharitably. At certain angles, as she had once overheard at the Remembrance Club, he did look uncomfortably like Adolf Hitler.

Eventually, Pa turned to Carrie, put his hand over the receiver, and said, 'Yes?'

A command rather than a greeting.

'This arrived for you at home,' said Carrie. 'Ma asked that I bring it over.'

Pa nodded and held out his hand for the letter, gesturing for Carrie to stay. He propped the telephone receiver between ear and chin, picked up a metal letter opener and slit the envelope open. He carried on telling the person at the other end of the phone exactly what he thought of their latest delivery as he unfurled the letter and quickly scanned the contents.

Whatever was written inside clearly shocked him.

'I've got to leave it there, Herbert,' he barked, and slammed the receiver down.

He carried on staring at the piece of paper – a muscle

going like the clappers in his cheek – occasionally muttering 'damnation' under his breath.

Carrie cleared her throat. 'Did you want to talk to me, Pa?' she asked.

Her father looked up sharply. He had clearly forgotten she was there.

'Not any more,' he said. 'Tell your mother I'll be late for supper, but don't forget it's the darts championship at the club this evening. Dress appropriately, if you please. No slacks.'

Carrie almost groaned out loud as she shut the office door behind her.

Chapter Three

Tuesday 4 June 1940

Later that evening, Carrie sat upright on her uncomfortable wooden chair with the other "important" women in the panelled games room of the Remembrance Club.

With her sensible pale-blue suit and seventeenth-birthday pearls, her hands folded primly in her lap and a silly half-smile on her face, she felt a bit like the Queen. But, of course, she was nothing like the Queen; everyone was inordinately interested in Her Majesty, but no one took a blind bit of notice of her!

Carrie sat quietly with half an eye on the darts tournament; she didn't have much of a clue as to what was going on but, judging by the cheers, Sarah's father seemed to be doing predictably well. Bored, she cast her eye around the room, her gaze settling on the other young estate residents. There had been a time when there had been almost a dozen girls roughly her age living on the estate, but almost all had left school at fourteen or sixteen and had already moved away. Some had gone to London for clerical or war work or to go into domestic service, whilst others had married their childhood sweethearts; indeed, Carrie had heard on the estate grapevine that sweet, giggly Hattie Evans already had two children at the ripe old age of nineteen! That just left her, and Sarah – and now Mabel – preparing for examinations at the Richmond County School for Girls before life could begin in earnest. It was the same with the boys; of the original eight lads her own age, only irritating Johnny Bates was left – and he would be scooped by the army as soon as he turned eighteen.

There were, of course, plenty of younger children still living on the estate and Sarah – wearing rather racy red-and-white checked slacks – was larking over by one of the window seats with her brothers and a handful of other youngsters. They all seemed to be having a very jolly time – Sarah's head thrown back in laughter – and, for a moment, Carrie felt a pang of pure jealousy. And here was Mabel, backing into the room with a heavy tray of beers and distributing them without fuss. She caught Carrie's eye, gave a tiny nod, an even smaller smile . . . and was gone.

Carrie sighed and tuned into Ma and Mrs Armstrong, who were sitting on either side of her and keeping up a steady stream of inconsequential chatter whilst clapping politely every time the cheers increased in volume.

'My cousin Connie in America has sent me some powdered egg,' Mrs Armstrong was saying.

'Lucky you,' replied Ma. 'I would love to have added a couple of hard-boiled eggs to this evening's salad. Not that Dennis was there to enjoy it . . .'

'What good would *powdered* egg be in a salad?' said Carrie, crossly.

Honestly, her mother *never* listened!

'But it certainly has its uses in a cake,' said Mrs Armstrong with a wink at Carrie. 'Mind you, there are bits of shell in it – just fragments, but enough to set your teeth on edge.'

Ma made a face. 'How horrible,' she said.

'Indeed,' said Mrs Armstrong. 'Connie wrote that everyone's saying they're bits of old ping-pong balls.'

Despite herself, Carrie let out a bark of laughter. Across the room, over by the wooden cabinets housing a myriad of trophies, Pa looked up from where he was chalking up the scores and met her eyes with a frown.

Next to her, Ma's brows drew together in confusion. 'But, why . . . ?' she started.

'It's a *joke*, Ma,' interrupted Carrie, with a sigh. Honestly!

Her mother *did* have a sense of humour, but sometimes it was very well hidden beneath layers of disappointment and conditioning.

'I wish the Americans would send more than powdered egg,' said Mrs Bennett from two seats along. 'Surely, with the Germans seemingly hellbent on invasion, it's about time they *joined* the war . . .'

Carrie had had enough.

Her bottom was going numb . . . and it felt like her brain was going the same way . . .

'Just popping to the lavvies,' she said to no one in particular as she stood up.

She made her way across to the far corner of the room, pushing herself gingerly and apologetically through the crowd and out into the hallway. To her surprise, Sarah was there, sitting on the bottom step of the staircase that curled up the three storeys of Cardigan House. She was flanked by one of her brothers and Johnny, and, to Carrie's further surprise, the handsome young man she'd seen earlier in the factory was also there. Standing smoking by the window, he was framed by the late evening sun, his expression serious . . .

None of the little group shifted or spoke to her as she approached.

'Excuse me,' she said, politely, gesturing to show that she needed to go upstairs to the washroom.

The boys on the bottom step shuffled to the sides, but Sarah didn't move. She just sat there, smiling up at Carrie in a way that wasn't rude, as such, but certainly felt rather intimidating. She looked modern, cool and crisp in her slacks and a neat, white jumper, which showed off her chestnut hair, and Carrie couldn't have felt more like a dowdy, old matron – all buttoned up in her safe little suit – if she'd tried.

Sarah took a sip from her glass of amber liquid, which looked nothing like the lemonade Carrie had been offered on arrival. Then she turned to her companions.

'Miss Harper and I had an interesting conversation at school today,' she said, casually. 'It rather seems she doesn't believe in the war.'

Carrie stiffened.

That was awfully provocative.

It was also completely untrue.

Unlike the Great War, *everyone* agreed that Hitler needed to be stopped.

Carrie might not care to get directly involved with the war machine . . . but that was different. And how dare Sarah make that glib comment in front of the handsome young man who was, presumably, a disabled veteran.

'I don't remember saying that,' she said. 'Of course, I believe in the war. It's happening, isn't it? You might as well say you don't believe in rain or the post.'

It was an attempt to defuse the subject by being clever.

Carrie held her breath, hoping that it would do the trick, and for a moment, Sarah looked confused. But she rallied quickly, sticking out her bottom lip and staring challengingly up at Carrie.

'Don't be pert,' she said. 'You made it very clear that you don't intend to do your bit.'

Carrie exhaled slowly. 'That's not exactly what I said,' she said. 'I just said that I still intend to go to university in the autumn along with thousands of other young people.'

'Well, just count your lucky stars you've got that choice,' said Sarah coldly. 'Johnny here has been conscripted and is off in a couple of days; *he* doesn't have a choice about whether or not to put his plans on hold. Isn't that right, Johnny?'

Johnny nodded, his Adam's apple bobbing up and down. With his pockmarked skin and a light dusting of ginger fuzz on his upper lip, he didn't look a day over fourteen.

'And, of course, *Harry* here has already done his bit,' Sarah continued, pointing at the handsome soldier. 'What's more, he lost a foot in France for his troubles.'

Oh, goodness.

This was excruciating.

Harry took a deep draft of his cigarette and then exhaled, looking levelly at Carrie over the stream of smoke. Then he smiled unexpectedly and his whole face lit up, revealing small, even teeth and a dimple in one cheek.

'Let's all play nicely, shall we?' he said, mildly, in a broad Yorkshire accent. 'And what do you mean "lost it"?' he added, turning to Sarah. 'That makes it sound as if I accidentally left it in the boulangerie whilst I were picking up me morning baguette. And it weren't France, anyway – it were Heligoland. Either way, I were one of the lucky ones. I made it back to Blighty!'

Sarah stuck her tongue out at him — as if to dismiss those mere details — in a manner that Carrie found terribly forward. Harry, to be fair, didn't look as though he very much minded. He even gave Sarah a little wink!

Carrie saw her chance. 'Well . . . I'm glad you made it home,' she said. 'And, now, if I might just head upstairs.'

She squeezed through the tiny gap between Johnny and the bannisters and ran upstairs, thanking her lucky stars that Harry had managed to defuse the situation so effectively.

But '*I'm glad you made it home*'? she echoed quietly, shaking her head in disgust at herself in the mirror.

What sort of a thing was that to have said? She would have to make some sort of self-deprecating joke when she went back downstairs, or there was every chance that Sarah's relentless needling would start up again.

But when she emerged a couple of minutes later, the four had gone.

Only Sarah's nearly empty glass remained on the bottom step.

Relieved, Carrie walked cautiously downstairs. She wouldn't put it past Sarah to be lurking behind one of the doors or hiding down the steps to the cellar, with some humiliating practical joke up her sleeve.

But there was nothing.

No one.

Tentatively, Carrie picked up the glass and sniffed the contents.

Yes, it was definitely beer.

She took another quick look around her, screwed up her face, and took a little sip of the contents.

Yuck; it was horribly bitter – almost burnt tasting.

To be honest, she preferred lemonade.

Laughing at her lack of sophistication, she pushed open the door to the bar. She couldn't face going back to her seat watching the competition just yet, so she would loiter in there under the pretext of returning Sarah's glass.

The room was empty save for Mabel drying glasses behind the bar.

'Here you are,' said Carrie.

'Aw, thanks,' said Mabel. 'You didn't have to do that.'

'I know. But Sarah . . .'

'Giving you a hard time, was she?' said Mabel. 'Only the door were open a crack. I couldn't hear what she were saying, but I got the gist.'

'Oh.' Suddenly Carrie was close to tears. 'I just meant that it was her glass but, yes. Sometimes Sarah can be a little . . .'

'She's a bully, that's what she is,' interrupted Mabel, fiercely. 'I knew it as soon as I saw her. There's lots like her in the East End. A big family, not enough attention, always having to fight to get noticed. It don't mean she's right. Try not to let it get to you . . .'

Carrie nodded and swallowed hard. 'Would you like to get a lemonade sometime?' she ventured.

Mabel hesitated a second. 'That would be really nice,' she said. 'I'd love to when the exams are over and everything calms down a bit.'

The bar door opened and Pa poked his head in. '*There* you are,' he said to Carrie. His tone was jovial enough, but there was an underlying hint of steel. 'We thought you'd been kidnapped.'

'I was just bringing in an empty glass,' said Carrie.

'That's not your job,' said Pa, coolly. 'Come along, please.'

Carrie left with an apologetic backwards glance.

Carrie followed Pa back into the games room and took her seat between Ma and Mrs Armstrong. She was just in time to see Sarah's father accept the trophy for the darts competition . . . and to see Sarah surreptitiously attempting to balance an empty glass on her forehead.

Thankfully, the evening was nearly over, and for Carrie it couldn't come soon enough. She'd be able to escape to her bedroom and perhaps even get a little studying in. She had been awfully lax earlier that day, dozing in the sun . . .

'A word if I may,' said Major Armstrong, his authoritative tones cutting across the chatter. 'I don't want to spoil the occasion or detract from the celebrations, but I think it would be wrong for this evening to end without my sharing with you extracts from a speech Mr Churchill made in the Commons today and which was reported in this evening's papers.'

He took a rolled-up copy of *The Times* from under his arm and shook out the front page. Then, without preamble, he started reading:

'The Battle of France is over. The Battle of Britain is about to begin. Upon this battle depends the survival of Christian civilization. Upon it depends our own British life, and the long continuity of our institutions and our Empire.

The whole fury and might of the enemy must very soon be turned on us. Hitler knows that he will have to break us in this island or lose the war. If we can stand up to him, all Europe may be freed and the life of the world may move forward into broad, sunlit uplands.

We shall go on to the end. We shall fight in France, we shall fight on the seas and oceans, we shall fight with growing confidence and growing strength in the air, we shall defend our island, whatever the cost may be. We shall fight on the beaches, we shall fight on the landing grounds, we shall fight in the fields and in the streets, we shall fight in the hills; we shall never surrender.'

There was utter silence as Major Armstrong finished reading. This was followed by a smattering of applause and a couple of subdued cheers . . . but rather more gasps of shock and surprise. Somebody started crying loudly, somebody else rather incongruously shouted 'God Save the King' and old Mrs Baldwin at the front sagged and had to be helped into a chair.

Major Armstrong opened his mouth to say something more, but suddenly the ear-piercing and undulating shriek of the air raid siren on the Remembrance Club roof split the air in two.

Carrie jumped, her heart thumping nineteen to the dozen, and let out a little shriek. All around her, people were doing the same. Faces, white with fear, called out for their loved ones. Ma laid a hand on Carrie's shoulder and Carrie could feel that it was shaking.

Air raid sirens were nothing new, of course; in fact, the first alarm had gone off minutes after war had been declared last September. At first, the dreadful racket – quickly dubbed Wailing Willie – had made Carrie's scalp prickle with fear. Since then, however, the alarm must have gone off at least a dozen times and nothing had ever happened. No falling incendiaries, no enemy fire, certainly no chemical attacks – just isolated German reconnaissance missions and the odd skirmish miles away along the coast. And the trouble was that, over time, people had become lax and complacent – many (not the Harpers) simply ignoring the alarm and choosing to stay in their own homes.

But that evening felt different.

The timing was unnerving, to say the least.

'Did the Germans wait for Major Armstrong to finish reading out his speech?' the crystal-clear voice of a child rang out, and there was a ripple of nervous laughter.

Either way, no one was going to ignore the alarm tonight.

And here was Miss Arnott, the local Air Raid Precautions Warden, striding flatfooted into the room and briskly clapping her hands together. A tall, thickly set woman with a shrewd gaze and a strong jaw, she immediately commanded attention.

'Take cover immediately, everyone,' she called out, authoritatively. 'Everyone who's here now, straight down into the basement, regardless of which shelter you're usually allocated to.'

Up until now, Miss Arnott had been almost a figure of fun amongst the youngsters. It wasn't that people didn't respect the ARP; everyone understood that it would play an instrumental role in firefighting, first aid and evacuation should the threat of aerial bombardment actually materialise. The problem was that Miss Arnott had rather let her newfound power go to her head. She strutted around like a sergeant-major in her regulation tin hat – no doubt resenting the holes drilled in the brim to distinguish it from a regular military helmet – and her voice was more abrasive than Wailing Willie himself.

Tonight, however, no one was laughing, even though her piercing tones – 'No smoking, no entry without a gas mask, no congregating in the entrance and absolutely no dogs,' – would have been heard by any Germans within ten miles. There must have been over a hundred people crammed into the Remembrance Club games room, and they all trooped hastily out into the corridor and thence down the steps into the cellar at Miss Arnott's command. Even the Turners – whom Carrie had never known to go to *either* shelter – were doing as they were told; Carrie could see Sarah ahead of her on the stairs, her father's trophy upside down on her head in an obvious parody of Miss Arnott. Next to her, Pa stumbled on the steep, narrow steps, but Carrie resisted the temptation to reach out and grab his elbow. Proud at the best of times, she knew the gesture would not be appreciated in public . . .

At the bottom of the stairs, Mabel's father was shepherding everyone to the air raid shelter at the front of the building; the room at the back was apparently dangerously damp and was thus strictly out of bounds. Carrie couldn't help thinking that she would far rather take her chances against a bit of damp than a German bomb, but she didn't demur.

She never did.

And then she was filing into the cavernous space with everyone else, wrinkling up her nose at the musty air. The shelter was very basic – little more than a series of benches and chairs around the walls with some mattresses in the middle and a couple of bunks at the far end. The Harpers made a little base with the other managers and their wives in one corner and prepared to sit it out. Carrie felt safer down there – the basement should survive everything but an unlucky direct hit – and, after a while, her main emotion was boredom. Daisy had reported that there was a positively party spirit at some of the public shelters in town in a bid to encourage attendance. Richmond Green had community singing to songs played on a radiogram whilst the Police Concert Party had been known to visit the shelter under the arches of Richmond Bridge complete in their scarlet jackets and fancy sashes – but there was nothing like that here. Carrie cursed her own lack of forward planning; even in the gloaming, she could have done a little swotting had she thought to pack her history books.

Instead, her eyes roamed around the shelter. There was Sarah, surrounded by a little group of youngsters and, once again, laughing at Miss Arnott.

There was Mabel – quiet and self-contained – helping her parents distribute tea from a large urn.

Carrie blinked away the tears prickling her eyelids. They were all in danger of being blown to kingdom come and, instead, she was bemoaning the fact that she didn't have any friends on the estate, let alone being part of the fictitious Poppy Girls.

It was ridiculous . . . and she needed to distract herself before she became a blubbering mess of self-pity.

Next to her, a family was doing a jigsaw on the floor. Carrie recognised them as the Coles who lived in the block of flats opposite theirs – Mr Coles cut out silk petals in the factory, Mrs Coles kept house and Eloise and Maggie were about nine and eleven – and asked if she might join in.

The puzzle depicted a jolly – and defiantly non-war-related – Christmas scene and boosted Carrie's spirits. It was calming fitting the pieces together, and Carrie could only hope that the various pieces of her own life would start to slot into place as neatly as the summer progressed.

By the time the all-clear sounded an hour later, Carrie was full of resolve.

Damn her parents.

Damn the estate.

Damn Miss Bateman for making everything worse.

Damn the non-existent Poppy Girls.

Against an uncertain and frightening future, it was time to move on.

The summer couldn't come quickly enough.

Chapter Four

Week commencing 10 June 1940

But, first, she had to pass her exams.

Carrie still had some last-minute revision to get through and she tried her best to put the war out of her mind.

It was hard, though.

Less than a week after the Dunkirk evacuation, Italy declared war on the United Kingdom, and British forces crossed the Frontier Wire into Italian Libya to start the Western Desert Campaign. The threat of imminent invasion hung over them all and with it – perhaps inevitably – came more frequent daytime air raid alarms. And, each time Wailing Willie started up, everyone had to troop outside to the air raid shelters on the school field and stay there – often for hours – until it finished. Sometimes the younger children were picked up by parents and taken home, but Carrie and her cohort were not allowed to leave of their own accord. The teachers did what they could – distributing iron rations along with Horlicks tablets for energy and ensuring there was a big bucket of water so that nobody went thirsty – but it was still nigh-on impossible trying to focus in such cramped, dark conditions.

And what would happen if the alarm went off during the actual exams?

Would they be expected to take their papers underground in such intolerable circumstances?

Carrie rather expected that they would. But, as it happened, the exams themselves passed without incident in the large, airy school hall. And, as far as Carrie was concerned, they really went rather well. She managed to avoid Sarah Turner the whole time, for one thing, leaving home earlier than usual and walking the slightly longer way down Richmond Hill to make absolutely sure that their paths didn't cross. Once or twice, she saw Mabel ahead of her and was tempted to run and catch up – but, in the event, she decided against it. This was a time to keep calm and unruffled and to brace herself for tricky exam questions; not a time to try and make new friends. But, as it happened, the examiners were kind and there was nothing hugely unexpected in the papers – and certainly none of the wildcards Carrie had come across in the practice papers. She planned her answers carefully and wrote calmly and methodically – no need to panic and scribble away – confident that she had plenty of time to get her ideas across and to do herself full justice.

And she was pretty sure that it was more than enough.
Birkbeck College, here she came!

Weeks commencing 17 and 24 June 1940

But first was the long-awaited summer holiday 'up North'.

Ma and Pa originally hailed from the Wirral and, every year, without fail, the Harpers revisited their roots. Ma was somewhat more enthusiastic about these trips than Pa – although he always came along with reasonably good grace – and Carrie had the distinct feeling that the arrangement was part of some non-negotiable agreement stretching back into the mists of time. It was probably something to do with the fact that Ma had been more or less forced to move down South after Pa's lower leg had been blown off in the Battle of Verdun. Carrie had the impression that the Liverpool streets had hardly been paved with gold for disabled war veterans. Until Pa fortuitously met Major George Howson, the founder of the Poppy Factory, in the Philharmonic pub, he had been pretty down on his luck.

As Pa was fond of saying, the Poppy Factory had saved them all.

All Carrie's grandparents were dead, but Pa's brother and Ma's sister had remained in the North West. Pa's brother and his wife still lived on the Wirral, but Ma's sister had married a farmer and relocated to the Lake District. Carrie disliked the Wirral visits – a gloomy, two-bedroomed Victorian terrace where Carrie slept on a very lumpy sofa – but the Lake District visits were a different kettle of fish altogether. Auntie Anne and Uncle Stanley had three children, and Carrie adored them in equal measure. Twins Charlie and George were barely a year older than she was, whilst Violet was just over a year younger, and all were such enthusiastic livewires that you couldn't help but get pulled along in their wake. Every year, they scooped Carrie up into their big, boisterous family and she basked in the fun and attention. Oh, she made a big point of moaning to her parents that she didn't want to trail all the way up to the frozen wastelands where there was nothing but windswept hills and sheep with dirty bottoms and not a whiff of a

Lyon's coffee shop for miles and miles. And, of course, her cousins teased her mercilessly for pronouncing words like 'bath' and 'grass' all wrong and for her clumsiness, which was second to none. But the truth was that everyone got on like a house on fire and had a magnificent time. And, every year, it was as if another Carrie emerged. A Carrie who could be as noisy and boisterous and exuberant as everybody else. She always vowed to stay in touch during the year but, despite the odd, sporadic letter to Violet, that didn't tend to happen.

It didn't matter though.

The Lake District was always there – just waiting for the summer.

The Harper family generally drove whenever they headed up North.

This was unusual amongst Carrie's peers, but Pa was lucky enough to have access to a specially adapted, neatly stencilled Poppy Factory van to visit clients and suppliers, and it was much easier for him than taking the train.

Driving long distances could be a problem, however, and – as Ma couldn't and wouldn't drive – Pa had made it his business to get Carrie competent behind the wheel when she was barely fifteen. On paper, it was completely uncharacteristic for her father to encourage – nay, demand – such independence, but in practice, it made sense.

Either way, Carrie loved it!

She enjoyed the freedom of the open road and, whilst she might be all elbows and knees in everyday life, she was a natural at driving.

Even Pa had seemed quietly impressed.

Last year, he had let her drive all the way from Oxford to Birmingham on the way north and, on the way home, his remaining leg had seized up and she had taken the wheel all the way from Birmingham to Richmond.

This year, Carrie had assumed that they would take the train.

Private road travel had more or less been banned — just recently, it had been decreed that all cars should have their wheels taken off! But then, almost at the eleventh hour, Pa had announced that he needed to pick up some goods — something to do with the new poppy centres — from a factory near Liverpool and that they would take the van after all. It all sounded a little suspicious to Carrie — weren't the bitumen centres being replaced by cardboard, and couldn't cardboard be obtained from anywhere? Presumably, it was all just a wheeze so that Pa didn't have to take the train — and who was she to complain? Pa could be extremely loud and embarrassing on public transport.

In the event, the journey went smoothly. Carrie drove the section from Birmingham to Chester, driving at a fair lick along the nearly deserted roads and enjoying the lush British countryside in all its verdant summer glory. From time to time, she needed to pull over to allow a convoy of military vehicles to pass and she enjoyed the many looks of surprise and admiration she attracted from the soldiers.

She was a woman of surprising talents: an independent spirit, very soon to be a university undergraduate . . . and the future started here.

She had a feeling that it was going to be a summer she would never forget.

*

To begin with, however, it was a summer to forget.

To Pa's chagrin, the mysterious materials weren't ready to be picked up. Pa's fuss and bluster that they weren't passing the factory on the way down South fell on deaf ears; parts and manpower were both hard to come by during wartime – 'No one's fault, guv'nor, blame Jerry,' – and, like it or not, they would have to make a detour on the way back.

And then, when they finally arrived on the Wirral, tired and hungry after over eight hours on the road, they found both Uncle Bernard and Auntie Flo with stinking summer colds and not at all in the mood to cosset and entertain. Ma and Carrie ended up doing much of the fetching, carrying and cooking and Carrie was dog-tired by the time she retired to the most uncomfortable sofa in the world and an eiderdown so dusty it made her throat rasp.

All that, however, faded into insignificance by the time they reached the Lake District.

Here, the air was sparkling clean, their welcome couldn't have been warmer, and the food was hearty and relatively plentiful compared to Richmond. After half an hour's mutual wariness, she and her cousins were as thick as thieves, enjoying the same old banter and easy camaraderie. Carrie felt that she had never been away.

In many ways, the Lake District seemed much further from the war but, dig beneath the surface, and there had been changes galore. With the recent emphasis on agricultural output, much grazing and recreational land had been turned arable for food production. Farming was a protected occupation, so George and Charlie were exempt from enlisting, but many men *had* been conscripted, and labour shortages were biting deep. To help address this, the government had introduced the Women's Land Army – quickly dubbed the Land Girls – who did a wide range of jobs, from milking cows and gathering crops to digging ditches and – ugh! – catching rats.

Against this backdrop, all three of Carrie's cousins, as well as her uncle, were out from dawn to dusk, working the land, tending the remaining animals, and supervising the Land Girls who were billeted in the nearby town of Ulverston. The largely unspoken expectation was that Carrie would do the same, and she was happy to oblige. After all, sitting around the house with a bored and disgruntled Pa was far less appealing.

And, to her surprise, she had a ball.

The work, of course, was repetitive, back-breaking and dirty, but Ma and Pa largely left her to her own devices and – oh! – the fun they all had when they were off duty.

Sitting on the daisy-strewn bank at breaktime, sipping lemonade and chewing the fat with the Land Girls.

Eating lunch in the shade of the gnarled old oak tree on the furthest paddock, swapping treats and confidences with Violet.

Impromptu evenings in the farmhouse garden under the starry sky, drinking cocoa and singing patriotic songs with the whole gang.

Carrie loved it all.

Best of all, there was Ned from the neighbouring farm, who was always at the centre of everything.

Ned, who seemed to have been dipped in gold, from his floppy blonde hair to his lightly tanned skin to his brown eyes with sparkling hints of honey. Ned, with his infectious smile and his strong, capable hands and his love of animals. Ned, who was friendly to everyone but who, as the days went by, seemed to be being just a little more friendly to Carrie than to anyone else . . .

She could hardly believe it.

And then, on the fourth day, just as Carrie was getting used to – revelling in! – it all, a letter arrived for her father. Everyone was at the breakfast table and Carrie had just spread her toast extra thick with raspberry jam – a luxury that was hard to get hold of in Richmond – when Violet brought in a telegram. Carrie didn't see Pa actually open it, but she was very aware of him taking off his spectacles and pinching the bridge of his nose tightly between thumb and index finger . . . and it was very hard to miss his groan.

'I have to go back, Gladys,' he said, cutting across the breakfast chatter. 'No time to lose – I need to leave straight away.'

No.

Not when everything was going so marvellously.

Not when Ned . . .

Ma's face fell, echoing how Carrie felt, but she rallied quickly.

'I'll go and start packing,' she said, without pressing Pa for details. 'Carrie, your case is in the boxroom. Can I leave you to sort yourself out?'

'Of course, Ma,' said Carrie demurely.

After all, what else could she say?

'Does Carrie really need to go?' asked Violet.

Carrie's heart soared.

This was how it must feel to have a sister.

'Can't she stay for the summer?' said Charlie. 'She could

become a Land Girl. Goodness knows, we need all the help we can get.'

Carrie suppressed a smile.

She wasn't sure she'd been much help with most of the tasks she'd been allocated thus far. Drystone walling had been a disaster; it was *difficult* and, despite the smiles and the friendly encouragement, she had a sneaking feeling she'd been a bit of a liability. Digging ditches had been better but, as she wasn't the fastest or the strongest, she had tended to fall behind. But she'd enjoyed mucking out the stables and talking to the horses, and she'd really come into her own driving the tractor and transporting supplies from one side of the farm to the other.

'Please can Carrie stay?' added George, in an altogether more serious tone. 'After all, we've all just received a pamphlet entitled "If the invader comes." I'm sure she'd be much safer here.'

Carrie held her breath.

'She will do no such thing,' said Pa firmly. 'Can you imagine what it would look like if a Harper left the Poppy Factory for safer climes? It would give everyone else carte blanche to do the same. A holiday is one thing, but Carrie needs to set a good example to the estate, pamphlet, or no pamphlet.'

'The estate!' giggled Violet, behind her hand. 'It sounds like you live in Buck Palace.'

Carrie was close to tears. 'It's a three-bedroom flat!' she whispered back, fiercely. 'And I *hate* it.' She wiped her mouth with her napkin, pushed back her chair and said, 'I'll go and pack,' in a louder voice, which wasn't entirely steady.

'Don't be ridiculous girl,' said Pa, waving his hand

imperiously at her to sit down. '*You* can't come back *now*. You and your mother need to stay here and drive the special materials back from Liverpool when they're ready. It's a blasted nuisance, but I'll have to take the train by myself. I can't see any way around it.'

Hope flared in Carrie's chest.

Violet clapped her hands together. 'Oh, that's just marvellous,' she squealed. 'The fun we're going to have!'

But Ma, hand fluttering to her pearl choker, looked shocked. 'You mean drive all the way back from the Lake District on our own,' she said, rattling her teacup back into its saucer. 'And in the middle of a war, to boot! It's an awfully long way for Carrie to drive – supposing we get lost?'

'We'll be just fine, Ma,' interrupted Carrie, hastily. 'I'm very happy to drive all the way and we've got maps. Nothing will go wrong.'

The plan was perfect.

She couldn't bear for it to be snatched away from her at the last minute.

To her relief, her father was nodding. 'I'm afraid we don't have a choice, Gladys,' he said. 'I'm not at liberty to share the details, but rest assured that this is a matter of huge importance. I've no choice but to report back on duty in the national interest . . .'

Luckily, Pa didn't seem to notice the muffled giggles . . . but Carrie was well aware of them. Why did her father have to be so pompous and why, oh why, did he always feel the need to exaggerate his influence and importance?

Whatever Pa might think, cardboard poppy centres were hardly a matter of national importance . . .

'Are you really sure, Dennis?' Ma was saying.

'It's the best way,' said Pa. 'If you come home with me, I'll need to send one of the men up in a couple of weeks anyway.'

'A terrible waste of petrol . . .' Charlie interjected.

'And not really in the national interest . . .' agreed George solemnly.

'I shall book a hotel near Macclesfield to break your journey on the way home,' said Pa, as if the boys hadn't spoken. 'It's an awfully long way in one stretch for a young lady.'

Carrie let the last comment lie and concentrated very hard on her third piece of toast. This wasn't the time to engage Pa in a discussion about exactly what young women could and could not do. She just exhaled gently and tried to stop herself from beaming too widely.

Over a week without Pa.

Oh, she was sure somewhere deep down there was love – and no doubt she would miss her father if something happened to him – but this was a treat indeed. She would be able to stay out longer, get dirtier and be herself – or, at least, the self that she wanted to be.

Carrie would make sure that it was a week to remember.

And what a week it turned out to be.

The world seemed to pause and life seemed to start because, as Carrie had somehow always known would happen, Ned became hers. Even the sudden news that France had fallen to Nazi Germany, leaving Britian as the only country to resist Hitler, couldn't detract from her happiness . . .

They snatched any free moment they could to explore the hills and wander the tranquil lake shores together. Feet in step and hands entwined, they talked about everything and nothing, their laughter echoing across the valleys. Somewhere near Windermere, Carrie decided to change her name to Lyn; Carrie was silly and childish, whereas Lyn was glamorous and sophisticated. And then, one balmy evening, beneath the star-strewn sky, 'it' happened. Lingering behind the others as they walked along a country lane, the two paused at an old oak tree. Ned turned to her and Carrie felt his breath warm against her cheek, and then the brush of his lips against hers.

Her first kiss.

The days sped by – each one a perfect bubble – but Carrie knew it wasn't forever.

She had heard the others talk of Mary – beautiful, charismatic Mary – who dangled Ned's heart on a string and who would be back from her own holiday a few days after Carrie was due to leave. She knew their parting was inevitable; Ned had gently made it clear all along that it was best for the two not to keep in contact once they went their separate ways.

When it was time to return home, Ned came to see her off and their parting was gentle and casual.

'Cheerio, Lyn,' Ned had said, patting the bonnet of the Poppy Factory van.

'Toodle-pip!' Carrie had replied.

Flippantly.

Ridiculously.

Despite it all, she had driven away with bittersweet tears in her eyes.

Nothing would ever be the same again.

*

The journey started well.

The summer sun cast a golden hue on emerald fields and rolling hills, as Carrie navigated the winding, semi-familiar roads homewards. Next to her, Ma – for all her earlier panic – dozed with the map open on her lap, and Carrie would glance across at it whenever she was unsure which way to turn next.

Everything was fine.

Enjoyable even.

Somewhere between Lancaster and Preston, Carrie arrived at a crossroads and realised she wasn't sure which way to head next. It was only then that she noticed the road signs had been taken down. Too late, she remembered her uncle and aunt chatting about it at the supper table – a precautionary measure given the threat of invasion – and her heart ratcheted up a gear.

This could be *bad*.

They were lost, in the middle of nowhere, the Germans expected at any moment. She should wake her mother up, seek advice, work out what to do next . . .

But, for some reason, all Carrie could see was Pa's 'I told you so' face . . . the one that implied that Carrie was incapable of doing anything on her own.

She took a deep breath and tried to stay calm.

There might be no road signs, but all was certainly not lost.

She still had the book of maps and, once she knew for sure where she was again, they would keep her on the right track. Besides, it was a clear and sunny day; she only had to follow the sun south. Surely, she couldn't go too far wrong . . .

There was nothing to worry about – nothing to dread.

She could sort this out on her own; no need to worry Ma.

She set off again, stopping a labourer walking along the road to check that she was on the right route – and then carried on with renewed confidence. The roads were quiet but hardly deserted – and the new barrage balloons would surely keep them safe.

She was on her way.

Arriving without incident at the factory near Liverpool, Carrie was met with interest and respect. A young woman driving a company van without a male escort was by no means unique these days, but it was still unusual enough to invite attention and comment.

Carrie revelled in the praise.

She and Ma accepted the offer of a cup of tea and returned to the van in time to see the last of several bulky packages being loaded into it. They looked too lumpy and irregular in shape to simply be cardboard for the new poppy centres but, of course, it wasn't hers to wonder why or to ask any questions. Perhaps Pa *hadn't* said it was the cardboard for the centres.

Perhaps it was the machinery to help produce them.

She really should listen more closely in future . . .

Back on the road, the shadows lengthened, but there was enough light for the rest of their journey to Macclesfield and the hotel Pa had booked for them. It was rundown and shabby – she and Ma joked they could trace the entire outline of Africa in the mould above their bed – but even that couldn't dampen Carrie's spirits.

She had changed beyond measure in the Lakes, and she was on the cusp of a new chapter in her life.

The next morning, the two were up early, speeding along the open road with the wind from the open window rushing through Carrie's hair and the sun kissing her forearms.

As she drove, a newfound determination flickered within her.

From now on, she resolved, she would be different.

She would stand up for herself.

She would no longer allow herself to be defined by the limitations her father imposed, nor would she let the likes of Sarah bully her. As they skirted Birmingham, she told herself that whatever challenges lay ahead, she would face them head-on with courage and conviction.

By the time they finally drove down the A316 to the bustling streets of Richmond, Carrie felt alive with the promise of new beginnings. She negotiated the narrow roads that led over the bridge and to the Poppy Factory and finally – *finally* – she brought the van to a standstill outside the factory warehouse doors.

Carrie triumphantly flung open the door.

She had done it.

'We've been expecting you,' said a chap who had come to help unload the van. 'This is an important delivery.' He paused and then added sombrely, 'Heard the news?'

'What news?' said Carrie, brightly, as she climbed down and stretched her legs.

'German forces have landed in Guernsey. The Channel Islands are under occupation.'

Chapter Five

Sunday 30 June 1940

Carrie took a deep breath of sooty Richmond air whilst the van was being unloaded and tried to process her thoughts.

There was shock, obviously, and a frisson of fear. After all the talk and worry and preparation, the Germans had finally invaded the United Kingdom . . . who knew how quickly they might try to advance.

Closer to home, there was the slight disappointment that Pa wasn't there to greet them. The van had been expected; surely, she and Ma would have been expected too. She didn't expect a red carpet or a welcoming committee, and she knew that Pa was a busy man, but it had been a long journey in difficult circumstances, and it would have been nice.

Underlying everything was a great big dollop of anticlimax. It had been a very eventful couple of weeks for very many reasons and now it was all over, everything seemed a little grey and drab . . .

'Need a hand with your stuff?' said one of the men, gesturing to their trunks still in the back of the van.

Ma opened her mouth to speak, but Carrie was too quick for her. 'No, thanks,' she said. 'You're clearly busy and we can manage.'

She handed over the ignition keys and, before Ma could protest, pulled both small trunks out herself. She should start as she meant to go on and, manager's daughter or not, an independent woman didn't need a man to carry her luggage when she was perfectly capable of doing so herself. One trunk in each hand, she started marching down the path that led around the side of the factory and over to the flats, Ma trailing in her wake. She walked smartly down the road to their block – thinking that something looked a little different, but really not sure what – then paused whilst Ma opened the front door. Finally, she wrestled both cases up the two flights of stairs to the penthouse.

'Home, sweet home,' said Ma, opening the front door and heading immediately for the kitchen.

Stepping through the door, Carrie found she could hardly catch her breath. It was partly the heavy cases, of course, but it was much, much more than that. The flat was messy and dusty – Pa obviously hadn't done an iota of cleaning or tidying since he had arrived home. Unopened mail and circulars were scattered haphazardly over the hall shelf, the floor was grubby, and Pa's one slipper had just been discarded on the rucked-up hall runner.

It was all so depressing.

Worse still, the air was heavy with the same oppressive atmosphere and the old familiar tension. Carrie could almost taste it. She put the cases in their respective bedrooms and then just stood in the hallway, heart pounding, and one hand on each wall as if to stop them closing in on her.

Then Ma's voice floated down the hallway, over the shriek of the kettle coming to the boil. 'Pop over to the factory, will you?' she said. 'Tell Pa we're home and ask him if he wants supper at the usual time?'

Carrie sighed.

It seemed that absolutely *nothing* had changed.

Despite it all, Carrie was quite looking forward to seeing her father.

After all, having single-handedly driven the van over two hundred miles without a single signpost to guide her way, even Pa wouldn't be able to find anything to criticise.

She could only wonder if he would immediately recognise that she had changed – grown up – over the preceding ten days.

Surely it was written all over her face?

There was no sign of Barney on the factory door, and she didn't recognise the other doorman who was deep in conversation with Sarah's father. She gave an airy wave, which encompassed them both, slipped inside and crossed the lobby.

Pushing open the big doors to the main factory floor, she stopped in surprise.

Everything was in a state of disarray and upheaval.

The men were working as usual – and apparently as hard as ever – but everything else was different. For a start, all the desks and workstations had been pushed much closer together – so much so that some of the men almost seemed to be rubbing shoulders as they worked. It must be hell for them all to get in and out. New desks and workstations had been added to fill the space that had been gained, and it looked as though the wreaths might now have been moved further down to be assembled in there as well. Groups of men she had never seen before were standing around talking and scratching their chins, whilst others were assembling machines with an air of busy enterprise.

Goodness! Carrie had had no idea that the changes to the poppy design and assembly had been so fundamental and required so many adjustments.

No wonder Pa had had to come home from the Lake District early.

Carrie picked her way across the factory floor. It was much more difficult than it used to be, given that the 'corridor' down the centre was now almost non-existent – and even that was blocked by bins, crutches, and other paraphernalia.

But here was Pa himself, emerging from the lift to the upper floors with his characteristically lopsided gait. Carrie was filled with her usual kaleidoscope of feelings on seeing him; a smidgen of fear, an undercurrent of love. But her hatred for the dreadful thing he had done the year before seemed to have intensified after her time away. What she *hadn't* anticipated was the way her father's expression would change when he saw *her*. In a matter of seconds, his normal bombastic expression went through surprise, pleasure, discomfort and even . . . especially? . . . anger.

Carrie stopped walking, her smile dying on her lips.

Pa marched straight over to her and grabbed her just above the elbow. 'What on earth are you doing in here?' he hissed.

'What?' Carrie twisted her body in a bid to get free. Her father's grip was vicelike, and it hurt. 'I've just come to say hello and . . .'

'And nothing,' said Pa, beginning to frogmarch her out. 'You can't just barge in here without so much as a by-your-leave.'

'Why not?' said Carrie. She was close to tears and stumbling over her own feet. All around her, embarrassed faces turned discreetly away.

'Firstly, because I said so,' said Pa, as if Carrie was six years old and asking why she couldn't have a second slice of chocolate cake. 'And secondly because there are changes being made. Some of the machines need to be replaced and others retooled.'

'But I already *know* that,' cried Carrie. 'I've just driven all the way back from Liverpool with the wherewithal for the cardboard centres. There's no secret.'

Pa didn't answer. He let go of her arm but gestured for her to precede him out of the main factory door. He then turned his back on her, bearing down on the new doorman.

'What was the meaning of letting this girl into the factory?' he demanded, poking a finger into the poor fellow's face. 'She had no right to be in there.'

The doorman took a step backwards. 'I were speaking to Mr Turner,' he said, defensively, 'and *he* said that the lass were your daughter, so I thought . . .'

'Damn it, fellow, you're not paid to *think*,' Pa shouted, a vein throbbing ominously in his neck . . .

'Pa?' said Carrie, tentatively.

She was shocked. This was hardly the reaction of a sane man – let alone a loving father – greeting his only child after ten days apart.

Pa turned towards her. 'Hurry along now,' he said, in a

slightly softer tone. 'There's no need to worry. We're just tightening security around here.'

'But . . . ?'

'No buts.' Pa's tone hardened. 'Tell your mother I'll be in for supper at the usual time.'

He turned away and, as Carrie obediently started trudging home, she could hear him still berating the hapless doorman.

Carrie dashed a couple of tears from her eyes.

So much for a fresh start.

Carrie might be nearly eighteen, but nothing had changed.

It didn't matter how many boys she had kissed or how many miles she had driven, she was still the same old, silly Carrie Harper, who couldn't quite break free of her father . . .

A noise and movement from above caught her attention. It came from the top floor of the block of flats to her left. Sarah's flat. A smallish boy was lugging a heavy, red bucket out of the window until it was precariously balanced on the window ledge outside.

Carrie started in surprise.

What a strange thing to do.

Almost like the Tudors tipping their waste onto the street below . . .

The small boy paused for a few seconds, glancing back over his shoulder, and then slowly began to tip the bucket. Carrie's eyes went instinctively to where its contents would land and realised exactly what the small boy was up to. Sarah was standing in the flowerbed directly below the window, half hidden from Carrie by a wigwam of runner beans. She had a patterned scarf tied tightly around her head and was picking beans into a trug – totally oblivious to what was going on above her.

Carrie should warn her . . .

On the other hand, Sarah was a nasty drop of work. No doubt, she had crossed her brother and it would serve her right to get a jolly good splattering.

But, on the other hand, what would that make Carrie . . . ?

'Sarah! Watch out!'

Carrie darted down the short path to the flowerbed, grabbing Sarah by the elbow and dragging her into the safety of the covered porch over the front door of the block of flats. The trug went flying and the beans scattered across the ground . . . but it wasn't a moment too soon. A split second later, the contents of the bucket came thundering down, drenching the beans and the surrounding flowerbed. The liquid had a distinctly brownish hue and carrot and potato peelings now hung languidly over the vines.

'God,' exclaimed Sarah, hand to heart, as a distinct cackle floated to their ears. 'The little so and so!' She stepped out from under the porch and peered up at the window, hands on hips. 'Wait until I get my hands on *you*, Alfie Turner.'

Carrie turned away and headed up the path. She was still shaken after the encounter with her father and she just wanted to go home. Besides, Sarah was a nasty bully and really not worth the time of day. Maybe Carrie *should* just have allowed her to get soaked.

'Oi!' called Sarah.

Reluctantly, Carrie turned around.

'Thank you,' said Sarah. 'That was jolly decent of

you – and mighty quick reactions if I might say so. You kept those well-hidden on the hockey pitch!'

Almost despite herself, Carrie found herself smiling. 'They always seemed to desert me as soon as there was a bully-off,' she said ruefully, as she turned to leave.

'I'm sorry about the other week,' said Sarah, suddenly. 'You know, in the Remembrance Club. No hard feelings?'

Carrie turned around again. Sarah was smiling, clearly confident that Carrie would quickly fall into line. But something hardened inside her. If she was serious about doing things differently from now on, she had to make a stand and tell Sarah how she felt.

'Well, actually, there *are* hard feelings,' she said, coolly. 'You were utterly beastly to me that night and there was no excuse for it.'

Sarah's eyes widened and she stepped backwards as though she'd been slapped. There was a long silence, and Carrie waited for her to rally with a stream of vitriol and insults.

But finally, Sarah just sighed. 'You're right,' she said. 'I was a prize idiot. I don't even really know why. I think I was showing off in front of Harry.'

'That's as may be,' said Carrie, in the same calm tone. 'But, whatever the reason, you are never to talk to me like that again. Do you understand?'

Sarah laughed, but her laugh was surprised and embarrassed rather than unkind. 'I certainly do,' she said. 'Wow, who would have thought Carrie Harper had such a backbone. If only you had shown *that* on the hockey pitch!'

This time, Carrie laughed out loud. 'Yes,' she said, in an altogether more jocular tone. 'About that.'

'What?' said Sarah.

'You always picked me last.'

'Because you were the worst,' said Sarah, matter-of-factly. 'I'll apologise for being a pig, but I shouldn't have to apologise for that.'

Carrie was indignant now. 'Irene Philipps and Joyce Skilling were *much* worse than me.'

Sarah shrugged. 'I'm afraid they weren't,' she said. 'Irene could actually be pretty nippy when she put her mind to it and Joyce didn't spend most of her time running away from the ball. Sorry, but on balance, you *were* the worst, and it was my job to pick the best team.'

'It's not always all about winning,' said Carrie, a trifle sulkily.

'What else is it about, then?'

'Giving people a chance, learning to be a good sport, teamwork, resilience . . .'

Sarah smirked. 'Shall we tell the Germans that?' she said. 'I'm sure they'll be interested to hear we're happy to come second in the war if it teaches us to be jolly good sports.'

Carrie gave a rueful smile. 'Fair point,' she said. 'But what about the tennis ball?'

'What tennis ball?'

'The one you deliberately whacked at me the day Miss Bateman called us the Poppy Girls.'

'I did nothing of the sort,' said Sarah, looking thoroughly bemused. And then she laughed. 'You're meant to move out of the way if the ball's coming for you. It's the whole point of tennis.'

Carrie sighed.

How had she got it all so wrong?

'But, to be fair, I *was* somewhat miffed at you,' Sarah added. 'Not to the extent of personal injury . . . but still.'

'You were miffed at me?' echoed Carrie. 'Why?'

'Oh, hark at you, Miss Innocent.'

'I honestly have no idea what you're talking about.'

'The History Cup, of course.'

'The *History* Cup?' Carrie was perplexed. 'Do you think I should have chosen you?'

'Not necessarily,' said Sarah. 'But you could at least have *considered* me.'

'But . . .' Carrie trailed off. It had never even crossed her mind. Sarah was popular. Sporty. Not a historian. 'You never said. You never *asked*.'

'I shouldn't have had to,' said Sarah. 'I came third in the year in the history exams. Above Joanna Byrd. Even above Daisy.'

'I didn't know that . . .'

'Well, you should have made it your business to know,' retorted Sarah, 'rather than just automatically choosing your friends. I had every right to be in that team. It wasn't fair.'

Carrie thought about it, head on one side. 'You're right,' she said, finally. 'I was horribly judgmental and I'm sorry.'

'Apology accepted.'

The two girls looked at each other and then burst out laughing.

'Friends?' said Sarah.

'Friends.' Carrie took a deep breath and then pointed to the upstairs window. 'Trouble with your brother?' she asked.

Sarah made a face. 'There's always trouble with at least

one of them,' she said, picking up the trug. 'At the moment it's the youngest one. I thumped him for pinching some of my chocolate allowance, and now the little bugger's out to get me. God, I wish I was an only child.'

'No, you don't,' Carrie burst out. 'You don't know how much I'd love some siblings to take the heat off me – especially with a father like mine!'

The words were out before she could stop them and, despite everything, Carrie felt a pang of disloyalty.

Sarah pulled a sympathetic face. 'I couldn't help but hear the shouting,' she said gently. 'Want to talk about it?'

Carrie hesitated. Confiding in Sarah was a novel concept – and not one without risk. But, then again, who else could she speak to? There was Daisy of course, but she lived almost half an hour's walk away and, besides, the two didn't tend to see each other much during the holidays. Her cousins and Ned were two hundred miles away . . .

There was no one.

Carrie puffed out her cheeks and shrugged. 'Pa was furious about me going into the factory,' she admitted. She was still totally baffled about it. 'He kept going on about the "changes."'

'Oh dear.' Sarah screwed up her face in sympathy. '*All* our fathers are extra grumpy nowadays.'

'Even yours? He always seems so jolly.'

'Even mine. I think he's narked beyond words that he can't fight this time around. Anyway, I'm sure yours will have calmed down by the end of the day. We're not in his good books either, if that helps.'

'Whyever not?' said Carrie.

'Haven't you noticed?'

Sarah smirked and pointed at the washing lines above their heads. Carrie followed her finger in confusion and . . .

Oh!

The lines belonging to the ground and first-floor flats duly stopped at the pole by the road, close to where the two girls were standing. But the one belonging to the Turner's top-floor flat now continued right over the road and was brazenly attached to the pole outside Carrie's flat.

That had been what had registered as different earlier on.

Carrie started laughing. 'Well, I have to admit that's a definite advance by the Turner Line into enemy territory,' she said.

'I'm glad you can see the funny side,' said Sarah, starting to pick up the scattered beans. 'Your father really wasn't very impressed.'

'I'm sure,' said Carrie, bending down to help Sarah. 'How soon before he noticed?'

'Oh, straight away,' said Sarah. 'It turns out he had a lot to say about it and most of it was very loud.'

'A lot of what Pa says is very loud. I'm surprised he didn't get you to take it down straight away.'

Sarah laughed. 'Oh, he tried,' she said, starting to pluck more beans from the vine. But Mummy's been complaining for ages that there simply isn't enough space on the line for six people so, one night, my brother Bertie took the law into his own hands and shinned up your pole to make it longer. And I said to your father that surely the Poppy Factory has an obligation to make sure we can get our washing dry. If we were walking around with damp, musty-smelling clothes, it would be a health hazard and reflect very badly on the place.'

'Very clever,' admitted Carrie, chucking a few beans in the trug. 'Pa wouldn't like *that* at all.'

'He didn't,' said Sarah. 'He backed down straight away. And the reason I'm telling you is that I'm sure it will be the same for you. Your pa will have calmed down by this evening and all will be forgiven.'

'But I don't know what I need forgiving *for*,' said Carrie, plucking a bean with unnecessary venom. 'I went into the factory to tell him we were home and it was as if the hounds of hell had been released.'

'I suppose it's really stressful for them with all the hush-hush changes going on,' said Sarah. 'My dad isn't a shouter, but even he's been very tetchy.'

'"Hush-hush changes?"' scoffed Carrie. 'You mean replacing the metal poppy centres with cardboard and maybe doing something different with the stems? I know it's a faff for them — and it's a shame Pa had to leave our holiday early — but it's hardly the end of the world. There's a *war* on, don't you know?'

Sarah smiled. 'Seriously, Carrie, I don't think it's poppy centres your father is worried about.'

'What is it, then? New wreath designs? Petal fabric shortages?'

Sarah touched Carrie's arm. 'I *know*, Carrie,' she said. 'You don't have to keep up appearances with me. My father might have to move departments, and he told us the big secret. He made me promise not to tell anyone, of course, and I absolutely won't . . .'

Carrie stared at Sarah in confusion, trying to make it all make sense.

'I honestly have no idea what you're talking about,' she said.

Sarah pulled away to get a good look at Carrie's face. 'Goodness, you really don't,' she said. 'Well, I'll be blowed. I assumed that your father would have told you.'

'Told me *what*?'

'I shouldn't . . .'

'Come *on* . . .'

Sarah sighed. 'Well, Dad told me in the strictest confidence, so you didn't hear it from me,' she said.

'Hear *what*?'

Sarah took a deep breath. 'In for a penny, in for a pound. I'm pretty sure the real reason your father returned home was that he'd just discovered the Poppy Factory is being partially repurposed by the Ministry of Aircraft Production. They want us to assemble radios for them.'

Carrie was so surprised – so shocked – that she wasn't sure how to respond. She just stood there, foolishly opening and shutting her mouth like a goldfish.

'No!' she said finally.

'*Yes*. But you mustn't tell *anyone*.'

Carrie exhaled noisily.

This was *huge* news.

Huge and . . . somewhat devastating.

For one thing, it would make the factory a legitimate target for enemy bombers and Carrie knew, without a doubt, that she would sleep a little less soundly once the news got out.

But there was more to it than that.

Making and assembling artificial poppies was a lovely, positive thing. As well as providing work for her father and all the others, they were so important for ritual and remembrance and for keeping morale high . . . especially during the war.

But manufacturing military aircraft parts was different. However you dressed it up, those planes were being made to kill and maim human beings. Oh, Carrie knew that all was fair in love and war, and she also knew that the aeroplanes would be used for defending Britain as well as attacking Germany . . . but still.

It just seemed very ironic and rather sad that the same men who spent their lives producing something to remember the horror and loss of war, were now being asked to help manufacture the very machines that would help make it happen all over again.

Carrie vowed right there and then to have nothing whatsoever to do with it.

She shook her head in frustration. 'I can't believe it,' she said. 'He never breathed a word.'

'They're trying to keep it under wraps,' said Sarah. 'That new doorman is meant to stop anyone who's not an essential worker from wandering in.'

Carrie pulled a face. 'Well, if Pa had kept me in the picture, I *wouldn't* have just wandered in,' she said. 'Thanks, Pa. Yet another example of you landing me in it.'

Sarah wrinkled up her nose. 'Talking of that . . . the awful thing that happened last year, I mean . . .' she started, tentatively.

Carrie's throat constricted. 'Please don't say it out loud,' she said. 'I can't bear for it to be spoken about, even now . . .'

'Sorry,' said Sarah. 'I just want to say that everyone felt terrible about what happened . . . about what he did . . .'

'But no one ever *said*. It might have helped, but no one said a thing. It was as though it hadn't happened.'

'We tried. We really did. But you just walked away if anyone tried to talk to you . . .'

'It was difficult . . . *impossible* . . . !'

'Carolyn!'

Carrie jumped in shock.

It was Ma, peering down at her from their balcony and looking none too pleased.

'I hope you're not expecting me to do all this unpacking on my own. Come up here at once.'

Chapter Six

Sunday 30 June 1940

Carrie debated long and hard whether to tell Pa what she'd discovered.

She really didn't want to provoke an argument, especially because – as Sarah had predicted – Pa arrived home in a fairly conciliatory mood. He didn't actually apologise for what had happened earlier, but he praised Carrie for driving the company van without incident – what a shock about the signposts! – and expressed an interest in how the remainder of their Lake District visit had gone. He told them his concerns about Guernsey and, to Carrie's surprise, even made a relatively jovial comment about the Turner's rejigged washing line . . .

All in all, it would be a shame to spoil the mood, but Carrie decided she didn't really have a choice.

If what Sarah had told her was true, she had a right to know.

Carrie waited until they were seated at the kitchen table, and Mother was doling out her store-cupboard, invariably disappointing, corned beef hash.

'Why didn't you tell us, Pa?' she demanded, and immediately cursed herself for not leading up to it more gently.

Her and her big mouth.

'Tell you what?' asked Pa, from behind *The Times*, a curl of pipe smoke appearing above the paper.

Ma paused with the ladle midair. 'Tell us what?' she echoed.

Carrie hesitated.

She had no idea if Ma knew that part of the Poppy Factory was being repurposed for nefarious ends.

'The real reason Pa came back from our holiday,' she said carefully.

There!

The perfect opportunity for Pa to come clean, without Carrie declaring her hand.

There was a short, stunned silence, which reverberated in the steamy kitchen.

Then Ma started slopping the hash into bowls with a slightly shaking hand. 'Don't be impertinent,' she said. 'Your father told you he needed to come back for his job, and that's all you need to know.'

Pa slowly lowered his newspaper and fixed Carrie with a level stare. 'Agreed,' he said. 'Since when have I needed to tell you the ins and outs of what I do?'

Oh, for goodness' sake.

'Since it started affecting me?' said Carrie, heatedly. 'Since it started affecting everyone else? You've already done much too much behind my back and, if part of the factory really has just been commandeered to help the war effort, it will put us in the line of fire . . .'

'Who told you that?' interrupted Pa. He thumped one hand down on the table so loudly that Carrie jumped. 'That's classified information.'

Yes, he was definitely even more short-tempered nowadays and Carrie hesitated before she answered.

This was scary stuff, and she couldn't implicate Sarah.

Oh, she knew that she didn't owe her erstwhile adversary anything, but she had warmed to Sarah that afternoon, and she didn't particularly want to see her get into trouble. Besides, the last thing she wanted was for Father to think that – dare she say? – the Poppy Girls couldn't be trusted.

'I'm just putting two and two together,' she said. 'New security on the door, everything squashed up together on the factory floor, you unhappy I was in there . . . it doesn't take a genius to guess that it's something to do with the war.'

Pa relaxed an iota. 'There are changes going on all over the country,' he said, in a slightly softer tone. 'I promise I'll tell you what you need to know, when you need to know it. It's much safer that way. And, in the meantime, I want you to promise not to repeat what you've just said. Is that perfectly clear?'

'Yes, Pa,' said Carrie, taking a mouthful of hash, and realising that she was absolutely starving. 'But, if there is extra work, who's going to do it?' she added, genuinely interested in the answer. 'Are they cutting the poppy quotas?'

'Not a bit of it,' said Pa, with an exaggerated groan. 'The buggers have actually *upped* the order.'

'Language, Dennis,' said Ma.

Carrie and Pa ignored her.

'Even though you said Armistice Day isn't happening this year?' persisted Carrie.

'Even so,' said Pa. 'The nearest Sunday is still being observed as a "day of dedication" and it's particularly important everything is shipshape and Bristol fashion for that. We don't want the Germans thinking that standards are slipping, do we?'

Carrie couldn't tell if he was joking. She couldn't help thinking that Hitler had other things to occupy him than scrutinising every wreath that came out of the Poppy Factory.

'So, what are you going to do?' she persisted. 'Are you going to bring in people from outside?'

'Certainly not!' said Pa, tetchily. 'All work here is reserved for disabled war veterans. You know that!'

'Even if it's not poppies and wreaths?'

'Enough,' said Pa, taking a huge mouthful of steaming hash and then wiping his mouth on his plain white serviette. 'I have never said that any of it is not poppies and wreaths, and, anyway, none of this is any of your business. In the meantime, mum's the word or I'll have your guts for garters. Understood?'

Monday 1 July 1940

Carrie woke late the next morning, feeling discombobulated.

She hadn't slept well; she had tossed and turned into the small hours, and when she finally dropped off, she was plagued with horrible dreams about Ned being taken prisoner of war in Guernsey.

She pulled on her dressing gown and padded into the kitchen in search of company.

Goodness – it was almost nine o'clock!

There was no sign of either of her parents. Pa would already be at work, of course, and a note on the table informed Carrie that her mother had gone to queue for meat.

Now what?

The truth was that there wasn't an awful lot for Carrie to do.

She was in limbo until she got her exam results and – hopefully – her place at Birkbeck. Only then would she have access to the curriculum and be able to get stuck into the pre-course reading lists . . .

The kitchen was close and stuffy and the day weighed heavily.

She could hardly believe it had only been yesterday that she had been bowling through the green country lanes of middle England with the sun as her guide. How far away all that felt now. Now the same sun was streaming in the smeary windows, making the dust motes shimmer and shine. How far away Ned felt. She knew they had agreed no contact but how she longed to write to him . . .

Enough of that.

She'd go to the library.

She might not be able to request her university books yet, but maybe she'd see if she could get her hands on the new Agatha Christie; she'd been longing to read *Sad Cypress* ever since March, but she'd held off because of her exams. Maybe she'd take it down to the river, buy an ice from the cart by the bridge and, war or no war, while the day away perfectly pleasantly.

Decision made, Carrie rifled through her wardrobe. She settled on her powder blue summer frock. It was hardly the height of fashion – ever since war had been declared, there had been a trend towards versatile neutrals and practical earthy tones – but, then again, nothing Ma made her ever was. This dress was also a little dressy for a visit to the library, but it was a pretty colour and Carrie knew the fitted bodice and flared skirt suited her well. For once, Mother hadn't made the whole thing hideously long – the hem dipped and swayed just below her knees – and the sweetheart neckline and hint of puff to the sleeves finished the whole look off very satisfactorily. Carrie added a cream belt to cinch in her waist, pinched her cheeks to give them a little colour, and then gave herself a little twirl in the mirror.

She looked like the bees' knees, if she said so herself!

She scribbled a note to her mother, slipped on some simple sandals and her trusty straw hat and headed out.

It was barely a ten-minute walk to Richmond Library, but Carrie was thoroughly hot and bothered by the time she arrived at the redbrick, gothic building on Richmond Green. So much for pinching her cheeks – they were, no doubt, glowing bright red by now.

Far for her to wish for cloudy skies, but when would this heatwave ever end?

Carrie skipped up the front steps with a sigh of pleasure. She had been coming to the library ever since she was a little girl; her education had always been taken very seriously and Ma had made a point of weekly visits as a child. Once she was older, she had often popped in on the way back from school, so it was very much a home from home. Even in wartime, not much had changed. The blackout curtains were new, of course – and some of the windows had actually been *painted* black. There was a sign to an area designated as an air raid shelter, and a poster plastered to the wall promoting the latest salvage drive. Apart from that, all was reassuringly familiar.

Inside, the cool, vaulted interior embraced and calmed Carrie as it always had done. Less had changed, at least on first glance. For a while, Carrie just wandered around, breathing in the exotic, musty smell of thousands upon thousands of books.

All those words.

All that *knowledge*!

Heading over to the fiction shelves, Carrie went in search of Agatha Christie. There were loads of them – almost a whole shelfful – but, sadly, no sign of *Sad Cypress*. Carrie glanced along at the other titles, but not only had she read them all, she could remember whodunnit in every case . . .

Damn!

There were thousands of other books, of course – but Carrie had had her heart set on Monsieur Poirot. She turned away from the shelves, puffing out her cheeks in frustration, and her eyes met those of a nice-looking young man who was sitting at a nearby table, idly tapping his fingers on the surface. He held her gaze – possibly for a heartbeat longer than was strictly necessary – then gave her a polite half-smile and looked determinedly down at his fingers.

The merest hint of appraisal, maybe, but certainly none of flirtation.

Carrie felt a tiny flicker of response. The man wasn't in Ned's league, of course; with his light brown hair, stubbled jaw and slightly hooded eyes, there was nothing particularly golden about *him*. But the eyes were the most piercing blue, and the lopsided half-smile lit up his face and . . .

Carrie suddenly found herself wondering what it might be like to kiss him.

Flushing, she melted away into the next aisle.

What on earth was wrong with her?

It was as if kissing Ned had opened a door which hitherto had been bolted shut. A door she hadn't even noticed really existed! She had barely registered boys until a couple of weeks ago ... and now look at her, practically having palpitations at the first man she had seen aged between eighteen and twenty-five.

It was ridiculous, because if Ned had been Champagne, this man was dandelion and burdock.

It was the heat, the long drive, the war, the aircraft radios ...

It must be.

She wasn't being herself.

She headed upstairs to the general history section. That should cool her ardour!

She had no idea what period they would be focussing on at university, but it wouldn't hurt to get back in the habit of some academic studying. She grabbed a copy of H.G. Wells' *The Outline of History* – you couldn't get much more general than that – and headed downstairs to the front desk.

She would not look over her shoulder to check if Mr Blue Eyes was watching her.

She would *not*.

She was – hopefully – a university student, an academic; not a shopgirl getting giggly and coy at the sight of anything in trousers ...

The queue to check out her book and to reserve *Sad Cypress* seemed to stretch on and on; the library was clearly experiencing staffing shortages, as everywhere else. Carrie passed the time by perusing the posters in front of the counter: 'Air Raid Wardens wanted; a responsible job for responsible men' and 'Serve to Save – women volunteers needed now'. 'Careless talk costs lives' brought her up short and reminded her of what she had learnt the day before. Like it or not, she was now in possession of classified information and she mustn't be found wanting . . .

'Next, please!'

The harried middle-aged woman behind the counter stamped Carrie's history book without a word; indeed, without even looking up at her. Carrie suppressed a smile; there wasn't much chance of careless talking costing lives here . . .

'I'd like to reserve *Sad Cypress*,' she said politely.

The librarian pushed a piece of paper under her nose. 'Fill this form in, please,' she said shortly.

A younger woman, busy with a stack of books, beamed over her colleague's shoulder. 'I couldn't help overhearing,' she said. 'And I think it might be your lucky day. I've just put a copy of *Sad Cypress* on the A–C fiction returns trolley. If you hurry, you might even be able to grab it before it goes back on the shelves.'

'Ooh, thank you.'

Carrie abandoned her form and turned around. Yes, there was the trolley, even now being wheeled over to the shelves she'd browsed in vain. Grabbing her hat and bag, she hurried after it.

She dismissed the thought that Mr Blue Eyes might think she was returning because of him.

To be fair, that *was* an added bonus.

Maybe once she had got her hands on *Sad Cypress*, she could 'accidentally' drop it at his feet. He would bend over to pick it up for her and, straightening up, his ridiculously blue eyes would stare into her altogether less dazzling ones. He would hand the book back with a little courtly bow and . . .

Carrie arrived back at the shelves just in time to see Mr Blue Eyes stand up, smile at the lady pushing the trolley, and leisurely pick out *Sad Cypress* for himself.

Then, before Carrie had time to react, he slung his bag over his shoulder and, whistling under his breath, headed for the front desk without a backwards glance.

Carrie watched him go, unsure whether to laugh or cry.

That was jolly annoying.

Infuriating, in fact!

And now she was going to have to go all the way to the front desk and order the damn book all over again. Well, she would jolly well wait until Mr Blue Eyes had gone.

Otherwise, he really *would* think that she was following him.

Then she noticed the scarf.

It was lying on the floor, underneath the table where he'd been sitting. A strange design, it had been fashioned from stitching together long, thin strips of material in wildly clashing blacks, blues, crimsons and greens. It was loud, garish . . . and a million miles away from the one-plain-one-purl scarves she sometimes helped Daisy knit for the Royal Navy.

Carrie's first reaction was to leave it lying on the floor.

It would serve him right!

But would that be being ridiculous and uncharitable at a time when everyone was supposed to be pulling together?

With a sigh, Carrie picked up the scarf. She resisted the temptation to hold it to her face and breathe in the fragrance, and stuffed it any old how into her bag. There was no sign of the chap by the front desk – typically, the queue was suddenly much shorter – so Carrie, with a deeper sigh – and a tiny flutter of excitement – hurried outside.

There he was, a few yards down the pavement, lighting a cigarette with cupped hands and inhaling sharply. He was shorter than she had realised (much shorter than Ned), although he nonetheless had a good couple of inches on her.

She walked over to him.

He saw her approach and watched her with narrowed eyes – and yet she could tell that he hadn't been waiting for her. He genuinely had just stopped outside the library to light up before he continued on his way.

'No, you can't have it,' he said, without preamble, as she drew level. 'And I'm afraid I'm not accepting bribes.'

He exhaled, the smoke from his cigarette narrowly missing Carrie's face, and gave her an amused smile. He had an everyday Surrey accent – the sort of voice you heard all the time at school or on the streets.

'I don't want it,' Carrie replied, a little confused. Why should she want his *scarf*? 'They're really not my colours.'

The man looked nonplussed. 'The book . . . ?' he started.

Carrie started laughing. 'Your *scarf!*' she replied.

She pulled the offending item from her bag and waved it triumphantly at him.

'My scarf!' the chap echoed, taking it from her outstretched hand and tossing it nonchalantly around his neck. 'By Jove – thank you! I hadn't even noticed I'd forgotten it!'

'It was under the table where you were sitting,' said Carrie. 'It's very striking – although slightly too warm for a hot July day, I might have thought.'

Goodness. Was that very forward?

Carrie found she didn't care. The scarf *was* an unusual choice for summer attire and, anyway, Carrie suddenly felt as confident and self-assured as she had on the long drive home.

Thank goodness she had chosen to wear a pretty dress.

Mr Blue Eyes was smiling. 'You're right,' he said. 'It's absolutely boiling! Maybe that's why I didn't miss it. But it's a university rowing one and I'm meeting some of the chaps at lunchtime, so it seemed to fit the bill.'

Mr Blue Eyes was at university! Carrie felt the lure of a kindred spirit. That and the fact that he obviously liked Agatha Christie. Her stomach was beginning to soar and swoop.

'It's ever so unusual,' she said, resisting the temptation to reach out and touch the scarf. 'All those stripes. I've never seen anything like it.'

The chap picked up one end, as if considering it for the first time. 'They couldn't get hold of big enough pieces of material to do it the old way once the war started, so now they make them up with these long, thin strips.'

'How funny,' said Carrie.

'Yes. And mine's even funnier because they clearly didn't have enough fabric even for the strips, so some change from green to crimson halfway down. I tried to get a discount, but apparently that makes it unique!'

Carrie laughed. 'Which university is it from?'

Wouldn't it be funny if . . . ?

'Peterhouse. Cambridge.'

'That's where LSE have relocated for the duration!'

'That's right.' The chap looked at her with more interest. 'Do you go there?'

'No. I was going to before . . . things got in the way.'

Mr Blue Eyes made a sympathetic face. 'Another one with messed-up plans?' he asked. Carrie nodded. 'What were you going to read?'

'History.' She raised her eyebrows at him. 'You?'

'Mathematics.'

'Oh,' said Carrie. And then, without really meaning to, she added, 'That's a shame.'

So, he wasn't as much of a kindred spirit as she had first thought.

Mr Blue Eyes gave her a quizzical look. Then he started laughing, revealing even, white teeth. 'Why's reading mathematics a *shame*?' he said. 'Isn't history more of a shame? What's the point of dwelling on the past?'

'Every point!'

'Musty, fusty old books . . . ?'

'Knowledge. Experience. Warnings . . .'

'We need a brave *new* world.'

'But how can you forge a new world without understanding what went wrong with the one that came before?'

'How can you forge a new world without science and technology,' countered Mr Blue Eyes. 'Being the best at maths and physics and chemistry *is* the way forward.'

'But you'll just repeat the same old mistakes with new shiny tools,' said Carrie.

'Without science, we won't have the opportunity to *make* mistakes.'

'I'm not sure that even makes sense,' said Carrie. 'I suppose we'll have to agree to disagree.'

'I suppose we will,' said the chap

The two stared at each other and then, as one, burst out laughing.

'I never thought when I popped into the library this morning that I'd end up having this conversation,' said Mr Blue Eyes.

'Me neither.'

Carrie found that her heart was beating a little faster than usual.

This was fun!

Everything around them seemed to have been thrown into sharp relief. The bright green leaves on the plane trees bordering the park. The clip-clip of the heels of the young mother pushing a pram to the playground. The roar of the aeroplane overhead . . .

The man glanced sharply upwards. 'One of ours,' he said, almost to himself, and visibly relaxed. He turned back to Carrie. 'I'd better get going or I'll be late for the chaps down by the river. Are you going that way?'

Carrie hesitated.

She should really go back into the library and order *Sad Cypress.*

Then again, she could do that any time.

'I am,' she said, and the two headed off in step together.

'So, you've had to change your university plans?' said the chap conversationally as they set off around the park. 'How many years did you get in first?'

Carrie shook her head. 'I haven't even started yet,' she said. 'I've only just done my Highers.'

Mr Blue Eyes made a sympathetic face. 'Bad luck,' he said. 'I got in two years – two marvellous years, I might add. So, what are you doing instead? WAAF? FANY?'

'Neither of the above,' said Carrie, secretly thrilled that the chap could see her in the Air Force or driving an ambulance. 'I mean, I'm still going to university – I've just switched to Birkbeck. It's stayed in London, which means I can still live at home in Richmond.'

'Oh, I see,' said the chap. 'Sorry, I misunderstood.'

There was a short silence. Was she imagining it or did the chap seem suddenly a little disapproving? Not, of course, that he had any right to be but, to be fair, it did all sound rather parochial, even to Carrie's ears.

Then again, the chap didn't know how hard she had had to battle to get thus far.

He didn't know Pa.

'Are you volunteering over the summer?' the man asked. 'My sister is doing factory work at Hayes.'

Carrie shook her head. 'I don't want to make weapons,' she said, firmly. 'I'm still finalising my plans, but I live on the Poppy Factory estate and I'll be helping out there, of course.'

She crossed her fingers behind her back. Stopping a small boy from pouring dirty water on his sister's head and running the odd errand for her parents hardly constituted 'helping out' – and she wasn't even allowed inside the factory anymore . . .

'You live up there, do you?' said the chap. 'Quite the building!'

'Yes,' said Carrie. 'It's marvellous. Very light and spacious inside as well. Everyone agrees it's a super place to work.'

'So, being "modern" does have *some* advantages then?'

Carrie laughed. 'It does,' she conceded. 'Occasionally.'

'And how, exactly, do you help out? Cutting out petals? Threading leaves?'

'Oh, no!' said Carrie, instinctively. 'All that is strictly reserved for disabled war veterans.'

As soon as the words were out of her mouth, Carrie realised it had been totally the wrong response. Her tone of voice had been far too earnest.

The chap was teasing her, for goodness' sake!

'I see,' said the man, with a chuckle. 'What about the stems then? Do they let you loose on those?'

Carrie had a chance to put it right.

'Only every other Wednesday,' she said, and was rewarded with a boyish laugh.

That was better.

For a second, Carrie thought of telling him that the Poppy Factory had just been requisitioned for war work. That would have him laughing on the other side of his face! But, remembering Pa's stern warning the evening before and the posters in the library, she resisted temptation.

'So, what about you?' she asked instead. 'What did you leave university to do?'

The chap shrugged. 'Well, for starters, I'm an ARP volunteer,' he said. 'All pretty mundane stuff at the moment – checking blackout blinds and the like – but with the Germans already knocking on our door, I fear it might get very lively quite quickly.'

Despite herself, Carrie shuddered. 'I hope you're not as much of a tartar as the woman who runs our section,' she said. 'We're all petrified of her!'

'Miss Arnott?' said the chap with a chuckle. 'Yeah, she certainly takes her duties very seriously. I think it comes with the territory, to be fair. One of the women on our patch is absolutely terrifying. She's a headmistress during termtime and she makes most sergeant majors look like pussycats! They're always looking for more volunteers, by the way . . .'

Carrie laughed. 'You're not really selling it to me,' she said. 'So, what else do you do? Have you been conscripted?'

When war had been declared the previous year, the National Service Act had been expanded to make military service compulsory for all men aged eighteen to forty-one who were both fit for service and not in exempted occupations.

'No such luck,' said the young man, morosely. 'I'd sign up in a heartbeat but one eye's not up to scratch, I'm afraid.'

He pointed to his right eye, but Carrie was none the wiser. The chap wasn't wearing spectacles and the 'bad' eye was just as piercingly blue as the other.

'So . . . ?'

'I'm working up at Richmond Park. There's all sorts going on up there, you wouldn't believe.'

'Oh, I would,' said Carrie. 'I've seen some of them! It's my favourite place to walk, or at least it was, before the war changed everything. So, you must be at the rehabilitation unit, or working with the anti-aircraft guns or something to do with those strange structures made out of chicken wire . . .'

The man laughed. 'Starfish,' he said.

'Sorry?'

Carrie had a sudden memory of digging on the beach down at Bexhill-on-Sea. One day she had found a perfect gold starfish. She had placed it carefully in her red plastic bucket and just stared at its five perfect legs before letting it go again.

'The chicken wire structures,' said the young man. 'They're nicknamed Starfish. Or, at least, so I'm reliably informed.'

'Why?'

The young man shrugged. 'I'm not entirely sure,' he said.

'What is it, anyway?' asked Carrie. 'It looks ever so strange out there in the middle of the park.'

The chap tapped the side of his nose. 'I've already said too much,' he said, as they turned onto the high street and headed towards the bridge. 'Mum's the word and all that.'

Chastened, Carrie nodded. 'Sorry,' she said. 'Me and my big mouth. I should know better than to ask questions like that.'

'Not at all,' said the young man. 'Besides, it's a perfectly formed mouth, if I might be so bold.'

Oh!

That had come from nowhere and Carrie simply didn't know how to respond.

She just stood there, gawping at him.

And, suddenly, the young man was shuffling from foot to foot and looking thoroughly discomforted. Then he glanced at his wristwatch.

'Lord, look at the time!' he said. 'I really can't dawdle any longer. But, before I dash off, might I ask you a couple of questions?'

'Oh, yes. Of course.'

He was going to ask to see her again, Carrie was sure

of it. And she found that she rather liked that idea. There could never be another Ned, but Ned was with Mary . . . and this chap was handsome and intelligent and combative and . . .

'Might I know your name?'

'It's Lyn . . .'

There it was again; out before she could stop it.

Glamorous, sophisticated Lyn rather than childish, homely Carrie.

At some level, she clearly wanted to impress this chap.

'Well, Lyn, I'm much obliged to you for returning my scarf. I'm Bobby.'

Carrie rolled the name around her tongue.

Bobby.

A nice, solid, reassuring name.

Should she immediately agree to meet up again – or would he think her fast?

Should she play hard to get – or would he think her cold or, worse, a tease?

Oh, what should she do?

Bobby opened his mouth and time seemed to slow down.

'One last thing,' he said.

'Yes?'

'I was right, wasn't I?'

'Sorry?'

'You *were* after that copy of *Sad Cypress*.'

Oh!

'Well, yes. But . . . ?'

'I thought so,' said Bobby with a grin. 'All that hanging about, going away and then dashing back! It didn't take

Poirot to work it out. And I feel ever so unchivalrous for hanging onto it – especially after you returned my scarf – but I promised my mother I'd try and borrow it for her. The woman with the trolley had given me a heads up that she would be round with a copy soon, so I'm afraid I was lurking with intent the whole time.'

'I see,' said Carrie. 'So, you're not the Agatha Christie fan?'

'Oh, I'm a fan all right,' said Bobby. 'I think she's marvellous. Did you read her last one?'

'The one where they were all trapped on an island . . . ?'

'Yes. Goodness, that was atmospheric.'

'And such a twist at the end!' said Carrie.

'Indeed,' said Bobby. He paused and then exhaled loudly. 'And, on that note, I'm late and I'd better be off. Lovely to meet you, Lyn.'

Then, without another word – *certainly* without giving Carrie a chance to reply – he strode away without a second glance.

Chapter Seven

Monday 1 July 1940

Carrie stared after Bobby's retreating back.

What on earth had caused that volte-face?

They had been chatting so animatedly for the past ten minutes . . . and then he had just dashed off.

It had been so abrupt that Carrie was tempted to run after him and demand an explanation.

But then, she saw her mother walking down George Street, laden down with bags and with a characteristic frown.

Carrie, without thinking too hard about it – without thinking about *anything* – dashed into Woolworths.

Carrie blundered through the store.

She pushed through the throng of shoppers and only stopped when she reached the empty shelves at the back of the store. There were *loads* of empty shelves nowadays; these ones seemed to have been for aluminium pots and pans before the war effort had commandeered them all to make weapons.

Carrie took a deep breath, half-expecting her mother to suddenly appear and to start interrogating her about Bobby.

Nothing.

She removed her hat. The shade was very welcome after the scorching midday sun.

How much had Ma seen?

Had she noticed Carrie standing open-mouthed in the middle of the pavement, people swirling around on all sides?

Had she seen Carrie conversing animatedly seconds earlier – before Bobby had abruptly turned heel and fled?

Or hadn't she noticed Carrie at all?

Either way, Carrie simply wanted to be alone and process what had just happened.

Why on earth *had* Bobby just dashed off without so much as a by-your-leave?

Was it because he was embarrassed about making a slightly risqué and clumsy comment about her mouth?

Did he regret his indiscretion in telling her about the chicken wire structures on Richmond Park?

Or was she thinking too deeply about it all?

Maybe it simply *was* that they had dallied too long and that he was running late for his rendezvous.

Whatever the reason, it was disappointing that Bobby hadn't mentioned meeting up again. She had enjoyed their conversation, and she would very much have liked to see him again. She consoled herself with the fact that he knew where she lived, so he should be able to track her down fairly easily.

Carrie was about to emerge from her hiding place when she began to tune into some voices from the neighbouring aisle.

She couldn't see who was talking, but the shrill and

somewhat aggressive tones sounded like they belonged to a group of girls or young women who were not being terribly kind to someone else.

'You're not from around here, are you?' came the first, somewhat mocking tone.

'What if I ain't?' came a second, exasperated, voice. 'Stop blocking me way; I need to go.'

Carrie stiffened.

The accent . . . the pitch . . . the timbre . . .

Carrie was pretty sure that the second voice belonged to Mabel.

Senses now on full alert, she edged closer to the empty shelves separating the two aisles. She liked Mabel – wished they had gone for that lemonade together – and couldn't bear it if people were being unkind to her.

'"*Ain't*"? We don't use words like that around here.' This third, rather la-di-da voice, was unusually low for a girl. 'Everyone knows it's "I'm not" – not "ain't".'

'*She* doesn't know that,' said the first voice. 'And that's because she's one of *them*. She's one of those refugees from London?'

Carrie inhaled sharply, feeling suddenly protective of Mabel.

Whatever should she do?

'Stop pushing me,' said Mabel. She sounded furious rather than frightened or upset. 'It don't matter to you *where* I'm from.'

Carrie held her breath.

'I rather think it matters quite a lot,' said the girl with the la-di-da voice. 'You and your sort, coming out here – without jobs and money – and expecting to be housed and fed. There may not be too many of you at the moment, but my father says that Richmond is about to be swamped.'

'And then you have the cheek to turn up your noses at what you're offered,' said another girl – this time one with a very shrill voice. 'My aunt says you're always complaining that the food isn't spicy enough and that you want to add peculiar ingredients to everything. Well, there just won't be enough of everything to go around soon, so I think you'll find it very *much* matters to us.'

'You're talking rubbish,' said Mabel, hotly. 'I had bangers and mash for tea last night.'

'Ah, but who paid for it?' said the first girl, spitefully.

'*We* did,' said Mabel. 'Me and me parents. We've all got jobs.'

'Bet you haven't.'

'Have so. I'm working at the Chrysler Factory. But, even if I weren't, whatever happened to pulling together and all being in it together?'

Goodness me, Mabel sounded feisty.

Carrie craned closer to the shelves to make sure that she could hear every word.

Should she intervene?

Rush around and have her tuppence worth?

'Well, perhaps you should give us that chocolate bar you're about to buy to prove that we're all "pulling together",' said the girl with the low voice nastily.

'Not on your Nellie,' Mabel shot back.

'Oh, don't be silly,' said the shrill girl, scornfully. 'She's not about to *buy* that chocolate, is she? People like her pilfer all the time. My mother says it's a way of life.'

'*My* mother says they spread all sorts of diseases. I bet she's riddled with hair lice . . .'

'Should we take a look?'

'Careful; you don't know what you might find in there!'

There was brief silence and then a little shriek. 'Get your bleeding hands off me hair!' yelled Mabel.

There was a scuffing sound from the other side of the shelves, and Carrie had had enough.

How *could* the girls be so beastly?

She straightened up, preparing to march around and give them all a piece of her mind but tripped and lost her balance, banging her hip hard against the units.

Reaching out blindly, she grabbed the shelving to steady herself . . .

Too little . . .

Too late . . .

The unit wobbled precariously and then collapsed into the neighbouring aisle with an almighty bang.

Carrie landed in an ungainly heap on top of it.

Four pairs of startled eyes turned to hers. Carrie vaguely recognised the three bullies as being a couple of years younger than her and Mabel at school. A girl with red hair abruptly let go of Mabel's hair and then the three of them scarpered.

Mabel's eyes bored into Carrie's and, as people appeared from all directions, she turned tail and fled.

The Woolworths staff were very kind, all things considered.

They clustered around Carrie, fetching her a chair and a glass of water and making sure that she wasn't too badly hurt.

Yes, the shelving could be a liability, they admitted; it didn't take much to make it wobble, although they had never known it to actually fall over like that. The trouble was that without goods weighing the shelves down and keeping them stable . . .

Carrie brushed away the fuss.

She'd scraped her knee and grazed an elbow where she'd tried to break her fall, but it could all have been so much worse.

As the staff provided cotton wool, antiseptic and adhesive bandages from their first aid kit, they plied her with questions.

Carrie started with the truth.

She'd just been getting out of the sun — it was blistering, wasn't it? — and she had been trying to cool down by the empty shelves out of everyone's way. And then she'd leant against the shelving unit because she was feeling a little faint . . . and the whole thing had given beneath her.

She was ever so sorry for giving everyone such a fright and she could quite see why some shoppers might have thought it was an explosion and had run for their lives, quite forgetting to pay for their purchases.

And she was ever so sorry that one old lady had drooped in a dead faint and was even now asking for her smelling salts.

And, no, thank you, she didn't need anything else, let alone a doctor.

She would just be on her way.

It was all hideously embarrassing and it really wasn't anyone's fault but her own. The reason the shelves had fallen down was because she had pressed her ears right up to the dividing panel in an attempt to eavesdrop.

In many ways, she had got what she deserved.

Mabel was waiting for her outside the shop.

Somewhat predictably, there was no sign of her tormentors.

'What were all that about?' Mabel demanded without preamble. 'Gave me the fright of me life.'

No expression of sympathy.

No asking if Carrie was hurt.

Carrie began to feel a little miffed.

'Thanks very much for waiting to check I was all right,' she said stiffly. 'I *know* you saw it was me lying on the ground. You could at least have helped me up.'

'I don't understand why you was there in the first place,' said Mabel, as though Carrie hadn't spoken. She looked so angry and intense – her face all screwed up so that the freckles ran together – that Carrie was on the verge of laughing.

'It's Woolworths, Mabel,' she said, gesturing to the large windows and – despite the war – quite a vibrant display of household goods, stationery and clothing. '*Woollies*! Not some secret military site. *Everyone*'s allowed in there – even though those bullies were suggesting you weren't.'

Mabel's hands clenched into fists by her side. 'So, you *was* listening in.'

'Of course I wasn't,' said Carrie. 'Not deliberately, at least. But I couldn't help overhearing what those beastly girls were saying . . .'
'You was in the middle of a load of empty shelves! Pull the other one!'

Carrie moved closer to the windows to get away from the hordes of shoppers streaming by. Honestly! To think she had wanted calm, level-headed Mabel as a friend. Where had *this* rude and spiky character come from?

'It's actually none of your business *why* I was in Woolworths,' she said, coolly. She really didn't want to explain that she was hiding from her mother! 'But I do promise it had absolutely nothing to do with you. And, just so you know, the reason the shelves fell over was because I was planning to run round to stick up for you and I accidentally barged into them.'

Mabel looked sceptical. 'It seems to me you was just standing there listening . . . not trying to help at all.'

'Well, you'll have to take my word for it. As soon as I recognised your voice and realised what those vile girls were doing, I tried to help.'

'I don't need your help, ta very much.'

Oh, for goodness' sake.

What was *wrong* with the girl?

She was being stubborn and ungrateful . . . and just downright unpleasant!

'I'm not saying you did,' said Carrie, resisting the temptation to stomp off. Her knee was beginning to sting and her elbow was throbbing for good measure. 'But I'm on your side. I heard you saying you're working at Chrysler, so suggesting you're sponging off us was terrible . . . '

'No,' interrupted Mabel. '*No*! That ain't the point at all. You're suggesting that if I hadn't got a job, those girls would have had the right to pull me hair and steal me chocolate?'

Carrie glanced down at the bar of Cadbury's Dairy Milk still in Mabel's hand.

Had she paid for it?

'Of course not,' she said. 'Who cares where you're from? As I told you, I lived in the East End until I was four . . .'

Mabel shook her head. 'It ain't the same. You're Richmond through and through. You're management.'

Carrie sighed. 'My father might be management, but I certainly am not.'

'If that's the case, why don't you muck in with the rest of us?'

Carrie was shocked. 'With what?' she said.

Mabel shrugged. 'If you have to ask, then I rest me case,' she said. 'In case you ain't noticed, folks is leaving the Poppy Factory in droves. Richmond might be safer than the factories and docks where I'm from, but it's only designated a neutral area and it certainly ain't as safe as moving to the countryside.'

'I know all that . . .'

'Yes, but did you know the lad who slopped out in the bar has gone to Shropshire, or that the woman who helped with the Brownies has gone to Cornwall? The allotments need tending, me Ma needs help cleaning the Remembrance Club . . . to say nothing of what's going on *inside* the factory. Chaps who come into the bar are complaining that they're rushed off their feet, and that the systems ain't working as they used to. There ain't enough people unloading supplies, so oftentimes they're twiddling their thumbs waiting for this or that. Worst of all, June, who used to man the tea trolleys, is about to be off to Gloucestershire to be with her sister and that's got *everyone* up in arms. The place will grind to a halt if everyone don't get their cuppas and biscuits twice a day. And the worst of it is that I've only been living here for a couple of months and I know all this and you – who have been here most of your life – ain't got a clue. So, no, we're not all in this together. And now, if you don't mind, I must be on me way.'

'I suppose that lemonade isn't going to be happening any time soon . . . ?'

Mabel gave her a scathing look. 'Good day to you . . . *Miss*.'

And she disappeared up the street.

The Poppy Girls, indeed!

Carrie started walking slowly down the high street.

What a day!

Her elbow and knee were throbbing like crazy, but she didn't want to go home until she'd got her thoughts and emotions into some sort of order.

Without really thinking about it, she found herself walking down to the towpath. There was no sign of Bobby in the crowds of men – many in military uniform – who had spilt out of the riverside pubs and who were drinking watered-down beer in the sunshine. If she was being totally honest with herself, she had probably walked that way because of the chance of seeing him again . . . but she certainly wasn't going to venture into any of the public houses to look for him. It would be embarrassing enough if he came out of the pub and saw her lurking!

Carrie scurried along the towpath and sat down on a bench a couple of hundred yards away. With a sigh, she pulled the history book out of the bag and opened it.

Seconds later, she snapped it shut.

With all that had happened over the past couple of

days – to say nothing of the past couple of *hours* – she simply couldn't concentrate.

Instead, she just sat there, taking in the busy riverbank scene. Boats of all shapes and sizes were going to and fro along the Thames or coming into dock, the faces aboard tight with concentration. Men and women were promenading along the towpath without an apparent care in the world, some alone, some laughing and chatting together. A child was crying noisily because the ice cream had fallen off his cone; his mother bent in silent supplication. Seagulls were wheeling and diving overhead or bobbing placidly on the navy-blue water. It was all as it ever had been, ever since Carrie could remember and, at first glance, you could be forgiven for thinking the riverside had escaped the war . . .

But look a little deeper, and the signs were everywhere.

Take the pillboxes that had sprung up along the river, strategically positioned and designed to delay the enemy. The nearest was a small brick building covered with a large sign declaring 'Teas, Wines, Eats' and further along was another disguised as a public convenience. Carrie had become so used to them that they just merged into the background and occasionally she was tempted to ask for an ice or to try to spend a penny . . .

Or what about the members of the Local Defence Volunteers, armed with rifles, stationed at either end of the bridge? Carrie recognised one as Daisy's father – the quietest and most mild-mannered of men – and smothered a smile. He certainly looked the part in his steel hat and khaki uniform, but if he was all that stood between them and an enemy invasion, God help them all . . .

Or even the A-board on the towpath, proclaiming that the boatmen had recently donated a day's takings to Richmond's Spitfire Fund and had raised a magnificent £59 in the process . . .

Carrie leapt to her feet and started marching down the towpath.

Even the *boatmen* were doing their bit to help . . .

Everyone was doing their bit: Daisy's father, Mabel at the Chrysler Factory, Bobby at the ARP *and* at Starfish . . .

Everybody except her.

It was all very well worrying about history repeating itself and bleating on about learning the lessons of the past . . . but what about when history was already knocking on the door? What about when it was already here?

Deep in thought, Carrie continued striding along the towpath, until Richmond was far behind and the houses had given way to fields and woods.

Maybe Mabel was right. She *should* be helping.

She should certainly be doing her bit until she went to university . . . and probably beyond – for as long as the wretched war lasted. As long as it wasn't directly involved with the fighting or with killing anyone, there was really no reason why she couldn't do so with a clear conscience.

Bobby was doing it.

Mabel was doing it.

Daisy's father was doing it!

By the time Carrie was approaching Ham House – a beautiful seventeenth-century English country house perfectly situated on a bend of the river – she was full of resolve.

Mabel had made it clear that there were plenty of jobs

that needed doing around the Poppy Factory. She would ask Pa where she could most usefully get involved until she headed off to university – and even whilst she was studying.

And she wouldn't give up until she had a satisfactory answer.

Chapter Eight

Monday 1 July 1940

Carrie was thoroughly hot and discomforted by the time she arrived back at the estate and her knee was stinging like crazy.

It had been an eventful day.

As she approached the penthouse, her thoughts strayed to Bobby. Was there a chance he might have regretted rushing off without a proper goodbye? He knew where she lived – but why, oh why, had she called herself Lyn . . . ?

'Hello!'

It was Sarah's voice. There she was, crouched over in the middle of the vegetables and wrestling with an enormous cabbage. Carrie was surprised quite how pleased she was to see her. Against all odds, she wanted to continue their conversation, might even confide in her about Bobby . . .

'Do you actually live in that flowerbed?' she said in amusement. She walked a little way down Sarah's front path, casting a quick glance up to make sure Alfie wasn't up to his antics again.

Sarah stood up with an expression that was halfway between a grin and a grimace.

'Feels like it sometimes,' she said. 'Mum's had her eye on this cabbage for ages and she doesn't want Mrs Perkins on the ground floor flat getting to it before we do. Not that

Mrs Perkins has any right to it – she's barely lifted a finger all season.'

Carrie made a little face. The flowerbeds in front of each block of flats were the responsibility of the residents and it was up to them how they divided up the fruit and vegetables they grew. Carrie was painfully aware that she did nothing to help in her block's flowerbed – the difference being that old Mr McLoughlin in the flat below had recently retired and had made it clear that this was to be his contribution to the war effort.

'Help me with this beast, will you?' said Sarah, pointing at the cabbage.

'Not likely,' said Carrie, pointing, in turn, at her light-blue frock. 'This is one of my favourite dresses and it's *ages* until washday.'

'Ooh, Carrie Harper. Don't be so prim and proper.'

'I'm not,' protested Carrie. She *certainly* hadn't been prim in the hayloft with Ned, although she had been careful not to let him go too far. 'I'm just sensible. Anyway, you don't need me to help pull it out. You're Sarah Turner – the school sports star. Just give it a yank.'

'Right you are.' Sarah gave Carrie a wide grin, gritted her teeth and duly pulled.

Somewhat predictably, she ended up on her back with both the cabbage and a large shower of earth on her stomach.

Both girls started laughing so loudly that Mrs Perkins shut her window with a rather pointed *thud*.

Still giggling, Sarah got up and sat on the front step of the flats. Carrie brushed the step clean and sat down beside her.

'Thanks for not dropping me in it yesterday,' said Sarah, cradling the cabbage like a baby.

'I'm not a sneak,' said Carrie. 'I told you that I wouldn't and I'm generally as good as my word. Anyway, how did you know I didn't?'

'Your father told mine that you knew about the factory being repurposed,' said Sarah. 'I was worried for a moment, but Dad said you knew because you'd been inside and had guessed.'

'It was the best I could come up with on the spur of the moment,' admitted Carrie. 'Even so, my father had kittens. Went on about it being classified information at the same time as trying to pretend that nothing had changed.'

Sarah laughed. 'I don't know how they think they can keep it a secret with hundreds of people working there. Anyway, never mind that. Guess what I've just gone and done?'

'I have no idea,' said Carrie, wryly. 'Joined the circus?'

'Silly!' Sarah gave her a friendly shove. 'I've signed up for the ARP! I'll be marching around and giving you all orders before too long!'

'Wow.' Carrie was amazed. After all, Sarah had never hidden her disdain for Miss Arnott. 'Here? At the Poppy Factory?'

'Yup! I'd been thinking about it for a while, even though Miss Arnott gets right up my nose. But the news coming out of Scotland this afternoon made me realise we've got to take this seriously . . .'

Carrie's heart rate stepped up a gear. 'What news?' she said.

'You haven't heard?'

'*No.* I've been out all day. What's happened?'

'A German bombing raid in Wick,' said Sarah, soberly. 'Several civilians were killed. Children, too.'

'That's *terrible*,' said Carrie.

'It is.' Suddenly, Sarah's eyes were shiny with tears. 'The BBC said the Germans were probably going for the nearby airfield or the Scottish coastal defences, but that's hardly a comfort, is it?'

'Not at all,' said Carrie. 'I can hardly believe it. Guernsey and now this. The enemy's getting closer all the time.'

She glanced up at the sky, half expecting a dozen German bombers to suddenly swoop into view.

'That's why I'm volunteering for the ARP,' said Sarah. 'Miss Arnott or no Miss Arnott, who knows how long we've got before they reach Richmond?'

Carrie gave her a shaky smile. 'You're a braver girl than me,' she said, trying to lighten the atmosphere.

Sarah laughed. 'Because of potentially flinging myself into bombed buildings, or because of Miss Arnott?'

'Both!' said Carrie. 'Let's hope she's all bark and no bite.'

'She seemed all right when I went along to volunteer, and she's already signed me up for first aid training at the Star and Garter.'

'And are you still planning to train as a physiotherapist?' said Carrie, shifting on the hard stone step.

'Course I am,' said Sarah. 'If I've passed my Highers well enough, I'm off to St Thomas's in September. There are already so many soldiers needing rehabilitation, and I can't see things getting better. Our fathers didn't get the help they needed – Dad often says he wouldn't walk with such a limp if he'd had proper physio back in the day – and it would be nice to be part of doing things better this time around.'

Carrie shuddered. She could think of nothing worse than looking after the poor soldiers' broken bodies, although, of course, she could see that the work was important. She felt a pang of guilt that studying history wouldn't be doing anything immediately to help and doubled down on her resolution to do some voluntary work.

'They're looking for more volunteers at the ARP if you're interested,' said Sarah, cutting across her thoughts. 'Or are you absolutely committed to not getting involved?'

'I want to help!' said Carrie. 'I just don't want to do anything that kills people. Volunteering for the ARP would be absolutely fine. In fact, maybe I'll ask my father . . .'

'Just *tell* your father . . .'

Carrie gave her a severe look. 'You *know* my father.'

Sarah's answering smile was sympathetic. 'True,' she said. 'In the meantime, maybe I should start my first aid practice on *you*. What on earth have you done to your knee?'

Carrie glanced down. The gash on her knee had oozed through the dressing and there was dried blood all down her shin.

'Oh!' She took out her handkerchief and started dabbing ineffectually at the stain. Then she told Sarah all about bumping into Mabel in Woolworths, overhearing her being bullied and then accidentally knocking the shelving over.

'Mabel wasn't in the slightest bit grateful to me for trying to help,' she finished, a little bitterly. 'She said she didn't need my help because I was "management" and more or less accused me of spying on her.'

'She's a queer fish,' Sarah agreed. 'She's polite and friendly enough in the Remembrance Club, but I bumped into her on Richmond Hill the other day – she was walking down the road just as I came out of the estate – and she scuttled past me like a rabbit in the headlights.'

Carrie shrugged. 'I'd hoped we might be friends,' she said, hauling herself to her feet. Now she was thinking about it, her knee had really started hurting and her elbow had joined in for good measure. 'I'd better go and get tidied up,' she said. 'And aren't you going to take that cabbage in for your mother?'

Sarah didn't move. 'Not just yet,' she said with a little smile. 'I'm keeping an eye out for "him". They'll be out soon.'

'Him?' echoed Carrie.

'Harry,' confirmed Sarah, two spots of colour appearing high in her cheeks. 'Don't you think he's a bit of all right?'

Carrie considered, her head on one side. There was no doubt Harry was a good-looking man with his dark, brooding good looks, but Carrie had barely given him a thought over the past couple of weeks. For a second, she was tempted to tell Sarah about Ned – and even about Bobby – but she stopped herself. Ned was a secret to keep close and Bobby had had his chance.

'He's certainly very handsome,' she conceded. 'But maybe a little too close to home?'

'Oh, he doesn't live here,' said Sarah quickly. 'He has rooms in Twickenham – or so I'm told – but he often passes this way to get his bus.'

'I see.' Carrie couldn't resist a smirk. Walking through the estate was hardly the quickest way to the bus stop. It sounded very much as though Sarah had already caught his eye. 'But . . .'

She trailed off.

How could she explain her reservations about getting involved with someone very similar to their fathers? Someone scarred from an experience that the home front could never fully understand.

'I thought you two were already . . . friends,' she said. 'You certainly seemed that way at the darts competition.'

Sarah shook her head. 'Not a bit of it, sadly,' she said. 'He'd only come out to the hallway for a ciggie and we – or, rather *I* – more or less accosted him. As soon as he'd finished his smoke, he scarpered.'

'Right!' said Carrie.

How different it had seemed from the outside looking in.

'I've barely seen him since,' Sarah continued. 'We've been away visiting relatives in Scarborough and I think he must have been away too. But then I spotted him from my bedroom window and, to be honest, that's part of the reason I've been lurking out here for the past couple of days.'

Carrie smirked and glanced at her watch. 'It's already five o'clock,' she said. 'You don't have long to wait.'

As if on cue, men started streaming from the Poppy Factory doors. Some lingered by the exit – getting into wheelchairs, chatting to colleagues, lighting a smoke. Others started walking – alone or in little groups – down the main thoroughfare of the estate, peeling off in turn to the various blocks of flats or carrying on out of the estate and onto the Petersham Road. They called out to each other – hoping for a quiet night or commenting on the heat still left in the day – with one or two cheerfully greeting Carrie and Sarah and remarking on the size of the cabbage that Sarah was still cradling. And then the wheelchair users started streaming past – some self-propelled, others pushed by a colleague – everyone looking happy to be clocking off.

But there was no sign of Harry.

'I think you're out of luck,' said Carrie, sympathetically.

'No. Don't make it obvious, but here he is now,' said Sarah.

Carrie ventured a little glance. Yes, here was Harry, using a stick and walking slowly in their direction. His hair was a glossy blue-black in the sunshine.

'Shall I go?' offered Carrie. 'I don't want to play gooseberry.'

'Please don't,' said Sarah. She got to her feet in one fluid movement. 'But you can take this, if you wouldn't mind.'

And, without warning, she thrust the huge cabbage into Carrie's arms. Carrie held it disdainfully at arms' length. So much for keeping her dress clean!

'Hello,' said Sarah, as Harry drew level.

'Afternoon,' Harry replied. He stopped at the end of the path and looked from one girl to the other. 'What's this? Pass the cabbage?'

Sarah grinned. 'It's all the rage,' she quipped. 'Fancy a go?'

She grabbed the cabbage from Carrie's arms and playfully thrust it towards Harry. Harry took an awkward step – almost a stumble – backwards and hastily righted himself with his stick.

There was an awkward silence.

In making a simple – silly – joke, Sarah had inadvertently drawn attention to Harry's disability and, in the process, seemed to have totally discomforted the poor fellow.

Carrie cleared her throat. They needed to change the subject quickly and Sarah seemed to have lost her tongue.

'How many down today?' she asked brightly.

It was the first thing that came to mind.

Carrie couldn't have given two hoots what the answer was, but Harry would know.

Pa always made a big deal about announcing that shift's tally.

How many petals had been cut out, how many stalks had been twisted, how many completed poppies had been boxed up.

Targets were important, Pa always said.

Focussing the men's minds on the bigger picture was important.

That was why the factory had recently introduced monetary bonuses linked with high productivity . . .

But Harry's brows were pulled together in confusion. 'Pardon me?' he said.

'The poppies, silly,' Carrie clarified. 'How many leaves or whatever did you make today?'

'Ah,' said Harry. 'Not really my department, I'm afraid . . .'

'Not your department?' echoed Sarah, suddenly finding her voice. She turned to Carrie, chestnut eyes shining with mischief, and added in an exaggerated whisper, 'Maybe he's an imposter. He could even be a spy. Do you think we should report him?'

'Probably wise,' replied Carrie, with a little grin. 'You

keep him talking and I'll go and fetch the Local Defence Volunteers.'

Harry laughed. 'Then again, maybe I've simply been drafted by the Ministry of Aircraft Production to help get the radios up and running,' he said.

Carrie and Sarah both gawped at him, then exchanged a little glance.

'I thought that was meant to be top secret, classified information?' said Sarah, wrinkling up her nose.

'Hardly,' said Harry, looking surprised. 'Maybe need-to-know would be a better way of describing it?'

'But my father gave me the third degree when he discovered I'd found out!' interrupted Carrie, almost indignantly. 'Said he'd have my guts for garters if I breathed a word.'

Harry blinked in confusion. 'Well, it's always best to be on the cautious side,' he said diplomatically. 'We certainly wouldn't want the man on the Clapham omnibus – or even the Richmond omnibus, for that matter – knowing the details. But I think it's pretty pointless trying to keep it from people living on the estate.'

Huh!

Trust Pa to have thrust out his chest in self-importance and to have exaggerated everything.

He *could* have told her all about the radios.

He had just chosen not to!

'Wizard!' said Sarah. 'So does that mean we can ask you questions about it?'

'Within reason,' said Harry with a grin. 'But, if you're about to give me the Spanish Inquisition, I might need a smoke!'

'So, how's the new department coming along?' asked

Sarah. She chose that moment to oh-so-casually whip off her headscarf so that her hair cascaded in loose waves around her shoulders and Carrie nearly laughed out loud.

Harry pulled a packet of cigarettes from his pocket and flipped it open.

'Slowly and with difficulty,' he said.

He extracted a cigarette with his lip, shut the packet, and slid it back into a pocket.

Sarah sprung forwards, hastily passing the cabbage to Carrie, and produced a silver lighter from her own pocket. With a swift flick of her thumb, the lighter sparked, fluttering slightly in the late-afternoon breeze. Sarah cupped the flame, held it up to Harry and, seconds later, Harry's cigarette was alight. He took a deep draught and then exhaled slowly, looking down at Sarah with an expression that made Carrie feel very much a gooseberry.

'Thank you,' he said softly.

Sarah smiled. 'My pleasure,' she said, flushing gently.

You could have cut the tension with a knife.

Carrie cleared her throat, embarrassed, and Harry stepped back.

'Would either of you like a cigarette?' he asked, his voice back to its usual volume.

Carrie waved the offer away and Sarah shook her head.

'No, thanks,' she said. 'This lighter is officially for allotment bonfires. Mum would have a fit if she saw me smoking down here.'

Carrie wondered if she should make her excuses and creep away. She had no wish to cramp Sarah's style, so she put the cabbage down on the pathway and picked up her bag. But Sarah reached out and touched her sleeve and gave her an almost imploring glance.

Carrie understood at once.

It was one thing two girls chatting with a young man, but if Mrs Turner should look out of her window and see Sarah dallying alone . . . well, that would be another matter entirely.

She stayed put.

'Are you an expert on radios?' she asked brightly.

Harry smiled. 'It's safe to say I know my way around one,' he said. 'I studied electrical engineering at college and then I was a wireless-operator on a Wellington bomber.'

The girls looked at him in admiration.

'Wow,' said Sarah. 'That must have been exciting.'

'*Terrifying*,' countered Carrie.

'Both,' said Harry. 'We just did what we had to do and kept everything crossed that we'd see Christmas Day. And that's quite enough said about that. The important thing is that I'm really lucky to be here and helping to set up a new unit for the Ministry is right up my street.'

'So, you're not just helping to *make* the radios?' said Sarah.

'No. Not at all. Me and two more senior chaps have a matter of weeks to get the factory organised, staffed and up and running.'

Both girls stared at him in newfound admiration. Harry was not just handsome; he was brave and accomplished and had clearly been given responsibilities way beyond his tender years.

'So, what's proving to be the difficulty in getting things off the ground?' asked Carrie. 'Is it just everything?'

Harry sighed and puffed on his cigarette. 'No, not everything to be fair,' he said. 'It's a super building and we're being allocated the whole top floor, which is marvellous, although I know it means everyone else has had to squash up a bit. And, by and large, we're slowly getting hold of all the materials we need. I gather you were kind enough to drive some important pieces back from Liverpool for us, Carrie?'

'I did?' said Carrie, who had begun to suspect as much.

'You did?' said Sarah, who clearly had no idea.

'She did,' said Harry, and the three laughed easily together. 'She brought us a couple of precision lathes and a coil winding machine all the way from Liverpool. No, the problem is manpower. We're not getting all the men in the factory, as we have elsewhere. We're not even getting most of them, because – as I'm sure you know – the Poppy Factory quotas are going *up*, not down. And there's more to it than that. Assembling radios is painstaking, fiddly work and, to be brutally honest, it's not really suited to the workforce we have here.'

'In what way?' asked Sarah.

'How much do you know about radios?'

Both girls gave elaborate shrugs in reply.

'Well, they're tricky little devils,' said Harry. 'There are lots of key components – transistors, resistors, capacitors, inductors – and that's just for starters.'

'Is there a law that they all have to end in "tor"?' interjected Sarah with a grin.

She was rewarded with a loud bark of laughter.

'I'd never really thought of it like that,' said Harry. 'The point is, though, that all these "tors" have to be meticulously placed onto a circuit board and then soldered into place. There's no room for error. If the darn thing is going to work, everything has to be just so. The job requires both an eye for detail and very steady hands.'

'I see,' said Carrie thoughtfully. 'The men here are already used to making fiddly artificial flowers – they've got great attention to detail – but many of them have one arm.'

'Precisely,' said Harry. 'You need to be stable and you need dexterity – even the chaps with both arms will struggle if balance is an issue. I had a go just this morning, and I found it well-nigh impossible to work quickly enough with this artificial leg throwing off my centre of gravity. And I'm not saying it's impossible – of course I'm not. Look how efficiently the Poppy Factory runs when each process is carefully tailored to the strengths and weaknesses of the worker. When the bench is designed to give extra support to the men with amputated legs, when those with one hand are given specially adapted frames to hold things in place. But all that takes time – lots of time – and time is one thing we don't have. We need to hit the ground running in just a couple of weeks with the standard equipment and with quotas that would be difficult to reach at the best of times. It's a conundrum, I'm telling you. No wonder my hair is going grey.'

Both girls laughed. Harry's hair might have chestnut highlights, but there wasn't a single silver strand.

'You'll just have to bring people in from outside, then,' said Sarah. 'It's the only practical solution. That's what they're doing everywhere else. Chrysler, Hayes . . .'

Harry smiled. 'The trouble is that the Poppy Factory isn't "everywhere else", is it?'

His eyes flicked to Carrie, who understood his implication immediately.

Pa had obviously made his views abundantly – and forcibly – known.

'I can imagine,' she said, wearily. She took a deep breath. '"It's the principle of the matter",' she parroted. '"Work at the Poppy Factory is strictly reserved for disabled servicemen and we don't want to establish a precedent for breaking that contract, even in wartime when we're not making poppies."'

Harry gave her a wry smile. 'Bullseye,' he said. 'And I do understand his point of view. I'm one of them. I get it. Opportunities for disabled people still aren't where they should be – even after all this time – and this is a very special place. But it leaves me stuck between a rock and a hard place. I want to honour the ethos of the factory . . . but this is wartime and things are different . . .'

'It's clear what you need to do, then,' Carrie interrupted him.

Two pairs of brown eyes turned to her.

'Is it?' said Harry with a quizzical smile.

'Yes,' said Carrie. 'Use us, of course. Use the Poppy Girls.'

'The Poppy Girls,' repeated Sarah, almost to herself. 'That's what Miss Bateman called us at school.'

A window was hurled open above them. 'Sarah Turner, will you stop gossiping and bring that cabbage up here right now, otherwise no one's getting any dinner tonight!'

Sarah, blushing furiously, picked up the cabbage. 'I'd better . . .' she said, gesturing inside.

And here was Pa heading down the road from the factory towards them.

'I'd better scarper as well,' said Carrie.

Harry glanced at his watch. 'Goodness me, is that the time. I must dash too, or I'll find myself walking back to Twickenham! I'm very glad we had this chat, ladies, and we'll hopefully talk again very soon.'

Seconds later, the street was empty.

Ten minutes later, Carrie was sitting on a chair pulled up to the sink in the kitchen whilst Ma dabbed her knee and elbow with cottonwool dipped in TCP.

It smarted like anything, of course, but the sharp sting soon subsided to a prickle and, after the day she had had, there was something very comforting about Ma tending to her grazes as though she was five years old again.

'Any chance of a cup of tea?' said Pa, stomping into the kitchen as Ma stretched Elastoplast over Carrie's knee. 'Goodness me, girl; what on earth have you done to yourself this time?'

There was scorn and even a soupcon of amusement in his voice, and Carrie bristled.

'A slight mishap in Woollies,' she said airily.

She held her breath. Hopefully Ma wouldn't suddenly remember she'd seen Carrie abruptly – and rudely – scuttling into the shop as she'd approached. But Ma just turned her attention to Carrie's elbow without comment.

'In *Woolworths*?' said Pa, eyebrows heading towards his heavily Brylcreemed hair. 'Good God, girl; it's hardly the Somme. What the devil happened?'

Carrie shrugged, embarrassed. 'Some empty shelves gave way when I brushed against them,' she admitted.

Pa's face split into an incredulous – and not especially

kind – grin. 'You must have "brushed" against them with quite some heft,' he said, guffawing loudly. 'Goodness me, you are a clumsy Clara! Always have been, and always will be, I suppose.'

Carrie turned away, furious.

Why did her father always make her feel so *wretched*?

Still, there was no point in rising to it.

She needed Pa on side.

'Actually, I bumped into Mabel Green in there . . .' she started, carefully.

'Who's she when she's at home?' interrupted Pa.

'Daughter of the new couple who run the Remembrance Club, dear,' said Ma mildly, repacking the first aid kit. 'Seems a very calm and capable young lady.'

'Mabel was telling me about her new job at the Chrysler Factory,' said Carrie. 'And it made me realise that I should be doing something as well. Particularly after what happened in Scotland today.'

'I'm not having you being a factory girl,' said Pa immediately.

Carrie almost laughed out loud at the sheer hypocrisy.

'*You* work in a factory,' she shot back. 'Is that how you feel about *your* workers . . . ?'

'Of course not. That is entirely different.'

'You can help me sort the flowers in the Remembrance Club, if you like,' interrupted Ma quickly, before her father had the chance to reply further. 'That would be very helpful.'

'Flowers in the Remembrance Club?' echoed Carrie weakly.

'Yes,' said Ma brightly. 'They've got the police coming over for billiards, and I promised Mrs Green I'd see if there are any flowers I can "borrow" from the allotments. It looks like Mr Harman has rather sneakily grown some delphiniums behind one of the sheds where he thinks no one can see and I'm sure he won't mind donating some of them to the cause. Slice these for me, will you, love?'

Carrie gave her mother a weak smile and took the small brown bag of tomatoes.

Arranging flowers seemed rather like King Canute pushing back the tide. And Mabel would no doubt have plenty to say about Carrie doing something so genteel.

So *managerial* . . .

'I was rather thinking of something more directly related to the war effort,' she said, coolly, starting to slice the tomatoes. They were woody and had clearly been plucked before their best. Nothing was at its best nowadays, including, it seemed, her and her family. 'Actually, I was thinking about volunteering for the local ARP.'

Carrie held her breath.

Hope sprung eternal.

But Pa had gone puce in the face. 'Absolutely not,' he roared. 'It's bad enough being shoved from pillar to post by that dreadful harridan Miss Whatnot . . .'

'Arnott,' interjected Ma, mildly.

'Miss Whitwhat,' Pa repeated rudely, as if Ma hadn't spoken. 'I can barely put up with her clomping around on her flat feet – and I certainly could *not* put up with being given orders by my own daughter. What would people think? *"Muster here, keep quiet, close that blind . . ."* It's out of the question.'

'Oh, for goodness' sake,' snapped Carrie. 'So, being a factory girl would be too lowly but volunteering for the

ARP would be getting ideas above my station? You can't have it both ways. Besides, Sarah Turner has already signed up. She's doing *her* bit.'

'Oh, so that's what you were talking to her about outside, was it?' said Pa sourly. 'Well, remember, if you please, that Sarah Turner is not the daughter of the factory manager and she shouldn't be putting ridiculous ideas in your head . . .'

'It's not a ridiculous idea . . .'

'It is where you're concerned,' said Pa, nastily. 'If you can't stay standing upright in Woolworths on a run-of-the-mill weekday, what use are you going to be when Jerry invades and it's all hands to the pump? You'd be a blooming liability!'

'Pa just wants to keep you safe,' interjected Ma. 'What about the Poppy Factory Brownies? I know Mrs Jennings is desperate for some help.'

'The Brownies would be seemly,' conceded Pa.

'I don't want to help the blasted Brownies. I want to do something *useful*!'

'Language, Carolyn,' growled Pa. 'Sixpence in the swear jar.'

Carrie resisted the temptation to let her chair clatter to the floor and to storm from the room.

'All right, then,' she fairly hissed. 'I'll help with the Brownies.'

'Your results will be back in a couple of weeks,' said Ma, soothingly. 'Then you can confirm your place at university and things will start to change. In the meantime, why don't you freshen up before supper? Spam salad tonight.'

Carrie nodded, close to tears, and went to her room.

She hated Spam and she hated her father.

Chapter Nine

Tuesday 2 July 1940

Next day, there was a knock on the front door around four in the afternoon.

Carrie answered it to find Sarah standing there, wreathed in smiles.

'It's such a lovely day – again,' she said. 'I wondered if you'd like to take a stroll with me?'

Carrie beamed with pleasure.

The invitation couldn't have come at a better time. Carrie had spent most of the day helping Ma with the laundry and both her hands and her temper had been rubbed raw. She also realised that, despite everything, her heart had been rubbed a little raw as well. It was the first time she had really had a chance to take stock since she'd arrived home and she realised that – despite her determination to put him firmly from her mind – she missed Ned. She really missed him; indeed, had been hard-pressed not to put pen to paper when she woke up that morning to tell him exactly that. All in all, it was lovely to have someone actually knocking at the door for her and to help take her mind off things. Her potential friendship with Mabel was clearly doomed not to get off the ground and Daisy lived so far away, but this made her feel as though Sarah might really become a friend.

What a strange summer this was turning out to be.

'I'd love to,' she said, untying her pinny. 'We've just hung the last of the washing out, so it's perfect timing.'

'I know,' said Sarah. 'I've been watching you from my bedroom. One of the advantages of living directly opposite.'

Carrie laughed and went to find her hat and her mother. Ma waved her away with a smile.

'Skedaddle,' she said. 'You've worked hard today. Have a little fun before your father gets home.'

'Where do you fancy strolling?' asked Carrie, as she and Sarah fairly skipped down the stairs. 'Shall we go down to the river?'

Sarah grinned. 'I was using the word "stroll" loosely,' she said. 'I thought we might just go to the Remembrance Club and grab something to drink. My mother's asked me to pass on a message to Mrs Green, so we could kill two birds with one stone.'

'Oh!' That put a completely different spin on 'stroll'. 'By "drink" do you mean "beer"?' she added cautiously.

Sarah laughed. 'Of course not,' she said. 'Even if I fancied one, Mrs Green would be hardly likely to sell me one at four in the afternoon. Not if she values her licence.'

That left Carrie feeling a little naïve.

'But do you like it?' she persisted.

Sarah shrugged. 'Not particularly,' she said. 'Dad bought me half a pint at the darts competition because I'd just turned eighteen, and I couldn't even finish that. Why? Do you?'

'No reason,' said Carrie, remembering how cool and

sophisticated she had thought Sarah that evening. How looks could deceive. 'And no, I don't, either. Horribly bitter.'

'Lemonades all round then,' said Sarah, with a grin. 'My treat.'

'No need,' said Carrie.

'Every need. Partly to apologise for the last time we were in there and partly to say thank you for not dumping me in it when I told you about the radios.'

Five minutes later, Sarah had passed on her message to Mrs Green – something boring about her father and the billiards match against the police that evening – and Mrs Green surprised them with lemonade on the house. The girls installed themselves at a scrubbed table near the window in the empty bar and Carrie gazed out at the bowling green and the old pet cemetery beyond . . .

She brushed away the thought that Pa might not find her sitting in the bar very seemly.

'Penny for them,' said Sarah, cutting across her thoughts.

'Nothing, really,' said Carrie, turning away from the window. 'At least, nothing worth owning up to. A question for *you*; weren't you tempted to wait outside your flat for "him" again this afternoon?'

Sarah coloured prettily. 'Of course I was,' she said. 'But that would be a little predictable – no? – and there's only so much gardening I can do in that flowerbed! Besides, I'm sure he'll track us down at some point. Apart from anything else, he seemed intrigued by your Poppy Girls comment . . .'

'Yes. Hopefully he'll realise it's the obvious thing to do . . .'

Carrie trailed off because Mabel had just come into the room, carrying a wooden crate of beer bottles. She hesitated when she saw Carrie, but continued on her way, depositing the crate on the bar with a little grunt. Seconds later, she was back, running a hand through her wayward curls.

She glanced at Sarah and then turned to Carrie. 'I want to apologise,' she said. 'I were ever so rude and ungrateful outside Woollies and I'm ever so sorry.'

Carrie nodded. 'That's all right,' she said. She gave a little self-deprecating grin. 'It must have been quite a shock to see the shelving collapse, with me on top of it.'

Mabel gave a relieved giggle. 'Not half!' she said. 'But that don't explain me rudeness.'

'What I don't understand is why you thought I was following you,' said Carrie. 'I mean, without being rude, why on earth should I *want* to?'

Mabel shrugged. 'I don't know why you'd *want* to,' she said, 'but you admitted you was standing next to some empty shelves and listening in.'

Carrie smiled. 'When you put it like that . . . !' she said. She paused and then decided honesty was the best policy. 'The truth of the matter was that I was hiding from my mother!'

To her relief, Mabel and Sarah both started chuckling.

'Fair enough,' said Mabel, with a sideways glance at her own mother, now unpacking the crate of beer behind the bar. 'We *all* want to hide from our mothers sometimes.'

'And then I couldn't help hearing those girls being perfectly beastly,' added Carrie.

'That were so embarrassing . . .'

'You should be *angry* – not embarrassed,' interrupted Carrie. 'I promise that most people round here don't feel like that. By the way, I recognised at least one of them. The one with red hair and the low voice was definitely a couple of years younger than us at school.'

'Hmm – that sounds like Betty Folger,' said Sarah. 'Knows her way around a hockey pitch, to be fair, but can be a spiteful little cow.'

'Should we tell Miss Bateman?' said Carrie.

'No, thank you,' said Mabel, firmly. 'I don't want to waste another moment on Betty Folger and her ilk.'

'I seem to remember she has refugees from London living with her family,' said Sarah. 'She was having a good moan about having to bunk down with her sister to make space. That doesn't excuse anything, of course, but . . .'

'Mind if I join the party?'

The three girls had been so busy in conversation, that none of them had seen or heard Harry approach. Seconds later, Harry had fetched chairs for himself and Mabel and the four of them were squashed around the small table.

'Well, this is a delightful surprise,' said Sarah, wreathed in smiles.

'I can't claim it's a coincidence,' said Harry. 'I came looking for you, but before I started ringing on random doorbells, a smallish boy – presumably your brother? – helpfully told me where you were.'

'Well, it won't have been Alfie,' Sarah said with a grin. 'He would have taken great pleasure in sending you on a wild goose chase!'

There were chuckles all round as Harry pulled his chair a little closer to the table.

'I wanted to talk to you about something you said last night,' he said. 'After our – er – need-to-know discussion.'

Mabel got to her feet. 'I'll leave you to it,' she said, slightly awkwardly. 'I'm sure Ma needs help behind the bar.'

'No, sit down,' said Harry. 'I didn't mean to exclude you. I'm presuming you know all about the changes going on in the factory, along with everyone else?' he added.

Mabel looked surprised. 'It . . . er . . . depends what changes you're talking about, Sir,' she said, warily.

'No need for the "Sir" here,' said Harry briskly. 'And news spreads like wildfire around a place like this.' He gestured around the bar. 'I'd be extremely surprised if you *hadn't* heard.'

Mabel gave the ghost of a smile. 'Do you mean the *special* poppies?' she said carefully. 'The special poppies that will, er, find themselves airborne very soon . . .'

Everyone laughed again and Sarah clapped her hands in glee.

'"The special poppies!"' she echoed. 'I like that.'

'Me too,' said Harry.

'That's what we call them in here,' said Mabel. 'Pa says it's common knowledge – everyone's moaning that there ain't enough men to go round as it is – but the important thing is to make sure that word don't spread beyond the estate and into the wrong hands.'

'Precisely,' said Harry. 'Now, I don't think there *are* sufficient men who can be freed up from the Poppy Factory to meet our objectives and you, Carrie, said that we should use the Poppy Girls. I think I can hazard a pretty good guess what you meant, but I'd quite like to hear you say it in your own words, if you don't mind.'

'Of course,' said Carrie, suddenly feeling self-conscious. 'I was suggesting you use the wives and daughters living on the estate to build your . . . special poppies. That way, you're keeping the faith by not bringing in outside workers.'

Harry nodded. 'Yes, that's what I thought you meant,' he said. 'And I thought – think – it sounds perfect. I was dreading telling the management team that we were going to have to recruit beyond the estate. This would be a far more palatable option. The workers may not be disabled or war veterans, but they would live here.'

Mabel's eyes were shining. 'I think it's a marvellous idea,' she said. 'Good for you, Carrie. And of course it needn't be just for the 'special poppies', need it? They're really struggling in the warehouse and deliveries now that a lot of the workers have enlisted. We could help out all over – so long as we're not making the actual poppies.'

'Absolutely,' said Harry. 'But I mentioned the idea to a few of the men today and I got a mixed response. My immediate supervisors think it's a marvellous plan, of course, but then – like me – they're outsiders without a personal stake in the factory. As for everyone else, the feeling I got was that they think it's a great idea in theory, but it didn't exactly get a ringing endorsement. Something's holding them back and I'm not sure what it is. Which is partly why I'm reaching out to you. The Poppy Girls.'

Carrie, Sarah and Mabel smirked at each other.

There it was again.

They turned back to Harry, all talking at once.

'The trouble is that the men in Richmond set a lot of store by being the man of the house,' said Carrie.

'Our fathers *want* to be able to provide for their families,' said Sarah.

'There's a lot of pride in wives and daughters *not* having to work,' said Mabel.

Laughing, they all stopped talking and then politely tried to speak one at a time.

'My father is happy for my mother to make blackout curtains and dresses for people,' said Carrie. 'But he makes a great deal out of referring to it as her hobby or saying that she is just doing it for pin money.'

'My dad really doesn't want my mother to work at all,' said Sarah. 'He always says that bringing up the five of us *is* her job.'

'Me Da don't mind so much,' said Mabel. 'But he were very clear when we came to work here that he's the Remembrance Club manager and me Ma just helps him out. Even though the way I see it is that she does at least half the work.'

'Yes, I understand all that,' said Harry. 'My father is largely the same. He works at the bank and my mother keeps house. But surely the war has changed all that?'

'I think it has,' agreed Carrie, working it out almost for the first time. 'That said, I do think things are different here. I really think the need for our fathers to provide and to prove themselves is stronger here than elsewhere.'

'Yes,' agreed Sarah. 'I think it's even more important for them to be seen to "be a man" because they've been injured and because they can't fight this time. I think they worry that a wife out working would reflect badly on them.'

'That's really interesting,' said Harry, thoughtfully. 'The trouble is, what do we do about it?'

'Concentrate on their daughters,' suggested Mabel. 'I don't think our fathers have quite the same reservations about us working.'

'Speak for yourself,' muttered Carrie crossly.

'No, I think Mabel has a point,' said Sarah. 'My father is much happier for me to work outside the house than he is my mother. The trouble is, there aren't enough of us. Lots of the veterans have older children who have already left the estate or younger children who aren't yet old enough to work. You'd need to get at least some of the wives involved.'

'So where does that leave us?' asked Harry.

'Who knows?' said Mabel.

The four laughed easily together and Carrie thought, once again, how strange the past few days had been. From constantly feeling as though she was on the outside looking in, she now felt as though she was in the thick of the action.

'Stress that men all over the country are "allowing" their wives to work for the duration and that it's our fathers' patriotic duty to do the same?' she suggested.

'Yes, that's one tack,' said Harry.

'But I seriously wouldn't mention it's my idea,' said Carrie. 'My father would dismiss it out of hand if he knew.'

'I'm sure you're doing him a disservice.'

'I promise you I'm not,' replied Carrie flatly

'Never mind the men,' interrupted Sarah. 'If you – we – want women to work in the factory, shouldn't we be speaking directly to *them*.'

'Exactly,' said Mabel. 'It's all very well hoping the men will talk to their wives and chivvy them along, but that might take *weeks*—'

'Or, most likely, it won't happen at all,' said Carrie. 'Could you send a letter to all the women telling them what's involved and inviting them to a meeting to find out more?'

Harry pursed his lips. 'We prefer to travel light,' he said. 'No formal records, nothing in writing unless we absolutely have to.'

'I could get me ma on board to tell the women who come into the Remembrance Club,' said Mabel. 'It's mainly men, but wives sometimes come along too . . .'

'I've joined the gardening club and there are quite a few women there nowadays,' said Sarah.

'And I've been roped in to help with the Brownies,' said Carrie, pulling a face. 'I'm really not sure about it but . . .'

'Oh, do step in,' said Mabel. 'It's good fun and Mrs Jennings is desperate for help . . .'

Carrie sighed. 'So my mother keeps telling me,' she said. 'Anyway, one advantage is I can talk to the mothers when they drop off or pick up. But what am I asking them exactly?'

Harry made his fingers into a steeple. 'I'm thinking of a meeting, here, say next Monday,' he said. 'We'll call it "Lend a hand in the factory" or something like that. I'll ask the men to tell their wives, but if you could work on the women, that would be marvellous.'

'Consider it done,' said Sarah, and Carrie and Mabel nodded in agreement.

'Super,' said Harry. He leant back and took a swig of lemonade. 'Something quite different,' he said, looking a little diffident. 'A couple of chums and I are thinking of going to the dance at the Castle Hotel next Wednesday.

Bob Garganido and his Band play there and I hear they're rather good. I wondered if you girls would like to come along too. We could treat it as a celebration of the new scheme.'

'I'd love to,' said Sarah, immediately, eyes shining. 'That sounds like fun.'

Mabel was shaking her head. 'I'm sorry,' she said. 'It does sound like fun but I'm working a late shift that night and it's too late to swap.'

It was on the tip of Carrie's tongue to turn down the invitation as well.

She hadn't been to a proper dance before and, frankly, she wasn't sure she really wanted to. She was clumsy and ungainly . . . and, besides, wouldn't she just be in the way? It was clearly all a ruse so that Harry could be with Sarah.

Just look at the two making cow eyes at each other . . .

But then Sarah kicked her hard under the table and she relented. Sarah might not be allowed out unless it was part of a bigger group and Carrie certainly didn't want to spoil her fun.

'All right,' she said lightly. 'If my father agrees, I'd be happy to come.'

Although, for once, she found herself half-hoping that Pa would say no.

Chapter Ten

Tuesday 2 July 1940

Shortly afterwards, the little meeting broke up.

Sarah stood up to leave and Carrie did the same.

'I'll walk you two home,' said Harry, getting to his feet a little unsteadily.

Carrie was about to demur – it was broad daylight and a matter of yards – when Mabel surreptitiously tapped her leg. Carrie briefly met her eye and the penny dropped.

'On second thoughts, Mabel,' she said, sitting down again, 'I think I'll hang around for a while. What about that lemonade à deux we've been promising each other for ages?'

Mabel smiled. 'Cor, yes,' she said. 'Although we'll have to sneak it outside so me mother don't rope me in to making a hundred rounds of sandwiches.'

'Oi! I heard that,' said Mrs Green from behind the bar. Then she laughed. 'Go on, the pair of you. Take your drinks outside and get some sun on you.'

The four said their goodbyes and went their separate ways – Sarah and Harry leaving arm in arm from the main entrance and Mabel and Carrie heading out of the back door and onto the drive.

'Are they courting?' asked Mabel without preamble, sitting down on a bench against the wall and tilting her face towards the afternoon sun.

Carrie smiled. 'I'm not sure they are yet, but it's surely only a matter of time,' she said. 'I'm pleased for Sarah; he seems a really lovely chap.'

Mabel turned to face Carrie and gave her a shrewd glance. 'You've changed your tune,' she said. 'It seems only yesterday we was agreeing she's a bit of a bully.'

Carrie laughed. How much had changed in so short a time!

'She's actually a good egg,' she said. 'She apologised for that night in the club and it turned out there had been a misunderstanding over something *I* had – or rather, hadn't – done and I needed to apologise too.'

Mabel grinned. 'I shall take your word for it,' she said. 'Especially now we've been thrown together on our special poppy mission. But, much more importantly, what about you?'

'What about me?' Carrie was perplexed.

'Are you courting? Any special men in *your* life?'

'Oh!' Carrie was thrown. 'No – not really. Only that's not entirely true because, well, there are sort of two but . . .'

She trailed off, suddenly feeling thoroughly confused.

Mabel burst out laughing. 'Now, this I have got to hear,' she said. 'Spill the beans, please.'

And, so, Carrie ended up telling her all about her summer fling with Ned and her meeting with the elusive man the day before.

'I feel a bit silly now I've said all that out loud,' she said, once she had finished. 'Because, of course, now it's clear to both of us, that I don't have any men at all.'

Mabel grinned. 'Oh, I don't know,' she said. 'What happens when Ned realises that beautiful Mary is just playing fast and loose with his feelings? And as for the other guy – no, don't tell me his name if he works somewhere security is an issue – well, maybe he were just late for his lunch. You could wake up one morning to find both of them knocking at your door.'

Carrie laughed and wondered how *that* might feel. 'How about you?' she asked. 'Are you courting?'

Mabel shook her head emphatically. 'Not a glimmer of a man,' she said firmly. 'And perhaps a good thing too, since I've just had to leave everything and everyone I know and start again in a strange town, which don't seem to want me very much.'

Carrie heard the uncertainty and loss behind the words and looked beyond the pretty freckled face and dark curly hair for perhaps the first time. Mabel *was* different. Her sensible white shirt, knee-length skirt and the knitted cardigan tossed around her shoulders were much what a girl born and raised in Richmond might wear to work, but the devil was in the detail. A skirt which had been let out and darned so many times the pleats had all but disappeared, a cotton rather than a silk shirt, with buttons that didn't quite match and a complete dearth of either watch or jewellery . . . The war – with its emphasis on doing your bit and avoiding waste – might have ironed out some of the differences between the two young women . . . but they were still there.

'It must be really hard for you,' said Carrie, gently. 'Leaving all your friends behind.'

Mabel shrugged. 'I've never really been a great one for friends,' she admitted. 'Always too busy with me head in a schoolbook.'

'I know exactly what you mean,' said Carrie, with feeling.

'Facts and figures are much easier to get along with, aren't they?'

'Too right they are,' said Mabel. 'They play by the rules, they don't judge . . .'

'They don't get their feelings hurt or hold grudges . . .'

'They certainly don't say one thing when they mean quite another.'

The two looked at each other and then burst out laughing. Maybe they had more in common than divided them after all.

'To be honest, I miss me old maths teacher, Miss Ellison, most,' Mabel continued. 'She saw something in me that no one else did and really encouraged me to stay at school. She spoke to me parents and practically bullied them into letting me apply for a scholarship to do me Highers. And then she invited me to join a little maths group she started on a Thursday afternoon – she set the trickiest problems you can imagine – and it all were the most marvellous fun. I really miss it.'

'She sounds fabulous,' said Carrie. 'I felt a bit like that about my history teacher . . .'

'Miss Ellison even helped line me up a job out here after I found out we was moving,' added Mabel, as if Carrie hadn't spoken. She was staring into the middle distance, in a little world of her own. 'Her brother works out this way and he were recruiting. A couple of tests, a quick interview . . . and I were in.'

'Chrysler, wasn't it?' said Carrie.

'Mm,' said Mabel. She got to her feet as a van drove slowly down the drive. 'Shall we move? Otherwise, we'll get roped into unloading the deliveries.'

'I don't mind helping . . .'

'I do,' said Mabel, firmly. 'I do enough around here as it is and I've already done a full day's work. Let's go to the pet cemetery. We won't be disturbed there.'

Carrie's heart sank.

Tucked away behind the old bowling green and right on the periphery of the estate, the little cemetery had been used to bury pets ever since the Remembrance Club had been owned by Lord Carlton. The residents of the Poppy Factory had continued the tradition and the little plot of land – backing onto the adjacent park – now contained a few dozen modest gravestones, each with a simple inscription. The trouble was that one was where Marigold was buried. Carrie – still devastated – rarely visited and, when she did, she preferred to be alone with her thoughts.

But how to explain all that to Mabel, who had already set off at quite a clip across the bowling lawn? Carrie had been enjoying their conversation and wanted to continue, so she had no choice but to follow in Mabel's wake, over the grass, through some overgrown bushes and into the little clearing. As Mabel had predicted, it was empty; but, then again, it was nearly *always* empty save for the odd clandestine courtship and the occasional group of giggling children on their way to or from school.

Carrie was only surprised Pa hadn't suggested digging it up for turnips.

She sat down desultorily on a bench with her back towards Marigold's grave. The last thing she wanted was to cry in front of her new friend. Meanwhile, Mabel drifted around the clearing unawares, quoting snippets from the inscriptions.

'"*Stepper – always bright and merry.*" "*Fusi – much loved*",' she read out. 'Ain't this grand?'

'You were telling me about Chrysler,' said Carrie, hastily, before Mabel had a chance to reach Marigold's headstone. Her beloved cat's death had not been "grand" at all.

'Oh yes.' Somewhat reluctantly, Mabel sat down on a bench facing her. 'Only, there ain't much more to tell. Me old teacher's brother fixed me up with a job – I were ever so honoured that Miss Ellison thought to put me forward – and that were that.'

Carrie frowned. Something wasn't adding up. 'But is Chrysler the sort of place you even need a personal recommendation?' she said. 'I was under the impression they're desperate for anyone.'

'Oh no!' Mabel drew herself up to her full height. 'No, I ain't working on the factory floor. I'm in *accounts*. I'm responsible for helping make sure the figures are sorted out proper – it's ever such a lot of responsibility.'

Carrie suppressed a smile. Mabel seemed so delighted and so proud of herself, as well she might be. 'That's marvellous,' she said. 'It's a wonderful opportunity for you and, with a bit of luck, something you'll be able to keep doing after the war.'

Mabel nodded.

'And, of course, I should have guessed,' Carrie added.

Mabel narrowed her eyes. 'Why?' she asked.

Carrie waved at Mabel's outfit. 'You're wearing smart office clothes rather than overalls.'

Mabel opened her mouth to answer, but then both girls turned their heads as the bushes behind them rustled . . . and Sarah emerged. Carrie and Mabel briefly locked eyes;

Sarah and Harry clearly wanted a private moment together and had been caught in the act.

But, seconds later, it was clear that Sarah was alone.

'Hello!' she said. 'I wondered if I might find you two here.'

Carrie got to her feet. 'Is everything all right?' she asked. 'Harry . . . ?'

Maybe the two had had a row. Or Harry had gently let her know that he was promised elsewhere. Or . . .'

But Sarah suddenly flung her arms skywards, threw her head backwards and twirled around.

'Harry is wonderful!' she said, laughing with sheer joy. 'I just had to tell someone. I'm completely wild about him!'

Carrie and Mabel couldn't help but grin at her excitement.

'Wild About Harry!' said Carrie, in reference to the popular 1920s song. 'Oh, Sarah, I'm so happy for you.'

'Better still, he says he's wild about me,' said Sarah, sitting down with a thump on the bench beside Carrie. 'And you have no idea how lovely that feels.'

'I might not, but Carrie here certainly does,' said Mabel with a grin. 'After all, she's got *two* chaps after her.'

Sarah turned to Carrie with an incredulous smile. 'Have you?' she said. 'You dark horse! You've certainly kept quiet about *that* over the past couple of days.'

Carrie laughed. 'Because it's not true,' she said.

'She's lying,' said Mabel in a sing-song voice. 'Go on, tell Sarah about Mr One and Mr Two.'

'But I only met Mr Two two days ago,' protested Carrie. 'It hardly compares to Sarah and Harry.'

'But it's such a good story, ain't it?' said Mabel.

'Come on,' said Sarah. 'Tell me all. You know you want to. You don't have to name names. Mr One and Mr Two will do.'

And so, for the second time that afternoon, Carrie found herself telling Sarah all about Ned and Bobby. She *didn't* name names – the last thing she wanted was Sarah knowing someone who knew Bobby and deciding to get involved, even with the best of intentions. Sarah listened with flattering intensity, a little smile playing around her lips.

'Jolly good show, old girl,' she said when Carrie had finished talking.

Carrie smiled. 'It's not a hockey match,' she said.

'More's the pity,' Sarah shot back. 'Ned sounds completely dreamy. But, if you want to know what I think, I'd forget about Mr Two. Three days is plenty enough time for him to have tracked you down if he really wanted to.'

Carrie nodded. 'I know,' she said. 'And I'm wondering why I'm quite so disappointed about that.'

Mabel had continued her perambulation around the graveyard. '"*Our special pal, Marigold . . .*"' she suddenly announced to no one in particular.

Carrie stiffened and glanced up. 'Stop it,' she said sharply. She swallowed hard, not trusting herself to say anything else.

'Stop it?' echoed Mabel in confusion. 'Why?'

'Because Marigold was Carrie's cat,' said Sarah, putting an arm around Carrie's shoulders.

'Oh, I'm so sorry,' said Mabel, continuing to look at the gravestone. 'She weren't very old when she died, were she? And why does it say, "Forgive us, little friend"?'

'Stop it, Mabel!' shouted Carrie, dissolving into tears. 'Tell her, Sarah. *Tell* her.'

Pa had had Marigold destroyed at the beginning of the war.

Carrie had been presented with the ginger moggie on her tenth birthday. Not having any brothers and sisters, Marigold had been sibling, best friend and confidante all in one adorable furry bundle, and Carrie had loved her with all her heart. Living in the penthouse, she was supposed to have been an indoor cat, but she'd soon had other ideas, jumping out of the windows, and climbing down the plants that grew against the side of the building.

Oh, how Carrie had loved her.

But just before the beginning of the war, the National Air Raid Precautions Animals Committee had started a public information campaign encouraging pet euthanasia.

The fear was twofold; keeping animals safe if Britain was bombed or invaded and the simple lack of food, meaning animals were in danger of slowly starving to death. A pamphlet was distributed, which concluded, 'It really is kindest to have household animals destroyed,' and the advice was reprinted in almost every newspaper and announced on the BBC.

Pa, being Pa, took it all to heart.

'Don't you see,' he'd said. 'It's up to us to set an example. Just as we need to make sure we have the blackest of blackout blinds, we need to do the right thing by Marigold.'

Carrie hadn't seen.

The very idea was preposterous.

She had, of course, refused point-blank to go along with it. How could she part with Marigold? How could they have a perfect, healthy – nay, absolutely perfect – animal destroyed? But Pa had been adamant and Ma had simply retreated into her sewing-nook.

Carrie had tried.

She really had.

She had started to research where she might send Marigold; their relatives in the Lake District, perhaps, or the various charities offering refuge. She had even considered running away with Marigold herself.

It was all in vain.

A couple of days after war was declared, Pa had taken Marigold to be put down. Worse still, he had then chosen to make a big song and dance about it around the estate in an effort to encourage others to do likewise.

It had all been for nothing.

Although three-quarters of a million British pets *were* killed in that awful week, nobody else on the estate had followed suit.

A few had made alternative arrangements for their animals – the Sinclairs sent Jasper to Battersea Dogs' Home and the Fairchilds sent Bramble to a sanctuary founded by the Duchess of Hamilton – but everyone else totally ignored both the National Air Raid Precautions Animals Committee *and* Pa. At first, people tried to keep their animals indoors and out of sight – Carrie could hear Misty in the flat below miaowing furiously to be let out – and the estate echoed to the sound of indignant dogs howling piteously for their daily walks. But, after a few days, it was business as usual. Carrie was aware of eyes swivelling away from her in embarrassment and pity and her heart broke for how she had failed Marigold.

Pa had had Marigold buried in the pet cemetery, and Carrie still hated him with every fibre of her being.

There was silence when Sarah finished describing the bare bones of what had happened – a silence broken only by Carrie's storm of weeping. She cried bitterly – head bent over her lap – and her tears were of sorrow, guilt and fury.

She was vaguely aware of Sarah's arm tightening around her shoulders and Mabel coming to sit on her other side and placing one hand gently on her knee.

And it helped.

It really did.

'I'm sorry,' she said eventually, straightening up and drying her eyes.

'Don't ever say that,' said Sarah fiercely. 'You have nothing to be sorry for. What your father did was despicable.'

'He *is* despicable,' said Carrie, bitterly. 'He's definitely got worse since the war started, but he's always been despicable and my mother's always been weak.'

'All our fathers are . . . complicated,' said Sarah. 'What happened to them in the Great War definitely changed them in some way . . . and this war has only made it worse.'

'Maybe that's true,' said Carrie. 'My friend Daisy's father was too young to properly fight in the Great War and he's definitely not as closed away and steely as Pa. I don't think she's ever really understood what it's been like growing up in a flat and on an estate where it still affects everything.'

'I think it's been harder for you because you've had no brothers or sisters to dilute it all a bit,' said Sarah. 'My brothers drive me mad, but at least they represent the future and not the past.'

'Me gran always used to say that you can't choose your family, but you can choose your friends,' said Mabel. 'So, choose us. We understand exactly what it's like and we'll be there for you.'

'Yes, choose us,' echoed Sarah. 'We understand and we'll be your family. Choose us. Choose the Poppy Girls.'

Carrie smiled around at the two of them.

Not just friends – but the closest thing she had ever had to sisters.

Chapter Eleven

Thursday 4 July 1940

In the usual course of events, the Poppy Factory Brownie Pack would be gearing up to take a break over the fast-approaching school holidays.

However, as with everything else, plans had been turned topsy-turvy by the war. Because many holidays and beach trips and other family jollities had been put on hold for the duration, Mrs Jennings – Brown Owl – had decided that the weekly meetings should continue over the summer so that the children could have at least *some* organised fun. Besides, it was a good opportunity to get the youngsters involved in some war-related projects, whilst giving their mothers a bit of a break . . .

A couple of days later, Carrie set off for the Remembrance Club.

Pa, predictably, had never let her join the Brownies when she was a little girl – although, to be fair, she had never really asked if she could. As such, she didn't have any clear idea of what they actually did . . . apart from maybe dancing around toadstools. She also had no experience of interacting with younger children, so – all in all – she felt more than a twinge of nerves.

What if the little girls didn't like her?

What if they poked fun at her clumsiness?

What if they point-blank refused to do what she asked?

But, in the event, it was all rather marvellous.

Brown Owl was patently grateful for the extra pair of hands. She greeted and introduced Carrie warmly, and then – to Carrie's surprise – set her straight to work supervising a gaggle of nine-year-olds who were working towards their Cook badge. Carrie rather expected that, before the war, it would have been all scones and Victoria sandwiches but, of course, rationing had put a stop to that. Instead, the Brownies were being put through their paces making potato piglets, which seemed to involve removing sections of a large potato using an apple corer and then stuffing the holes with wartime 'sausage meat'.

Nervous at first, Carrie soon started to enjoy herself. She vaguely supervised the girls as they combined minced meat of indeterminate provenance with oatmeal, breadcrumbs and grated carrot, then bound it together with milk.

But largely, she left them to it.

They seemed a cheerful, earnest and resourceful bunch and Carrie was sure they would learn a lot more if she wasn't butting in all the time. So, she praised and encouraged and joined in the general merriment when Eloise managed to weigh out twice the necessary amount of oatmeal and Maggie's breadcrumbs ended up all over the countertop.

'You're not like the other helpers,' said Maggie, as she scooped up the errant breadcrumbs and deposited them into the mixing bowl.

'Aren't I?' said Carrie.

Goodness; was she doing something wrong?

'No,' said Eloise, a serious little thing. 'Brown Owl is lovely but the others who help are more like teachers and tell us off if we do something wrong. I really hope you come again.'

'Oh, I plan to,' said Carrie, with a little glow of happiness.

Gouging holes with the apple corer proved tricky all round but – perhaps predictably – Carrie's was the first to go flying across the kitchen. The laughter that followed was companionable and supportive and Carrie was just picking up the offending potato when Mabel walked into the kitchen.

'Hello, Brownies,' she said in a sing-song voice as she tossed her curls over one shoulder. She poured herself a glass of water and took a deep draught.

The girls all smiled and greeted her warmly, clearly familiar and at ease with her.

'I'm just back from work and I thought I'd see how you're getting on,' Mabel added to Carrie.

Carrie smiled. She had grabbed a quick cup of tea with Mabel and Sarah the evening before and both girls had been anxious to check on her welfare after her breakdown over Marigold. They'd also talked more about their fathers and about the challenges – and pride – of living with men whose lives had been so dramatically altered by the Great War.

'Well, apart from throwing my potato across the room, I'm doing well,' said Carrie. 'Luckily, the Brownies are here to keep me on the straight and narrow.'

Mabel grinned. 'Keep an eye on her for me, please, girls,' she said. 'This one managed to knock a load of shelves over in Woollies the other day. She's still got the graze on her elbow to prove it.'

The girls, wide-eyed, giggled long and loud and Carrie joined in. When Mabel was relaxed, she could be ever so funny.

Then Mabel touched Carrie on the shoulder. 'Might I have a quick word?' she said, gesturing to the scullery leading off the kitchen.

'I'm meant to be in charge here . . .'

'I'll finish your potato for you, if you like,' said Eloise.

'It won't take a minute,' said Mabel.

Carrie nodded and followed Mabel into the scullery, positioning herself so that she could still keep an eye on her charges. 'What's the matter?' she asked.

Mabel pushed Vim, Ajax and Sanitas Powder to one side and hauled herself up onto the counter. 'I think it's going to prove more difficult than we thought to get Operation Special Poppies off the ground,' she said, gloomily.

Despite everything, Carrie felt a pang of disappointment. She had known it was a long shot and not generally the way that things were done at the factory, but it had seemed the perfect – the *obvious* – solution.

'Ah well,' she said, trying to keep her voice light. 'I suppose it was one step too far for some of the men. No doubt Pa was amongst the naysayers.'

Mabel shook her head. 'No,' she said. 'I'm talking about the women.'

'The women?' echoed Carrie in surprise.

'Yes. Ma and I collared the flower arranging committee, who was holding a meeting here last night. They ain't keen, I'm afraid. I doubt any of them will come along to the meeting . . .'

'Finished,' chorused the Brownies from next door.

Carrie ran a hand through her hair. 'Give me two ticks,' she said to Mabel. 'I want to hear more.'

Carrie hurried back into the kitchen. The girls hadn't made a bad stab at the potatoes, but the kitchen was a mess with dirty utensils and discarded potato scraps scattered everywhere.

'Jolly good,' she said. 'Let's pop them in the oven and hopefully they'll be ready for you to take home when your mothers come to pick you up.'

'How are we doing in here?' said Brown Owl, popping her head through the door.

'Marvellously,' said Eloise.

'We really like Carrie,' added Maggie.

Brown Owl smiled at Carrie. 'It sounds like you're a hit,' she said. 'Happy to keep an eye on them for another half an hour? We're running late with the First Aid badge and, to make matters worse, little Annie Parsons has managed to hurt her ankle for real.'

'That's fine,' said Carrie. 'We've still got the washing up to do and then I wonder if we might cook something else?'

Brown Owl nodded. 'There's a bag of veg I brought in as contingency,' she said. 'They could make . . .'

Smiling, Carrie put her finger to her lips. 'Shhh,' she said, with a wink. 'I'd like to set a little challenge, if I may. I can see lots of lovely leftover potato and sausage meat and I'd like to think about how we might use them in a different dish. Would that be all right?'

'Yes!' chorused the girls.

'Of course,' said Brown Owl with an approving nod. 'Very clever. Good luck, girls.'

And she was gone.

'I'll take the washing up through to the scullery and make a start on it,' said Carrie. 'And I'd like you to write a recipe for me and come up with a name? Can you do that?'

The girls nodded enthusiastically and Carrie brought the dirty utensils through to the scullery, clattering them down in the sink. Mabel slid down from the counter and started filling it with hot water.

'You're an absolute natural with them,' she said, adding a handful of soap flakes.

'Believe me, no one is more surprised than me,' said Carrie. 'But tell me, what did the women *say*?'

Mabel shrugged and started the washing up, elbows and soap suds flying. 'All sorts of things,' she said, over her shoulder. 'But mainly that they're too busy to help out in the factory – or anywhere else for that matter.'

'Too busy?' echoed Carrie, so loudly that the Brownies looked up. 'Whatever happened to getting stuck in and doing your bit?!' She picked up a cream bowl from the draining board, gave it a cursory wipe, then slammed it back on the counter with more force than was strictly necessary. 'Whatever happened to *patriotism*?'

'Careful!' said Mabel, inspecting the bowl for damage. 'And I don't think it's a lack of patriotism that's holding them back. It seemed more that a lot of the women have children – and the school holidays are about to start.'

'That's no excuse.' Carrie was outraged, and she didn't care who knew it. 'Women all over the country have children and Richmond isn't the only town with school holidays.'

'I know,' said Mabel. 'I don't understand either. Let's see if the Brownies' mothers have anything different to say.'

Carrie nodded and headed back into the kitchen to be briefed all about Brownie broth, thickened with the potato plugs, to be served with Patriotic Patties made from the leftover sausage meat. To be honest, there was very little else that the girls could have come up with with the ingredients at their disposal, but Carrie made sure that she praised the ideas fulsomely. And then it was all hands on deck to make the ideas a reality. As they peeled and chopped and simmered – and Eloise excitedly told them all about going to visit her grandparents in the Peak District that weekend – Carrie wondered *why* the women on the estate didn't want to do their bit with the 'Special Poppies'.

Surely there had to be a solution.

But the mothers who duly arrived half an hour later did nothing to allay her fears or to provide any answers. Carrie and Mabel set out the case for them working on the aircraft parts or in the warehouse or around the estate, and duly invited them to the meeting, but came across the same answers again and again.

'No point in coming to the meeting. I'm already run ragged.'

'Sorry, love. There's no one who can help me.'

'The school holidays are about to start and we're all already on our knees.'

It all seemed hopeless.

To Carrie's disappointment – but not really to her surprise – the 'Lend a hand in the factory' meeting a few days later was a complete flop.

None of the management attended and – worse – barely a dozen women came along. Most of them were Ma's age or older and, although many *did* sign up to start working on the aircraft radios, it wasn't enough.

Not nearly enough.

Afterwards, Harry was stoical. 'It's a step in the right direction,' he said. 'We've got a bit of time and hopefully now we've started, the whole thing will start gathering pace.'

Carrie, manning the tea urn, wasn't convinced.

Where were the *young* women? She thought of the poem they had learnt at school – 'In Flanders Fields' – and the lines:

To you from failing hands we throw
The torch; be yours to hold it high.

It had been written about men, of course – about soldiers – but it could equally be applied to the women of her generation.

This was *their* time.

So, where were they all?

Maybe, like her, they were disillusioned and had no wish to be part of the war machine. But there were plenty of other things they *could* do. She certainly had no intention of assembling radios, but she would be very happy to do her bit in the Poppy Factory warehouse. No one could have any problem with *that* . . .

'Chin up,' said a voice, cutting across her thoughts.

It was Mrs Armstrong, smiling at her over the brim of her teacup.

Carrie smiled warily back. 'Hello, Mrs Armstrong,' she said.

She'd been surprised to see the older woman at the meeting and wasn't entirely sure of her agenda.

Did her husband know she was here?

Did Pa?

'I gather all this was your idea?' she said, waving vaguely around the games room.

Carrie pulled a little face. 'I thought it might help,' she said. 'The men have so much to deal with with all the normal poppies and now switching to the cardboard ones, and the special French ones, and now . . .' she trailed off.

'I gather you're calling them the "Special Poppies"?' interjected Mrs Armstrong with a smile.

Carrie started.

Had Harry told her that?

Was Mrs Armstrong laughing at her?

'Yes,' she said. 'I'm sorry if we got ideas above our station, but, as I said, we just wanted to help . . .'

'Not at all,' said Mrs Armstrong. 'As soon as I heard about it, I knew it was a marvellous idea. The men are taking a little longer to come round to it, but they're getting there. Even your pa,' she added, with a smile.

'Really?' said Carrie.

'Absolutely. It's the perfect way forward. All of us pulling together – and the young ones leading the way. Just like the old days. Just like it should be.'

Carrie smiled sadly. 'Only it hasn't worked,' she said, gesturing round the nearly empty room.

Mrs Armstrong nodded. 'For now,' she said. 'But nothing worthwhile was ever easy, was it? We've just got to work out why.'

*

Carrie had wondered if the meeting's failure would mean they didn't go dancing. After all, Harry had specifically linked the two events when he'd issued the invitation and, as it happened, there really wasn't much to celebrate.

But not a bit of it.

Harry made a point of confirming the outing as they finished the washing up and Sarah reiterated that she simply couldn't wait. They then both looked expectantly at Carrie.

'I haven't had a chance to ask my father,' she said, as they left the club together. 'Of course, he's likely to put the kibosh on it and that will be that. But you two could still go . . . ?'

'I think my parents would be happier if they knew you were coming,' said Sarah, carefully. 'Please ask him.'

'In fact, we can ask him now,' added Harry. 'He's heading this way.'

Carrie followed his line of sight and, yes, there was Pa coming out of the Poppy Factory and heading towards the Remembrance Club.

Her heart sank.

'Evening all,' he said, as he approached. 'Meeting over already?'

'Yes, sir,' said Harry, practically standing to attention. 'Not as many people there as we might have hoped.'

Pa looked smug. 'I did think that would be the case,' he said. 'Mrs Armstrong's little idea is all well and good – and goodness knows we need all the help we can get nowadays – but the good women of the estate are all busy with home and hearth.'

Mrs Armstrong's little idea . . .

It had been *her* idea.

We need all the help we can get . . .

Her father had certainly changed *his* tune.

Carrie opened her mouth to protest, and then shut it firmly again.

It was probably better this way.

'Sir, I was wondering if Miss Harper might accompany me and a couple of others from the new division to a dance at the Castle Hotel on Wednesday?' said Harry. 'After all, we're new in town, and don't really know our way around. Miss Turner is coming and, if you give permission, I promise to personally pick them both up and deliver them home at a sensible hour.'

Honestly!

It sounded as if Carrie was one of the Brownies – not nearly eighteen!

And Pa was still going to say no . . .

'An excellent idea, Flight Sergeant Hooper,' said Pa. 'I'm all for fostering good relationships across the estate. By the way, did I tell you young people that I've been personally invited to join the Local Defence Volunteers? You know all about them, of course? We're tasked with defending the home front against invasion or sabotage.'

Carrie sighed. Why did Pa always have to boast in such a booming voice? She supposed she could only be grateful he had said 'we' rather than claiming to be the one person standing between Jerry and total victory.

'That's very impressive, sir,' said Harry politely.

'Quite rightly, they've realised that someone with my experience could make all the difference in whipping the troops into shape. I'll be out several evenings a week from now on, so anything to help entertain the womenfolk . . .'

He touched his cap and was gone.

Carrie puffed out her cheeks and smiled round at her friends.

Like it or not, it looked like Cinderella would be going to the ball after all.

Chapter Twelve

Two evenings later, Carrie duly arrived at the riverfront Castle Hotel with Sarah and Harry.

Was there a chance that Bobby might be there?

The impressive façade – all huge windows and fancy signage – was already dulled by a year of wartime neglect, but the grand double doors stood invitingly open and faint strains of a lively swing tune spilt out into the warm summer air.

Carrie's stomach tightened with nerves as she stepped inside and followed the others to the ballroom. She had had no idea of what to wear – her wardrobe had proved completely uninspiring – so she had settled on her favourite pale-blue frock.

Next to Sarah's tight mustard number, it felt hopelessly gauche.

Harry bought three tickets at the entrance to the ballroom and the three stood and surveyed the scene. At the far end, Bob Garganido and his Band were already in full swing on a small raised stage, their brass instruments gleaming dully, an eponymous banner above their heads in swirling script. A polished wood floor dominated the room and around the edge were clusters of small, round tables with simple white linens, where revellers could rest between dances. To Carrie's relief, it all somewhat brought to mind the games room at the Remembrance Club. They weren't really alike, except that they both had once been elegant rooms that had now seen better days. The dance floor was scuffed, the chandeliers hung with uneven light – some bulbs missing entirely – and floral paper, long past its prime, curled faintly on the walls.

There was nothing to intimidate her here.

Oh . . . but the dancing!

The floor was alive with young couples twirling, spinning and swaying to a lively tune in a way Carrie knew she could never emulate. Many men were in uniform and the others wore neat, well-worn suits, whilst the women wore dresses in muted wartime fabrics with bright lipstick and carefully styled hair. It only took a second for Carrie to confirm that Sarah had got it spot on and she had got it oh-so-wrong. Her pastel dress was positively babyish and her careless updo – already unravelling – was far too casual . . .

Damn!

'There are the chaps,' said Harry, lifting an arm in greet-ing to two young men sitting at a table close to the dancing. Carrie recognised them vaguely as newcomers from the estate and her heart promptly sank. One of the men had sharp features, an impatient expression and the practised, appraising glance of the rake and the other – who had got to his feet to greet Harry – was clearly a good four inches shorter than she was.

Carrie lingered by the door for a moment, awkwardly tugging at the hem of her dress. She wasn't sure what was going to be worse: sitting at the table trying to make small talk or risking the dance floor . . .

'Come on, Carrie.' Sarah came back and fairly pulled her towards the table. 'Don't look so glum, it's going to be fun!'

Carrie plastered a smile on her face and allowed herself to be swept along in Sarah's wake. Despite her sinking stomach, she didn't want to be a killjoy and spoil the evening. She would just have to make the most of it. So, she accepted the port and lemon that Harry pressed into her hand, greeted the men as pleasantly as she could, and did her best to chat and nod and laugh along with the rest.

All too soon, Sarah and Harry headed for the dance floor and joined the crowd in a very creditable quickstep. Then came the moment that Carrie had dreaded.

'Would you like to dance?' asked the sharp-featured man, already standing up and holding out his hand.

Carrie didn't know how to refuse and, seconds later, he was guiding her onto the dance floor with a practised smile.

'Let's have some fun,' he said, spinning her around to face him.

'Fun' wasn't how Carrie would have described what happened next.

She knew the basics of the quickstep, of course; they had been taught it in the gym at school, although Carrie, being tall, had often had to dance as a man. But her partner's idea of dancing involved spinning her around faster than she could keep up, and leading with flourishes that made her stumble. Every time she missed a step – which was often – he tutted softly under his breath and, by the time the song ended, Carrie was totally humiliated.

'Great dance,' said the chap, with barely disguised sarcasm.

He bowed with exaggerated swagger before sauntering off to find another partner.

The short chap was next, although Carrie suspected it was more out of obligation than enthusiasm. That dance, too, was little short of a disaster; clearly uncomfortable by the height difference, the man held her at arm's length and carefully avoided any steps that might bring them too close together. They shuffled around the floor like a couple of wooden mannequins and, when the dance finished, he too scuttled away with almost indecent haste, muttering something about having seen a friend over by the bar . . .

Embarrassed, Carrie slunk off the dance floor and sat down, trying not to feel too sorry for herself. Around her, couples whirled and twirled, their laughter and cheers whenever someone attempted an ambitious move making her feel more awkward by the second. Across the room, Sarah and Harry swayed together in harmony and Carrie was right back to school days, on the outside looking in . . .

'Lyn!'

Carrie twisted round on her chair. She recognised that voice.

Sure enough, Bobby was approaching her, an easy grin on his handsome face.

Despite everything, Carrie felt her mood lift. Of course, it wasn't ideal that he had discovered her being a wall-flower – and goodness knew if he had witnessed her performance on the dance floor – but Carrie suddenly found that she couldn't keep a silly grin off her face.

'Hello,' she said, warmly. 'No scarf today?'

Bobby's grin broadened. 'I thought I would give it the

evening off,' he said, and then he added, 'Would you care to dance?'

Carrie's heart sank. 'Me?' she said.

'No, the woman sitting three tables behind you who can't hear me,' said Bobby. 'Of course, you, silly.'

'Must I?' said Carrie with a little groan. For some reason, she didn't feel she had to keep up appearances with Bobby. 'It's my first ever dance, and I've just made an idiot of myself doing the quickstep.'

'That makes two of us,' said Bobby, with a wink. 'Come on. We can make idiots of ourselves together.'

Grumbling, Carrie took his outstretched hand – his warm in hers – and let him lead her onto the dance floor. The moment his hand settled lightly on her waist and they began to move, Carrie could sense the difference. Quite apart from the bolt of electricity that Bobby's touch was generating, he guided her through the steps with a confidence that made her feet feel a little less clumsy.

'There you go,' he said, as she managed a half-decent spin. 'You're getting the hang of it.'

Carrie let out a startled laugh. 'I can't believe I didn't fall over.'

'Believe it,' Bobby said, grinning. 'Now, just follow my lead.'

The music swelled, and for the first time that evening, Carrie let herself go. She forgot about Sarah and Harry, forgot about just how out of place she'd been feeling. She even forgot to worry about tripping over. Bobby's confidence was infectious and soon they were dancing with an easy rhythm between them.

When the song ended, they were both breathless and

laughing. Bobby bowed dramatically, and Carrie curtsied in response, her cheeks flushed.

'Thank you,' said Carrie. 'You've saved my evening.'

'Always happy to be a hero,' Bobby replied lightly. 'Fancy another go? Practice makes perfect . . .'

Carrie laughed. 'Yes, please,' she said.

One more dance turned into four and, this time, Bobby didn't let go of her hand immediately after the music stopped.

'Shall we get some air?' he asked, nodding towards the open doors. 'It's sweltering in here.'

Carrie hesitated, glancing around the room. Harry and Sarah were still going strong on the dance floor, the sharp-faced man was entwined with a bottle-blonde in the corner and the short one was engaged in heated conversation with a group of men by the bar. For once, there was no one to ask permission from and no one to miss her if she went outside.

'Good idea,' she said lightly.

Outside, the cool evening air was refreshing after the stuffiness of the ballroom. Carrie and Bobby carried their drinks to the river's edge, where the last vestiges of light danced on the rippling water.

'I'm much happier out here,' Carrie admitted, sipping from her glass.

'Me too,' said Bobby. 'The dancing is just for show. This . . .' He gestured to the water and the other couples who had had the same idea. 'This is where the real conversations happen. By the way, you were wearing that dress the first time we met. I like it. The colour really suits you.'

'Oh!' Carrie started laughing.

'What's funny? Did I say something wrong?'

'Not at all,' said Carrie. 'I was just having second thoughts about it . . .'

'Well, I think it's smashing. And I'm *very* glad I bumped into you tonight.'

Carrie wrinkled her nose at him. 'That's nice,' she replied. Well, that made two of them! 'But you certainly beetled off quickly enough the *last* time we chatted.'

She kept her tone carefully light and casual but, even so, she fancied that she saw Bobby blush in the gathering darkness.

'Did I?' he replied, not very convincingly.

'Yes!' said Carrie. 'I paused to take breath . . . and you'd gone!'

'Hardly! I think I'd just suddenly realised how late I was for the chaps . . .'

Carrie let it go. 'Perhaps,' she said, in a conciliatory tone.

What was important was that they were here now and she certainly didn't want to spoil the magical evening. So, they talked about books – *Sad Cypress* was positively stuffed with red herrings, Carrie's history book less so – and the strangeness of living through a war that seemed to be edging closer to Richmond all the time. Bobby had a way of listening, head on one side, which made her feel as though her words – however trivial, however serious – really mattered . . .

'Bobby!'

Carrie had been so engrossed in their conversation that she hadn't noticed the young man approach until he clapped Bobby on the back. Bobby made the introductions – 'Cousin James, meet Lyn from the Poppy

Factory' – and after a few affable words all round, James peeled off to rejoin his party.

'How lovely to have a cousin in Richmond,' said Carrie, wistfully.

'I've got dozens of them,' said Bobby, with a laugh. 'My ma and pa are both one of six, so there are a *lot* of us.'

'And they all live around here?'

'Pretty much.' Bobby shrugged. 'Where else would they go?'

'Well, *anywhere*,' said Carrie. 'I don't think I've got a single relative within two hundred miles.'

'What . . . no aunts and uncles, no cousins . . . ?' Bobby sounded incredulous.

'I've got all of those but they're all up near Liverpool or in the Lake District . . .'

'Wow,' said Bobby. 'I've never been north of Birmingham . . .'

He followed up with another question, but Carrie didn't register it.

Couldn't register it.

This new information was significant, she was sure of it. She just needed a second to fit the jigsaw pieces together . . .

'I've got it!' she shouted out, thumping her hand triumphantly down on the railings.

'Got it?' Bobby's voice was confused. 'Got what?'

'Why the women on the estate are reluctant to work. It isn't that they're lazy or unpatriotic . . .'

'Heaven forbid . . .'

'Stop it!' said Carrie, with a laugh. 'This is important. They're not stepping up in the factory because they haven't

176

got anyone nearby to help with their children. Other people in the area have family on tap – grandparents, parents, sisters – to share the strain. But we're different. Just about everyone on the Poppy Factory estate has had to move here from somewhere else, and sometimes from hundreds of miles away. It's one of the only places that disabled war veterans could find employment.'

She thought of little Eloise off to visit her grandparents in the Peak District that weekend; or Sarah visiting hers in Scarborough several weeks back; of Mabel moving out from London . . . and, of course, of herself – spending part of every summer up north. It was such a pattern to all their lives that she often forgot it wasn't the same for everyone.

'Step up to what?' asked Bobby. 'Making poppies?'

Carrie sidestepped the question. 'The quotas have gone up this year,' she said. 'The government think people are going to want to be extra patriotic this year and it's stretching the factory to the limit.'

'But does poppy production *need* to increase?' said Bobby. 'I mean, I can understand people wanting to be patriotic, but in wartime there's lots of things people want but can't get. Besides, shouldn't the women on your estate be doing genuine war work? Fake flowers are hardly a priority when the world is at war . . .'

'They're not just fake flowers . . .'

'But they are . . .'

'No. Their symbolism goes much, much deeper . . .' said Carrie, parroting what she had heard a thousand times.

She didn't mind Bobby challenging her – in fact, she was all for a good philosophical discussion – so long as they were both still smiling.

'They're a trifle. A distraction . . .' Bobby persisted.

'They're better than making things to blow people to pieces, Bobby! I can't believe you're getting so worked up about them . . .'

'I can't believe you're not. We have factories doing important war work that are desperate for workers and you're going on about silk petals and felt leaves . . .'

Oh!

Now it was getting personal.

'I'm not "going on" about anything,' said Carrie, hotly. 'Besides, as I told you the last time we met, women aren't even allowed to do that sort of work. It's reserved for the disabled veterans who – if you really want to know – have also just been given a huge quota of military aircraft radios to assemble. And that's something that we *can* help with. All right?'

As soon as the words were out of her mouth, Carrie regretted saying them.

What had everyone said about keeping it within the estate? And now she had gone and blabbed practically the first time she'd spoken to someone outside the estate and potentially put them all at risk.

How could she have been so stupid?

But then she told herself not to be melodramatic.

She might only have met Bobby twice, but, somehow, she trusted him implicitly. The same way he had obviously trusted her when he'd told her he worked at Starfish. There was nothing to worry about.

'All right,' Bobby was saying. 'That makes perfect sense . . . and mum's the word, of course.'

'Thank you. I knew you'd understand.'

'Shall we head in? It's getting a tad chilly.'

Carrie nodded. She hadn't realised how cold she was until he'd mentioned it. They drifted inside, just as Bob Garganido announced the final number of the evening and the band struck up a soft, romantic tune.

Bobby turned to her. 'One last one for the road?' he asked, with a smile.

This time, Carrie didn't hesitate. She simply nodded and let Bobby lead her back into the crowd. This dance was different – slower and more intimate – but Bobby steered her with the same steady confidence, his movements unhurried. Carrie relaxed into his arms and the world beyond the ballroom seemed to melt away. The low hum of conversation, the soft glow of the chandeliers, the gentle sway of the music – it was all perfect and their earlier slightly heated conversation and Carrie's regrettable indiscretion simply melted away.

All too soon, the song came to an end.

Bobby slowed their steps and released her hand with another slight bow. 'There,' he said. 'You've officially survived your first dance.'

Carrie laughed softly. 'Only thanks to you,' she said.

Bobby's smile lingered, but his tone turned practical. 'How are you getting home?' he asked.

Carrie hesitated.

Was he about to offer to walk her back?

Oh, how she hoped so. The soft summer night, the romantic moon . . .

'I'm here with friends,' she said carefully, glancing over to where Sarah and Harry were chatting and glancing over at *her*. 'I think we were planning to all walk back together, but I'm very happy to . . .'

'Good,' interrupted Bobby. 'Well, lovely running into you again. Marvellous evening.'

'Oh! Yes, it was wonderful but . . .'

'Good night, then.'

Bobby reached out and shook her hand.

Shook her hand.

Then, before Carrie could say anything, he tipped an imaginary hat and slipped away into the crowd. Carrie stood frozen, her words caught in her throat.

She could still feel the warmth of Bobby's palm . . . and now he had gone!

Again!

She had been dismissed as easily as one might discard a napkin.

'Who was *that*?' asked Sarah, as she and Harry came over arm in arm.

Carrie shrugged. 'Mr Two!' she said, bitterly.

By the time they all began the short walk home, disappointment had started to crystallise into anger. It was terrible form to dance with someone all evening, and then neither offer to see them home, nor ask to see them again.

It was so bad-mannered, it was almost insulting.

Bobby may have stopped her evening from being a complete disaster – she liked him, she really did – but she would never, *ever*, let herself be fooled by him again.

Chapter Thirteen

Thursday 11 July 1940

Carrie woke the next morning, desperate to share her revelation with the others.

She was eating her breakfast alone in the kitchen, wondering how best to rally the troops, when she spotted Sarah sitting in *her* kitchen on the other side of the road. Abandoning her porridge, Carrie ran onto the balcony, waving frantically in a bid to catch her friend's attention.

It worked.

Seconds later, Sarah appeared on her balcony, shielding her eyes from the sun.

'What's the matter?' she called, making a silly face for good measure.

'I need to talk to you.'

'Will you come back inside and stop making a spectacle of yourself?' said Ma from behind her. 'What's wrong with walking around and knocking on someone's door? By the Lord Harry . . .'

'Sorry, Ma,' Carrie giggled.

What fun it was having a friend to be silly with and how she had missed that growing up.

Carrie bolted the rest of her breakfast and ran downstairs, meeting Sarah in the hallway by her front door.

'I thought I'd come over to you,' Sarah said. 'Great

evening last night. Is that what you wanted to talk about?'

'It isn't,' said Carrie. 'But you and Harry were looking *very* cosy together. I'm so happy for you both.'

'Thank you. But what about *you* and Mr Two? He could hardly keep his eyes off you all evening!'

Carrie shrugged. 'Ha! He clearly thinks he's Cinderella because he had to dash off before the stroke of midnight,' she said, trying to keep the bitterness out of her voice.

Sarah laughed. 'He'll be back,' she said. 'He looked totally smitten.'

'I don't *want* him back,' said Carrie, firmly. 'That's the second time he's run out on me, and he doesn't get any more chances. Anyway, more importantly, I've had a thought about getting women to sign up for the special poppies. I need to get the Poppy Girls together.'

Oh, it felt good to refer to them like that.

'I'm off to the allotments now,' said Sarah. 'But I'm meeting Harry at six for a stroll.' She coloured prettily. 'Maybe we could all get together then if Mabel's back from work?'

'Good plan,' said Carrie. 'I'll pop over to the club now and try to catch her before she leaves.'

And, sketching a wave, she was off, running up the alleyway beside Sarah's flat and thence up the path to the Remembrance Club. Once again, she thought how strange and lovely it was to be so connected within the estate. And it was just as well. She was disappointed about Bobby. She had really liked him; he was clever and quick-witted, and challenging, and she had never been able to talk to a chap like that before. Even Ned, for all his sparkle and golden boy good looks, had never been able to challenge her in the same way.

She found Mrs Green in the bar, assembling a huge plate of cheese and onion sandwiches and busy in conversation with Mrs Armstrong.

'Sorry to interrupt,' said Carrie, politely. 'Is Mabel around?'

'You've just missed her, love,' said Mrs Green.

Damn!

'Thank you,' said Carrie, already spinning on her heel. She hadn't passed Mabel walking through the estate, so she must have gone the other way, onto Richmond Hill.

'Someone's in a hurry today,' she heard Mrs Armstrong laugh as she rushed out.

Seconds later, Carrie emerged panting onto Richmond Hill and craned down the hill for any sign of Mabel.

Nothing.

She had – as ever – been too slow.

Disappointed, Carrie turned and looked up the hill, wondering if she had time for a quick stroll in the park before she went home to help Ma with the laundry.

But wait?

That figure, walking up the hill away from her?

Was *that* Mabel?

The short stature, the purposeful stride, the bouncy dark curls . . .

It certainly *looked* like her.

Carrie frowned in confusion.

Mabel worked at the Chrysler Factory – and that was in completely the opposite direction. Whatever could she be doing heading towards Richmond Park at this time of the morning . . . ?

Carrie debated running after her, but doubted she would be able to catch up. Besides, she couldn't be entirely sure that it was Mabel. So, she headed back to the Remembrance Club – dodging various delivery lorries – and found Mrs Green and Mrs Armstrong exactly as she'd left them.

'She's back!' said Mrs Armstrong with a smile.

'I've missed Mabel,' said Carrie

'Happy to pass on a message, love,' said Mrs Green, still buttering furiously.

'I just wondered if she was free this evening and if we could meet her here,' asked Carrie, politely.

'No problem at all, love.'

Almost as an afterthought, Carrie added, 'Would you two like to join us?'

Mrs Green blinked in surprise. 'If you like, love,' she said. 'Though I might still be making these blasted sand-wiches for the billiards tonight . . .'

But Mrs Armstrong just smiled. 'I would like that very much, dear,' she said. 'It sounds as if you've thought of your way?'

Carrie smiled.

'I think I have,' she said.

'So, what's all this about then?'

Harry was the last to join the little group in the Remembrance Club bar that evening and arrived wreathed in smiles. Carrie noticed his gait seemed to be a little better and wondered, inconsequently, if Sarah had been helping him. Judging by Sarah's adoring look and cat-that-got-the-cream expression, Carrie suspected she was right . . .

'I think young Carrie here has got a plan,' said Mrs Armstrong, cutting across her thoughts. 'And I, for one, am all ears.'

Everyone sat forwards expectantly and Carrie suddenly felt a flutter of nerves.

What if she had got this wrong?

Or what if it was so obvious that everyone knew it anyway?

Or . . .

She took a deep breath. 'Not a plan, as such,' she said. 'More a sudden realisation about why the mothers on the estate aren't exactly falling over themselves to make the radios.'

'Why?' asked Mabel, sitting a little straighter. 'Although I still prefer to think of them as "special poppies" so I don't forget and blurt it out to the wrong people.'

Carrie defiantly pushed down a wave of guilt. She really shouldn't have told Bobby . . .

'The fact is that very few of us are from around here,' she said. 'We don't have mothers and sisters and cousins and aunts who can help out whilst we do our bit. That makes it very difficult for mothers of school-age children; they can't just drop everything and step up to the plate – even if they'd like to – because there's no one to pick up the slack.'

There was a short silence, and then Harry sat back and clapped his hands together.

'By Jove, you're absolutely right,' he said. 'I mean, I knew the facts, of course, but I'd never joined the dots . . .'

'I don't think any of us had,' said Mrs Armstrong. 'Because we're all so used to being from somewhere else, we forget that other people have a network of family members to help them in times of need. Brava, Carrie.'

Carrie smiled. 'The other thing, of course, is that most

of the children are still *here* and the school holidays are about to start,' she said. 'We're still a neutral zone, so they haven't been evacuated away to safety, and I reckon that's how many mothers in other areas have been freed up to do war work.'

'Of course,' said Harry. 'But what to do about it. . . ?'

'I've had a couple of thoughts about that, too,' said Carrie diffidently. 'What about if a group of us arranged to look after the children during the working day? At least during the school holidays.' She glanced at Mrs Green. 'I was thinking that perhaps we might use the Remembrance Club for that?'

She held her breath.

She really had no idea how the idea would be received.

There was a brief silence, and then everyone started talking at once.

'What a marvellous idea.'

'Tip top. Why didn't we think of that before?'

'Brava, Carrie, indeed.'

Carrie exhaled and beamed around at everyone. 'I was thinking maybe we could make it a summer club with all sorts of fun activities for the children,' she said. 'Sort of like the Brownies, but with quiet times too.'

'Oh, yes,' said Mabel. 'What do you say, Ma?'

'You'd be very welcome here,' said Mrs Green. 'After all, the whole point of the club is to be of service to the community. So long as I'm not left to look after the little blighters on me own!'

'You wouldn't be left on your own, Mrs G,' said Sarah. 'We'd get a big team of people to help run it. Maybe we could call it Little Poppies?'

'Little Poppies – I like it!' said Carrie, delightedly. She turned to Mrs Armstrong – who had hitherto kept quiet – knowing that the older woman's reaction would likely make or break the entire idea. 'What do you think, Ma'am?'

For a moment, Mrs Armstrong didn't react – and then her face slowly split into a huge beam. 'Well, I think you've certainly found your why,' she said. 'But I'm just sitting here wondering if we could do a little more than that.'

'*More?*' said Harry, with a grin.

'Yes, young man,' said Mrs Armstrong. 'As well as looking after the children, I'm thinking we might provide an evening meal for the women working in the factory, so they don't have to cook a meal for their families once they're off duty. Perhaps we could look after their allotments too, if they wanted; even have a sewing posse to help with the darning. I'm running ahead of myself here, but we could arrange to take their children to and from school once term starts up again in September. All the things that a mother or an older sister would automatically do for a family member signing up for war work. I'm not sure my old fingers are up to making . . . special poppies, and I don't want to be paid, but I miss my grandchildren terribly and I'd love to help look after the little ones. I'm sure there are many others in the same boat . . .'

There was a little silence, and everyone spontaneously started clapping.

Harry looked from one to the other. 'I think that that might be the answer to our problems,' he said. 'Thank you, Mrs Armstrong.'

'No, it's all thanks to Carrie, Mabel and Sarah,' she said, firmly.

'The Poppy Girls to the rescue,' said Carrie with a wink.

Mrs Green made another pot of tea, and full of enthusiasm, the little team got down to practicalities.

Mrs Armstrong would tell Major Armstrong the plan that very evening – although she assured them all that his approval was merely a formality.

They would arrange another estate meeting within the next few days, and Mabel would put posters around the estate to announce Little Poppies. In the meantime, everyone would make sure that the news spread by word of mouth.

'How many women will you need in the factory?' asked Sarah.

Harry pursed his lips. 'Well, there are a few men we can move over from the main factory – I'm working on how to accommodate their disabilities – but we can't take too many given the increased poppy quotas. So, I think we need at least forty – maybe fifty – women making the special poppies, plus all those who will be needed to look after the children. We have ten or so who have already signed up – or at least have signified that they are available – so we have a long way to go. Think we can do it?'

'We *have* to do it,' said Sarah staunchly. She sounded so fierce and so passionate that Carrie was hard-pressed to swallow her smile. 'It's a tall order, but consider it done! Think about what our fathers did in the last war . . .'

'Exactly,' said Mabel. 'Anything to help our fathers. And anything to win the war.'

Carrie was silent.

It was interesting that the others were doing this to *help* their fathers.

Although she hated to admit it to herself, she was doing it for the opposite reason.

She wanted to show Pa up.

It didn't reflect well on her, but it was the truth.

Carrie was on cloud nine as the meeting finished.

'Well, that went rather well,' she said, when most people had dispersed and Sarah was waiting for Harry to return from the washrooms.

To her surprise, Sarah pulled a little face. 'It's all well and good,' she said, 'but I can't help but worry it's like trying to bail out the sea with a bucket.'

'That's a bit gloomy when we've just discovered a potential solution to our problem . . .'

'Sorry. I'm totally on board with it and it's not that I don't think it's a marvellous idea. It's just Miss Arnott keeps on telling us that major, devastating air attacks are inevitable and that they could happen at any time and no one seems to be giving two figs about that. If we're all blown sky-high, it doesn't matter how many people we get signed up. Meanwhile, there are loads of vacancies at the Poppy Factory ARP and no one stepping forward to fill them . . .'

'I'm sorry,' said Carrie. 'Maybe we can use this recruitment drive to send a few people your way.'

'Maybe.' Sarah didn't look terribly convinced. 'The trouble is, it's just not as glamorous and exciting as everything else, is it? No one takes the sirens seriously, and the blackout is boring until we get bombs rained down on us and, by then, it will be too late.'

'You should have mentioned it. It was the ideal opportunity.'

'I know. But I didn't want to be a killjoy and then I got swept along with everyone else.'

'Look,' said Carrie. '*I'll* volunteer.'

'I didn't mean that.'

'I know. But I will. You're right – it's important work and we need to be stepping up. I'll ask my father again tonight. He's just volunteered for the Local Defence Volunteers so I'm sure he'll see sense.'

But Pa was having none of it.

'I've said no once, and we'll not talk about it again,' he said.

'But Pa . . .'

'Enough, Carrie . . .'

'We just want to keep you safe,' said Ma.

'I'm just trying to keep us *all* safe,' countered Carrie in frustration.

Pa put his cutlery down and fixed her with a gimlet stare. 'I am sick and tired of confrontation,' he said, coldly. 'I work darned hard in that factory and I deserve a bit of respect when I come home in the evening. Instead, I've had to put up with this carping and questioning of my authority over and over again. I'm not an ogre – I allowed you to go to the dance yesterday and no doubt you'll be asking me to let you get involved in the new schemes very soon . . . but it never ends. I don't like your attitude, young lady, and I won't put up with it any longer. You can't join the Poppy Factory ARP – and that's that. Now go to your room and let me finish my meal in peace.'

Carrie glanced at Ma, who suddenly seemed very interested in dabbing her mouth with her napkin and wouldn't meet her eye.

There would be no support coming from *that* quarter.

Fuming, Carrie put down her own napkin and left the room.

Chapter Fourteen

Monday 15 July 1940

But before Carrie could do anything at all, her exam results arrived.

The brown envelope was sitting innocuously with the other letters in the shared hallway when Carrie went downstairs after breakfast. She was almost surprised to see it there; after thinking about almost nothing else for months, examinations and even starting university had hardly crossed her mind over the past few days. She snatched the envelope up and held it to her heart before ripping it open without ceremony, fluttering open the single sheet of paper and casting her eye over the contents. She had done enough – she was sure she had – but she couldn't believe it until she saw the results in black and white . . .

A distinction in every single subject!

Carrie exhaled a ragged breath, her heart thumping uncomfortably in her chest.

Everything seemed thrown into sharp relief: the sun streaming through the glass doors and catching the dust motes in a shower of gold; the other letters and circulars still scattered at her feet on the doormat; a thump of footsteps on the stairs. Hastily, Carrie gathered up the remaining letters; it might be a red-letter day, but it would still be terribly bad form not to distribute the other letters around the block. Finally, she returned home and brandished the letter triumphantly at Ma.

'I've done it,' she panted. 'All distinctions.'

And then Mother was twirling her around the room in jubilation. 'My clever little bluestocking girl,' she said. 'I never doubted for a second you could do it, but with the war turning everything topsy-turvy, I was worried that you wouldn't get your due. Thank goodness your hard work paid off!' She stopped dancing and stood back; her hands heavy on Carrie's shoulders. 'This is *your* time,' she said seriously, looking Carrie in the eye. 'I know you'll still be coming home each evening, but don't let anyone stop you from doing what *you* want to do.'

Ha! That was quite the change after not standing up for her over the ARP. The 'anyone' hung between them; understood but unacknowledged.

'I won't,' Carrie said simply. 'Not anymore.'

And, somehow, she didn't mind quite so much that she would be commuting to London each day. Life in Richmond seemed richer and more interesting nowadays.

'So, how are you going to celebrate?' asked Ma.

Carrie didn't skip a beat. 'With Sarah and Mabel, of course,' she said. 'We've got plans to meet once Mabel's back from work this afternoon. Fingers crossed they're as happy with their results as I am with mine.'

There were other people she would love to share her good news with as well, of course. Ned for starters; she had wittered on about her exams far too often in the Lake District but although Ned had always expressed an interest, she had felt he didn't really 'get' it. He had left school at fourteen and always said that he had learnt far more from the mountains and the fields than he had from his schoolbooks. Bobby would understand, of course, even if he took the opportunity to tease her about studying history . . . but, again, Bobby had burnt his bridges with her . . .

And then she hesitated. There was a time when the first person she would have wanted to confide in was Daisy, but her friend had also been far from her mind over the last few days. To be fair, theirs had been mainly a class-room friendship – but, even so, it was strange how much everything had changed.

There was a knock at the door. Ma went to open it and, seconds later, Sarah appeared. She looked expectantly at Carrie and when Carrie gave a little nod, Sarah gave a little whoop of exhilaration.

'All distinctions?'

'Yes!'

'Me too! University here we come! I'm just going to tell my father and then shall we head down to school together to confirm our new university choices?'

Carrie paused, suddenly uncomfortable. She hadn't even contemplated sharing her good news with Pa. Her father would no doubt immediately find some way to burst her bubble.

'Yes, you go ahead,' said Carrie. 'I'll wait for you outside the factory.'

'Your father has his big Monday morning meeting, so best not to disturb him,' said Ma, papering over any awkwardness. 'Congratulations, girls. I'm very proud of you.'

*

Carrie and Sarah fairly skipped down to the school.

They were still arm in arm, chatting nineteen to the dozen, as they made their way down the corridor to Miss Bateman's office.

'How much *smaller* everything looks.'

'It still *smells* the same, though!'

'Yes! Eau de smelly old plimsoll.'

'Carrie?'

For the first time, Carrie noticed the figure standing outside the office. 'Daisy!'

She unlinked her arm from Sarah's and ran to greet her old friend. But Daisy, hanging back, was looking at her warily.

'Hello,' she said, somewhat coolly.

That was a strange reaction!

Then the penny dropped!

The last thing Daisy would have expected to see was Carrie arm in arm with her erstwhile enemy. Carrie gave Daisy an enormous bearhug, nonetheless. There would be time enough to explain everything later.

'I didn't know you were back from the Lakes,' said Daisy, slightly sulkily. She pulled away, looking at Sarah over Carrie's shoulder.

'We haven't been back long and I've got *so* much to tell you,' said Carrie. 'First things first, though; how were your results?'

Despite it all, Daisy's face split into a huge beam. 'Distinctions,' she said, face flushing with pride. 'Oxford, here I come!'

'Well done, Daisy,' said Sarah, warmly, from behind Carrie.

The door opened and Miss Bateman appeared. Daisy disappeared inside with a rather uncertain backwards glance.

'I don't think she's very pleased to see me,' said Sarah dryly.

Carrie laughed. 'I think she was just taken aback to see us arm in arm,' she said. 'You were hardly my favourite person at school.'

Sarah grinned. 'I know,' she said. 'Likewise. Seriously, I'll go in next and then I'll scarper so that you and Daisy can have a heart-to-heart.'

'I don't want to just *dump* you,' said Carrie, doubtfully.

'You won't be,' said Sarah. 'I have some errands to run anyway.'

'Really?'

'No,' said Sarah. 'But still . . .'

Carrie laughed. 'Thank you,' she said. 'That's really thoughtful.'

The office door opened. Daisy emerged and Sarah, with a subtle wink to Carrie, went inside.

Daisy rounded on Carrie before the door was properly shut.

'Sarah *Turn*er?' she hissed, confusion and derision jostling for supremacy in every syllable.

'Yes,' said Carrie. 'But I've seen a different side to her this summer and she's lovely. She really is.'

'She made your life a *misery*.'

'A lot of that was in my own head,' admitted Carrie. 'And it turned out that I'd hurt her too . . .'

'A likely story,' scoffed Daisy. 'Are you sure she isn't just taking you for a ride?'

'Yes, I'm absolutely sure. Come on, Daisy – give me *some* credit.'

But Daisy just shook her head from side to side in confusion.

'Look, wait for me whilst I see Miss Bateman?' said Carrie urgently. 'We can have a proper catch-up . . .'

'Good morning, Carolyn!'

Carrie blinked. The door had already opened and Miss Bateman was smiling up at her.

And then she was being ushered into the office with no real idea of whether Daisy would be waiting for her afterwards or not. She accepted Miss Bateman's congratulations and signed the requisite forms. Miss Bateman was muttering that everything was different because of the war, but Carrie didn't know what it had been like before and, besides, what did it matter? She was going to university! The only slight fly in the ointment was that Pa also needed to sign the forms, which would necessitate a separate trip . . .

Gah!

This time it wasn't his fault, but his tentacles really did get into every facet of her life.

'What have you been doing with yourself this summer?' asked Miss Bateman as Carrie slid the lid back onto her fountain pen.

'Rather a lot, actually,' said Carrie. Proudly, she told Miss Bateman all about helping out as an honorary Land Girl and then driving the van back from the Lake District.

'Brava,' said Miss Bateman. 'And how about now you're home? There are still a couple of months before university starts.'

Carrie told her the bare bones about Little Poppies – positioning it only that it would allow mothers on the estate to do general war work, and not mentioning that the factory had been partially requisitioned. 'I intend to volunteer with the children,' she finished off.

Miss Bateman nodded. 'Sarah told me a little about that and it all sounds very creditable,' she said. 'And what about during the evenings? I know the Poppy Factory ARP is desperately looking for volunteers and I'm sure Miss Arnott would snap you up in a heartbeat to work alongside Sarah.'

Carrie sighed. 'I've been thinking about the ARP,' she admitted. 'Everything I've seen and heard has convinced me that it's going to be crucial in the months ahead. But I'm not sure the Poppy Factory branch would work for me . . .'

'Really? Not because of Sarah?'

No, because my father thinks I'm about eight . . .

'No, absolutely not. But I'm the daughter of the manager and . . .'

Miss Bateman laughed. 'Goodness me, politics gets everywhere, doesn't it? Well, why not volunteer at my section?'

'*Your* section?'

'Yes. I run the St Mark's Avenue area,' said Miss Bateman, leaning forwards in her chair. 'Usually, we look for someone who's very local; someone who knows everyone and everywhere like the back of her hand. That said, we're very short-staffed, and I'm loath to let someone who can already drive slip through my fingers. How do you fancy being an ambulance driver?'

Carrie gasped and suddenly realised she would like that very much indeed. *Here* was the challenge she'd been looking for . . .

'Do I need to get my parents' permission?' she asked.

Miss Bateman laughed. 'Not now you're eighteen,' she said.

'But I'm not eighteen for another month,' said Carrie mournfully.

'Ah, yes,' said Miss Bateman. 'You're tall, so I always forget you were one of the babies of the year. Whenever I saw you next to Mabel Green, I found it hard to believe that she's nearly a year older than you.'

'So that's that then,' said Carrie, feeling thoroughly deflated.

'Not a bit of it,' said Miss Bateman, rubbing her hands together briskly. 'We just need your father to write a quick note, and then seventeen will do very nicely. I can help you draft a letter now, and your father can sign it alongside your university forms this evening.'

Carrie tried – and failed – to stop a hollow laugh escaping her lips.

'Not going to be as easy as that?' Miss Bateman asked gently.

Carrie shook her head, her eyes filling with tears. 'It would be impossible,' she said simply. 'I don't think it's just the Poppy Factory ARP he disagrees with.'

'Come now,' said Miss Bateman. 'I can't believe a girl who's just driven a van cross country would give up without a fight.'

'You don't know what he's like . . .'

'I remember him from Parents' Day, and he was certainly

a force to be reckoned with,' said Miss Bateman with a smile. 'But where there's a will, there's a way. I can understand that the Poppy Factory ARP might be too close to home. I can also understand him wanting to protect you; after all, it's a natural parental instinct. But the thing is that we're all having to do things and accept things we wouldn't have contemplated before the war. You tell your father that one alumna – Lorna Hawley – from this school has already been sent to the Naval Signal Office in the caves under Dover Castle, and Muriel Glass – remember her? – is doing her bit as an establishment officer in Cairo. Given that, I really think your parents can let you do your bit in Richmond. The Germans are coming, there's no doubt about that!'

Against the odds, Carrie felt her resolve strengthen.

Desperate times called for desperate measures.

'Would you like me to speak to your father?' Miss Bateman was saying. 'I could try to put his mind at rest?'

Carrie shook her head. 'No, thank you,' she said firmly.

There was a significant chance Pa would say no and Ma, of course, would be no use at all. Either way, the cat would be out of the bag.

There was no other way around it.

She would have to forge Pa's signature.

She smiled resolutely at Miss Bateman. 'If you could help me draft a note, I'll make sure I get it signed this evening, and then I'll be available to report whenever you need me.'

Miss Bateman gave her a shrewd look and the ghost of a smile. 'Right you are,' she said. 'Why not drop off all your forms at 56 St Mark's Avenue at two o'clock tomorrow and we'll get going straightaway? Once you're all trained up, we'll need you for three nights a week. That suit you?'

Carrie swallowed hard. 'Yes, Ma'am!' she said, resolutely.

'Welcome aboard the good ship ARP.'

Daisy was waiting for Carrie outside the office.

'Your new friend has already left,' she said, somewhat pointedly.

A wave of irritation washed over Carrie. 'Yes, she left so that we might chat,' she said, equally pointedly. 'Come on, let's go and sit in the park.'

Five minutes later, the two were lying on the cool grass of Richmond Green.

'So, your news?' said Daisy, clearly trying to be cheerful. 'Does it involve men?'

Carrie laughed. 'Two,' she said and duly told Daisy everything.

Despite the earlier coolness, she trusted her friend implicitly; there was no need to edit what she said or leave anything out for fear of it being judged or repeated. By the time she had finished speaking, Daisy was laughing.

'What do they say about buses?' she said. 'None at all and then two at once!'

Carrie grinned. 'It's not like that,' she said. 'I really liked Ned but that was just a holiday fling, and, as for Bobby — well, he's lovely, but he's already run out on me twice.'

'I think the lady doth protest too much,' said Daisy, her smile hiding a shrewd glance. 'Otherwise, why tell me about him at all?'

'You said to tell you everything . . .'

'Hmm.'

'There's more,' said Carrie. She stopped and then announced proudly, 'This is a total secret, but I'm going to join the ARP as an ambulance driver.'

'What!' Daisy scrambled into a sitting position. 'What are you thinking, Carrie? That's incredibly dangerous. And why is it a secret, for goodness' sake?'

'Because my father must never, ever find out about it.'

'Oh, for heaven's sake, this is ridiculous!' said Daisy hotly. She paused and then added, '*She's* put you up to this, hasn't she?'

'Sarah?' said Carrie. 'No, of course she hasn't . . .'

'She mentioned when you were in with Miss Bateman that she's volunteering . . .'

'Yes, but that's got nothing to do with it . . .'

'She's a bad influence, Carrie.'

'She *isn't*. I'm not even . . .'

'She *is*. You should stay well away from her. Why don't you join my knitting circle instead? You can still do your bit and . . .'

'Because I don't want to join your knitting circle,' Carrie interrupted. 'That won't help if the Germans start bombing, will it?'

'Maybe not but at least you won't be deliberately putting yourself in harm's way.'

'Well, *someone's* got to put themselves in harm's way . . .'

She trailed off and the two girls stared angrily at each other, chests heaving.

'I don't want to argue,' said Daisy in a more conciliatory tone.

'Me neither,' said Carrie. 'But there's clearly no point in my asking you what I was going to.'

Daisy's face softened. Absentmindedly, she picked a buttercup and tucked it behind her ear. 'The answer is yes,' she said.

Carrie wrinkled up her nose in confusion. 'And what was my question?' she asked.

'Your question was, "May I tell my parents I'm at yours knitting comforts for the sailors whenever I have to report for duty?"'

There was a short silence.

'Thank you,' said Carrie simply.

Daisy hesitated. 'You'd do it anyway, whatever I said,' she answered softly. 'And, for the record, I think you're mad, but I won't give you away. Those sailors are going to be awfully warm at night with all the knitting you're going to claim to be doing.'

Carrie's heart and her thoughts flip-flopped for the rest of the day.

There was a time she would never have *contemplated* deceiving Pa. Lying went completely against her principles and, besides, she would have been too scared.

But this was no longer that time. The war was real and coming closer and, to be frank, forging Pa's signature would serve him right for what he had done to Marigold last year . . .

By the time she met up with Mabel and Sarah at the Remembrance Club, she was full of resolve. It was a jolly, upbeat occasion; Mabel was thrilled by her results – the third highest maths mark in the *country*, she announced proudly – and Mr and Mrs Green produced cider and cake all round to celebrate and left the girls to it.

Carrie waited until she had downed every last drop of the amber liquid before she announced her plans. She had debated whether or not to share her intentions after Daisy's reaction, but she trusted the Poppy Girls implicitly and she really wanted their support.

'Good for you,' said Sarah warmly. 'You'll be an asset to them! But are you sure about not telling your father?'

'He'll just say no,' said Carrie.

'It's an awfully big secret to keep from your parents,' said Mabel. 'And secrets can wear you down.'

'I know,' said Carrie, dabbing the cake crumbs off her plate with her thumb. 'But I can't spend my whole life being pushed around by my father.'

'We're right behind you whatever you decide, but give him a chance to say yes?' persisted Mabel.

Carrie sighed.

Maybe she should give Pa one last opportunity to be reasonable.

It was only fair.

'It's a deal,' she said, holding her empty glass up to her friends.

At suppertime, Pa was at his most charming.

Clearly thrilled by Carrie's results, he produced a hitherto hidden bottle of Champagne and proposed a toast to her. He then slightly blotted his copybook by praising himself for his support and forbearance in getting her to this point, but Carrie supposed that it wouldn't be fair to judge him solely on that.

You couldn't expect a leopard to completely change its spots!

Then he moved on to the creation of Little Poppies. It had obviously been discussed at length that day and Pa now seemed to think it was *Major* Armstrong's idea and therefore to be taken seriously.

'An interesting idea,' he conceded. 'I'm curious to see how it works in practice.'

'Well, I think it all sounds marvellous,' said Ma. 'I can't wait to do my bit.'

Carrie smiled at the unexpected support. '*Do* you, Ma?' she said. 'That's wonderful.'

'Absolutely,' said Ma. 'I think it's a very ingenious solution.'

Carrie basked quietly in her mother's second-hand praise.

Pa grunted. 'Major Armstrong has got a whole list of tasks for you ladies,' he said. 'I'm sure we can find something suitable that means you don't neglect your duties at home.'

'I thought I might help in the factory,' said Ma brightly. 'I rather enjoyed it during the Great War and assembling radios sounds quite the challenge. How about you, Carrie?'

Carrie hesitated. For all her wanting to get stuck in and help, she was still determined not to get involved with anything that could kill or maim. 'I'd like to look after the children,' she said, firmly. 'I'm really enjoying the Brownies.'

'That's very fitting,' said Pa, approvingly. 'I hear you're doing very well with the Brownies and it will all prove useful when you have a family of your own.'

Goodness.

Was Pa being almost reasonable?

Carrie put down her knife and fork, swallowed a mouthful of special-occasion chicken and smiled brightly at her parents.

'Then again, I rather fancy manning the factory tea trolley when June goes off to Gloucestershire,' she said casually, sprinkling more salt over her potatoes.

'Less fitting!' said Pa, mildly enough, spearing a piece of carrot. 'We're *management!*'

'*You're* management,' Carrie clarified. 'Besides, what better way to demonstrate that we're all in it together than having the manager's daughter mucking in and serving the tea? Actions, not words . . . ?'

'And absolutely out of the question,' Pa interrupted. 'Apart from anything else, I fear much crockery would be broken and many men would be scalded before the summer was out.'

He laughed long and loud at his own joke and Carrie silently went in for the kill.

'When I asked if I could join the ARP, you refused because I'd be lording it over you all,' she said calmly. 'You seem to want it both ways.'

Her father put his cutlery down. 'We couldn't have you barking instructions at Major Armstrong, now, could we?'

'But what about volunteering at another branch of the ARP?'

She held her breath.

'No, darling.' It was her mother speaking. 'That just wouldn't be safe.'

'*War* isn't safe!'

'I agree with your mother,' said Pa with finality. 'Besides, it would look very strange for you to be volunteering at another ARP. The point is that you know the neighbourhood . . .'

'But you've just said that I can't volunteer at ours!'

She was pleased Pa was being so rigid and, frankly, ridiculous. She *wanted* to join Miss Bateman's branch of the ARP and – by being unreasonable – he had just handed it to her on a plate.

'Don't let's argue on such a lovely day,' said Pa. 'We've agreed to you looking after the children in Little Poppies. Let's leave it at that.'

Carrie smiled. 'Of course,' she said, in a conciliatory tone. 'In the meantime, I have some university forms for you to sign. I told Miss Bateman I'd return them to her tomorrow.'

Pa nodded. 'That's better,' he said. 'Bring them to me after supper.'

'And one more thing. I saw Daisy at school today. Would you have any objection if I volunteered at her knitting circle over the summer? They're making comforts for the sailors and they've set themselves a very ambitious target.'

'That's more like it,' said Pa. 'A very suitable occupation for a young lady.'

'It will be a lot of evening work, though. How would you feel about me staying over with her some nights?'

She held her breath.

'No objection, at all,' said Pa. 'Mr Thornton is a very respectable businessman – and a stalwart volunteer, to boot. Besides, it's better than walking home in the dark.'

'And you'll be a darn sight safer in their home than you are on the estate now that we're involved in war work,' added Ma. 'I gather they have an Anderson shelter in their garden?'

'They do.'

'Then that's settled,' said Pa. 'You see, Carrie, we're quite reasonable really. Not quite the dreadful tyrants you make us out to be.'

Carrie didn't answer.

Chapter Fifteen

Tuesday 16 July 1940

After all the angst – and a fair bit of tossing and turning that night – it took seconds to forge Pa's signature the next morning. Carrie had planned to practise on a blank piece of paper until she was confident she could achieve a good approximation of Pa's looping scrawl but, in the event, that wasn't necessary. She got the signed university form, put it on top of the ARP letter and traced Pa's signature with a pin. This left an indentation of his signature on the letter below, which she simply filled in with pen. It was an old trick – one she had seen Sarah and her friends implement dozens of times at school – and it worked a treat.

She still had her doubts, though.

Apart from the deception, volunteering for the ARP was hardly playing to her strengths. If the worst came to the worst and Richmond *was* attacked or invaded, she would probably be useless at rescuing people. She wasn't especially brave – look at her skulking behind Pa's back rather than really standing up to him! – and she was so clumsy and unco-ordinated she would probably be more hindrance than help. Sarah would be able to clamber walls and shin down the smallest of holes in the rubble, whereas she would probably fall over or get stuck and end up having to be rescued herself.

Maybe she should put the whole silly idea behind her

and concentrate on Little Poppies and her reading list for university. Yes, that was precisely what she should do. She would go to St Mark's Avenue that afternoon, give Miss Bateman her university forms and simply say that she'd changed her mind about the ARP . . .

There was a rap on her bedroom door and Carrie hastily shoved the letter with its incriminating signature under her pillow. Ma came in, an envelope in her outstretched hand.

'Letter for you,' she said, pleasantly. And then, 'I'm so pleased we've settled on what you're doing this summer. Looking after the children and knitting with Daisy sounds perfect. Pa only wants what's best for you, you know.'

'I'm not sure about that,' said Carrie, taking the envelope and recognising cousin Violet's handwriting. 'But I'm glad it's all settled too.'

Ma left and Carrie threw herself back onto her eiderdown to read her letter. She and Violet had already exchanged a letter in the two weeks since she had left the Lake District, and it was lovely to hear from her again so soon.

Violet started without preamble.

She wrote with news.

Developments.

Unbeknown to any of us, Charlie has applied to and been accepted by the Royal Airforce. We're all reeling with shock, but my parents are putting a brave face on it. Between you and me, I think they're rather proud of him as well as being worried sick. He's off to join Bomber Command in Lincolnshire in a matter of days and – in another twist – Ned is going with him. The two were in cahoots all along . . .

Carrie sat bolt upright. The letter dangled from her fingers before slowly fluttering to the floor. Heart thumping, Carrie picked it up and scanned the contents again.

Oh goodness!

There was the danger, of course; everyone knew that flying a bomber was a huge risk to life and limb. Carrie was already sick to her stomach with nerves for both of them.

But . . . Ned?

She had thought the two of them were so close, and yet Ned had kept this a secret from her. Amongst the admiration and the anxiety, there was also anger. It felt like she had hardly known him at all.

Should she write to him? Tell him she had heard the news and was wishing him well. Should she even advise him not to enlist or, at least, to choose something less dangerous?

No.

Neither would be appropriate.

It had been left to Violet to tell her that he had signed up and it simply underscored the fact there was nothing left between the two of them. She assumed that beautiful Mary was home and sharing Ned's honeyed kisses and there was nothing more to do except hope that he would return to his beloved mountains and lakes when the war was over.

But if Ned was willing to put his life on the line, then to hell with playing it safe with Little Poppies.

She *was* going to join the ARP, after all.

Ma had received a letter from Aunty Annie that morning and, naturally, all she and Carrie could talk about as they did the housework was Charlie signing up and their fears for his future.

At lunchtime, they shared a quick sandwich.

'I need to drop my university forms off at Miss Bateman's this afternoon and then I thought I might go to Daisy's and make a start on the knitting,' said Carrie.

The words stuck in her throat and she was sure she was blushing bright pink.

But Ma just smiled. 'Good idea,' she said. 'Nothing like keeping busy when you've had bad news.'

'Will you be all right on your own?'

Ma smiled. 'Thank you, darling, but I'll be just fine. Mrs Jones has rather foolishly washed her blackout curtains, which has made them go see-through, so I've plenty to keep me occupied.'

Carrie laughed and then made a big show of getting her knitting paraphernalia together. Just as she was about to leave, Ma presented her with a couple of balls of wool and an old jumper to be unravelled and reknitted.

'I'm proud of you, darling,' she said, kissing Carrie on the cheek.

Carrie's guilt ratcheted up a gear. 'I'll be off then,' she said, carefully avoiding her mother's eye.

And then, without a backwards glance, she left. She was already running a little late – especially as she wasn't precisely sure which of the warren of roads on the other side of Richmond Hill was St Mark's Avenue – so she headed up the hill at a jog. She was just emerging from the estate onto the hill when someone almost collided with her . . .

A male someone with light brown hair, pale skin and a colourful scarf wound around his neck . . .

Someone, in fact, who looked a lot like . . .

'Bobby!'

Carrie stared at him in surprise.

Presumably, he was simply using the Poppy estate as a short cut between Richmond Hill and the bridge, although might there be a miniscule chance he was looking for her?

Either way, it really didn't matter.

She had already resolved not to have anything more to do with him and, anyway, she really didn't want to be seen in his – or in any man's – company. The last thing she needed was some busybody telling her parents she was sneaking out to meet a boy. And Miss Arnott, busy sweeping the steps outside her flat on the corner, was certainly one such busybody . . .

Bobby, meanwhile, was smiling down at her, all relaxed bonhomie.

'Lyn!' he cried expansively. 'How are the stems?'

'Hello, Bobby,' Carrie replied coolly. 'I'm late for an appointment and I'm afraid I can't stop to chat.'

And you ran out on me. Twice!

Carrie went to push past him, gas mask bouncing, but suddenly the scream of a loud engine split the air in two. Carrie stopped and quickly scanned the skies . . .

'Over the river. A German plane, flying low,' shouted Miss Arnott.

'A Messerschmitt,' confirmed Bobby. 'We need to take cover.'

Carrie was rooted to the ground in shock.

Take cover?

Where?

There might be time to run to the shelter underneath the Remembrance Club . . . but it would be touch and go. Maybe they should simply spreadeagle themselves on the ground. In the meantime, should she put on her mask in case of the gas attack the papers had been warning about for months . . . ?

Before anyone had time to react, there was a burst of fire and then a screech of several more planes. Carrie's heart plummeted and then, to her exquisite relief, she saw that these were Spitfires – their smooth curves and elliptical wings sleek and elegant against the sky. They raced after the German plane, following it into a bank of cloud . . . and then they were gone, leaving nothing but an eerie silence.

Carrie and Bobby turned to each other.

'First time I've seen a dogfight around here . . .' said Bobby.

Carrie pushed out her cheeks. 'I thought we were all goners,' she admitted.

'No time even to sound the alarm,' Miss Arnott called over. 'Let's hope they gave Jerry a good pummelling.'

'*I* just hope our boys get back safely,' said Bobby. 'I'm sorry to say that we're no match for the German planes.'

Carrie gave him a sharp look. If that was true, it was very frightening indeed.

She glanced at her watch and – golly! – she really was late now.

'I must be going,' she said.

'Of course,' said Bobby. 'Only . . . I was wondering if I might see you again?'

Completely unexpectedly, happiness surged through Carrie. Bobby *had* come to find her . . . and part of her very much wanted to see him again too. But he always blew so hot and cold and it really unsettled her. She couldn't let him do it to her a third time . . .

'I don't think so,' she said, gently enough and walked away without giving him the chance to reply.

She didn't glance around until she'd crossed Richmond Hill and then the hurt and disappointment on Bobby's face almost made her hurry back to him.

But she mustn't.

She turned on her heel and walked resolutely away.

Carrie hurried up Richmond Hill, the river below her to the right, and then turned left into the warren of suburban streets. She had walked them often enough over the years – occasionally using them as a cut through to the station or school – but she wasn't totally au fait with the street names, nor the cul-de-sacs that led off many of them. Luckily, she had sneaked a glance at Pa's map that morning, so she knew St Mark's Avenue was half a dozen roads along on the right and that it headed directly towards the park. It was all somewhat further than she had anticipated and she was panting well before she finally turned the corner.

Like the streets around, the houses on St Mark's Avenue were detached redbrick Victorian villas, interspersed by more modern, semi-detached houses. The road was wide and tree-lined and the whole ambience was one of quiet prosperity, despite the fact that fences and garden gates had been melted down to help the war effort.

A group of neatly dressed little girls played hopscotch on the pavement, whilst a couple of older boys wheeled around on bicycles, excitedly calling out to each other about the dogfight and debating whether to go off in hot pursuit. As Carrie marched past, an air raid siren started up from close by and anxious mothers opened doors and urged their offspring inside. Carrie picked up her pace and followed the sound as, of course, the siren would be coming from the ARP base. And there it was: an imposing double-fronted Victorian house with an acceptably tidy – but far from manicured – front garden and a large khaki car painted with red crosses parked on the drive.

Carrie hurried up the flagstoned pathway – resisting the temptation to clamp her hands over her ears against the piercing shriek – and knocked smartly on the door.

There was no reply – perhaps unsurprisingly over the din – so she knocked again.

Still nothing.

Feeling rather self-conscious, Carrie took a couple of steps sideways into a neglected bed of roses and peered through the front window. The window gave onto a sitting room stuffed with mahogany furniture and an abundance of knickknacks. It was, however, empty of people save for one tiny old lady who was fast asleep in an overstuffed armchair, a ginger tabby curled on her lap. It didn't look very promising . . .

As Carrie stood debating what to do, an internal door swung open and Miss Bateman strode into the room. Ah, the right house, but how embarrassing to be caught in the flowerbed with her nose pressed against the window! Carrie tried to back away . . . but too late. Miss Bateman looked up, saw Carrie, and started in shocked surprise. Then, her face relaxed into a smile, and she gestured for Carrie to walk round to the front door.

'So sorry, Carrie,' she said, seconds later, as she opened the door. 'One can't hear a thing with this racket going on. I do hope you haven't been standing there too long.'

'No, Miss. I've just got here,' said Carrie. Somewhat embarrassingly, her jumper was attached to a prickly rose briar, so she was still standing in the flowerbed. 'And, if you wouldn't mind calling me Lyn?'

She had planned this in advance. She didn't want word of what she was doing to get back to the estate and perhaps using a slightly different name would help with her 'disguise'. Luckily, Miss Bateman didn't bat an eyelid.

'Right. Lyn it is,' she said, with a little smile. 'Come along in, or are you still wrestling with that bush?'

Carrie yanked herself free and knew her cheeks were flushing as pink as the roses. Over Miss Bateman's shoulder, she could see a blonde-haired girl suppressing a smirk.

It was hardly the most auspicious of starts.

'Everyone else is up on the roof,' said Miss Bateman. 'Evelyn, Madge and I have stayed down here awaiting orders and to keep an eye on Mother. Let's hang fire until we get further instructions.'

'I saw the planes,' said Carrie, wiping her feet. 'I think they've gone – for now at least. They disappeared into the clouds towards Kingston . . .'

A phone rang somewhere in the depths of the building and, seconds later, a female voice shouted, 'All clear.'

Miss Bateman smiled with satisfaction. 'There you are,' she said. 'Confirmation twice over.'

Wailing Willie stopped and Carrie was suddenly aware of the loud ticking of a grandfather clock and the gentle snoring of Miss Bateman's mother. Then the all-clear sounded.

Miss Bateman set off at a clip down the hallway and Carrie fell into step with the blonde girl who regarded Carrie coolly from beneath heavily mascaraed eyelashes.

The hall led to a large room at the back of the property, which opened directly onto the garden, the glass-panelled doors crisscrossed with adhesive tape.

Carrie stood and drank it all in.

The telephones, radios and files crammed onto wooden tables pushed against one wall were clearly the nerve-centre of the operation. A redheaded girl was standing over them, scribbling something into a large ledger. On the wall behind, there was a large noticeboard studded with sheets of paper and a heavily annotated map of the local area. Carrie stared at it in fascination. This was where the response to air raids was coordinated and where information was disseminated to the civilian population.

It was both sobering and exciting beyond words.

Then, Carrie turned her attention to the rest of the room, which was much more comfortably and informally furnished. This must be where the ARP staff and volunteers gathered during their quieter periods. The space was dominated by a full-sized table tennis table, the brightly coloured bats scattered haphazardly on the surface. There were several battered armchairs and an old sofa with books, knitting projects and handbags lying across the seats and a table and chairs, which had recently been used for playing whist or suchlike – the cards face down in their hands. The whole impression was at once homely and officious, comfortable and slightly scary.

No sooner had Carrie begun to take it all in than the door to the garden opened and three young people trooped in, chatting animatedly amongst themselves.

'That was the shortest air raid in history . . .' said a pretty, round-faced brunette.

'Hopefully the break served to remind you not to trump too low,' said a short man with a strong French accent. 'You were about to get a proper drubbing.'

'Oh, it would take longer than that to remind Tilly of the fundamentals of whist!' laughed a taller girl with mousy hair and protruding teeth. 'Although I'm delighted to hear you use the word "drubbing" so confidently. Your English is really coming on!'

Carrie stood self-consciously; a nervous smile plastered on her face. The three newcomers seemed so relaxed together and that sort of banter never came easily to her. Again, she couldn't help thinking that Sarah was far better suited to it all.

'Never mind all that,' interrupted the blonde-haired girl. 'Did you think of a name for us? We can't let the Kings Road Glamour Girls have all the attention.'

'Not all the ARP stations have to have a name,' interjected Miss Bateman, mildly, leaning over the ledger beside the redhead. 'The Poppy Factory's doesn't.'

'But where's the fun in that?' laughed Tilly good-naturedly. 'No, we must have a name. We just didn't have time to think of one.'

'Besides,' added the man, 'as I am not a female, we must take care not to include the word "Girls".'

'What about the Saints?' interrupted Carrie, the name popping fully formed into her mind. 'You know, from St Mark's Avenue.'

She held her breath.

Would her contribution be welcomed . . . or would it be seen as too much, too soon?

'Ooh, I love it,' said Tilly, earning Carrie's eternal gratitude.

'Me too,' said the redhead. 'And it doesn't exclude you, Bobby and Benoit.'

Bobby!

Carrie stiffened at the mention of his name.

Was it the same Bobby?

It must be!

'I think the name will do nicely,' said the blonde girl, cutting across Carrie's thoughts. 'I think *you* will do nicely too.' She smiled and her whole face lit up, displaying unexpected dimples. 'Cuppa?' she added. 'I'm just popping the kettle on.'

'I'm glad you're all making friends,' said Miss Bateman. 'Some of these posts can be worse than the Upper Thirds on a wet lunch break. But I'm afraid tea for Lyn will have to wait. I need to process her paperwork and then she's got her first driving lesson with Benoit.'

Carrie started in surprise.

'Now?' she squeaked to a chorus of friendly laughter.

'There's no time like the present,' said Miss Bateman briskly. 'You're no use to us until you're trained up.'

Carrie swallowed hard. 'Well, I'm as ready as I'll ever be,' she said.

Miss Bateman smiled. 'You've driven vans before, so you'll be fine. If you could just let me have your university forms and your permission slip . . .'

With shaking fingers, Carrie opened her leather bag and extracted the paperwork, wondering if the signature on the permission slip would pass scrutiny. But Miss Bateman simply took both without comment, placing the permission slip in a cardboard folder on the desk and popping the university forms into her handbag underneath it.

Carrie exhaled gently.

She might as well have signed Pa's name in her own hand – or even written her own name – such was the lack of scrutiny . . .

Miss Bateman straightened up. 'We'll provide you with a steel helmet and an armband, but you'll need to smuggle out some Wellingtons next time,' she said quietly.

Carrie started in shock.

So, Miss Bateman *did* know she was here without permission.

Goodness me, she could *never* underestimate the woman.

Outside, the little girls were back playing hopscotch and the boys were wheeling around on their bikes again. It was as if the air raid siren had never sounded.

'So, this is the ambulance,' said Benoit, pointing to the car. 'I'll give you a tour first, and then we can take her for a little turn.'

'You mean a spin,' said Carrie, with a grin, warming to him. 'Although my driving might give you a turn!'

Benoit laughed. 'I pray that you will be kind on me,' he said. 'I'm feeling a little delicate today from the drink. Tilly and I went to the Rose and Crown yesterday.'

Carrie smiled. 'I'll do my best,' she promised.

'They all say that,' said Benoit, gloomily. 'Tilly – she was like a kangaroo in the car. I was very happy when she decided it was not for her.'

He opened the rear doors and Carrie peered inside. The interior had been stripped bare of its previous fixtures and fittings and a foldaway bed had been attached to one interior wall, a wooden stretcher strapped on top of it. There were storage compartments and racks along the other wall – already full of first aid kits, bandages and splints – and a foldaway seat ready for the ambulance attendant.

Carrie gulped hard.

It all looked very real and very scary.

'Come and take your seat inside,' said Benoit.

He opened the passenger door and Carrie let out a little shriek.

'It's all back to front,' she yelped. 'The driver isn't supposed to sit *there*!'

Benoit laughed. 'They are in Belgium,' he said matter-of-factly.

'But we're not in Belgium!'

'This is true,' said Benoit. 'And also, to be true, this is not a car from Belgium. It's an American Packard – very much admired for its status – so we must remember to be grateful for its use.'

'That's all very well,' grumbled Carrie. 'But why can't we have a *normal* ambulance?'

Benoit's answering shrug was so elaborate that his shoulders almost touched his ears.

'Because this is wartime?' he said, gesturing for Carrie to take a seat inside. 'Because the Americans are helping us? Because we fear there will be a greater need for ambulances than the number of "normal" ambulances available? Enough . . . ?'

'Enough.' A little chastened, Carrie took a seat behind the wheel. 'Everything looks completely different. The gear stick is on the wrong side, and how on earth am I supposed to know which pedal is which?'

Benoit slid into the passenger seat. 'Most things are

exactly the same,' he said reassuringly. 'The pedals are all where you would expect them to be. The main things you need to watch out for are your position on the road – it can be difficult to judge how far you are from people or parked cars. Also, be careful when overtaking. And, of course, reversing and parking can be a big problem . . .'

'Stop!' said Carrie, half-laughing and half-groaning.

'Sorry,' said Benoit. 'Never mind what Gertrude Bateman thinks, it's harder if you've driven before. Anyhow, why don't you drive slowly down the street and we'll look how we go.'

Carrie nodded, storing away Miss Bateman's Christian name to share with the Poppy Girls.

Concentrate, Carrie – or should that be Lyn?

She fumbled the key into the ignition – *everything* was back to front! – and then struggled putting the car into first with the 'wrong' hand on the gear stick.

Next to her, Benoit remained still and quiet, but Carrie could tell that he was poised to grab the steering wheel or pull on the handbrake if need be.

Slowly, she inched forwards and – keeping a sharp eye out for the little girls and the wheeling Jack-the-lads – set off down the street. It felt strange changing gears with her right hand and, as Benoit had warned, it was hard to tell how far away she was from the kerb, but she managed with the minimum of lurching and without hitting anything. Luckily, there were very few cars around and there really wasn't much to hit!

'Very good,' murmured Benoit. 'Now, Tilly, she had nearly hit many trees by this point. Let us go around the blocks and then we will go out onto the main road.'

'Yes, boss.'

By the time Carrie had driven around the local streets for a while, she had learnt two things. The first was that driving a car was very similar to riding a bicycle. Regardless of the internal layout, once you had mastered the basics, you were absolutely fine provided you kept your wits about you.

The second thing Carrie learnt was that Benoit was in love with Tilly. His desperation to say her name, his shoe-horning her into conversations she really had no reason to be in, the dreamy tone in his voice . . . his devotion was palpable and really rather touching. Carrie found herself hoping against hope that his feelings were reciprocated . . .

'Let us now go up Richmond Hill,' said Benoit. 'We will drive around the park a little and then we will stop at the Star and Garter and book you in for your first aid lessons.'

Carrie nodded and duly turned left onto Richmond Hill. This was a busier road – at least with regards to pedestrians and bicycles – and it was also home territory as it bordered the Poppy Factory estate. Carrie was torn between winding the window down so that everyone could see that she was *driving an ambulance* . . . and keeping her head well down for fear that news of her doing so would get back to Ma and Pa.

'Watch up ahead,' said Benoit, as they approached a parked car. 'That vehicle has been filled with stones.'

'Why?' said Carrie, giving it a wide berth.

'In case of invasion,' said Benoit, simply. 'It will be positioned in the middle of the road to slow the enemy down, along with a plank of wood through the windows to make it wider.'

Carrie grimaced as she slowed to overtake a group of soldiers marching in the road.

The war really did get everywhere.

They drove on up the hill and then through the ornate wrought-iron gates into Richmond Park.

'So, you're not the only man volunteering for the Saints?' she asked, desperate to turn the conversation to Bobby.

'The only one doing twelve hours on, twelve hours off.'

Carrie gulped inwardly. Twelve hours on and twelve hours off?

That would have been an awful lot of knitting to explain away. Luckily, she had only committed to three nights a week.

'But people work different hours?' she clarified.

'Most do. They have work elsewhere, for example. Turn around up ahead, please.'

'In that driveway?'

'*S'il te plaît.*'

Concentrating hard, Carrie turned the ambulance around without either hitting the kerbs or crunching the gears and was rewarded with a grunt of approval.

'You said there's another chap who works these different hours?' she asked, as she started to drive back the way they had come.

'Yes. Bobby. A hearing chap.'

'Hearing?' Carrie was confused. 'You mean he's not deaf?'

Benoit laughed and hit himself lightly on the side of his head. 'My English, sometimes it is not so good. I mean he is a decent fellow. I do not know about his hearing.'

'Oh, a *sound* chap,' said Carrie with a giggle.

'That is correct,' said Benoit. 'He works somewhere up

here as it happens. I have no idea what he does because he has to keep mother about it.'

'I've met him, I think,' said Carrie. 'He sometimes wears a very distinctive scarf.'

'Oh, that scarf,' said Benoit, pulling a face. 'It is so bright, I am surprised the enemy do not see it from the skies.'

Carrie giggled. 'Did you teach him to drive too?'

'No, no,' said Benoit. 'Bobby do not drive. His vision is not good and that is why he is not conscripted.'

'I see. So, what's his role at the ARP?'

'He is part of our rescue squad,' said Benoit, matter-of-factly. 'He will enter the bombed buildings to bring out survivors.'

Carrie swallowed hard. The rescue squad really was the front line – men and women deliberately putting themselves in harm's way to help civilians to safety. Carrie honestly didn't think that she could do it. Driving an ambulance during a bombing raid was hardly without its risks, of course, but it was nothing by comparison.

They were approaching Richmond Gate and, as Carrie slowed down to negotiate the narrow entrance, her eyes were suddenly drawn to one of the pedestrians heading into the park.

Short, dark, curly hair . . .

Was it Mabel?

It certainly looked like her and Carrie was almost tempted to toot the horn in greeting.

Seconds later, Benoit was directing her to pull up outside the Star and Garter Home. Carrie drew the ambulance neatly to a stop outside the grand, columned building and applied the handbrake with a little sigh of satisfaction.

That wasn't bad for a first lesson!

'I'll wait here and keep my eyes on the ambulance,' said Benoit. 'You pop inside and put your name down for the next ARP first aid course and then we'll head back.'

Carrie did as she was told. Despite living nearby, she had never been inside the convalescence home and, as she stood in the queue for the front desk, she took the opportunity to have a good look around. The reception hall and the rooms leading off it looked almost like a hotel with their ornate detailing, luxurious furnishings and fancy artwork commemorating military service. But it was the men in recovery that set it apart. Wheelchair users, or men learning to use crutches, many of whom had recently lost limbs. In many ways, it reminded Carrie of the Poppy Factory, only the men here were so much younger than the typical employee. Carrie suppressed a shudder at the terrible consequences of man's inhumanity to man and wondered how many of the men here would eventually end up working under Pa.

When she got to the front of the queue, the receptionist informed her that the next ARP first aid course started in just two days' time. Carrie was lucky – she had secured the last place. She should present herself at seven pm sharp, together with a sheaf of forms she needed to complete in the meantime. Carrie bundled it all up and hurried outside, pleased with how the afternoon had gone. Benoit was leaning against the ambulance, talking to another man who was partially hidden from her and shrouded by a cloud of cigarette smoke. She approached, a smile on her face . . . and then realised that the other man was Bobby.

In her surprise, Carrie stumbled over onto one ankle on the cobbles, dropping her gas mask and her handbag at her feet. The bag tipped over and her recently acquired paperwork spilt out together with her pen and a rather grubby handkerchief. Cheeks flushed with humiliation, Carrie crouched down to gather them up.

Seconds later, Bobby was by her side. 'What a dark horse you are,' he murmured.

Carrie kept her head down, unsure of quite how to respond.

He might think she had joined Miss Bateman's branch of the ARP because of *him* . . .

In the meantime, Carrie certainly didn't want to compound her indignity by mumbling back to him whilst they were both on their hands and knees. So, she continued gathering up her belongings, stacked them neatly in her bag and then, still without answering, stood up with as much dignity as she could muster.

'I'm grateful for your help,' she said coolly but clearly, making perfectly sure Benoit could hear every word. 'Miss Bateman is my old headmistress and she suggested I volunteer for the ARP. It came at a very apposite time; my cousin and his friend have just enlisted for Bomber Command and everything seems really raw and personal at the moment . . .'

She had said what she did mainly to wipe the smirk off Bobby's face and to try and regain the upper hand. But, from seemingly nowhere, a lump appeared in her throat and her voice thickened. The full ramifications of what Ned and Charlie were doing suddenly hit home and she found that she was dangerously close to tears.

Without waiting for a response, Carrie walked swiftly over to Benoit. 'Shall we be getting back?' she asked crisply.

'Of course,' said Benoit. 'And, as driver, you may decide whether we give our friend Bobby here a lift back home before he has to report on duty.'

Carrie ventured a glance at Bobby who was watching her warily.

'If he behaves himself,' she said lightly, jumping into the driver's seat.

Seconds later, both Bobby and Benoit had squeezed onto the passenger seat.

'First lesson?' asked Bobby.

Carrie nodded.

'Am I taking my life into my hands?'

'Very probably,' said Carrie, dryly. 'I should strap myself in tightly if I were you.'

Bobby gave a chuckle. 'To be honest, I thought that the moment I met you . . .'

Carrie caught her breath. Glancing across, she met Bobby's eyes, holding them for a moment longer than was strictly necessary.

'You should not tease, Lyn, thus,' Benoit was saying. 'She is the best driver I have ever known. No need for straps.'

Minutes later, they were dropping Bobby off at a Victorian house a couple of streets away from St Mark's Avenue.

'Excellent driving,' he said to Carrie. And then, in a lower voice. 'If you change your mind . . .'

Carrie considered for a moment – and then shook her head. 'No, thank you,' she said and drove away.

Chapter Sixteen

Friday 19 July 1940

Meanwhile, there were only days to go until the Little Poppies meeting and Carrie spent most of her spare time helping Mabel and Sarah drum up interest around the estate.

Posters started appearing in the Remembrance Club and on the doors to the blocks of flats, urging all 'Poppy Girls' to come along and learn how to do their bit. Sarah gathered support at the Gardening Club and Carrie continued talking to the mothers picking up their Brownies. She also worked on the Brownies themselves, extolling the virtues of Little Poppies so enthusiastically that she feared she may have totally oversold the venture! Either way, there seemed to be a genuine buzz of excitement running through the estate – Carrie could *feel* it – and she held her breath and crossed her fingers that it would be enough to get the idea off the ground.

And, to Carrie's exquisite relief, the second meeting was everything that the first had failed to be.

This time, the games room at the Remembrance Club was standing room only. Women of all ages turned up in droves – many with their husbands in tow – and there was a palpable buzz of anticipation in the room. This time, the scheme was introduced by none other than Major

Armstrong, although he wisely left his wife to flesh out the details. Mrs Armstrong, for her part, made a big deal of crediting Carrie, Mabel and Sarah both with coming up with the idea and with helping to iron out the logistics. And, if Carrie felt a slight pang of disappointment and anticlimax that the 'grown-ups' were now in charge, she had to admit that the venture had been given a boost of both credibility and gravitas.

And it worked.

When the speeches were over, there was practically a stampede to sign up and, fifteen minutes later, most of the shifts had already been spoken for. Carrie was amused to see just how quickly the younger women put their names down to have their children looked after so that they could work in the factory – but luckily, there were plenty of older women who were happy to staff Little Poppies.

It was all perfect.

At the end, Ma sidled up to her.

'I'm so proud of you, darling,' she said.

Carrie swallowed a wave of guilt. Her mother might not be quite so proud of her if she knew her daughter had been driving an ARP ambulance around behind her back!

'Might you sign up?' she asked, hesitantly.

'Rather,' said Ma, enthusiastically. 'I've already put myself down for the factory. But I was also thinking I could do the odd shift in Little Poppies teaching the older children a bit of sewing; simple things like the blackout blinds I'd be making anyway. Might that be helpful?'

'It would be the icing on the cake,' said Carrie.

And she really meant it.

Saturday 20 July 1940

The next day happened to be the Poppy Factory rowing race, an annual tradition in which eight men who had one arm took on eight who had one leg – the whole thing designed to demonstrate how disabled men could still take pleasure in sport. The timing was coincidental but, to Carrie, it was almost like a planned celebration for getting Little Poppies off the ground.

It was a glorious summer day, and it seemed the entire estate had made the short journey down to Eel Pie Island. The riverbank was alive with the chatter of families and the laughter of children darting in and out of the willows. Carrie sat on a tartan blanket with Sarah and Mabel – their skirts fanned out in the relentless heat – and thought how different it was from the darts competition a couple of months ago when she had sat stiffly to one side with Ma and Mrs Armstrong. Here she was, in the middle of the action, with her new best friends. She took a sip of lemonade and looked around at the smiling faces of her neighbours with a sudden wave of affection.

There were Major and Mrs Armstrong sitting under a huge parasol; Mrs Armstrong pleased as Punch because her grandchildren were visiting for the occasion.

There were the Brownies – Eloise, Maggie and their friend Clara – chattering away as they threaded daisies into chains to make bracelets and headdresses.

Even Pa, who had been decidedly prickly recently, was walking up and down with a little smile on his face.

'Look, there's Harry!' said Sarah, jumping to her feet as

the two boats rowed past on their way to the start of the race. 'Come on! Let's go and follow them.'

The three girls ran downstream and arrived just in time for the starter's pistol. The boats surged forwards and – despite the rowers' disabilities – their oars sliced cleanly through the water. And there was Harry in the middle of one of the boats, his face taut with concentration and a sheen of sweat already glistening under the brim of his cap.

'Go on, Harry!' shouted Sarah, running alongside the boat and frantically waving her arms.

Carrie and Mabel and a whole host of other children and young adults started running and cycling along the towpath. The two boats stayed level for a while, but slowly . . . slowly . . . Harry's boat began to pull ahead.

'Come on, Harry,' shouted Sarah, her voice squeaky with excitement.

'He's a natural,' said Mabel, shielding her eyes against the sun.

'He really is,' said Sarah, proudly. 'I'm so proud of him. He's never rowed before . . . and look at him now!'

Harry's boat continued to press home its advantage until there was a length of clear water between the two.

'Don't slow down,' shouted Sarah. 'They're just behind you . . .'

But the finish line was in sight.

Harry's boat raced over it in first place . . . and the crowd erupted into cheers.

'That was marvellous,' said Sarah, her eyes shining.

'It really was,' said Carrie, as the three girls flopped down onto their blanket. 'Phew, I'm quite worn out from all that running.'

'Yes, worse than running up Richmond Hill,' said Mabel, fanning herself with a hand.

Carrie laughed. 'I try not to!' she said. 'Luckily, if I'm going up the hill, it's just for a stroll in the park.'

'Well, you won't be doing that for much longer if the rumours are true,' said Mabel, lying back, her arm over her eyes.

'Whyever not?'

Mabel shrugged. 'I heard it's closing to the public,' she said.

'Really?' Carrie was dismayed. 'Oh, no – that's such a shame. Where did you hear that?'

Another shrug. 'I can't remember. Someone in the club, I think.'

'Oh, I'm sad about that,' said Carrie. 'You must be too, Mabel. I've seen you up there, twice recently – once whilst I was driving the ambulance!'

Sarah laughed. 'I'm surprised you haven't been roped in as a spy, Carrie,' she said. 'You seem to know exactly what Mabel's been up to.'

Mabel was laughing too. 'Pity I were only going to the dentist,' she said. 'Not very exciting.'

'Ouch,' said Carrie. 'Toothache's a pig.'

'It really is. And I hate the dentist; I'd been putting it off for ages and I ended up having to go twice.'

Harry, his face flushed and his forehead damp with effort, dropped onto the blanket.

'You were brilliant, darling,' said Sarah, handing him a handkerchief to mop his brow.

Harry shrugged modestly. 'We're all only as good as our team,' he said. 'And, believe me, our practice sessions didn't always go so well. I had a horrible feeling we were just going to go round in circles.'

Carrie laughed. 'Both boats were as straight as a die,' she said.

Harry smiled. 'And that's the miracle of it,' he said. 'It's ruddy difficult rowing with one foot, let me tell you – although I think the other chaps had it harder. But it's amazing what you can do when you put your mind to it and work together.'

Mrs Armstrong bustled over. 'Well done, young man,' she said, beaming down at Harry. 'Sterling effort. No, don't get up.'

'Thank you,' said Harry. 'And thank you again for all you've done to help at the factory.'

'Not at all,' said Mrs Armstrong. 'It's really thanks to these young ladies. And whilst I've got you girls, can I just confirm where, if at all, you'll be working?'

'Sorry, Mrs A,' said Sarah. 'We were so busy getting everyone to sign up that we haven't done so ourselves. I'll be making the radios with Harry.'

'Marvellous,' said Mrs Armstrong. 'Mabel, you already have an outside job, of course . . .'

'Yes, but I'll do what I can for Little Poppies when I'm home in the evenings.'

'Super. And how about you, Carrie? Will you be in the factory with Sarah?'

Carrie gave an involuntary shudder. 'No,' she said, perhaps too forcefully. 'I'm happy to help with Little Poppies but being part of the war machine is not for me.'

Harry raised an eyebrow. 'Why not?' he asked.

Carrie hesitated, suddenly flustered. 'I just don't want

to be part of it,' she said firmly. 'The war, the killing. Any of it.'

Silence fell over the group, filled by the distant laughter of children and the soft lapping of the river. Mrs Armstrong took the opportunity to discreetly melt away.

'It's not that simple,' said Harry, eventually. 'You're not building bombs, Carrie. You're helping people like me – people who need all the help they can get to stay alive out there. Men are dying out there in their thousands – just look at the *Lancastria*.'

News had just broken of the dreadful bombing of the *RMS Lancastria* off the coast of France with the loss of at least five thousand men. It had happened a month previously, but the government had suppressed the news to avoid demoralising the public and it had only just reached the papers. Carrie was, of course, as horrified as everyone else about it, but her mind went stubbornly back to Santayana's quote.

'Those who cannot remember the past are condemned to repeat it.'

'I understand all that,' she said, carefully. 'But you only have to look at the books – to look at the *facts* – to know that war doesn't solve anything. It just kills people and ruins the lives of others. And, even then, the problems don't go away . . .'

'Stop kidding yourself, Carrie,' Mabel broke in. 'We're all part of this, whether we like it or not.'

Carrie's jaw tightened, but she didn't reply. Mabel's voice had been calm, but her words were almost unkind. Could Mabel be upset that Carrie had put her on the spot about being spotted near Richmond Park? No, that didn't make sense; everyone needed to go to the dentist from time to time . . .

Harry left to get ready for the prize-giving ceremony, Mabel went to join her parents and the little group disbanded. The sun continued its relentless march across the sky and, for once, Carrie felt no relief in its warmth.

An hour later, Carrie and Sarah were walking home along the towpath together, Mabel having opted to walk separately.

They talked idly about this and that but, as they approached Richmond, Sarah suddenly said, 'I thought that comment of Mabel's a bit unkind.'

Carrie shrugged. 'I suppose my views on the war aren't always popular,' she said.

And here, right on cue, was Mabel, running up to join them from behind. 'I'm ever so sorry I were grumpy with you just now, Carrie,' she said. 'I've had the most awful headache all day but that ain't no excuse. I shouldn't have snapped at you like that.'

'That's all right,' said Carrie, linking arms with her.

'But it ain't really, because it ain't that I don't respect your views about the war. It just came out all wrong.'

Carrie squeezed her arm. 'No offence taken,' she said.

They were nearly home by now and, as they emerged onto the main road through the estate, Sarah suddenly gave a shriek of shock. Carrie followed her line of sight and saw a single pair of white frilly bloomers hanging over the middle of the road from the Turners' washing line. Despite it all, she felt a smile tugging at the corners of her mouth.

'Yours, I presume,' she said.

'Yes,' shouted Sarah. 'The little so and so. I told on him to my parents for pinching my chocolate again, and he wasn't allowed to come today . . .'

Carrie composed her features.

After all, she would be mortified if the situation was reversed.

It was one thing having your smalls hanging out to dry with the rest of the family's clothes on washday, but quite another for a single pair of knickers to be left fluttering alone forlornly above the street for all to see. *That* broke all societal norms of modesty and privacy and would be utterly humiliating.

Sarah was already bounding down the path to her block of flats.

'Now it's war!' she shouted.

Chapter Seventeen

August, 1940

The fine weather continued to hold.

The summer days were golden and warm, but the air was thick with unease, as though the nation was holding its breath. Britain still stood alone against Hitler's Germany and the Luftwaffe's campaign to dominate the skies intensified. Across the Channel, German forces gathered, poised for an invasion which now felt inevitable.

As July slid into August, waves of bombers and fighters swept over the Channel, targeting airfields, radar stations and supply depots. In response, RAF pilots scrambled daily, outnumbered yet defiant. The roar of engines and the chatter of machine guns became as much a part of the landscape as the summer sun. Ned and Charlie were never far from Carrie's mind; as far as she knew, they were still training, but it was surely only a matter of time . . .

And then Birmingham was hit.

The Luftwaffe struck the city hard, aiming for factories and railways, but also flattening residential areas, leaving entire streets of terraced houses reduced to rubble. Over a hundred people died, burnt alive or buried in the debris of their homes.

Carrie – like everyone else – was stunned. Birmingham was just a hundred miles away and, if it could be struck, what was stopping the Luftwaffe from turning its sights on Richmond? Worse still, the Poppy Factory was such a distinctive building and Carrie was suddenly all too aware how visible it must be to enemy planes . . .

And, against this backdrop, Little Poppies was up and running.

The games room and the old cinema had been converted into a nursery and a playroom, with newly erected shelves hastily lined with second-hand toys and bits and bobs for making things. The older volunteers – most of whom had raised children of their own – quickly took charge of the babies and toddlers, their movements calm and assured as they soothed cries, changed terry nappies and sang soft lullabies. Carrie, on the other hand, had been assigned a group of girls aged between five and ten, which included Maggie, Eloise and Clara.

And she loved it!

The girls were lively and curious – absorbing the world around them like little sponges – and Carrie quickly settled into a rhythm, the days a blend of laughter, occasional tears and the steady hum of activity. Mornings tended to be busy and lively – the girls seemed to have boundless energy – and Carrie organised endless games of hide-and-seek, British bulldog and grandmother's footsteps. The girls had the run of the estate, but the pet cemetery was out of bounds; it didn't seem fitting for the children to be running around and over the graves. Sometimes they went further afield and she would lead her charges in scavenger hunts or scour the estate and surrounding streets for scraps of metal or glass bottles, which could be repurposed. Every now and then, the girls would stumble upon something unexpected – an old horseshoe, a broken buckle – and present it to Carrie with wide-eyed excitement. Carrie, for her part, made a point of praising every find and reminding the girls how much even seemingly small efforts could make a difference.

Afternoons tended to be quieter. Sometimes, they would gather around the radio to listen to a children's programme. Carrie might supervise crafts – teaching the girls to sew simple handkerchiefs or to knit squares for blankets that would eventually be sent to Daisy for the soldiers. Occasionally, she tired of threading needles, tying knots and encouraging patience, but it was a small price to pay for the satisfaction on the girls' faces when they completed their projects. Oftentimes, they ended up in the kitchen, helping to prepare simple meals under the guidance of Mrs Armstrong, who was nominally head of the whole operation and who had assumed the moniker of Big Poppy.

The work could be tiring, and Carrie occasionally caught herself yearning for something different. But then the mothers arrived to pick up their daughters, full of the work they were doing on the aircraft radios, and Carrie knew that it was all worthwhile. In the meantime, she grew close to 'her' girls, relished the camaraderie of the women working around her and tried to make the most of every day.

One morning, about two weeks after Carrie had started work at Little Poppies, Mrs Perkins – the woman in charge of the boys – called in sick. Carrie immediately volunteered to supervise them for the day, and Mrs Armstrong gladly accepted.

Looking after a mixed group of children proved much

more of a challenge – Sarah's brother Alfie was more than enough to contend with on his own! – and after a particularly bruising game of bulldog, Carrie was exhausted.

'Right. Sardines,' she said, wanting the whole lot of them as far away from her as possible. 'Jack, you go and hide. The rest of you, count to a hundred and then join him in his hiding place when you've found him. Go wherever you want, *but do not leave the estate.*'

Jack scampered off and, a minute later, the others duly darted off in hot pursuit. Carrie, breathing a sigh of relief, went into the kitchen to make herself a well-deserved cuppa.

Children!

No sooner had she taken her first much-needed sip than Dorothea – five years old and fairly new to the estate – slunk back inside.

'I think they've all found Jack,' she said, miserably, around the thumb in her mouth. 'And I've looked everywhere but can't find any of them anywhere.'

Carrie sighed. She was clearly doomed not to finish her tea.

'They won't have gone far,' she said, standing up and taking Dorothea's hand. 'Shall we go and find them together?'

The two emerged into the sunshine and did a swift tour of the usual hiding places – the various dustbin sheds, round the back of the Remembrance Club, behind the bushes on the path leading to the factory . . .

Nothing.

Carrie was just beginning to wonder if the children *had* disobeyed her instructions and left the estate when a giggle near the allotments caught her attention.

Aha; now she knew *exactly* where they were.

Swallowing a wave of annoyance, she led Dorothea to the old pet cemetery, reminding herself that none of it was Jack's fault. She had made it clear he could hide anywhere on the estate, and she hadn't specifically ruled out the cemetery. She only had herself to blame.

Dorothea ran ahead, pushing through the bushes and emerging into the little clearing.

'I didn't know this was here,' she cried delightedly. And then she saw the other children, clustered behind a large oak tree. 'Found you!' she shouted, and they all emerged, laughing and pushing each other good-naturedly.

Carrie stood stock still staring at Marigold's grave.

'That was *your* cat, wasn't it?' said Jack, from behind her.

Carrie didn't answer.

'We wouldn't have come,' said Eloise, earnestly. 'Only Jack didn't know not to . . .'

Carrie still didn't answer.

She *couldn't* answer.

The last time she had been in here, the grave had been bare – but now it was surrounded by a glorious riot of colour. A sea of marigolds, beautifully tended and dead-headed, had been planted around the grave, the flowers dancing in the breeze.

Her eyes suddenly blinded by tears, Carrie reached out and touched one of the blooms. What a beautifully kind and heartfelt gesture – and, suddenly, she knew exactly who would have planted them and exactly how she was going to thank them.

Carrie, Sarah and Mabel had got into the habit of rendezvousing at the Remembrance Club after they finished work. It wasn't always possible of course – Sarah might be disappearing off to the ARP, and Carrie to a driving lesson or to her first aid classes – but at least twice a week, the girls would enjoy a cuppa or a lemonade together whilst helping Carrie put the toys away and putting the world to rights. Carrie looked forward to these meetings immensely; Mabel's harsh words were all but forgotten and she could just relax and totally be herself with her friends.

It was one of her favourite times of the day.

Carrie spent that afternoon making honey biscuits and paste sandwiches with some of the girls whilst the boys listened to the radio and played with the trains. By the time Sarah and Mabel arrived after work, she had already cleared the room of toys and had set up a table in the corner, neatly laid with the Remembrance Club's best crockery.

Sarah and Mabel arrived almost at the same time.

'What's all this then?' said Mabel, taking in the little scene.

'I just thought you needed a little spoiling,' said Carrie. 'Sit yourselves down, and I'll bring the tea over.'

'I would have thought it was *you* that needed spoiling,' said Sarah, sitting down with a little groan of exhaustion. 'I hear you've had to look after Alfie and the others as well as your usual girls.'

'True,' said Carrie, pouring out the tea. 'But I just wanted to say thank you.'

Sarah and Mabel exchanged a little glance. 'What for?' said Mabel, picking up a sandwich, doubling it up, and cramming it in her mouth. 'Cor, these are delicious.'

'You know exactly what for,' replied Carrie, with a little smile.

Mabel grinned. 'Well, we don't, because there are a million and one things you could be thanking us for,' she said. 'After all, if we ain't the best friends a girl could ask for.'

Sarah laughed. 'Too right,' she said. 'We help you put the toys away.'

'We ain't breathed a word to your ma and pa about the ARP.'

'We haven't pestered you with questions about Mr One and Mr Two.'

'Should we go on?'

Carrie smiled. So, this was how they wanted to play it. 'Well, just know that you're both very lovely and that I'm deeply appreciative,' she said. 'Have another biscuit.'

The conversation moved on. As ever, Carrie was keen to hear all the little details of working in the Poppy Factory. It had been a male preserve for – well – *ever*, and it both fascinated and intrigued her that women had now more or less taken over the top floor. If they had been making anything non-war-related, she would have volunteered like a shot but, as it was, she had to experience it all second-hand through Sarah, which wasn't really the same thing at all.

'Today was tough,' Sarah admitted. 'Welding really isn't for the faint-hearted. It took a while to get my eye in, but I was getting the hang of it by the end of the day. I've got a thumping headache though; I'm not sure if it's due to squinting at the circuit boards all day or because of all the sparks and electricity in the room.'

'I know what you mean,' said Mabel. 'I were staring at the same rows of figures for so long today that they started jumping all over the page.'

'Your pa paid us a visit today, though, Carrie,' said Sarah, as if Mabel hadn't spoken. 'He usually sticks to his part of the factory, but he was showing some bigwigs around. They were very impressed by our set-up here.'

Carrie sighed with satisfaction. 'Can you believe that from a simple idea, we helped to get it all up and running?'

It never failed to amaze her that the three of them had been instrumental in getting the scheme off the ground.

Sarah grunted. 'Let's hope it's not all in vain,' she said.

Carrie and Mabel rounded on her. 'Whatever do you mean?' said Mabel.

'I think we're struggling to meet our quotas on the radios,' said Sarah. 'The others wouldn't know but Harry says that's the truth of it. We're all doing well individually, but the wiring is so intricate and so exacting that it's taking longer than expected, and there simply aren't enough of us to go around. We need more women from the estate or more men from the factory, but it seems we've reached our limit. Harry says there's no need to panic yet, but if things don't pick up, we might have to bring in workers from elsewhere after all.'

'No!' said Carrie. 'The whole point of Little Poppies is that it means we don't need to recruit from outside the estate.'

'I know that and you know that,' said Sarah. 'But, at the end of the day, we can't let the Ministry of Aircraft down, can we? I dare say we will get quicker over time, but it might not be enough.' She paused and then added, 'I don't suppose I can persuade you to move across, can I, Mabel?'

Mabel reached out and touched her hand. 'Oh, Sarah, I've thought about it, I really have,' she said. 'If I were just doing regular factory work that anyone could do, I'd switch across in a flash. But I ain't. I'm doing specialised work and there ain't anyone else to do it.'

'I know,' said Sarah. 'And there's no point in asking you, is there, Carrie?'

Carrie bristled. 'I've been looking after scallywags all day so that *ten* women might work in the factory today,' she said pointedly. 'You might not agree with my views, but surely I shouldn't be feeling guilty . . .'

'Calm down,' said Sarah, with a grin, reaching out and patting her hand. 'I wasn't insinuating anything. I just meant that you – like me – will be at university in a matter of weeks and that everything is going to change.'

'Oh!'

Carrie hadn't even considered that.

University, it seemed, was further and further from her mind.

Chapter Eighteen

August 1940

Meanwhile, Carrie's ARP training continued apace.

She had completed her series of first aid lessons at the Star and Garter and, despite getting in a bit of a pickle with bandaging and almost tripping over her own feet when she ran with a stretcher, she had been judged competent to proceed with her training. Carrie was under no illusion; she had hardly been a star pupil but she would be driving rather than treating patients, so they could afford to let her through.

God forbid she would ever be responsible for first aid in the field!

Luckily, her driving lessons were going somewhat more smoothly.

Several times a week, she left Little Poppies on the dot of five and hurried to join Benoit at St Mark's Avenue. From there, they crisscrossed Richmond in the ambulance, often taking different routes down to the Richmond Royal Hospital and practising, over and over again, where Carrie would take her civilian casualties. Gradually, they began to go further afield, memorising the routes to Kingston or Ealing in case the hospital in Richmond had been bombed or was otherwise inaccessible.

Carrie had wondered if she might see Bobby again – if

their paths might cross as they had done outside the Star and Garter – but there was no further sign of him. Carrie wasn't sure whether to be relieved or disappointed. He was a queer fish, no doubt about that, and his blowing hot one minute and cold the next was, of course, perfectly intolerable. But Carrie had to admit his comment about strapping himself in for the ride with her had got *her* going hot and cold all over! Almost despite herself, she liked him – she really did – and there was no doubt that part of her couldn't wait to see him again.

The final 'test' in Carrie's ambulance training was a solo twenty-minute drive around Richmond.

The idea was that she would drive between five addresses – which she would be given in a series of envelopes just before she departed – without a map, in a set amount of time, and with Miss Bateman, Benoit and the others waiting at strategic points to confirm she duly arrived. Carrie had been looking forward to the challenge. She loved driving and, after three weeks with Benoit, she knew Richmond like the back of her hand. When the afternoon arrived, however, she found that she was unexpectedly nervous. Supposing her apprehension got the better of her and she messed things up? She really didn't want to let everyone down . . .

Carrie needn't have worried. Although the weather was finally on the turn, it was a still, dry August evening and, as soon as Carrie got behind the wheel, she knew everything was going to be all right. Calmly – almost casually – she opened the first envelope on the passenger seat and set off for Ennerdale Road, over towards Kew.

Easy!

There was Benoit, grinning broadly and making a big show of ticking her off on his sheet.

One down, four to go.

Carrie exhaled slowly and opened the second envelope. The next rendezvous was on Fife Road. Carrie knew exactly where it was – on the other side of Richmond, over by the park – but there was now a horse and cart in the middle of the road behind her and she would need to drive the long way round rather than do a quick three-point turn in the street.

No matter.

She had plenty of time.

With a jaunty wave to Benoit, she continued up the road, cut through to Sandycombe Road and headed back through the centre of town. Progress was slow because of some military vehicles parking – badly – near the station, and even a couple of soldiers standing to attention as she passed didn't quell her annoyance. There was rarely any traffic on the streets at this time of the afternoon and for a brief moment, she wondered if this had been pre-arranged as part of the test.

As if the British Army didn't have other things to worry about!

By the time Carrie squealed to a halt on Fife Road, Miss Bateman was looking meaningfully at her watch. Carrie gave her a tight smile and opened the third envelope . . .

Star and Garter Hill.

Carrie knew exactly where *that* was – after all, she'd been taking her first aid lessons just around the corner. She considered a moment, head on one side, and concluded that the quickest way would be through Richmond Park itself. It might be the same distance – even a tad longer – but it would almost certainly be quicker. She fancied Miss Bateman gave a tiny shake of her head as she headed off but carried on regardless.

Sheen Gate was closed; the wrought-iron gates pulled firmly shut.

Carrie could have wept.

Now she remembered that Mabel had told her the park was due to close. She really should have taken more notice, because it might cost her the test.

What now?

Carrie wasn't allowed to use her flashing lights but, still, she was in an ambulance.

Surely, she could bluff her way through?

She drove right up to the gate, wound down the window and leant out to the young soldier standing guard. 'Emergency,' she said, crisply. 'As quick as you can, please.'

The soldier snapped to attention. 'Yes, Miss,' he said. 'Sorry, Miss.'

And, seconds later, the gates swung open.

Carrie roared through the park as quickly as she could, heart thumping with anxiety. They hadn't said *not* to use the park but if Richmond Gate was closed on the way out, she would be getting perilously low on time. But there it was and – joy of joys – it looked like it was open. Carrie jutted out her lower jaw, set her eyes on the horizon and put her foot down. Only a minute or two to Star and Garter Hill and she was right back on track . . .

Carrie approached Richmond Gate at forty miles an hour and was just slowing down to negotiate the gates when she spotted Mabel – and it was *definitely* Mabel, this time – striding purposefully through the park.

Again!

Seconds later, Carrie saw Bobby strolling the same way.

He had every right to be there, of course; he had already told Carrie he worked there. But, glancing in her rearview mirror, it looked very much like he was calling something out to Mabel. Mabel, for her part, turned around, paused a moment, then continued on her way.

What was *that* all about?

Why on earth was Bobby hurrying to catch up with *Mabel*?

Did the two know each other?

Carrie couldn't let it lie. It was really none of her business either way, but it *was* all a little strange. Besides, why was Mabel in Richmond Park *again*? Surely not another dentist appointment! There was traffic behind her, so Carrie was forced to drive through the gates, but there were lots of places to turn around on the other side . . .

Carrie drove past the hedge-lined service entrance to the Star and Garter and stopped. Up ahead, she could see Tilly, her pretty face craning in her direction.

She really should carry on . . . finish the test.

Then again . . .

Decisively, Carrie slipped the ambulance into reverse. Hands gripping the steering wheel, she eased backwards into the driveway and . . .

Crash!

Carrie's heart leapt at the unexpected impact and the discordant clatter of metal. Glancing in the wing mirrors, she could see that she had knocked over a row of empty milk churns, which had been lined up in the shadows. They lay scattered like discarded skittles, metal flanks gleaming accusatorily, creamy streams trickling across the tarmac.

What to do?

If she wanted to confront Mabel and Bobby, she'd have to leave immediately. Then again, her training had drummed home the importance of checking for damage after an incident . . .

Right on cue, a horse-drawn milk float appeared round the corner of the driveway. Carrie sighed. Metaphorically caught with her hand in the biscuit tin, she certainly couldn't leave now. Cheeks flushed, she clambered out of the cab. The ambulance was thankfully undamaged, but the churns were completely blocking the narrow lane. The milkman – an old man with a bushy moustache – was already making his way over to her.

'Are you all right, miss?'

Carrie offered an apologetic smile. 'I'm ever so sorry,' she said, her voice not entirely steady. 'I was turning and I simply didn't see them.'

'No harm done. Is it an emergency?'

'No. Just . . . routine.'

'Then together we can have these churns righted and on the float in no time.'

Carrie gave him a small smile. To be honest, it served her right. With a little sigh, she righted the first churn and hauled it onto the back of the float. She wouldn't be able to check up on Mabel and Bobby, but fingers crossed she would be able to make the next checkpoint and finish the test on time.

*

'I hear you passed by the skin of your mouth,' said Benoit.

It was the next evening, and Carrie had reported for her first nightshift at the ARP. She had duly told Ma and Pa she would be staying at Daisy's regularly from now on and, to her relief, they had barely batted an eyelid.

She could hardly believe she was getting away with it.

It was true that she just scraped her driving test but, as Miss Bateman kindly pointed out, a pass was a pass. Carrie was now a fully trained-up ARP volunteer and, as such, she would be expected to report for duty three times a week. It was also her responsibility to make sure the ambulance was roadworthy – checking the tyres, radiator and battery at the beginning and end of each shift.

Meanwhile, she wrinkled her nose up at Benoit. 'I'm sorry,' she said. 'Just about everything that could go wrong, did go wrong. The park was shut, there were military vehicles outside the station and horse-drawn milk carts everywhere. It was *terrible.*'

'All the more reason you must keep practising,' said Benoit. 'In particular, you must practise driving at *night* with Tilly as your ambulance attendant.'

'In fact, Lyn, you can go out tonight, if you wouldn't mind,' said Miss Bateman. 'Wait until it's properly dark, but I have some helmets and armbands that need to be dropped off at other ARP stations. Tilly's off sick, and Benoit is overseeing the blackout patrol so . . .'

'I'll go with her, if you like,' interrupted a voice behind her. Bobby!

Carrie glanced around. She hadn't even seen him enter the room, and she hadn't been alone with him for several weeks.

259

All in all, she really wasn't sure what to feel.

'Marvellous,' said Miss Bateman. 'All taken care of.'

Carrie gave Bobby a level look. 'Brace yourself for the ride,' she said, coolly.

It was strange being alone with Bobby in the ambulance.

Or, at least, it would have felt strange if Carrie had had time to dwell on such things. Navigating the roads at night was *hard*. With the rigorously enforced blackout and the dimmed streetlamps, it was almost pitch black, and the special covers over the ambulance headlights barely illuminated a few feet ahead. Nonetheless, in the event of an emergency, she would be expected to drive at full tilt down to the hospital, so she needed to get used to it.

At first, Carrie was overly cautious, jumping at shadows and sensing danger at every turn.

'Your patient would have died of boredom by now,' said Bobby, as Carrie braked sharply at a bend.

'There could have been a child . . .' said Carrie defensively.

'Not at this time of night . . .'

'That's extremely presumptive,' said Carrie. 'Anyway, who's driving . . . ?'

'You are. Sorry. Just pretend I'm injured and will bleed to death if we don't get to hospital in the next five minutes.' He gave a theatrical groan and slumped back in his seat.

Despite herself, Carrie laughed.

Then she gritted her teeth, screwed up her eyes and sped down Richmond Hill more quickly than seemed even remotely safe.

*

For the next ten minutes, they crisscrossed the streets, stopping every so often so that Bobby could drop off his supplies or berate a household for breaking the blackout. And, apart from mounting several well-nigh invisible pavements and scaring both a cat and a courting couple, Carrie managed it all without incident.

'So, what happened on the test?' asked Bobby. 'Benoit's been singing your praises and you seem pretty competent to me . . . and yet you barely scraped through?'

Carrie puffed out her cheeks.

'Well, you saw part of it,' she said. And then when Bobby didn't immediately answer. 'You must have seen me in the park?'

'Of course I saw you,' said Bobby. 'It would have been hard to miss the ARP ambulance tearing through the park at sixty miles an hour. For a moment, I thought it was a real emergency and then I realised it was you taking your test.'

'But you just ignored me,' said Carrie.

'What was I supposed to do? Leap into the road and start waving like a madman when you were concentrating?'

Hmmm.

Carrie hesitated and then added, 'It looked like you were calling to the girl ahead . . .'

Bobby's face split into a grin. 'So?' he said. 'Do I detect a tiny hint of jealousy?'

'Of course not,' said Carrie. 'But I know that girl and I just wondered if you did too . . .'

'Seems to me you were spending far too much time looking in the rearview mirror rather than focussing on the road ahead,' said Bobby, good-naturedly. 'I'm not surprised you had an unexpected encounter with some milk churns shortly afterwards!'

'I really should have kept quiet about that,' said Carrie, with a wry grin. 'Either way, you haven't answered my question.'

'All right. I don't know that girl from Adam. I thought she'd dropped her hankie – you probably saw one fluttering along the pavement – but she said it wasn't hers.'

'I see.' Carrie hadn't noticed a handkerchief, but that was neither here nor there.

'And, now, might I ask you a question?' said Bobby.

Carrie shrugged. 'Of course,' she said.

'It seemed to me we got on very well at the dance and when we first met outside the library – and yet when I suggested we meet up again, you shot me down in flames?'

Carrie hesitated. She was about to come up with a bland reply, but surely it would be better to tell the truth.

'I thought we got on very well, too,' she said. 'And I really enjoyed the dance. But both times we met, you rather rudely dashed away without a backwards glance, and I've vowed that I won't let you do it a third time.'

'I see.' Bobby paused for a very long time, and it seemed almost that he was wrestling with himself. 'Well, thank you for being honest with me,' he said eventually. 'I wish that I could give you a satisfactory answer for my admittedly rude behaviour, but sadly I can't. I will just have to hope I can eventually persuade you that I am worth another try. Shall we head back to HQ?'

'How did the knitting go last night?' asked Ma pleasantly.

It was the next morning and Carrie had just arrived

262

home, bleary-eyed after her first night at the warden station. She hadn't got much sleep, but she hadn't knitted a single stitch either; it was safe to say that one-plain-one-purl hadn't crossed her mind once.

Instead, once she and Bobby had arrived back at Saints HQ, there had been a tea-fuelled meeting followed by several very competitive games of gin rummy. That had been capped off by some very energetic ping pong, including a version new to Carrie that involved hitting the ball, then dropping the bat and running round the table to wait in line for the next shot. It had been fast, exhausting . . . and absolutely hilarious; in fact, Carrie's cheeks still ached from laughing until she cried. All in all, by the time Miss Bateman had announced it was lights out and she had settled down to sleep in a rather uncomfortable bunk in the girls' 'dorm', she had been completely spent.

Oh, but it had been wonderful!

The fun, the banter, the camaraderie!

It was rather what she imagined boarding school would be like – and certainly what she hoped university life would offer. But it was more than that. It was being part of a team for a cause that was bigger than any one of them, and being with people she knew would have her back in the event of an emergency. It was feeling that what she was doing really mattered.

And, of course, there was Bobby.

Little glances and smiles, the way her skin reacted when their hands collided fumbling for the tennis table paddle, their shoulders touching as they stood silently waiting for their turn . . .

How could she ever have thought he was dandelion and

burdock? With the benefit of distance, she could now see that her relationship with lovely, brave Ned had been much more superficial. Bobby challenged her, stretched her . . . understood her.

In turning him down, had she just cut off her nose to spite her face?

But that morning, she just smiled at her mother and said, 'Fine, thank you,' and stuffed her knitting back under her bed to hide her lies and her subterfuge.

What a tangled web she was weaving!

Chapter Nineteen

August 1940

And then the weather changed.

Rain slicked the roads and paths of the Poppy Factory estate and turned the bowling green into a muddy quagmire. Brollies that had been gathering dust were shaken into action and sou'westers pulled from hooks and cupboards.

It looked as though autumn was arriving early.

Above the clouds, the Battle of Britain raged on. The Luftwaffe redoubled its efforts, intent on clearing the skies for invasion. But the rain and low cloud were working in Britain's favour, disrupting German formations and giving the RAF time to regroup.

Below the clouds, the rain was causing problems at Little Poppies. The weather had put a stop to the boisterous outside games and scavenger hunts so important for working off the children's excess energy. Carrie and the other volunteers did their best to keep things fresh and interesting, but it was difficult.

Really difficult.

Cooped up together, tempers were frayed, arguments broke out more often and Carrie found herself counting down the days until the children went back to school.

*

'I'm so bored.' The girls were supposed to be doing crafts, but Eloise and Clara had had their noses squashed hard against the windowpane for the past ten minutes, predicting which rain drop was going to be the first to reach the sill. 'Is it *ever* going to stop raining?'

Carrie sighed and put down the piece of embroidery she was helping Maggie with. 'I wish I knew,' she said. 'How's your knitting coming on?'

Eloise held up her needles. 'Holier than Daddy's socks,' she said with a giggle. 'Holier than crochet, which is *meant* to have holes in it.'

Carrie laughed. 'That's not going to keep the soldiers very warm, is it?' she teased. 'Want me to help you start again?'

Eloise shrugged. 'I'd rather play Sardines,' she said, hopefully.

The other girls looked up at this.

'Ooh, yes,' said Maggie. 'Can we?'

A couple of the boys who were supposed to be reading quietly on the other side of the room came over. 'Can we play too?' they asked.

Carrie glanced at Mrs Perkins. 'I don't see why not?' she said. 'It would do them good to work off a bit of steam before they go home.'

Mrs Perkins nodded. 'If they can find somewhere to hide,' she said. 'No waking the babies and no going upstairs to the private quarters,' she added severely to the children.

Seconds later, Sarah's brother Alfie had been nominated as the first to go and hide.

Sarah and Mrs Perkins breathed a sigh of relief as they all scampered off. It had been a long and trying week – and hopefully it would be some time before Alfie was discovered. In an ideal world, there would be time for a quick cuppa before any grown-up intervention was required.

But what was that?

Grown up shouting from somewhere beneath their feet.

Seconds later, Mabel marched into the room, followed by several sheepish-looking children. Carrie noticed that Clara was almost in tears.

'You're early! I didn't know you were back from work . . .' Carrie started.

'I've just discovered the children down in the cellar,' interrupted Mabel.

'So?' Carrie was nonplussed. 'I know the back room is out of bounds, but no one has said the rest of it is?'

'The storerooms are down there and we're due a big delivery,' said Mabel. 'Of *course* it's out of bounds . . .'

'I'm sorry,' said Carrie. Why was Mabel being so unreasonable? 'I understand it's inconvenient to have us here sometimes, but I didn't know about the delivery and your ma has never said that we're not allowed downstairs . . .'

'Ma probably didn't think that you would let your charges run riot down there nor that Alfie Turner would be helping himself to ginger beer from the storeroom,' said Mabel. 'Honestly, Carrie, when we let you use this place for Little Poppies, we thought we could trust you to supervise the children . . .'

'Hang on,' said Carrie, hotly. She hadn't seen this side of Mabel since the incident in Woolworths and had thought their friendship ran deeper than that. 'This is the only time they've ever been down to the cellar. We *do* supervise them, it's just that it's been raining all day and . . .'

'They can't be running around downstairs,' repeated Mabel, flatly. 'I've come back from work early to help with a delivery . . .'

'Oh, so you've actually been to work, today, have you?'

Mabel stopped, her hands on her hips. 'And what's that supposed to mean?' she demanded.

'It means that I saw you in Richmond Park again,' said Carrie. 'You've been up there recently more times than I've had hot dinners.'

Mabel exhaled noisily. 'About that . . .' she said. And then she glanced out of the window and saw a large white van approaching. 'I've got to go. Ma and Pa are at the wholesalers and I promised I'd deal with this delivery alone,' she added in more conciliatory tones. 'Just keep the children out of the way and the doors closed, please, will you?'

'Of course,' said Carrie, coolly.

'And, look, I'm sorry. It's been a very long week.'

Carrie gave her a tight smile. 'No hard feelings,' she said, remembering the flowers in the pet cemetery.

She would forgive Mabel almost anything for them.

Chapter Twenty

Late August 1940

The war continued to get closer and closer and preparations at Saints HQ continued in earnest.

Now that Tilly had recovered from the flu, she and Carrie were tasked with going out in the ambulance together as often as they could. Carrie needed to practise her nighttime driving whilst Tilly needed to sit in the back and practise caring for a casualty – in this case, a sandbag – whilst the vehicle was being driven at speed.

The first night they went out together, Carrie wasn't sure what to expect. She hadn't spent much time with Tilly, so much of what she knew came via the besotted Benoit.

Carrie wasn't sure she'd be worthy of such a saint!

She needn't have worried.

'Meet Sir Sandalot,' said Tilly, as Carrie arrived outside Saints HQ the first evening they were due to go out together.

'Pardon?'

Tilly gestured inside the ambulance – and Carrie snorted with laughter. Tilly had dressed the sandbag in an old threadbare shirt and battered bowler and had inked a cheerful face – complete with twirly moustache – onto the burlap.

'Sir Sandalot,' repeated Tilly. 'Despite his cheerful expression, he's not feeling very happy at the moment.'

'Right, Sir,' said Carrie with a grin, strapping on her helmet and armband. 'We'll get you to the hospital as quickly as possible.'

Carrie was still giggling as she slid into the driver's seat. She adjusted the rearview mirror to catch a glimpse of Tilly.

'All right back there?' she called, gripping the wheel with both hands.

Tilly, kneeling beside Sir Sandalot, grinned up at her. 'Perfect,' she said. 'In fact, he's the quietest patient I've ever had.'

'Let's see if we can keep it that way,' said Carrie, starting the engine.

The ambulance gave a reluctant sputter before roaring to life, shuddering slightly as Carrie guided it onto the road. Behind her, Sir Sandalot's hat tumbled to the floor. Tilly retrieved it with a flourish, setting it back at a rakish angle.

'There we go, old chap,' she said.

Carrie put her foot down and sped down the street, trying to remember all her training.

'Careful,' called Tilly, steadying Sir Sandalot. 'Our patient's leaking vital contents!'

Carrie smirked, glancing briefly over her shoulder. 'It's a good opportunity to practise your bandaging skills,' she said. 'Alternatively, you just could make a sandcastle.'

'You're far too slapdash about this,' Tilly laughed, as Carrie swerved to avoid a pothole.

Carrie sped up. 'If Sir Sandalot's going to make it through this journey, he'll need quicker bandaging.'

'What he *needs* is a better driver,' Tilly retorted, winding bandages around Sir Sandalot's shoulder. 'Lie *still*, please, Sir.'

Carrie grinned and eased the ambulance to a halt in front of a mocked-up casualty station. Tilly hoisted the sandbag onto her shoulder.

'Let's hope real patients are half as agreeable,' she said, through the front window. 'I could take quite a shine to Sir Sandalot.'

'Benoit will be disappointed,' Carrie replied.

It was out before she could stop it.

Tilly sighed. 'Benoit – sweet though he is – is not the man for me,' she said.

'Poor Benoit,' said Carrie.

He really was a lovely man.

Might he do very well for Mabel?

As well as maintaining the ambulance and practising her driving skills, Carrie was also expected to take her turn on the blackout patrols – and all the while ensuring that her parents were none the wiser about what she was up to.

The first time, she went out with both Bobby and Tilly to be coached on what to say and – perhaps more importantly – how to say it. It was eerily quiet as they patrolled their assigned street, the soft glow of their shaded lanterns bouncing off the puddles in the road. Bobby tapped his list of properties against his thigh as he glanced up at the darkened windows of the terraced houses.

'Looks good,' he said. 'Number 14's finally got the hang of it.'

Tilly laughed. 'It looked like a blooming lighthouse last week.'

They moved on, spotting a thin strip of light escaping from the edges of the blackout curtains at Number 22. Tilly sighed as she rapped on the knocker. 'Looks like someone didn't double-check their work,' she said.

The door creaked open to reveal a balding man with a frazzled expression. 'Evening,' he said, squinting out at them. 'Is there a problem?'

'Just a little sliver of light, Mr Allen,' Bobby said, pointing towards the lower window.

'Oh, blast it,' Mr Allen muttered. 'I thought I'd fixed that last night.'

'Bay windows are notoriously tricky,' said Tilly. 'Shall we give you a hand?'

'No, thank you, dear.'

Carrie was incensed. 'I think we should,' she said, sweetly. 'You wouldn't want to put your neighbours at risk, would you?'

As the old man opened his door, Bobby and Tilly were both suppressing smiles.

'*Someone*'s passed their training,' said Bobby, quietly.

Carrie soon discovered that she liked the whole ARP team, and didn't really mind who she was paired up with for the patrols.

But she had to admit that her favourite times were those spent with Bobby.

They talked about everything and nothing, at ease in each other's company and finding entertainment and humour in the most unlikely of places. Carrie teased Bobby about his striped scarf, which scarcely left his neck. Bobby teased her about the fact that she was so nervous of being recognised – and, particularly, about word of what she was up to getting back to Pa – that she rarely took her steel helmet off. And, of course, they both teased each other about their choice of university subject, with endless debates about the merits of humanities versus science.

The conversation turned to serious matters too, of course.

One day, Bobby told her the details about why he hadn't been able to enlist. His had been a tricky birth and a simple slip of the forceps clamped around his head had rendered him almost blind in his right eye.

Carrie was intrigued.

To all intents and purposes, Bobby was disabled, just like the men at the factory. But, of course, not having received an injury through service to his country, he wasn't eligible for employment there.

Instead, he had been left to make his own way in the world – and just look at all he had achieved.

A place at Cambridge . . .

A responsible position at Starfish . . .

A volunteer with the rescue squad for the ARP . . .

Carrie couldn't help but be impressed.

For her part, Carrie told him all about her father. Not everything, of course – she may never be ready for *that* – but she tried to get across something of the hold he had on the family. Bobby listened intently and was sympathetic, but she was grateful that he neither tried to dismiss her feelings nor attempted to give her any advice.

She liked him very much indeed.

*

Occasionally, the ARP volunteers socialised together.

One evening, some of them went to see *His Girl Friday* at the Premier. Another time, they had a few drinks at the Ship. And when they discovered that Carrie's eighteenth had been and gone – marked only by a 'special' meal at home – Tilly arranged a surprise trip to none other than Bob Garganido and his Band at the Castle Hotel. How different it was this time; her dancing hadn't much improved but, this time, no one gave a hoot. She was amongst friends, in the thick of the action . . .

But, most of the time, they simply practised for what was surely coming next.

At the end of August, German nighttime bombers aiming for the RAF airfields drifted off course, accidentally destroying several London homes and killing civilians. The next day, the RAF bombed Berlin in retaliation and an incensed Hitler promptly ordered direct attacks on London and other major British cities.

Surely an attack on Richmond was only a matter of time?

Chapter Twenty-One

September 1940

And it turned out that they didn't have long to wait.

It was a couple of weeks later and Carrie was on duty at the ARP.

To begin with, she assumed it was a storm approaching. The weather had really turned and it felt like autumn had arrived. A message came in to sound the air raid siren and Tilly went onto the roof to turn it on . . . but the distant rumble did sound for all the world like thunder.

Carrie put her cards down – a shame because for once she had loads of trumps and was about to wipe that smirk right off Bobby's face! – and ran to the window with everyone else.

At first, all she could hear was the drone of the bombers and the answering roar of the anti-aircraft guns on Richmond Park. Then the sky was split aside by jagged flashes and, seconds later, all hell broke loose . . .

An explosion, a couple of streets away at most, turned the night sky an eerie orange and, a split second later, the corresponding boom made Carrie instinctively clamp her hands over her ears . . .

'It looks like St Andrew's Avenue,' called Miss Bateman, her voice clear and calm. 'Action stations, please, everyone . . .'

For a moment, Carrie stood rooted to the spot. Another

boom reverberated around the room and her overwhelming instinct was to take cover . . .

Don't think, Carrie.

Just do.

Seconds later, Carrie was in the ambulance, Tilly slipping into the passenger seat beside her. There was no banter about Sir Sandalot this time; in fact, neither of them said anything, but the glance they exchanged spoke volumes. And then Carrie slipped the vehicle into gear and they were off, heading down St Mark's Avenue as fast as she dared. There was no need for instructions on where to go – no need for headlights, for that matter – the orange glow was staining the sky like a grotesque beacon . . .

Carrie turned the corner into St Andrew's Avenue and . . .

'My God,' said Tilly, her hand clamped to her mouth.

One of the large redbrick mansions had suffered a direct hit. Half of it had collapsed and part of the remainder was already on fire. Red and yellow flames billowed towards the heavens, highlighting clouds of dust and debris and the personal effects spilling out of the gaping hole . . .

Our turn, thought Carrie, suddenly strangely calm.

The same scene had been repeated up and down the country over the past couple of weeks; Carrie had seen the pictures in *The Times* of almost identical damage in Birmingham and Coventry and the coastal cities on an almost daily basis.

Please let them – let *her* – be up to the challenge.

The first aiders and stretcher bearers were already there and Carrie could only watch, heart in her mouth, as they approached the building – silhouettes against the flames – and then disappeared inside. Bobby was one of those silhouettes, and it would only take the beams to collapse or the flames to suddenly shift direction for . . .

Oh, please let him be all right.

Meanwhile, she and Tilly were required to stay with the ambulance – ready to leave as soon as the injured were loaded – and were strictly forbidden from entering the building. Carrie hated herself for feeling relieved that she wasn't expected to plunge into the wreckage herself; looking at what was being required of the others, she honestly didn't know if she had it in her.

The heat . . .

The smoke . . .

The roar and crackle of the fire . . .

Pushing away the uncomfortable thought that she was a coward, she did what she could whilst following the rules; approaching the clusters of horrified neighbours who had appeared on the pavements in their nightclothes – making sure that they were standing well back and trying to find out what she could about the occupants of the bombed house. She quickly discovered that a family lived there – parents and their three teenage daughters – together with a couple of Belgian refugees.

Seven in total.

How many were accounted for . . . ?

The first aid party were bringing out a couple of walking wounded and Carrie and Tilly rushed over to see if they could help. But the two young girls – although severely shocked – only had minor injuries and were dispatched to the sitting case car to be taken to the nearest first aid post . . .

'Lyn!'

Carrie wheeled around. Bobby was running at full tilt towards the ambulance, carrying the front half of a stretcher, with Madge bringing up the rear. On the stretcher was another teenage girl, alive and writhing with pain, her face and chest covered in blood.

'Head injury,' panted Bobby. 'She's for the hospital.'

'Right away.' Carrie stood back as he loaded the stretcher into the ambulance and Tilly started strapping it onto the bed. Her eyes locked onto Bobby's. 'Careful, now,' she said.

He nodded, touched her lightly on the shoulder . . . and was gone.

Carrie got behind the wheel and exhaled slowly. Everything felt so strange, as if she wasn't really there . . .

'Good to go,' called Tilly, banging on the roof of the ambulance.

Carrie nodded and set off, hands damp with sweat on the steering wheel, breath coming in raggedy little gasps.

The road ahead was full of debris and flooded by water – inky in the gloaming. She'd never get through . . .

No sooner had the thought come into her head than she crashed the ambulance into reverse and shot backwards . . .

'Steady,' called Tilly, followed by a loud groan from behind.

'Sorry!' Carrie gritted her teeth and completed the turn, then sped off down the street.

She could do this.

'You're doing ever so well,' said Tilly, from behind. At first, Carrie thought Tilly was talking to her and it was on the tip of her tongue to thank her. But Tilly continued to speak in a low, reassuring tone and Carrie realised she was trying to calm the patient and keep her conscious. 'We'll have you at the hospital in a jiffy and the doctors and nurses will get you back on your feet, you'll see. Now, can you tell me your name?'

There was a mutter from behind.

'Sorry, what was that?' said Tilly. More mumbling. 'Betty?' Tilly persisted. 'Betty Folger? Good. And do you have any brothers or sisters, Betty . . .'

Carrie tuned out.

Betty Folger.

How did she know that name?

She glanced in the rearview mirror, saw the long, red wavy hair hanging over the edge of the stretcher, and suddenly knew exactly why she'd recognised it.

It was one of the girls from Woollies who had been so beastly to Mabel.

Carrie's heart ratcheted up a gear.

It didn't matter; her job was to save lives – not judge them – and no one was perfect.

She set her jaw and navigated the streets as quickly and as smoothly as she could and, less than two minutes later, they were pulling up at casualty at the back of the hospital. Seconds later, two porters had appeared and extracted the stretcher and Tilly disappeared inside the hospital with them.

The whole thing had run like clockwork.

Carrie drove the ambulance over to one of the parking bays and sat there in the darkness.

A shiver ran through her and she noticed her hands were shaking.

Shock, she supposed – but there was no time for that. She needed to remain calm because who knew how many more trips she would need to make that evening.

It seemed an age until Tilly emerged and, meanwhile, several more ambulances had arrived at the hospital.

'I'm covered in blood,' Tilly said, inconsequently, as she got into the back of the ambulance. 'I'd better get myself and this place cleaned up whilst you drive us back for round two.'

There was no round two.

When they got back to St Andrew's Avenue, a couple of fire engines were plying water over the inferno, but there was no sign of Bobby and the others.

After a while, a very sober-looking Miss Bateman detached herself from her conversation with the fire crews and came over to the ambulance.

'Everyone's been accounted for and all the survivors have already left,' she said. 'And I hate to ask you this, but I wondered if you'd be happy to take one of the deceased to the mortuary. Ordinarily, we'd leave her for the mortuary ambulance, but it may be some time before it returns and it seems terribly insensitive to just leave her here.'

Miss Bateman indicated further along the pavement and, for the first time, Carrie noticed the small inert bundle wrapped in an army blanket on a stretcher.

'Oh no!' said Carrie, hand to mouth. It was the first time she had seen a dead body – even a shrouded one. 'Of course,' she added quickly, remembering her training.

'Thank you,' said Miss Bateman. 'You know where the mortuary is?'

'Yes, Miss. Next to the school in the old swimming baths . . .'

'That's the one. Now, the rest of the team has gone back to base, so why don't Tilly and I load her up and you can be on your way?'

'I'm happy to load her, Miss,' said Carrie.

Miss Bateman nodded. 'Thank you,' she said. 'In that case, I'll get back to HQ and we'll start the debrief.'

She bustled off and, in silence, Carrie and Tilly picked up the stretcher. The small bundle was so still and so small but what nearly broke Carrie were the little bare feet sticking out the bottom.

'Will you come in the front?' said Carrie, when the stretcher had been loaded and secured.

'No,' said Tilly. 'I'll stay with her in the back and keep her company.'

Carrie managed to keep it together until they got back to St Mark's Avenue but, as she pulled into the drive, she suddenly found that she was close to tears.

'Come along in and get a cuppa,' said Tilly, standing outside her window.

Carrie shook her head. 'I've got to check the ambulance over,' she said. 'I need to make sure the tyres have survived, check the oil . . .'

'Can't it wait?'

'Not really,' said Carrie. 'What if we're called out again?'

'I'll stay with you, then.'

'Don't,' said Carrie. 'You go in. To be perfectly honest, I could do with a few minutes to myself . . .'

Tilly nodded. 'Right you are. Well done, tonight, by the way. Sterling effort.'

'Well done, yourself.' Carrie gave Tilly a weak smile. 'Sir Sandalot would be proud of us.'

Tilly grinned and disappeared inside. Carrie got stiffly out of the ambulance and started working methodically through her checklist, finding comfort in the familiar routines and rituals . . .

'Does she pass inspection?'

Carrie, head in the bonnet checking water and oil, looked up. It was Bobby, holding out a cuppa.

'I think so,' said Carrie, putting the mug on the ambulance roof. 'How are you?'

Bobby shrugged, suddenly looking older than his years. 'It's not easy, is it?'

Carrie shook her head and then, to her mortification, the tears finally came. 'It was awful,' she said. 'I vaguely knew the girl with the head injury I took to hospital and all I could think was that I hadn't liked her. Does that make me a terrible person?'

'Just a human one,' said Bobby, taking Carrie into his arms. 'And I don't know – don't *want* to know – what dreadful thing she'd done to get on the wrong side of you, but I *can* tell you that she was very brave when it mattered most. She saved the life of one of the Belgian refugees, even if she couldn't save her own sister. If she survives, she can be very proud of that.'

For a moment, Carrie's weeping intensified and she just stood there, allowing Bobby to rhythmically stroke her back. Then she gently pulled away.

'There's good and bad in everyone, isn't there?' she said. 'Sometimes, I'm not very good at remembering that.'

Bobby nodded. 'We can all certainly strive to do better

and say sorry when we're wrong,' he said. 'But no one's perfect and everyone deserves a second chance.'

Carrie wasn't entirely sure whether he was talking generalities or specifics but, nonetheless, she put her head on one side and wrinkled up her nose at him.

'Or even a third chance?' she said.

And then, she wasn't sure entirely how it happened, but suddenly she was properly in his arms and they were kissing the hell out of each other.

Smoke and honey and his hand in her hair and the other clamped around her waist and . . .

It had taken a tragedy to realise it, but Bobby Roscoe *definitely* deserved a third chance.

Chapter Twenty-Two

September 1940

Carrie, washed and in a fresh set of clothing, was home in time for breakfast.

'Wretched business,' said Pa, patting her on the shoulder. 'Only a matter of time, I suppose. It was St Andrew's Avenue – a huge house completely destroyed. Sadly, there were three dead, including – I have to tell you – a couple of young girls.'

Carrie tried to nod as if this was all news to her.

'I'm so pleased you were at Daisy's,' added Ma, spooning out the porridge. 'You'd have been a lot safer and more comfortable in their Anderson shelter than under our bowling green, that's for sure.'

Carrie grunted.

'The only positive thing was that the local ARP apparently came up trumps,' said Pa. 'Call themselves the Saints, I hear. Their system worked like a dream. We can only hope that Miss Whitnot and her chaps rise to the challenge with such aplomb if we're ever put to the test.'

The guilt was almost unbearable . . . as was the urge to tell her parents what she'd really been up to the night before. All this lying – all this subterfuge – was bone-achingly exhausting. She was wrung out, body and soul – barely able to stand, let alone smile. Even when the others had finally gone to bed at HQ, she'd needed to wash her white shirt so as not to give the game away . . .

'I must send some flowers to Daisy's mother to thank her for putting up with you all summer,' said Ma casually. 'You've been staying there at least three times a week and every Tommy in the country must have scarves coming out of his ears.'

'Oh, please don't, Ma,' said Carrie hastily. 'I'm sure they won't expect anything and I'll make sure to pass on your thanks the next time I see her.'

'Nice for Daisy to have company, though,' said Ma. 'Two "only" children together and it can be lonely on your own.'

Carrie smiled blandly.

Her mother really had no idea.

Pa stood up decisively. 'Must be off,' he said. 'Let's just hope last night was a one-off. An isolated incident . . .'

It wasn't an isolated incident.

Not a bit of it.

By the twentieth of September, there had been four bombing raids over Richmond, although no more in the vicinity of St Mark's Avenue. Amongst the casualties were the Danby Girls – Margaret, Stella and Sybil – who Carrie vaguely remembered as Scholarship Girls from school. Miss Bateman was devastated at their passing, remembering them as the very best of pupils, and the whole thing just heartbreaking beyond words.

There was much chatter around the estate about whether Richmond was being specifically targeted. The town, of course, had important rail and road connections, which served as vital arteries for moving people, goods and troops, and although the town itself was largely residential, there were industrial and military targets galore in the surrounding areas. Maybe the Poppy Factory itself was a target, and the Luftwaffe wouldn't rest until they had destroyed it . . .

On the other hand, German bombers often relied on visual navigation and Richmond, with its prominent Thames bends and bridges, could be being mistaken for more critical central London targets. And it was widely known that German bombers often dropped their unused weapons indiscriminately when returning from central London . . .

At the end of the day, the consensus was that Richmond wasn't being specifically targeted. *Everywhere* – from major cities to small towns – was being targeted. London was being targeted *nightly* and even Buckingham Palace had been damaged.

When would it ever finish?

Meanwhile, life – of sorts – went on.

The children on the Poppy Factory estate – as elsewhere – had gone back to school and, with their departure, the role of Little Poppies had changed.

Some of the helpers – including Mrs Perkins – transferred to assembling radios in the factory, which was still crying out for new workers. But for those who remained in the Remembrance Club, including Carrie, there was still plenty to do. The babies and toddlers still needed looking after, the younger school-aged children needed walking to and from the local primaries *and* there was the after-school club to run until such time as their mothers finished in the factory. Carrie had wondered if she would miss Eloise, Maggie and the others, but she was often so exhausted after her nights at St Mark's Avenue it was all she could do to keep her eyes open. More than once, she found herself dropping off as she rocked a cradle or gave a baby its bottle . . .

How on earth was she going to cope when she went to university in a mere matter of weeks?

Because, one thing was for certain.

She certainly wasn't going to stop volunteering for the ARP.

And then there was Bobby.

Bobby.

From the moment the two had kissed outside Saints HQ, everything had changed. Carrie now couldn't believe how stupid – how *judgmental* – she'd been over the past few months. Who cared if Bobby had been a bit rushed over his goodbyes a couple of times?

It was hardly a crime.

Besides, it was how a person made you feel that mattered and Bobby made Carrie feel safe and excited at the same time. He made her feel like she had come home and suddenly she wanted to spend every waking moment with him.

The trouble was that it was virtually impossible to be alone.

The two saw each other regularly on duty at the ARP, of course. Carrie was sure everyone must be aware of what was going on, but they did their best to be professional and to keep up appearances. But, apart from that, there was virtually no chance to be together at all. To be fair,

Carrie was hardly seeing anyone; she hadn't seen Daisy for months and even her evening meetings with Sarah and Mabel had virtually ground to a halt now that they were all working so hard. And, of course, Bobby had his work up at Starfish where he was often working double shifts now the Blitz was ongoing and it was all hands to the pump. They managed a couple of river walks over the weekends, and one Saturday afternoon, they snuck off to the Premier to see *Rebecca*. Sitting in the dark, shoulders touching, Carrie did wonder if Bobby might hold her hand. At first, she sat resolutely on her hands until her fingers were numb – she certainly didn't want him thinking she was the sort of girl who came to the flicks simply to cavort in the back row – but after a while he reached for her and she quickly realised that she was *exactly* that sort of girl!

If her parents could see her now!

Carrie debated whether or not to tell Mabel and Sarah about 'Mr Two', but she so rarely saw them nowadays that there hadn't really been the opportunity. In the end, she decided to hug it to herself for the time being. It was so early, so new . . . and, for now, she preferred to keep it close to her chest as her very own delicious secret.

'Your mother and I have been talking,' said Pa one evening towards the end of September. 'And I'm afraid we've come to a decision that won't be to your liking.'

Alarm bells began to ring in Carrie's head.

'What's that, then?' she asked cautiously.

Had they found out about the ARP?

About Bobby?

'We want you to defer Birkbeck at least until January or

until the bombs stop,' said Pa. 'It simply wouldn't be safe travelling up and down to London at the moment.'

Carrie hesitated.

At one point – indeed, only a matter of weeks ago – this command would have felt like an utter disaster and something to be railed against with all her might.

She had had her heart set on university – on escaping Richmond – for years.

But now, not only could she see that this was a sensible decision, she was surprised to discover that it was also what she *wanted*.

She smiled at her parents. 'Actually, I agree with you,' she said.

Her parents exchanged a glance.

'*That* was easy,' said Ma.

'Well, trailing up and down to London during the Blitz *would* be utter madness,' said Carrie. 'I might often disagree with you, but I'm not *totally* pig-headed.'

There was more to it than that, of course.

This was wartime and everything had changed.

University could wait.

Chapter Twenty-Three

November 1940

The days shortened and the leaves turned brown – and still the Blitz continued.

In London, sixty-six people were killed when a German bomb penetrated Balham Station on the London Underground, which was in use as an air raid shelter.

In Richmond, there was an attack virtually every other day, and many people took to permanently sleeping in the various air raid shelters, many of which were fitting bunks as quickly as they could. It was absolutely petrifying going to bed and not knowing if you would wake up the next morning and Carrie couldn't believe that everyone was just carrying on with their everyday routine as if nothing was happening. To be honest, she found the nights at the ARP less frightening than those in her bed alone; there really was a safety in numbers and the thought of Bobby sleeping in the next-door room comforted and reassured her.

Meanwhile, at the Poppy Factory, it was all hands on deck to get ready for the fast-approaching Armistice Day and tensions were running high. Nearly fifty million poppies had been produced – many in the new designs – and Pa and Major Armstrong claimed they were turning grey. Day and night, vans arrived at the factory to load up – and, on occasion, Carrie was relieved of her duties at Little

Poppies to help in the warehouse or even to drive poppies to the British Legion Offices in the neighbouring suburbs. It was exhausting.

'Do your fathers and the chaps at the Poppy Factory sell the poppies as well as making them?' asked Bobby, one Saturday, as the two were strolling along the towpath. It was a chilly afternoon, and Carrie had Bobby's scarf wound around her neck.

'Oh no.' Carrie was shocked. 'No, that wouldn't do at all.'

'Why ever not? I would have thought that would be a fitting climax to all their hard work.'

Carrie hesitated.

She had grown up understanding why the poppies were sold by others, but how to explain it to an outsider?

'It's because of the Victorian flower girls who used to sell artificial flowers to support themselves,' she said. 'People think that if the disabled veterans sell the poppies themselves, it might be seen as too close to begging.'

Bobby nodded thoughtfully. 'So, instead, we have the "Poppy Girls", smartly dressed and cheerful, carrying trays of poppies through the city streets?' he said with a grin.

Carrie laughed. 'Something like that,' she said, tucking her hand under his arm. 'Up and down the country, it's usually volunteers from the British Legion, but there is a tradition that the girls from the estate can sell them in Richmond once they're eighteen. And, this year of course, that's . . . *moi*!'

She gave a little twirl, followed by a little curtsey, and Bobby grinned.

'Let's hope Herr Hitler doesn't create havoc with your plans,' he said.

'There hasn't been a raid in Richmond for a few days now,' said Carrie. 'Let's hope our luck holds.'

Their luck held.

Carrie, Mabel and Sarah had been allocated a slot outside the station. It was a cold morning with a nip of frost in the air, and it wasn't long before Carrie's fingers and toes started going slightly numb. Sarah, of course, was in her element; happily approaching all and sundry with a wide smile and an enthusiastic sales pitch. Carrie and Mabel, more reticent by nature, hung back at first, but the commuters were so friendly and supportive that, pretty soon, they too got into the swing. As Carrie pinned poppies onto more coats and jackets than she could possibly count, she was almost bursting with pride for all the Poppy Factory estate had achieved that year.

This was what it was all about.

Friendship, community, pulling together in tough times.

By midmorning, things had quietened down a little and Harry popped down to say hello. Sarah – uncaring – wrapped him in a huge bear hug and the two moved to one side, eyes only for each other.

'Almost brings a tear to the eye, don't it?' said Mabel, with an indulgent smile.

Carrie nodded. 'It's lovely,' she agreed, simply. 'They're so happy together.'

'Funnily enough, despite everything, the past few months *have* been lovely in many ways,' said Mabel, stamping up and down to keep warm. 'We've all been able to do our bit and, even though we ain't seen much of each other recently, making friends with you two really has been the icing on the cake.'

Carrie paused to sell a poppy and then turned to Mabel with a wry grin. 'I'm so pleased to hear you say that,' she said. 'I thought I'd been in your bad books ever since that afternoon Alfie went down to the cellar.'

Mabel made a face. 'Well, I've hardly seen you since,' she said defensively. 'And I know I've been a right old grump recently. There's stressful stuff going on at work and sometimes I take it out on me friends. Forgive me?'

Carrie felt a rush of affection and relief. 'There's nothing to forgive,' she said. 'You and Sarah have been so lovely to me over Marigold *and* you've kept my secret over the ARP. Honestly, you're like the sisters I never had.'

Mabel smiled gently. 'I don't think Daisy would be very happy to hear you say that,' she said.

Carrie shrugged. 'I think Daisy would say that it's not a competition,' she said with a laugh. 'And Daisy's a very dear friend, of course she is, and she has been for a long time. But we – the Poppy Girls – have got so much more in common; fathers who were scarred by the last war, living *and* working in close proximity. We *understand* each other . . .'

She broke off, deep in thought, as a little flurry of people approached to buy poppies. For all her protestations of sisterhood, she had kept one very important secret from Mabel and Sarah. She made a quick decision and, as soon as the customers had dispersed, turned to Mabel before she had a chance to change her mind.

'I want you to be the first to know something I've been hugging to myself for a while,' she said diffidently. 'Mr Two and I are stepping out together!'

Mabel's face split into a huge grin. 'I knew it!' she exclaimed, sweeping Carrie into a hug. 'You've got this sort of *glow* about you – it just *had* to be a man!'

'What's all this then?' Sarah – minus Harry – was coming over to join them, a quizzical smile on her face.

So, Carrie told her the news as well and then, to much laughter and squealing, she was being plied with questions. His name was Robert, she said – that made him sound ever so grand – and he had broken off his studies to help out at Starfish, which was why he couldn't be here today . . .

'The Poppy Girls!'

Carrie, Mabel and Sarah sprung apart.

It was Miss Bateman bearing down on them all with a wide beam. She bought a poppy, clapped them all on the shoulder and, as she left them – thick as thieves – Carrie could have sworn that she winked.

And then it all started to go wrong.

Chapter Twenty-Four

Monday 25 November 1940

There was usually a sense of holiday and a tangible sense of relief around the Poppy Factory estate in the days and weeks following Armistice Day. 11th November marked the culmination of all the hard work over the year and it was customary for everyone to celebrate and for some to go away on holiday afterwards.

This year proved different.

It wasn't because that year's Poppy Appeal had been unsuccessful – far from it. Indeed, more poppies had been produced and sold than during any year before, and in the most trying of circumstances. (No wonder Pa was strutting around like the cat that had got the cream.) But it was hard to celebrate or to arrange a trip away when the country was under constant bombardment. And, of course, the aircraft radios still needed to be assembled with the targets set by the ministry looking further and further out of reach.

Pa and the others tried to keep up morale – the customary tug of war between veterans still took place on what was left of the bowling green – but the overall mood was far more sombre than celebration.

For her part, Carrie kept on doing what she did and, ten days or so after Armistice Day, she was duly helping to supervise the Little Poppies after-school club.

About twenty minutes before she was due to go off-duty, the door to the kitchen burst open and Mabel came in, bringing a blast of cold air and woodsmoke in with her. She was carrying a heavy-looking shopping bag over one shoulder.

'Drinks for the darts match against the police tonight,' she grumbled to no one in particular, heaving the bag onto her other shoulder. 'Blooming heavy, too.'

Carrie paused from her kneading and the dough she was making popped and deflated with a little oomph. She stretched her fingers and turned to Mabel, ready with a little smile of welcome and the offer of a cuppa.

The smile froze on her lips . . . because on top of the bag, the ends trailing down on either side, was Bobby's scarf.

Mabel had Bobby's scarf.

In shock, Carrie glanced down at her floury fingers – maybe she had imagined it – and then looked up again. No, the scarf was still there; the achingly familiar stripes stuffed casually on top of the drinks.

What on earth was going on?

Of course, Carrie realised with a jolt of relief, the scarf might not be Bobby's.

After all, he was hardly the only young man to have gone to Oxford or to have rowed for his college. But no sooner had she latched onto *that* explanation, than the relief was cruelly snatched away. There was the unusual stripe – the one that started green and ended crimson – and it was clear for all to see, right next to the grocer's name on the bag.

Mabel had Bobby's scarf.

'Are you all right, Carrie? You've gone as white as a sheet.'

It was Eloise, looking up at Carrie with concern, even as her small fingers reached for the neglected ball of dough.

Carrie nodded distractedly and her eyes slid to Mabel's. She opened her mouth to say something – what, she had no idea – but Mabel just stuffed both ends of the scarf back into the bag and left the room.

Carrie finished making the bread and put it in the oven to bake. Her hands were shaking and she felt close to tears, but she had to carry on. Flour was too precious to spoil the bread – even in extremis – and she couldn't leave the girls unsupervised.

But neither could she let it lie.

No matter the explanation – and there were dozens of ever-more implausible ones running through her mind – she had to ask Mabel what was going on. She had to know, no matter how hurtful the truth might be. And so, when Sarah arrived in the kitchen, Carrie thrust her pinny at her, muttered a garbled explanation and set off in hot pursuit.

Mabel was nowhere to be found.

She wasn't behind the bar, stashing the drinks away. She wasn't in the new Homework Club, where a dozen boys and girls were bent over exercise books and Alfie and his chum were forming ink blots into shapes unrelated to any homework Carrie had ever been set! She wasn't playing bricks and toy cars in the back room with the younger children.

Of course, she had probably gone upstairs – she lived there after all!

Carrie was standing at the foot of the stairs, wondering what to do, when a noise from the basement caught her attention.

Aha!

Mabel had obviously popped *downstairs* to the storeroom.

Carrie leant over the balustrade – yes, the light at the bottom was on – and then, without second-guessing herself, ran lightly down the stairs.

The storeroom was empty.

No sign of Mabel, the bag or, indeed, Bobby's scarf.

Confused, Carrie headed further down the corridor to the air raid shelter. The door was unlocked but, as the lights were off, it was unlikely that Mabel was in there. There were a couple more storerooms – little more than large cupboards – and she opened the door to the first one . . .

'Can I help you?'

Carrie wheeled around as if she'd been caught with her hand in the biscuit tin.

'No . . . I mean . . . sorry . . .' She trailed off.

'Are you following me?' demanded Mabel. She was smiling, but there was steel behind her eyes.

'*No*. I mean, sort of. I mean, that scarf you were carrying earlier. The striped one. I just wondered how you came by it?'

'Me *scarf*?' said Mabel, pulling a little face. 'You came all the way down here to ask me about me scarf. Whatever I thought you was going to say, it weren't that.'

'It isn't *your* scarf, though, is it?' Carrie blurted out.

'Pardon me?'

Carrie paused.

What if Bobby had *given* Mabel the scarf?

'It's not, though, is it,' she repeated.

'Well, no,' conceded Mabel. 'A friend from work lent it to me.'

Carrie was so taken aback by the barefaced lie that she was stunned into silence. She just stood there mutely, a thousand thoughts running round her brain.

Bobby . . .

Mabel . . .

'Are you quite all right?' asked Mabel, eventually.

'I'm not as it happens,' said Carrie. 'Because that simply isn't true. I know the chap who owns that scarf and he certainly doesn't work at the Chrysler Factory.'

Mabel just gawped at her, opening and shutting her mouth like a goldfish.

'Have you *stolen* that scarf, Mabel?' Carrie asked, considering the possibility for the first time.

Mabel's eyes snapped to Carrie's. '*What?*' she exploded. 'Of course, I ain't.'

'So, who does it belong to then?'

Mabel paused. 'A friend,' she said. 'Although that ain't none of your business.'

'What sort of friend?' Carrie persisted, her tone sharper than she had intended.

Mabel drew herself to her full height – still a good six inches shorter than Carrie's.

'You might be the manager's daughter, but it really ain't none of your business which boy's given or lent me what. I think I'm allowed some secrets. Now, if you don't mind coming out of *our* cellar – which, might I remind you, is out of bounds! – I need to finish stocking the bar for tonight's do.'

She waved Carrie ahead of her up the stairs, then followed her without another word.

*

Carrie arrived back in the kitchen close to tears.

'Are you all right?' asked Sarah. 'You're awfully flushed.'

Carrie shrugged, swallowed . . . and then dissolved into tears. 'Not really,' she admitted.

'Let me pop the kettle on,' said Sarah, trying to shield Carrie from small, enquiring eyes. 'Want to tell me the problem?'

Carrie took a deep breath. 'Mabel,' she said, simply.

Sarah started in surprise. '*Mabel?*' she echoed. 'Whatever's happened?'

Carrie glanced at her watch and made an instantaneous decision. 'I promise to tell you everything a little later,' she said. 'Only, there's something I really need to do right now. Can you keep an eye on the girls and the bread for a few more minutes?'

Sarah nodded. 'Of course,' she said, without enquiring further. 'You take your time.'

Carrie gave her a grateful glance and dashed out of the Remembrance Club. Without stopping to think about the feasibility of her plan, she ran up the path to Richmond Hill. She should just be in time to intercept Bobby as he walked home after work. All she had to do was to ask him about his scarf. Somehow, she knew he wouldn't be able to lie to her . . . and one look at his face would tell her all she needed to know.

And, as if by magic, here he was, marching down the hill towards her, looking very bare without his scarf.

'*Lyn!*'

Bobby's face was wreathed in smiles as he walked towards her and Carrie knew that if it hadn't been for Miss Arnott sweeping her front steps – was the woman *always* sweeping her front steps?! – he would have taken her into his arms right there and then.

Suddenly she knew everything was all right. Bobby, straight as a die, was hers and she was a silly-ninny for ever doubting him . . .

She reached out and touched the rough wool of his jacket. 'Do you know a girl called Mabel Green?' she asked.

She might as well solve the mystery.

Bobby took a step back. 'Pardon me?' he said, rubbing the bridge of his nose.

'Mabel Green,' repeated Carrie, impatiently. 'We were at school together and she lives on the estate. But you probably know all that because I've just seen her with your scarf sticking out of her bag. The thing is, she told me some rubbish about you two working together. Of course, that's impossible because you work at Starfish and she works at the Chrysler Factory, but when I confronted her about it, she went all funny and clammed up . . .'

Carrie trailed off and the world ground to a halt whilst she waited for Bobby's reply. Even Miss Arnott paused in her sweeping, clearly straining to hear every word.

Please let Bobby laugh and tell her Mabel had recently moved jobs, but it was meant to be a secret or maybe that the two were cousins or . . .

Bobby took a horribly long time to reply and suddenly seemed very interested in a spot over Carrie's right shoulder. 'I don't know . . .' he started.

'You *don't* know her?' Carrie finished for him. 'Maybe she stole it. I've had my suspicions about her . . .'

'No.' Bobby's eyes snapped to hers. '*No!* Don't you dare think that about Mabel. I would trust her with my life . . .'

'I'm sorry?' Carrie stammered.

'I don't want to lie to you, Lyn,' said Bobby in a gentler tone. 'You'll just have to trust me on this.'

'*Trust* you?' Carrie took a step forward and thumped Bobby lightly on the chest. 'What does that even mean? Trust you on what?'

Bobby gave an infinitesimal shrug and a tiny regretful smile. 'I can't tell you why Mabel came to have that scarf,' he said. 'Not without telling you a lie . . .'

'*Carrie!*'

Carrie jumped at the voice behind her.

It was Ma. *Ma*, standing a few steps behind her with hands on her hips. Shocked, Carrie stumbled backwards, hastily trying to distance herself from Bobby.

How on earth to explain this?

How on earth to explain *Bobby*?

Ma could hardly have missed the fact that the two had been busy in conversation – even had she not seen Carrie thump Bobby on the chest.

Carrie plastered a smile on her face. 'I'll just be a moment, Ma,' she said, knowing her voice sounded unnaturally high. 'I've got . . . something to sort out here and then I'll be home to help with supper.'

'Home. *Now*,' replied Ma, and there was ice in her tone. 'Unless you want your father to come and fetch you himself.'

Carrie's blood ran cold.

That was the *last* thing she wanted.

Which raised the question of why was she being summoned home at all? What on earth had her parents discovered?

She turned to Bobby. 'I have to go,' she said, flatly, already turning away.

'Lyn, please . . .'

'*Now*, Carrie,' said Ma, sharply.

And Carrie walked away without a backwards glance.

Chapter Twenty-Five

Monday 25 November 1940

'I'm afraid your father knows everything,' said Ma, over her shoulder.

Carrie's heart, hitherto in her throat, plummeted like a stone. Wordlessly, she trailed behind her mother – half naughty little girl, half hardened criminal. Without knowing what Pa had discovered, she couldn't say anything without potentially incriminating herself further.

Everything seemed thrown into sharp relief; the workers streaming out of the factory, the children reunited with their mothers after Little Poppies. And here was Sarah, running up to her, then retreating with a little frown when Carrie waved her away with a face she hoped communicated the gravity of the situation.

Why on earth had she thought it was a good idea to lie to her parents?

As they emerged onto the road by the flats, Carrie considered not stopping. She could walk right out of the estate, onto the Petersham Road and just keep going. She was eighteen years old and many girls her age were already married with children or risking their lives in far-flung corners of the world.

Surely, she could strike out on her own?

But she had no money of her own, hadn't yet come of age, and the country was gripped by war . . .

She had no choice but to go home and face the music.

Pa was pacing up and down in the living room like a caged tiger. He wheeled around as Carrie and Ma entered the room.

'And what do you have to say for yourself, young lady?' he said, without preamble.

Oh, goodness.

'Perhaps you would tell me exactly what it is that I am supposed to have done,' said Carrie, with a nonchalance and bravado she really didn't feel.

Pa swung towards her, fury in his eyes. 'Don't even try to brazen this out,' he hissed, taking a step towards her.

Carrie took a couple of steps backwards until she was hard up against the armchair. 'I'm not . . .'

'I saw Mrs Thornton in town earlier on,' interrupted Pa. 'She told me about Daisy starting work at the Chrysler Factory and I thanked her for letting you spend so much time there over the summer. Only it turns out that's not where you've been, Carolyn. Is it?'

Carrie exhaled and shook her head.

This was just as bad as she'd feared it would be.

'That just leaves the question of where you *have* been,' said Pa, softly.

'It's *him*, isn't it?' interrupted Ma. 'I knew the moment I set eyes on him.'

'Him?' echoed Pa, turning to face Ma.

'I've just caught her having a tiff with a lad,' said Ma. She turned to Carrie. 'A couple of women have mentioned seeing you out and about with a chap, and that would all have been well and good if you'd *told* us . . .'

'Except that you've clearly got the morals of an alley cat,' interrupted Pa. 'Staying out with him night after night. You do realise your reputation is in tatters – even if you're lucky enough not to be with child.'

Carrie burst out laughing.

Talk about her parents making a mountain out of a molehill!

'Oh, goodness,' she said, trying to swallow her giggles. 'It's not like that at *all*.'

'So, who *is* the young man?' asked Ma, looking slightly mollified.

'His name is Bobby. He's . . . a friend.'

'And are you stepping out with him?' Ma persisted.

Carrie considered, head on one side. 'I honestly have no idea,' she admitted, sinking heavily into the chair. The possible ramifications of what she had learnt that afternoon hit her anew, and suddenly she didn't want to laugh at all.

'So, you've been bestowing your favours around town without the young man even courting you?' bellowed Pa.

Carrie looked up at him, coldly. 'Of course, I haven't,' she said.

'So, where *have* you been?' persisted Ma. 'If you haven't been at Daisy's and you haven't been with this Bobby, where exactly *have* you been spending your nights?'

Carrie took a deep breath.

In for a penny . . .

'I've been volunteering for the St Mark's Avenue ARP,' she said simply. 'And when I'm on duty, I need to stay overnight at HQ with the others.'

She shut her eyes and braced herself for the onslaught.

'St Mark's Avenue ARP!' said Pa incredulously, as though Carrie had just told him she'd been spending her evenings in Timbuktu. 'What on earth . . .'

'Well, you wouldn't give me permission to volunteer at the Poppy Factory ARP,' replied Carrie coolly.

Pa gave her a smile that was totally devoid of humour. 'So, it's *my* fault you've disobeyed us?' he said. 'And I'm assuming you forged my signature – or doesn't the warden over there care much for rules?'

Carrie hesitated.

The last thing she wanted was for Miss Bateman to get into trouble on her account.

'I forged it,' she said, in a small voice. 'The warden thinks I've got permission.'

'And was it worth it?' sneered Pa. 'Was it really worth going behind our backs just to check a few blackout blinds?'

Carrie inhaled in fury.

Why did her father *always* have to believe so little of her?

She had been driving the living and the dead through the pitch-black streets of Richmond whilst everyone else had been sheltering, for goodness' sake!

She opened her mouth but closed it again without uttering a word.

What was the point?

Even if she single-handedly managed to stop the war, Pa would doubtless still find something to find fault with.

Then Pa stepped to one side and, for the first time, Carrie noticed The Strap, curled almost obscenely on the coffee table in front of the sofa. The long tan belt had hung menacingly from a hook in her parents' cupboard through-out her childhood, although it had very rarely been used and certainly not for many years. Pa might be a dictatorial bully, but his weapon of choice had almost always been words. But now, here he was, wrapping the strap around his hand and giving it a couple of experimental flicks.

Carrie recoiled with shock.

He *wouldn't*.

And then, the thought flickered into her mind – as it had always done as a little girl – *at least the lounge window faced away from the estate* . . .

'You've gone behind my back, Carolyn,' said Pa in a low voice. 'And that hurts me much more than I'm – sadly – going to have to hurt you.'

Just refuse, Carrie.

Refuse.

But eighteen was still a child in the eyes of the law. She needed her father's permission to go to university.

She needed Pa's permission for *everything* . . .

Oh, how she hated him.

'Don't be ridiculous, Dennis,' came a sharp voice from behind.

Carrie wheeled around in relief.

Ma was standing there, hands on her hips.

'I'm afraid it's necessary, Gladys,' said Pa, wrapping the belt further around his hand. 'Our daughter has blatantly disrespected and disobeyed us.'

'That's as may be,' said Ma, stepping forwards and standing between Carrie and her father. 'But you'll have to hit me before you get anywhere near her.'

'Gladys . . .' There was a warning glint in Pa's eye.

'No, Dennis.' Ma's answering tone was calm but oh-so-firm. 'That's not the way. Not anymore.'

For a moment, no one moved or said a thing.

Then Pa lowered the strap onto the coffee table. Ma picked it up and left the room. She reappeared seconds later and went and stood beside Pa and it was as if he was suddenly a little smaller and she a little taller.

'I suppose you think we should just let her off scot-free,' said Pa icily and Carrie realised that the danger hadn't passed.

'Not a bit of it,' replied Ma briskly.

Pa nodded and drew himself up to his full height. 'Carolyn, from now until further notice, you will not leave the flat without our express permission and you will certainly not step one foot outside the estate. Do you understand, girl?'

Carrie nodded.

She would almost rather be beaten, but she understood.

'Go straight to your room,' said Pa. 'I don't want to see your face at the dinner table.'

Carrie turned tail and stalked out of the room.

She hated both of them.

She hated Pa for being beastly and for ruining her life – and she hated Ma for being weak. Her mother *had* prevented Pa from beating her, but she hadn't exactly taken her side. And, once they had stormed round to St Mark's Avenue, indignant that Carrie had forged Pa's signature, Miss Bateman would have no choice but to stand her down.

Carrie lay down on the bed, railing against the injustice.

A couple of times, she heard a knock on the front door

and the low murmur of voices outside. She had no idea who was calling and – although she had a pretty good idea that the visitors were for her – she wasn't summoned. Switching off the lights and peering out the window didn't help either – it was a moonless night, the blackout was doing its job and she had no idea who the various footsteps belonged to.

Damn it all.

Half an hour later, Ma rapped on her door and came in bearing a bowl of soup and some rye loaf.

'Your father and I have decided you aren't to send or receive letters for the foreseeable,' she said, putting the supper tray carefully down on the dressing table.

'Visitors, neither, by the sound of it,' said Carrie, bitterly. Her mother didn't answer, so she pressed on. 'There are people I need to get messages to if you really are going to keep me in here,' she said. 'I'm due on shift at the ARP tomorrow evening and they'll be expecting me at Little Poppies in the morning . . .'

'That's all taken care of,' said Ma, straightening up and stretching her back.

'What do you mean?'

'I've already told them you won't be at Little Poppies.'

'Oh, Ma. I can't just not turn up.'

'Perhaps you should have thought of that before you started trying to pull the wool over our eyes,' said Ma tartly. 'Anyway, with the children back at school, I gather you won't be much missed.'

Ouch. That stung.

'And the ARP?'

'Your father is on his way over there as we speak.'

Carrie shut her eyes in embarrassment and humiliation. It was to be expected, but it was still awful.

'By the way,' added Ma. 'I meant what I said about letters, but there *is* one here from your cousin Violet that I will allow you to read and reply to.'

Carrie turned her face away. 'So kind,' she murmured under her voice.

This was all so unnecessarily humiliating.

'I've just received a letter from your aunt, so I know there's likely to be some distressing news in it,' added Ma in an altogether gentler tone.

That got Carrie's attention.

'Distressing?' she echoed, sitting bolt upright.

'I'm afraid so,' said Ma. 'You'll remember Ned, from the farm next door?'

How could she ever forget?

Summer days with his mouth against hers and their laughter echoing across the hills and valleys . . .

Her mother opened her mouth to carry on speaking and everything slowed down . . .

He might have failed his training . . .

Or maybe he'd had appendicitis . . .

Or maybe he'd even been slightly injured and . . .

'Killed . . . training flight . . . North Wales . . .'

Her mother's words hit her like an express train and Carrie shut her eyes to protect herself from their force. When she opened them again, Ma was peering down with concern.

'Are you all right, dear?'

'Quite all right, thank you.'

How was her voice sounding so *normal?*

'I know it's a shock, but you hardly knew the lad.'

Carrie didn't answer.

How could Ma possibly *not* have known? 'Pop your tray outside the door when you've finished,' she said. 'And then think about your recent behaviour and why we're so disappointed in you.'

And she disappeared.

Carrie slit the letter open and read the news of Ned's death in Violet's looping scrawl. Then she lay back on the bed and stared up at the ceiling.

Ned.

His golden hair. His honeyed kisses. The sparkle in his brown eyes.

All gone.

She hadn't said goodbye properly, hadn't told him how much his friendship meant to her, hadn't even tried to stay in touch. Oh, they had agreed not to, of course – and she had always known, deep down, that he wasn't the man for her – but, still, she mourned him. Her stomach twisted as she thought of him up in the skies, flying into danger in one of the very planes she had refused to assemble radios for. She crumpled the letter in her fist, her eyes stinging with unshed tears.

The war was suddenly real in a way it had never been before.

It had taken someone she had loved and nothing would ever be the same again.

Chapter Twenty-Six

Monday 25 November 1940

Carrie stood up slowly, her hands shaking as she smoothed the letter and tucked it under her mattress.

She badly needed some fresh air.

She turned off the lights in her room and wedged her dressing gown under the door to extinguish the sliver of light from the hallway. Then she opened the blackout blind and the window and leant out, elbows on the ledge outside. She welcomed the cold blast of winter air that greeted her – at least it made her feel *something*. Over to the left were the stark lines of the factory, just visible now that the cloud had moved and a scattering of stars punctuated the inky blackness . . .

It was there that she needed to be.

She could no longer hide behind moral objections . . .

Ouch!

What on earth was that?

Something small and hard, hitting her cheek and pinging off the windows. It was almost like hail, except that . . .

'Psst! *Carrie.*'

The voice was coming from below and it belonged to Sarah. Carrie craned her head further out of the window and could just make out her friend's upturned face in the flowerbed below.

'What's going on?' Carrie hissed.

'You tell me!' came the disembodied voice.

Carrie groaned. 'I wouldn't know where to start,' she said softly into the darkness.

'Well, don't worry about that now because he's coming up.'

'Coming up?'

Who?

Then Carrie felt the ivy twitch.

For a wild moment, she thought the 'he' might be Bobby and, despite it all, she worried for his safety. The ivy might have been allowed to do its own thing during the war, but Carrie doubted it would be thick and sturdy enough to support an adult male. Then, a small figure clambered over the railing onto the Harpers' balcony.

'*Alfie!*'

'Sarah wants me to fix a wire between our flats, he said, with an enormous grin.

'What?'

'I've already attached it on our side, and I've just got to thread it through the hook here with your washing line and then I'll go back to our flat and . . .'

'*Why?*'

Surely Sarah didn't expect her to tightrope across to freedom?

'So, you two can send messages, of course,' said Alfie matter-of-factly. And, when Carrie didn't immediately answer, 'She's given me a peg and I've got a letter here explaining it all.'

Carrie paused, working it out. The Harper Line started at a hook in the wall just inches from Carrie's bedroom window. She could reach out of her window and touch it. Similarly, the Turner Line started near Sarah's bedroom window on the other side of the road. Most of the washing lines extended no further than the nearest pavement, but the Turner Line, of course, had already broken with convention and was attached to the Harpers' pole. That meant that if a second thin wire or string was strung in parallel at the same height, it would be unnoticeable to all but the most observant of eyes.

It was audacious, but it might just work.

But was it worth the risk?

On balance, she decided that it was. Ma rarely went onto the balcony at this time of the year except to hang out the washing and if Carrie started volunteering to do it for her, she was unlikely to get caught.

And there was no doubt that it would be useful to be able to send and receive messages.

'Sarah said you'd pay me for my services,' said Alfie, cutting across her thoughts.

Carrie gave an indulgent chuckle. She was sure Sarah had said no such thing but, nonetheless, she rooted around in her handbag for her purse and felt around for a thrupenny bit.

'Not a word,' she said, as she pressed the coin into Alfie's sweaty palm.

'On my life,' said Alfie, passing her an envelope in return.

Seconds later, she heard him make his way down the ivy, some muffled words as he rendezvoused with Sarah and, shortly afterwards, the front door opposite slammed shut.

Despite the extreme awfulness of the evening, Carrie couldn't help but smile.

It was a ridiculous plan – childish, audacious, very Sarah! – but suddenly Carrie did feel a lot less alone. She shut the window, pulled down the blackout blind – goodness, war made everything so *complicated* – switched the light on, and then sat down on the bed. Ripping the letter open, she hastily scanned the contents.

Sarah wrote that she'd been concerned both by Carrie rushing out of the Remembrance Club and by subsequently seeing her being practically frogmarched home by her mother.

Was everything all right?

She had taken the liberty of knocking on Carrie's front door but had been given short shrift by her father. She knew that Carrie wouldn't be out for a few days and, in the meantime, was forbidden from speaking with her friends.

What on earth was going on?

She presumed Carrie hadn't suddenly come down with an infectious disease and therefore that she was in trouble for something. Presumably, her parents had found out about the ARP and hit the roof?

Hence the Wire and the Plan. At ten o'clock every evening that Sarah wasn't on duty, she would wait in her bedroom. If she had a message for Carrie, she would peg it to the wire and send it over; if not, she would simply wait for any messages to come through. She would be in place that evening and every evening thereafter until Carrie was released.

Carrie glanced at her watch. There was just over half an hour until ten o'clock, and she was going to be very busy indeed.

*

Firstly, Carrie wrote to Miss Bateman. Her old headmistress would, of course, know what had happened by now and Carrie cringed as she tried to imagine how the conversation with Pa might have transpired. She apologised for lying and for forging Pa's signature, and thanked Miss Bateman very much for trusting her with driving the ambulance. She thought of adding that she hoped she could report back on duty in the not-too-distant future but decided against it. Technically, her parents could put a stop to her volunteering until she was twenty-one and, besides, Miss Bateman probably wouldn't *want* her back after all this fuss. She felt terrible about it all, not least because the ARP was so important. The others would, of course, rally around, but she *had* rather left them all in the lurch . . .

Next, she wrote a quick note to Daisy. Again, she apologised for what had happened – she seemed to be doing a *lot* of apologising at the moment! – and hoped that Daisy hadn't got into real trouble on her behalf. And fancy Daisy ending up working at Chrysler! Did she know that Mabel Green was also working there? Perhaps she would make a point of looking her old classmate up and saying hello . . .

Carrie's last letter was for Bobby. She had anticipated that this would be most difficult to write but, once she got going, she was suddenly in no two minds as to what she wanted to say. There was no mention of Mabel . . . no mention of the scarf . . . she simply wrote that their friendship was over and that she wouldn't be returning to St Mark's Avenue. She asked Bobby to respect her decision and not to try and contact her in any way . . .

Dry-eyed and clearheaded, she re-read what she had written. Was that really what she wanted?

The answer was an emphatic 'yes'.

Bobby had *never* played straight with her.

He had blown hot and cold from the beginning, stringing her along for weeks and, just when she'd been comfortable – *thrilled* – that they were finally stepping out together, *Mabel* had entered the equation. And it didn't so much matter what they might or might not be up to together, it was the subterfuge and the lack of transparency that upset her the most . . .

Carrie had run out of patience.

She had given Bobby multiple chances, and she wasn't giving him any more.

Finally, Carrie scribbled a quick note to Sarah. She thanked her friend for devising this brilliant, mad, ridiculous scheme and hoped she wouldn't end up getting into trouble as a result. She asked her to forward the letters (she'd addressed the envelopes, sending Bobby's via Saints HQ, and enclosed the necessary stamps). And, yes, it was all going horribly wrong at home. Her parents *had* discovered she'd lied to them, but there was more to it than that. She had just discovered that Mr Two was involved with *Mabel* in some way. Both of them were being very shifty and, at the very least, one or more of them had lied to her about where they worked. Perhaps Mr Two had transferred to Chrysler, perhaps Mabel had transferred to Starfish on Richmond Park – she didn't know and perhaps it didn't much matter. But, as neither of them were coming clean with her, she had to assume that something nefarious was going on and that they were romantically involved . . .

Of course, Carrie conceded, Mabel may not know that Bobby was involved with someone else, let alone a friend. Maybe she should give her the benefit of the doubt. But, on the other hand, no. If Mabel really was an innocent party, why had she been so secretive about being challenged over Bobby's scarf?

Carrie was almost in tears by this time. Almost for the first time, she acknowledged the strength of her feelings for Bobby. And Mabel was her *friend*; a relatively new one, to be sure, but one that she loved and trusted.

Their betrayal – because it really looked like one – was utterly heartbreaking.

Carrie sighed as she signed her letter to Sarah and popped it in a large envelope along with the three others.

She glanced at her watch; goodness, it was five to ten already. She snapped the light off, stuffed her dressing gown into place, and pulled up the blackout blind. She opened the window, groped across to the string and, with trembling fingers, started to peg the letter into place . . .

'What on earth's going on in here?'

It was Ma, struggling to push the door open against the dressing gown.

Carrie wheeled around. 'Quick, Ma; the blackout,' she hissed as light flooded the bedroom.

She started to pull down the blind, but Ma had already snapped the hall light off and pulled Carrie's bedroom door shut behind her.

'What are you doing?' Ma persisted.

'Just getting some fresh air,' said Carrie, holding the letter behind her back.

'I've come to get your supper tray,' said Ma, rather pointedly. 'Don't stand at the window too long – you'll catch your death of cold.'

And she was gone.

Carrie was left with a dilemma. She had a matter of seconds to pull the letter across to Sarah, but Ma would be in the kitchen, far too close for comfort to the wire outside. But Carrie didn't really have a choice. Time was of the essence and she really didn't want to wait until the following day.

Slowly, slowly, Carrie leant out of the window and pegged her letter into place. Its weight made the wire sag well below the washing line and, for a moment, she was afraid the whole contraption would simply collapse onto the road below. To her relief, however, it held firm and she began to pull gently on the wire. The letter set off jerkily across the road and, despite everything, she stifled a giggle.

This was absolutely ludicrous!

After a while, she realised the letter was moving of its own accord, which meant that Sarah must be pulling on the wire as well. Eventually, she felt three little tugs and assumed, with a little sigh of relief, that the envelope had been safely received.

Mission complete.

Carrie shut the window and pulled the blind back down. What a day!

Tuesday 26 November 1940

The full ramifications of everything that had happened hit Carrie the following day.

All things considered, she'd slept pretty well, but she woke early the next morning with a nauseous headache, which kept her bedbound.

She wouldn't have been able to help at Little Poppies even had she wanted to.

She dozed on and off throughout the day, and when she was fully awake, found that she couldn't stop crying for Ned. She knew she was mourning their past – there had never been the option of a future – but, still, her grief was very real. She had loved their time together and she had loved Ned, and it all seemed so arbitrary and unfair that Ned was dead and Bobby hadn't even had to fight.

By the end of the day, she felt well enough to pen a long letter to Violet together with a note to Ned's parents. To both, she wrote that she would make sure his sacrifice was not in vain – and that she would be honoured to start assembling aircraft radios in his memory.

By half past nine, Carrie was pacing her room, and by ten to ten, the lights were off and the window open in readiness for any 'deliveries'. She found her heart was thumping as the allotted time approached and was surprised just how relieved she was when there was a twitch on the wire. It started running between her fingers and, finally, a fat envelope nudged against her hand. Carrie unpinned it, gave three little tugs on the string, and shut the window as quietly as she could. Seconds later, the blackout blind was down and Carrie was back in bed, slitting the envelope open by the thin beam of her torch.

Sarah was clearly cock-a-hoop that her scheme had worked. She wrote that she had delivered all Carrie's messages, but there were no replies as of yet. She had also tried to talk to Mabel about what had happened the day before but, sadly, Mabel had shut her down straight away. It was all very strange and sad from someone they thought had been a good friend, but she would keep trying. She had thought it circumspect not to mention anything to Mabel about the wire and the messages for fear that she might give the game away.

And, in the meantime, there was nothing to do but wait.

Chapter Twenty-Seven

Wednesday 27 November 1940

They couldn't keep her locked up forever.

Early the next morning, Pa arrived at her bedroom door and announced that Carrie would be let out of her room under strict conditions. She would be allowed to resume her work within the estate, but she would not be allowed to step foot outside it until further notice. To that end, she would be chaperoned at all times by either her mother or by Mrs Armstrong.

At any other time, Carrie would have found these stipulations unbearable and would have railed loudly at the indignity. Today, devastated by Ned's death and buffeted both by Bobby's betrayal and Mabel's apparent duplicity, she simply didn't have the strength to fight.

'I understand,' she said. She took a deep breath and ploughed on before she could change her mind. 'But I'd like to assemble the radios rather than go back to Little Poppies.'

Her father blinked. 'And to what do we owe this volte-face?' he demanded.

Carrie shrugged. 'Well, the children are back at school, so I think I can be spared at the Remembrance Club,' she said. 'And I just want to do my bit. Everything feels different now Ned . . .'

She trailed off.

She really did *not* want to cry in front of her father.

Pa nodded. 'I'm sorry about the lad,' he said.

Carrie nodded. 'It just seems so final and so unjust.'

'That's war for you,' said Pa, bluntly. 'Now, about my meeting with that blasted Miss Bateman . . .'

Carrie sighed. 'Please Pa, can we not? Not now.'

Pa pursed his lips. 'Very well,' he said. 'Well, I dare say they'll be pleased enough for another pair of hands inside the factory, even one as clumsy as yours.'

Half an hour later, Mrs Armstrong – presumably plucked from her usual duties at Little Poppies – arrived to accompany Carrie for the short walk over to the factory.

She strode ahead of Carrie with a purposeful air, tall and austere in her tailored navy coat and, although her expression gave nothing away, Carrie could almost feel the weight of everyone's disappointment each time she glanced over her shoulder.

Carrie puffed out her cheeks.

It was all so ridiculous.

She gazed up at the familiar Poppy Factory building. The sweeping curves and geometric lines exuded an elegance totally out of place with the grim urgency of war.

Everything had changed.

She had changed.

But, when they reached the entrance to the factory, still she hesitated.

Part of her wanted to turn back, still hating the idea of contributing to the war machine. She stepped cautiously through the entrance of the factory, her heart pounding.

She wasn't sure if she was ready, or if this would ever feel right, but she had to try.

For Ned.

And for all the Neds who wouldn't come back.

The Ministry of Aircraft Production had taken over the top floor of the Poppy Factory.

As Carrie climbed the metal stairs, unfamiliar noises – high-pitched beeps, a soft hiss and pop, female chatter – were the first indication that things had changed.

Then came the smells: the pungent aroma of metal solder, the faint scent of heated electronics, the tinge of burning.

Finally, Mrs Armstrong led her into the room itself . . . and Carrie could only stand and stare.

Rows of long workbenches stretched out before her, each one equipped with screwdrivers, wire strippers and a variety of mysterious, shiny components Carrie couldn't yet identify. Women and men worked side by side, heads bent in concentration, faces set and focussed. Some used magnifying lenses to peer at fine wiring or circuit boards. Others, in goggles and protective clothing, used soldering irons to join wires and electronic components, their hands swift and sure. Despite the low thrum of conversation and the occasional bark of laughter, there was a tautness, an intensity to the air.

'I'm here to help,' she said, as Harry approached. 'Tell me where to start.'

Harry looked her over, surprised for only a moment, then nodded. 'Good,' he replied, simply. 'We can use every pair of hands we can get. Come with me.'

*

Carrie followed Harry to an empty seat. From the other side of the room, Sarah's eyes widened in surprise, and Carrie gave a tiny shake of her head by way of reply.

Despite appearances, nothing was back to normal.

Carrie sat down next to Eloise's mother, Nora, and Harry briefed her on what she needed to do. Her job was to connect wires to the various components on the radio's circuit board. Firstly, she had to measure and cut wires to specific lengths, ensuring they would fit neatly between connection points without excess slack or being too tight. Next, the plastic insulation needed to be stripped from the ends of the wires before they were welded into place with a soldering iron. Finally, each connection had to be double-checked — ensuring there were no loose wires or solder accidentally connecting two points — before testing the circuit with a multimeter.

There was so much to do.

So much to remember!

To say nothing of the need for accuracy, intense focus and nimble fingers.

Carrie tried to suppress the knot in her stomach and the pressure of unspoken expectations. She puffed out her cheeks and looked around the room with fresh eyes, full of admiration for the women who were already rising to the challenge. To be honest, it was hard to reconcile these women with the ones she'd grown up with on the estate. There was busybody Mrs Fenton from the ground floor flat, her brow furrowed in concentration as she fitted a component into place with the precision of a surgeon. And there was Clara's mother, hunched over a workbench, deftly assembling a tangle of wires Carrie couldn't begin to understand. These were women who had once been confined to domesticity – their concerns no larger than the day's errands – and yet here they were . . . already making a difference.

Carrie took a deep breath and reached for the wire-cutters. The radios were a lifeline for the pilots. Precision was key and there was no room for mistakes.

She couldn't be found wanting.

By the end of her first working day, Carrie was absolutely exhausted.

She was too wrung out to care that Mrs Armstrong materialised by her side whenever she queued for a sandwich or even dashed to the lavvies. What, exactly, did she think Carrie was going to do? Run to St Mark's Avenue or Richmond Park?

But there was an honesty to her tiredness, and Carrie was just relieved she hadn't made too much of a hash of things. She had a feeling she wasn't the quickest or the nimblest of workers – and she *had* made rather a mess of the solder from time to time – but Nora reassured her she had seen far worse. Almost nicest of all were the two girls in the washrooms who made a point of saying how lovely it was to see Carrie Harper mucking in with all the rest.

That meant more than anything.

Her erstwhile hero, Santayana, might not be too impressed that she wasn't learning the lessons of the past, but things seemed somewhat different when you were right in the middle of them. It had taken the death of someone she cared for, but if it was a choice between philosophy and saving someone she loved, well, she now knew which side of the fence she wanted to be on.

At ten o'clock, an envelope arrived from Sarah.

There was a brief message from Sarah herself, saying that she enclosed a reply from Daisy and adding that she had been tempted to add some treats for Carrie, but she'd been worried the wire would collapse under the weight! She would just send Carrie her love and would hang around for fifteen minutes for any reply.

Slightly nervously, Carrie opened Daisy's letter.

But, to her relief, it was lovely.

After reassuring Carrie that she wasn't in *too* much trouble, Daisy went on to apologise for how she had behaved at school the day of the results. The truth of the matter was that she was so proud of Carrie for volunteering for the ARP and only wished that she was half so brave. And she had been wrong about Sarah. She had been both jealous and suspicious of her new friendship with Carrie, but she could see now that Sarah was an absolute brick. She hoped that Carrie would forgive her for her pig-headedness and that they could go back to being friends.

Carrie smiled and a knot that had become lodged underneath her breastbone gently melted away. Daisy had been her friend for a long time and Carrie realised that she had missed her.

But as she carried on reading the letter, her smile turned to a frown.

Because Daisy wrote that Carrie must have been mistaken about Mabel. Daisy was actually working in the personnel department at Chrysler and, on receiving Carrie's letter, she had taken the liberty of looking up which department Mabel Green was working in.

And she could categorically tell Carrie that no one named Mabel Green had *ever* been employed by the company.

Stay calm.

Stay calm and *think*.

On automatic pilot, Carrie scribbled out a message to Sarah.

'Mabel has never *worked at the Chrysler Factory! What now?'*

Once the letter had been sent across the wire and Carrie had received the three little tugs by way of reply, Carrie lay down on her bed.

What now, indeed?

She had known, at some level, that Mabel had not been being entirely honest with her. There was her paranoia that Carrie was following or spying on her for one thing – as well as the fact that Carrie had simply seen Mabel in the environs of Richmond Park far too many times for someone who claimed to be working elsewhere.

But what did it *mean*?

Carrie, herself, had not been entirely honest with her parents – indeed, she had outright lied – but her intentions had undoubtedly been sound. She had wanted nothing more than to do her bit for King and Country and to save innocent lives.

She mustn't just jump to the worst conclusion with Mabel.

Her erstwhile friend deserved some grace. Maybe she simply worked at Starfish with Bobby and had gone above and beyond to keep it under wraps.

But the more Carrie thought about it, the more all sorts of nefarious possibilities started drip, drip, dripping into her mind.

Could Mabel be up to no good?

There seemed to be more to it than the whole Richmond Park thing.

Something much closer to home.

Carrie screwed up her face as she remembered following Mabel down to the cellar of the Remembrance Club a couple of days earlier. She had been so flustered at being caught snooping around that she hadn't really registered what was going on. But in the cold light of day, it was clear that Mabel had been coming from the part of the cellar that was allegedly horribly damp, very dangerous and completely out of bounds.

What on earth had Mabel been doing there?

Monitoring?

Repairs?

Or something more suspicious?

And then there was that time that Alfie and the others had played Sardines down there. Carrie could understand Mabel's annoyance at the bottle of ginger beer being stolen, but – that notwithstanding – she had completely overreacted about the whole thing.

Could there be something else going on?

Some sort of smuggling?

Could Mabel even be a spy?

After all, she had arrived at the Poppy Factory at the start of the war, and no one really knew anything about her.

Carrie was surprised at her visceral response to the idea

of Mabel being up to something underhand. Her heart rate ratcheted up a gear and she could almost taste her *rage*.

Goodness, how much had changed there too.

University had always been the ultimate goal; when, exactly, had doing one's bit and being patriotic become quite so important to her?

In the meantime, what to do?

She had missed her chance to ask Sarah to go up to Starfish and check if Mabel was working there, but she would do so the very next night.

But, the next evening, a message from Sarah arrived before she had a chance to send her own.

> I hope you don't mind, but I took it upon myself to go up to Richmond Park in my lunch hour. It took all my powers of persuasion to get in and to present myself at Starfish, but I told them I had important messages for both Bobby and Mabel.
>
> I wasn't particularly surprised to discover that no one called Mabel Green has recently started working there.
>
> But – brace yourself – it turns out that no one called Bobby Roscoe has ever worked there either.

Carrie held the letter to her chest.

Shocked to the core, she also felt utterly betrayed.

If Bobby had lied to her about something as fundamental as his place of work, where else might he have been selective with the facts?

And might he, too, be up to no good?

Carrie couldn't decide whether she was more devastated

that Bobby might be up to no good, or the probability that he was romantically involved with Mabel.

Either way, it was absolutely devastating.

How she wished she had never told him about the Poppy Factory radios.

Carrie wondered if she should tell someone. The trouble was, who? And what on earth would she say? Lying to someone about where you worked might be morally suspect in the usual scheme of things, but it wasn't actually against the law, and could actually make sense in wartime.

Unless she really suspected that Bobby or Mabel had committed a crime, there was really nothing to tell.

One thing was for certain, though, she was going to do anything she could to get into the Remembrance Club cellar and find out what they were up to.

Chapter Twenty-Eight

Thursday 28 November 1940

In the meantime, Carrie kept her head down in the factory as she tried to get to grips with the radios. The second day was much easier than the first and she began to enjoy sitting in the beautifully proportioned room with the autumn light streaming through the high windows. Her work picked up in speed and accuracy and Harry even made a point of praising her.

Emboldened by her success, Carrie asked Mrs Armstrong if she might take a walk that lunchtime. She had another rotten headache – it was hot and noisy and stuffy in the factory – and she was longing for a breath of fresh air. Even a few turns around the Remembrance Club might help.

Mrs Armstrong was happy to oblige and the two set off together, heading down the path from the factory to the club. And then Mrs Armstrong played straight into Carrie's hands by saying she needed to nip inside to talk to Mrs Green and to pop to the lavvies without queuing up with everyone else inside the factory.

'No problem, at all, Mrs Armstrong,' said Carrie, politely. 'In fact, I might do the same, if that's all right with you? I can pop down to the one in the cellar if you'd like to make sure I don't bump into anyone?'

Mrs Armstrong nodded distractedly. 'Of course,' she said. 'And, by the way, might I add that I think this charade is perfectly ridiculous? For what it's worth, I'm *proud* of you for defying the old man and volunteering at the ARP and I made a point of telling your father so. The only reason I suggested chaperoning you was to stop your parents incarcerating you day and night for the foreseeable future.'

Without another word, she bustled off to the ladies' lavatories on the first floor of the Remembrance Club. Carrie stared after her thoughtfully. Should she tell Mrs Armstrong her suspicions?

No point – they were nothing *but* suspicions for now.

Instead, she took a deep breath and hurried downstairs to the basement. Glancing around to make sure she wasn't being watched, she ran straight to the back of the building, stopping in front of the stout wooden door that led to the out-of-bounds room.

It was locked.

Of course, it was.

Carrie waggled the handle and applied a little force, but the door held firm. Then she noticed that there were three locks and one large padlock securing it. Damp was, of course, injurious to human health, but it was hardly a catastrophe. Was it really necessary to go to such lengths to keep people out?

Either way, there wasn't much else Carrie could do for the time being.

She scampered back upstairs and was waiting innocuously in the hallway when Mrs Armstrong reappeared from the upstairs washrooms. Once outside, she chattered brightly about nothing in particular whilst they walked around the Remembrance Club but, all the while, her eyes were peeled for . . . well, she wasn't sure exactly what.

No cellar windows.

No recessed doors that might give access to the lower room. Nothing at all.

Carrie sighed deeply, shutting her eyes momentarily, then tripped over her own feet and nearly went flying.

'Careful, dear,' said Mrs Armstrong, grabbing her forearm. 'These coal plates can be such a menace.'

Oh.

A coal plate.

A cast-iron metal plate with a small metal ring set into the pavement, it had been installed in the last century to allow coal to be deposited directly into the coal cellar without bringing it through the house. This one was circular and about eighteen inches in diameter.

Might a slim woman be able to fit through the coal hole that the plate was covering?

It would be a tight squeeze, to be sure, but it might just prove possible to lower herself feet first, holding onto the sides for control. It wouldn't be plain sailing, of course; the coal hole would open onto the cellar space below and there could be a significant drop. And all sorts of other things might also go wrong; cuts and scrapes from the edge of the coal hole to say nothing of not having anywhere to brace her feet and hands.

Maybe she should ask Sarah to attempt it.

Yes, she would explain it all that night.

Because, the more she thought about it, the more she was sure that Mabel – and perhaps Bobby? – was hiding something down there.

That afternoon, Carrie found it hard to concentrate.

Her mind was whirring, trying to think of how to put

her highly audacious plan into action. Whoever attempted it would need something like a pry bar to prise up the recessed coal plate. Most household metal objects had been swept away to make weapons, of course, but luckily there were metal objects aplenty on the factory floor. The closest thing to a crowbar was the base of her soldering iron, but Carrie knew she would never get away with pilfering that! But that large flat-headed screwdriver could be wedged under the edge of the coal plate to give a bit of leverage, and that large spanner with the adjustable head might work if the angled end was inserted just right. Even that metal file might do at a pinch . . .

Carrie tried to catch Sarah's eye. Maybe the two could rendezvous in the lavvies and Carrie could explain what she had in mind, because it would prove easier for Sarah to smuggle the various items home. But Sarah was concentrating hard and barely looked up. When Carrie eventually got her attention and tried to look meaningfully at her, Sarah simply mimed writing a note . . .

In the end, Carrie 'borrowed' all three items from various benches around the room — scooping them into her bag when everyone else was still coming back from their tea break. She would replace them all, of course — she wasn't a thief — but it might be that a combination of tools would be necessary.

If she ever had the opportunity — and the courage — to attempt it.

Chapter Twenty-Nine

Thursday 28 November 1940

As it happened, the opportunity presented itself that very evening.

Carrie spent a quiet evening with her mother – her father was out patrolling the streets with the newly renamed Home Guard and Ma made a big point of allowing her into the living room – and went to her room at a quarter past nine. She drafted a message for Sarah and then suddenly remembered that Sarah was on duty with the ARP that evening . . .

Drat!

Maybe she should just head out for the Remembrance Club herself.

If she waited until after Father was home at three am to avoid the chance of bumping into him, she was unlikely to get caught.

She set her alarm, popped it under her pillow so as not to disturb anyone else, and went to bed.

Carrie woke with the air raid siren ringing in her ears.

She froze, pulse quickening as the deep, undulating sound sliced through the night. Then she snapped the light on and quickly glanced at her watch.

Two thirty in the morning.

'Carrie!' Despite the number of times they had all been through this, Ma's voice trembled with urgency from the doorway. She bustled in, clutching her cardigan tightly around her shoulders, her face pale and taut. 'We must go. Quickly now!'

Carrie was already out of bed, slipping her coat on over her pyjamas and grabbing her capacious bag. Her thoughts turned to Sarah, up on the roof of the Remembrance Club, watching over the Poppy Factory with the ARP, and she pushed away the thought that *she* should be at Saints HQ . . .

She followed her mother down the stairs and out into the almost pitch-black street, alive with the sound of hurried footsteps and low, anxious murmurs. It was a cloudy night – the Luftwaffe clearly no longer waiting for perfect conditions in which to strike – and the familiar road was transformed by eerie shadows.

As the two emerged past the flats on the other side of the road, Carrie glanced towards the Remembrance Club. She could just make out a silhouette – a lone figure on the rooftop and very possibly Sarah – standing watch against the ominous horizon.

She really should be helping . . .

She shouldn't be trotting passively to the air raid shelter . . .

She should be at St Mark's Avenue with the ambulance, just in case . . .

Carrie stopped dead in her tracks. Ma kept walking, oblivious, and was quickly swallowed up by the night.

Carrie sensed rather than watched her go . . . and then she started running.

Every second mattered.

Heart pounding, she darted around to the far side of the Remembrance Club – well away from the people streaming into the basement air raid shelter – only stopping when she reached the coal plate.

So, this was what she was planning to do!

She wasn't going to rejoin her colleagues at St Mark's Avenue.

She wasn't going to help Sarah.

She had the 'borrowed' tools in her bag and she *was* going to find out what Mabel was hiding.

Carrie crouched beside the heavy iron lid, half-expecting to be confronted.

But it was quiet here. On the other side of the Remembrance Club, people would be filing silently in through the main doors and down to the air raid shelter – Carrie could hear the low murmur of voices and the odd cough – but there was no reason for anyone to come round to the weed-covered parking space on this side of the building.

Carrie pulled the borrowed tools out of her bag and started trying to lift the lid.

It wasn't easy.

The metal file quickly snapped under pressure – oops! – and both the screwdriver and the spanner proved to be insufficiently powerful levers. To Carrie's frustration, the heavy lid remained stubbornly in place, refusing to budge an iota.

Gah!

Maybe the damn thing had been cemented into place.

Carrie was just about to give it all up as a bad – *ridiculous!* – job when, on a whim, she decided to try both the spanner and the screwdriver together. Might that provide twice as much power? She inserted the tools, pushed with all her might and no one was more surprised when the lid slowly and silently rose a few inches . . .

Throwing herself to one side, Carrie managed to get her shoulder under the metal plate and pushed the lid over to one side. The resultant clang seemed to reverberate around the estate and she held her breath as the echoes died away.

Surely someone would hear and come to investigate now?

But no one did. With Germans overhead, no one was going to worry about a random clang close to hand . . .

Carrie crouched beside the coal hole and quickly turned her torch on. It didn't much help – merely illuminating a gaping black void – so she snapped it off again and tried to get her thoughts into some sort of order.

Was she mad?

Taking bold action and putting herself in danger was one thing, but was she sure she was doing it for the right reasons?

She was.

Mabel – and Bobby – might be a spy or a criminal.

Surely, that was enough?

The narrow opening was just wide enough for Carrie to wriggle through.

Carrie forced herself to breathe slowly but, even so, her heartbeat thundered in her ears as she carefully slid her legs inside, her coat snagging on the rough stone. She should have taken it off, but it was too late now. Inch by inch, she lowered herself into the cold, musty emptiness, the muscles in her arm screaming for mercy.

How much further was there to go?

The simple answer was that Carrie had no idea.

She should have put the illuminated torch in her mouth so that she at least had some idea of the drop but, clot that she was, she hadn't thought to do so and now she didn't have the strength to haul herself up again.

Why was she such an idiot?

Sarah should have been the one to do this.

She had ten times more bravery and common sense than Carrie did . . .

Panic rose in Carrie's throat. Her arms were fully extended and she was just going to have to let go . . .

She shut her eyes and let herself drop.

Oh, please don't let it hurt too much . . .

Carrie's feet landed with a soft thud on a wooden floor less than a foot below her.

She hadn't even fallen over!

She was tempted to laugh out loud in relief, but she wasn't out of danger yet. There could be anything in this room.

Any*one*.

Mabel and Bobby could be in here, part of a German spy ring, ready to do all sorts of unspeakable things to her. There could be weird surveillance equipment, banks of screens, interrogation equipment . . .

But it didn't *feel* like there was anyone in there.

It was pitch black, for one thing, and silent as the grave, for another.

The faint smell of dank coal dust clung to the air, but there was something else as well; a musty, earthy smell with an acidic undertone Carrie couldn't quite place.

One thing was for certain; it certainly wasn't damp . . .

Carrie pulled her torch out of her coat pocket and, after a moment's hesitation, switched it on. The beam flickered to life as she nervously swept it across the room.

No people.

No strange machinery.

Just some old crates, a couple of bags of coal and a few pieces of discarded wooden furniture.

Carrie exhaled a ragged breath.

She made her way through the cellar – the thin torch beam only able to illuminate a couple of yards in front of her – her palm against the cold, gritty stone walls. In front of her were some shelves, carefully covered in dust sheets. Somewhat disinterestedly – the shelves probably housed tools or tins of old paint – Carrie carefully tweaked the nearest sheet to one side, wrinkling up her nose in expectation of choking dust as she did so.

And then she took a step back, with an exclamation of surprise.

Of *shock*!

The shelves contained books; thick-spined volumes, their cracked covers almost indistinguishable in the darkness. Now Carrie could pinpoint the smell she'd noticed earlier. It was the mildew of old paper mingled with the scent of old leather bindings and the sharp tang of rusted metal. It brought her straight back to Richmond Library and the first time she'd met Bobby . . .

Pushing that firmly from her mind, Carrie reached for

the nearest volume and slid it carefully out from between its neighbours.

This wasn't any old book.

Bound in rich, worn leather, its edges were embossed in delicate gold leaf – dulled by time, certainly, but still gleaming faintly. Carrie turned a couple of thick, textured pages, marvelling at the meticulously inked calligraphy, dark and elegant against the cream parchment. There were swirling vines, gilded flowers and tiny depictions of mythical creatures; there were saints or kings dressed in jewelled robes, their faces alive with expression. The pigments were vibrant even in the dim torchlight: deep reds, lapis blue and bright verdant greens . . .

No ordinary book indeed . . .

The next volume was smaller but no less exquisite, its cover illustrated with an intricate knot embossed in silver. Inside, the text spiralled in an unfamiliar language, decorated with geometric borders inked in the same lustrous colours. Carrie felt a rush of awe – but also a shiver of fear. These books were priceless, and there was no knowing the lengths that whoever had secreted them here would go to to protect them.

She should get out.

But, somehow, she couldn't.

Open-mouthed, she prowled around the shelves – and there were rows and rows of them – lifting the dust sheets, inspecting the contents. Not all the books were ancient. Some were modern, their brittle pages rustling and crumpling slightly under her fingers. Carrie was no expert, but she recognised them as rare, controversial or culturally significant works. *All Quiet on the Western Front*, banned by the

Nazis for its anti-war sentiments. Shakespeare and Dickens and other books linked to English history. Philosophical or revolutionary texts by thinkers like John Locke, Karl Marx and Voltaire – books representing ideas about individual freedom, political philosophy or social justice. Scientific texts on physics and medicine, together with the journals of prominent scientists. She would probably even find Santayana if she looked hard enough. These weren't just pages bound together. They were pieces of human history . . .

The question was, what on earth were they all doing *here*?

Had Mabel taken – *stolen* – them alone or was she in league with others?

How did Bobby fit into the picture?

And what on earth did they intend to do with them all? Carrie knew that the Nazis raided and plundered valuable items of cultural significance across the Channel.

Is that where these were headed, too?

And why were they *here*, beneath a building on the Poppy Factory estate?

A volley of coughing close at hand almost shocked Carrie out of her skin.

Suddenly, she was acutely aware that there were people huddled in the basement room next door. Now she was attuned to it, low murmurs and the occasional laugh filtered through the walls, reminding her that any misplaced noise could draw unwanted attention. And, even as the thought crossed her mind, the cellar door rattled slightly. Carrie froze, her heart pounding, half-expecting the door to swing open at any second. Panic surged through her as she remembered she wasn't supposed to be there.

She switched off her torch and pressed herself against the wall, the cold stone biting through her coat.

Nothing happened.

It must have been the wind, or a figment of her over-wrought imagination. Either way, there was nothing more she could do for the time being. She needed to get out of there.

Trying to calm her breathing, Carrie started making her way back to the coal hole. The fear of discovery twisted in her stomach – she needed to be quick. Here was the coal hole; the clouds had parted and the moon was lighting it from above. Had she realised it was a good five feet above her head? It was much too high – even in her panicked state – to jump and grab.

Carrie's fear ratcheted up a gear.

What on earth should she do now?

She glanced around for a ladder; there might be one to access the top shelves – although they weren't particularly high – or even an older one for maintenance.

There was no immediate sign of one.

She would just have to stack some objects on top of each other. The largest, heaviest books were the obvious candidates, but, even in the circumstances, Carrie couldn't bring herself to press such beautiful and valuable man-uscripts into action. Instead, she hastily placed a couple of crates on top of an old wooden table and prayed that the precarious pile wouldn't shift and collapse under her weight. She clambered up the makeshift ladder as carefully and lightly as she could – holding her breath every time the crates creaked and grumbled – and reached up for the opening.

It was within her grasp.

Carrie pulled herself up, debating whether or not to kick the crates away to try and hide the fact that she had been there. She decided against it – the resulting crash was likely to attract unwanted attention. Even as it was, every small sound felt amplified, echoing through the cellar.

Eventually, and with some difficulty, she wriggled up through the coal hole, twisting around so that she ended up sitting beside it. She lowered the plate as silently as she could and melted into the shadow of the Remembrance Club.

She had done it!

Although what she was going to do now, goodness only knew.

She had discovered something far bigger than she'd ever imagined, and she could only hope that she was up to whatever came next.

Chapter Thirty

Friday 29 November 1940

Carrie stood, pressed against the Remembrance Club wall, and considered her options.

The all-clear hadn't sounded and the searchlights in the park were still punctuating the night sky, so the danger clearly hadn't passed. Carrie knew she should really make her way over to the air raid shelter and join her mother. She would come up with some feeble excuse to explain her absence; maybe she would say she'd left something at home or perhaps she had stopped to help someone who had fallen over . . .

Goodness, when had she turned into such a *liar*?

A movement from the Remembrance Club rooftop made Carrie change her mind. Suddenly, she wanted nothing more than to be with Sarah and to tell her what she had discovered. Two Poppy Girls were better than one and, together, surely, they could work out what to do next.

No sooner had the idea come into Carrie's mind than she dumped her metal tools behind the bushes and was off, dashing into the empty, echoing Remembrance Club and running lightly up the stairs. She had never been onto the roof before – hadn't been part of the little gang of children who had trespassed there back in the day – but it wasn't difficult to find the way. On the top landing, a wooden door was ajar with a metal ladder leading upwards . . .

Carrie's breath came out in sharp puffs as she climbed the final rungs and emerged onto the rooftop. The searchlights were so much brighter up here that it was all she could do not to screw up her face like a little girl. The air tasted of ash and danger and, in front of her, chimneys rose like watchful sentries, their silhouettes stark against the starry sky. A narrow terrace, with a low, ivy-covered retaining wall, wound ahead of her around the building. There was no immediate sign of Sarah – or of anyone else for that matter – so Carrie set off along the terrace, praying she didn't slip on the uneven surface or stumble over a creeping ivy tendril.

Eventually, Carrie spotted Sarah standing quietly, barely visible in the darkness. She was gripping a pair of binoculars and raking them across the empty night sky, her breath barely a whisper in the cool night air. Carrie couldn't help stopping and watching her for a moment. She looked so different from the silly, slapdash girl of just a few months ago. Carrie moved on, her footsteps muffled on the mossy tiles.

Sarah started as she approached. 'It's you,' she said, almost accusingly. 'What on earth are you doing here?'

Carrie opened her mouth and then shut it again.

How to explain what she had just discovered?

'Are you quite all right?' said Sarah, in an altogether softer voice.

'She's hiding things,' Carrie burst out. 'Books! In the cellar.'

It was a relief to say the words out loud.

Sarah's brow creased with confusion. 'Who is?' she said. 'What books?'

'Mabel!' shouted Carrie, still struggling to believe it herself. 'I think she's stolen them. Just like she stole those sweets in Woollies.'

Sarah blinked slowly. 'Right,' she said, shaking her head from side to side. 'Look, even if she *has* pinched a couple of library books, does it really matter?'

'*Yes!* You don't understand.'

'Maybe not. But I'm on duty and this will have to wait . . .'

Suddenly, a high-pitched whine cut through the air, growing louder by the second. Carrie's eyes snapped to the horizon, heart freezing in her chest. A German bomber was gliding through the black sky, its silhouette framed by the weak moonlight.

'Get down!' Carrie shouted, grabbing Sarah, and pulling her behind the low wall.

Seconds later there was a loud explosion in the town centre. The girls locked eyes and then put their heads over the parapet in time to see flames shoot into the night sky and turn the world orange. Sarah pulled out her radio and started talking urgently into it.

'It's the town hall or thereabouts,' said Carrie, her breath coming in little raggedy gasps. 'Oh God, those poor people.'

'It's not our patch,' said Sarah, putting the radio down. She sounded calm enough, but her eyes were wide and dilated with shock.

Carrie nodded. No matter how much one might want to help, it was one of the cardinal rules of the ARP that volunteers from one station didn't leave their positions until the air raid was over and they knew their area was safe. Then again, she wasn't on duty, and she didn't volunteer for the Poppy Factory ARP anyway. There was nothing to stop *her* going across and seeing what she could do to help . . .

But no sooner had Carrie stood up than another explosion tore through the air and the night sky lit up again. This blast was further away – down towards the railway station – but it was quickly followed by a third. Then another – and another – until when Carrie peeked over the parapet, it looked as though the whole of Richmond was on fire.

At a pause in the bombing, Carrie got shakily to her feet again.

She would head into town and . . .

Boom!

The bomb exploded so close to where Carrie was standing that it felt as if it had gone off in her head. The building below started shaking as though it might simply crumble away, and Carrie flung herself to the ground again. For a moment, she could only lie there, pressed against the cold rooftop, her ears ringing and her heart pounding in her throat. Other members of the ARP had joined them now – Miss Arnott and others Carrie didn't know – their faces illuminated by the hellish glow of the fires now consuming half the town.

'That could have been us,' Sarah breathed, her voice trembling.

Carrie nodded and swallowed hard. Then, as one, they got to their feet and ran around the side of the building to see what had been hit.

They stopped, simply unable to make sense of what lay below them.

Because the shelter under the bowling green – where people had taken refuge just an hour ago – was now a smouldering ruin.

Chapter Thirty-One

Friday 29 November 1940

Sarah was the first to move.

'Come on!' she shouted, yelling into her radio and sprinting away without a backwards glance.

The weight of what she was seeing settled over Carrie like a suffocating blanket. She let out a guttural cry.

'Ma,' she wailed.

And then she set off in hot pursuit.

Please let her be brave enough to cope with whatever lay ahead.

Carrie caught up with Sarah – still shouting into her radio – in the queue for the ladder.

When it was their turn, the two girls scrambled down as quickly as they could, feet barely touching the rungs. As they tore down the stairs, Sarah – naturally – pulled ahead. The smell of smoke clung to the air and the distant wail of sirens filled the night. But it was the panicked screaming closer to hand that turned Carrie's insides and made her heart pound faster.

Don't think, Carrie.

Just *do*.

Carrie followed Sarah out of the Remembrance Club. They raced down the path and across the lawn, dodging debris and disoriented people. The shelter, or what was left of it, was a scene of total devastation – twisted metal, crumbling walls and a gaping hole where the bomb had torn through. The rescue teams hadn't yet arrived, but survivors – their faces and nightclothes covered in dust and blood – were crawling out and stumbling around looking for their loved ones.

It was like a scene from a disaster film.

To Carrie's relief, she spotted Ma straight away, helping to reunite a little girl with her father. Ma spotted Carrie at the same time and came rushing over.

'I didn't know where you were,' she said frantically, folding Carrie into a bear hug and kissing her hair.

'I'm sorry, Ma . . .'

'I couldn't bear it if . . .'

'I know. I'm here. But I've got to go and help.'

Carrie waited for her mother to demur. To tell her not to be so silly and to insist Carrie accompany her to the other shelter.

But, to her amazement, her mother just nodded. 'What can I do?' she asked.

'Get yourself safe,' said Carrie. And then, when her mother didn't move, 'A lot of these people are very shocked and will get in the way of a rescue effort. Please can you take them to the other shelter, and give them some hot, sweet tea?'

'Of course.'

And her mother was off, rounding up a couple of clearly traumatised women and gently shepherding them away.

Carrie rushed up to Sarah, who had already found Miss Arnott. 'What can *we* do?' she asked.

'There are several injured and trapped,' said Miss Arnott shortly. 'Our first aiders and stretcher bearers are already in there, our ambulance is in position and . . .'

'We'd better get in there . . .' said Carrie, stripping off her coat.

'Wait,' said Miss Arnott, reaching out a restraining arm. 'Are you trained? We can't have every Tom, Dick and Harry rushing in here and becoming a liability . . .'

'St Mark's Avenue ARP,' interrupted Carrie. 'I'm an ambulance driver, but I'm up to date with my first aid . . .'

Miss Arnott nodded and stood back. 'Careful in there,' she said.

Carrie nodded and swallowed hard. 'Ready, Sarah?'

'But where's everyone else?' said Sarah, looking around in panic. 'Where's the fire brigade? And we need more rescuers, more ambulance drivers, more *everything* . . .'

'Half of Richmond has been bombed,' said Miss Arnott flatly. 'Everyone's busy elsewhere. I'll keep radioing for assistance, but I really fear there's no one to help us.'

'Come on,' said Carrie, ducking instinctively at another explosion.

'You're in your *pyjamas*.'

'It's half past three in the morning.' Carrie took Sarah's arm. 'Come *on*. We're wasting time . . .'

Sarah stood frozen, eyes wide with fear.

'I can't!' she said, almost to herself.

Carrie could hardly believe her ears.

Sarah, who had always seemed so brave, was holding back.

But there was no time to argue, no time for anything . . .

Without another word, Carrie let go of Sarah's arm and

ran full tilt towards danger. Other people were doing the same and Harry, his face streaked with dust and soot, was standing by what had been the entrance, obviously about to head back in.

'What can I do?' Carrie shouted, without preamble.

Harry gestured inside. 'I think there are people trapped over to the left,' he shouted over the chaos. 'We're still trying to free a chap to the right.'

Carrie nodded, took a deep breath and dashed inside. It seemed everyone who could had already left and the shelter was eerily empty. The heat was overwhelming, and the air was thick with choking dust. Carrie's heart hammered in her chest as she weaved through the wreckage, stepping over fallen beams and broken bricks.

Surely, no one could have survived this.

Suddenly, a groan from beneath a pile of rubble made Carrie freeze.

She dropped to her knees, frantically pulling away chunks of stone and twisted metal. Her fingers started bleeding from the sharp edges, but she didn't falter. She kept digging, arms burning with the effort.

'Help!' a faint voice called from below.

Carrie gasped. It was a child's voice and she recognised it instantly.

'Eloise! Hold on, I'm coming!'

She pushed a piece of plasterboard to one side and revealed Eloise's face – dusty, scratched, but alive. Her brown eyes focussed on Carrie's.

'I didn't think anyone would come,' she whispered, her voice trembling.

'I'm here and I'm not leaving you,' Carrie said, her voice

steadier than she felt. 'Are you hurting anywhere?' she added, continuing to pull debris off the little girl.

'My leg,' said Eloise. 'But,' she added stoically, 'it isn't too bad.'

Carrie pulled off some more plasterboard and, yes, Eloise's leg was trapped beneath a large wooden beam. Nearby, masonry tumbled to the ground and the smell of burning grew stronger. Time was clearly of the essence . . .

Summoning every ounce of strength, Carrie grabbed hold of the beam. Her arms screamed in protest as it rose inch by inch – but it was simply too heavy and she had no choice but to lower it back down as gently as she could.

'Help!' she called.

Hopefully Harry or one of the others would hear her . . .

But there was nothing.

And then someone materialised by her side.

'If we both lift at the same time, we might just be able to do it.'

Carrie recognised that voice too.

It was Mabel, already rolling up the sleeves of her pink flannel pyjamas.

Carrie had a thousand questions – Mabel's job, Bobby's scarf, the books in the basement – but she pushed them firmly away. She counted to three and together the two young women heaved the beam with all the strength they could muster. Slowly, slowly the beam rose above Eloise's legs and, this time, the child managed to roll herself free. There was blood oozing from a nasty wound on her leg, but otherwise she seemed to be relatively uninjured.

Carrie and Mabel manoeuvred the beam to one side and let it drop.

'We probably shouldn't move her until she's been checked over,' said Carrie, trying to remember her training.

Above them, the shelter groaned ominously.

'Bugger that,' said Mabel, succinctly. Crouching down, she scooped Eloise up and headed for the exit. 'By the way,' she said, over her shoulder, 'I have a horrible feeling there's another child still in here.'

Carrie's heart tripped into overdrive. 'What makes you think that?'

'Because until ten minutes ago I were helping Eloise, Maggie and Clara with their maths homework,' said Mabel. 'I'd promised them the next time there were an air raid – no matter how late – I'd join them in here and we'd have an improvised Homework Club. It helps stop them panicking. That's why I were in here rather than under the Remembrance Club. Clara's already out and reunited with her mother, Eloise is here, safe and sound, but I don't think Maggie's been seen. Have *you* seen her, Eloise?'

Eloise shook her head. 'No,' she said, her bottom lip trembling. 'But my head was covered up so I couldn't see *anything*. Please let me help look for her.'

Despite the situation, Mabel smiled. 'I don't think so,' she said. 'I'm not sure you can even stand. Let's get you out of here and get your leg looked at.' She turned to Carrie. 'I'll be back,' she said, simply.

And she was gone.

Quashing a wave of fear, Carrie turned back to the pile of rubble and started moving it to one side as quickly and carefully as she could, calling Maggie's name every few seconds. It was back-breaking work and, before long, she was covered in sweat, her hair limp and slick. She made a concerted effort to ignore the creaking sounds and could only pray the ceiling wouldn't suddenly crash down on her head.

But wait.

What was this?

A tangle of red hair in the debris.

Heart in mouth, Carrie redoubled her efforts, pulling away plasterboard and wooden planks, until she had uncovered Maggie's head and chest. The little girl's eyes were closed and she was so still and white that at first Carrie thought she was dead. Then, to her relief, she felt breath on the back of her hand and saw the weak pulse at Maggie's throat. The child didn't have any obvious injuries, but that was no reason for complacency; there was still the rest of her body to uncover, and goodness knew what was going on internally.

Carrie continued desperately pulling off the rest of the debris and crying out for help. There were men digging furiously in the furthest corner of the shelter but – although one shouted out something incomprehensible to her – no one came to her assistance. But here was Mabel – just as she had promised – crouching down beside Carrie and starting to pull away bricks and rubble like a Trojan.

Finally . . . finally . . . Maggie was free.

Carrie picked her up, and she and Mabel ran for the opening. And, just as they emerged from the smoke and ruin, there was a crash behind them. Turning around, Carrie saw that part of the shelter had collapsed.

They hadn't been a moment too soon.

Carrie's legs began to buckle beneath her. Sarah rushed forward, taking Maggie's weight, and easing her to the ground. Carrie collapsed next to her, panting, her hands shaking uncontrollably.

Sarah turned to Carrie, her face a mix of relief and shame. 'I'm sorry. I couldn't . . .'

Carrie shook her head. 'It doesn't matter,' she said. 'You're here now.'

As Sarah turned and started checking Maggie over, Carrie shut her eyes in exhaustion.

She had always thought that Sarah was the brave one, the one who could face anything without fear.

But, in that moment, Carrie had been the one to dive into danger.

Bravery, it seemed, wasn't always about being the strongest or the best at something.

It was about stepping forward when no one else would.

Chapter Thirty-Two

Friday 29 November 1940

But, of course, they weren't out of the woods yet.

'Both these girls need to get to a hospital as soon as possible,' barked Miss Arnott. 'Eloise is losing a lot of blood and, although Maggie has come round, I fear she might have internal injuries. The trouble is our ARP ambulance is already completely full and is about to leave. Their mothers are in there, but we simply can't fit the girls in, too. We'll need to find some other way of transporting them. Hopefully, when the wretched alarm goes off, some of the other ARPs will lend us theirs, but that might be . . .'

Carrie jumped to her feet, fully alert again. 'What about the Poppy Factory van?' she suggested.

It was the obvious solution.

Miss Arnott nodded, her brow clearing. 'Good thinking,' she said. 'Could you . . . ?'

'I could,' confirmed Carrie. 'I've driven it back from the Lake District, so I know what I'm doing. If I could have Sarah and Mabel giving first aid in the back . . .'

'Of course,' said Miss Arnott. 'Drive around here – don't worry about the grass. Go. *Go.*'

And Carrie went, running around to the back of the Poppy Factory. As always, the van was unlocked – the keys in the glove compartment – and moments later, she was roaring around to the Remembrance Club and pulling up on the lawn. Whilst she'd been gone, the others had found mattresses and blankets and, in no time at all, the back of the van had been fitted out as a makeshift ambulance and the patients carefully installed inside.

Moments later, they were on their way.

Carrie, glancing in the rearview mirror, could see the Poppy Factory men – backlit by fire – still desperately digging, and knew that the image would be burnt onto her brain forever . . .

But there was no time to dwell on that tonight . . .

She turned right out of the Poppy Factory and headed towards the bridge, desperately trying to get to grips with the controls being on the 'wrong' side. The whole town was lit by a ghostly, orange glow – how many bombs had there *been*? – but at least it meant that she could see, and she drove as quickly and as smoothly as she could . . .

Almost immediately, however, they hit problems; a huge backlog of ambulances, police cars and horse-drawn vehicles leading to the town centre and, soon afterwards, the traffic ground to a complete standstill.

A policeman on the side of the street stuck his head into the van.

'You'll not get through that way, love,' he said. 'The townhall's been struck – there's bricks and goodness knows what all over the road. It's completely impassable.'

'Oh no,' said Carrie, heart sinking. 'Only, I've got two injured children in the back that I need to get to hospital . . .'

'Kingston County's your best bet,' said the bobby. 'Should be a bit quieter too – the Royal will be stretched to breaking point. I'd turn around here if I were you.'

Carrie nodded. Thank goodness she had prepared for this eventuality and knew exactly where she was going. She executed a rather ragged three-point turn, and seconds later the van was hurtling down the country lanes to Kingston. It was darker here – the bombing clearly hadn't extended this far – and for the first time in what felt like hours, Carrie began to feel a little safer.

But what about everyone else?

Bobby and the rest of the Saints.

Daisy.

Even Pa.

'How much further?' said Sarah, from the back. 'I'm putting as much pressure as I can on Eloise's wound, and I've tied a tourniquet as best I can, but she's still losing blood.'

'Nearly there,' said Carrie, gritting her teeth and putting her foot down. 'You'll be all right, Eloise. Hang on in there, there's a good girl.'

Minutes later, they were pulling up in front of Kingston County Hospital and then it was all hands on deck, reassuring the girls, summoning porters and finding trolleys. Despite what the policeman had said, Kingston Hospital was rammed as well, and all this took quite some time, but eventually the children were taken away, leaving Carrie, Mabel and Sarah standing on the front steps.

'Will they be all right?' said Carrie, suddenly close to tears. 'They're so young and lovely – I couldn't bear it if anything happens to them.'

'Fingers crossed they'll pull through,' said Mabel, patting Carrie on the back. 'They're in the best place now, thanks to you.'

'Better head back, I suppose,' said Sarah. 'Not that I was much help last time . . .' she added somewhat shamefacedly.

'Rubbish,' said Mabel, robustly. 'You gave first aid to both girls – and that's just as important as anything else.'

Sarah smiled ruefully as the three girls piled into the front cab – Mabel in the middle – for the journey back to the Poppy Factory.

Only they couldn't get out.

Another ambulance, a police car and two private cars were blocking the exit whilst they offloaded their own patients.

There was nothing the three girls could do except sit it out.

'What a night,' said Carrie, stretching her arms above her head and suddenly feeling inordinately tired.

'Dreadful,' agreed Sarah. 'I really hope everyone is all right. It looked pretty grim in one corner.'

'It did,' said Mabel. 'Those poor sods. Still, at least Miss Bateman would be proud that the "Poppy Girls" pulled together when it counted.'

Carrie knew that Mabel was only making a jokey comment to lighten the atmosphere, but, nonetheless, the words rankled. She hadn't intended to say anything – not here, not now – but suddenly her mouth opened by itself and words she had no control over started spilling out.

'Only we're not the "Poppy Girls", are we?' she said coldly. 'I'd say that's never been further from the truth.'

She held her breath.

She probably shouldn't have said that, but there was no putting the rabbit back in the hat now.

*

366

For a second, there was complete silence. Carrie felt Mabel stiffen beside her.

'I say, that's a bit rum, old girl,' said Sarah, sounding hurt.

'Yes,' said Mabel. 'If you're talking about Sarah not coming into the shelter, we *all* did our bit . . .'

'Of *course* I'm not talking about that,' said Carrie.

'What then?' said Mabel. 'We've just worked together to rescue those girls, ain't we? *And* we set up Little Poppies – or at the very least, we came up with the idea. I'd say we're very much the Poppy Girls . . .'

'Oh, come off it, Mabel,' said Carrie crossly. 'Over the past few months, you've done nothing but lie to us. Lie upon lie upon lie. We know you don't work at the Chrysler Factory for starters and you seem to practically live in Richmond Park . . .'

Mabel opened her mouth to reply, but Sarah was too quick for her. 'I'm not sure this is the time or the place,' she said. 'But if we're really going to talk about it now, you told Carrie you worked with Bobby, so I went up to Starfish to check out your story and they'd never heard of you.'

Mabel gasped out loud. 'You did *what*?' she said. 'What's Starfish got to do with anything? How have you even *heard* of it?'

'Bobby told me,' said Carrie, with a wry laugh, although it really wasn't very funny. 'To be fair, they'd never heard of *him*, either, but that's neither here nor there. I don't know how you two know each other, but I'm not sure that matters. True Poppy Girls wouldn't be all secretive with each other's fellas, now, would they? All that malarky with his scarf . . .'

'This is just ridiculous,' said Mabel, looking from one

367

to the other. 'There ain't nothing between me and Bobby. And I wrote to tell you exactly that.'

'No, you didn't.'

'I did,' said Mabel. 'I promise you, I dropped it off with your parents after you found me with Bobby's scarf.'

Carrie hesitated. Was it possible that Ma and Pa *still* hadn't handed on all her mail? Maybe she should give Mabel the benefit of the doubt – on this at least.

Sarah had no such qualms. 'I'm beginning to think your promises don't mean very much, Mabel,' she said.

'Pardon me?' said Mabel. 'All right, so I lied about me job, but I can explain . . .'

'There's more to it than that,' said Sarah. 'I'm beginning to think you lie *and* you steal. Why, only this evening, Carrie came to find me all upset because she'd found out you've been stealing books.'

There was a charged silence, which seemed to go on for an eternity.

Damn Sarah and her big mouth.

Damn her!

Carrie really hadn't intended for that to get out, but – it was all her fault for starting it.

Mabel cleared her throat, turned to Carrie, and said in a quiet, flat tone, 'You know about the books?'

Carrie was suddenly wary. She had no idea what she had stumbled across, no idea who Mabel even *was* anymore. To be honest, she *had* hoped that Mabel would have no idea the books were even there.

'I'm probably putting two and two together and making twenty-two,' she blustered.

'What do you mean, Carrie?' burst out Sarah indignantly.

'In case you've forgotten, you've just interrupted my shift to tell me there are books in the basement of the Remembrance Club and that you don't know what to do about them.'

Oh, goodness.

Mabel flopped back on the seat. 'Oh, my God,' she said. 'You must both promise me here and now not to tell *anyone* about what's in the basement.'

There was another, even more charged silence, and then Carrie found her tongue. 'Why not?' she said hotly. 'You can't creep around and lie to us and then just expect us to keep your secrets. What exactly is going on down there?'

Mabel hesitated. 'You've actually seen the books? You know what's there.'

'Yes. All sorts of rare and, I assume, priceless manuscripts.'

'*What?*' exploded Sarah. 'I thought we were talking about half a dozen dog-eared Agatha Christies filched from Richmond Library!'

'Hardly,' said Carrie, dryly. 'I was so shocked I didn't manage to get across the significance to you, and then the bombs started going off.' She turned to Mabel. 'And now's the time for answers, don't you think?'

Mabel let out a huge sigh. 'All right,' she said. 'So, I don't work for Chrysler and I never have done.'

'Well, *that's* perfectly clear,' said Carrie.

The traffic finally began to move. Carrie slid the van into gear and eased out.

'I don't know why I ever said I did when it's completely in the opposite direction from where I *do* work,' Mabel continued. 'I suppose I were that flustered that day in Woollies I just said the first thing that came into me head. I never thought you would overhear, nor that we would become such good friends. I should have just told you I'd made up something to get those girls off me back . . .'

'So, where *do* you work?' asked Carrie.

Mabel sighed. 'I still can't tell you,' she said. 'And I know that sounds suspicious, but I *can* tell you it's a government department based in the park. Most of what I told you were true, Carrie; when we found we was moving to Richmond, me old maths teacher put in a good word for me with her brother and his department took me on. It just weren't at Chrysler! And, it's not the main thing we do, but we also help sort out taking books into safekeeping. Important books that could be lost forever if the worst happens.'

Carrie turned to Mabel and saw that her eyes were bright in the dimly lit ambulance. What she was saying seemed almost absurd, yet something in her voice told Carrie that she wasn't playing games.

'Why books?' demanded Sarah, sounding altogether less impressed. 'I mean . . . why not people? Surely keeping *people* safe is the most important thing of all.'

'Of course,' said Mabel. 'I ain't disputing that. But these books hold more than words. They're symbols, knowledge, memories. Some of them go back centuries . . . first editions, illuminated manuscripts, the very stories and ideas that make us who we are.' She paused, as if choosing her words carefully. 'If London falls, they'll need to be somewhere safe, tucked away for future generations.'

'But why here?' persisted Sarah. 'And why *you*, for that matter? I mean, five minutes ago, you were just a schoolgirl.'

Mabel laughed. 'Good point,' she said. 'There's nothing special about me at all. I were just in the right place at the right time. The books ain't going to *stay* at the Remembrance Club – they're en route to a coalmine in Wales where they really will be safe. But the powers-that-be were on the lookout for somewhere close to London; somewhere they could be gathered, catalogued and prepared for transport further afield. I just suggested the basement. It's close enough to London to make sense, we have deliveries all the time, so no one bats an eyelid at the extra vans and – we thought! – it were out of reach of the heaviest bombing. And, of course, at that point, we had no idea an air raid shelter would be created so close by. Me parents are in charge of the whole operation now. Not me.'

'Who else on the estate knows?' asked Carrie.

'Apart from me parents, just Major Armstrong,' said Mabel. 'No one else. I trust it will stay that way?'

'Of course,' said Carrie.

'It all begins to make sense, now,' said Sarah. 'You spending half your time in Richmond Park, bawling out everyone who went down to the basement of the Remembrance Club. And only a truly good egg would have thrown themselves into danger like you did tonight . . .'

Mabel smiled. 'Well, there's good and bad in everyone,' she said. 'So, I wouldn't say that last one necessarily rules out me being up to no good. But, still, it's good to know we're all on the same side . . .'

'What about Bobby?' interrupted Carrie. She hardly dared to ask. 'Where does he fit into all this?'

Time seemed to hang still whilst she waited for the reply.

'Bobby is incidental to the whole thing,' said Mabel, firmly. 'He works at the same place as me, and we're pals. That's it. He knows about the books because he sometimes helps with the logistics. And last week – the day you saw me with his scarf – a couple of books had arrived at work rather than being transported directly to the Remembrance Club. I should have gone through the official channels, but I decided to just sneak them back in me bag and pretend they was drinks. Bobby suggested I stuff his scarf on top to make sure the books stayed hidden. It were as simple as that, I promise you.'

'Oh goodness.' It was just dawning on Carrie that she had done Bobby a terrible injustice. She had believed the worst of him and shut off all communication without listening to anything he had to say.

'At that point, I didn't know he knew you,' Mabel continued. 'I certainly had no idea he were Mr Two! He'd once mentioned he were smitten with a girl called Lyn from the estate, but we're strongly encouraged not to form personal attachments. I know he were in a quandary as to what to do. Of course, I should have worked out that Lyn were you . . .'

Despite the awfulness of the night, happiness surged through Carrie.

Bobby liked her and she liked him.

If only it wasn't too late . . .

Chapter Thirty-Three

Friday 29 November 1940

The next couple of hours were bedlam.

The diggers were still digging when Carrie pulled up onto the Poppy Factory lawn and it looked like outside help *still* hadn't arrived.

Carrie had no sooner pulled on the handbrake than she and Sarah were called upon to transport more people to hospital. As the two loaded their patients into the back of the Poppy Factory van, Carrie tried to keep her eyes from a couple of figures lying over by the hedge, dressing gowns over their faces. The figures were heartbreakingly small . . .

When they arrived back from Kingston Hospital an hour later, the little pile of bodies had risen to seven.

'Oh, no!' Carrie's hand fluttered to her chest.

Miss Arnott nodded grimly. 'Help never came, so our menfolk and womenfolk have had to dig them out themselves.'

'Who were they?' Carrie hardly dared to ask.

Matter-of-factly, Miss Arnott reeled off a list of seven names, and Carrie broke down. She simply couldn't help it. Mothers, daughters and sons – children a few years older or a few years younger than her – who wouldn't live to see the new dawn.

Miss Arnott patted her on the shoulder. 'There was nothing that could have been done,' she said. 'They were all killed instantly. And, if it wasn't for the bravery of you and your friends, the total tonight would have been even higher. You can be very proud of yourselves for that.'

Carrie gave her a weak smile. 'Can I help take them to the mortuary?'

'No need,' said Miss Arnott. 'Help is finally on its way.'

'Carrie.'

She span around.

Pa was walking towards her, his face grave. Carrie braced herself for a verbal onslaught, but then caught herself. What, really, did she have to feel ashamed about?

She had done her best and Pa couldn't ask any more from her than that.

But, to her surprise – to her *amazement* – Pa wrapped her in a huge hug. Carrie's arms hung loosely by her sides for a moment, but then she allowed herself to hug her father back. For a long moment, the two just stood there and then Pa pulled away and placed his hands on Carrie's shoulders.

'It's a dark day for the factory today,' he said. 'Major Howson will be turning in his grave.'

The old, familiar resentment and irritation bubbled to the surface.

'It's a darker day for those whose loved ones have been killed,' she replied, hating the tartness clearly audible in her tone.

Pa gave her a sad smile. 'That's what I meant, darling,' he said. 'But, sometimes, the things I say come out wrong and I could curse myself for it. I don't have your gift of eloquence – you have your mother to thank for that.' Then, without waiting for a response, he offered Carrie his arm. 'Walk with me for a moment, will you? There will be all sorts of unpleasant duties to perform in due course, but first of all I want to do the most important thing and that is to apologise to you.'

Carrie glanced up at him in surprise. 'Really?' she said. 'What for?'

She didn't know quite why she was surprised. After all, there were many, *many* things her father might justly be apologising for – and, frankly, not before time.

'For trying to keep you safe,' said Pa. He sketched a wave at his leg with his free hand. 'And for trying to stop history repeating itself.'

A gasp escaped Carrie's lips.

'Like Santayana,' she burst out.

'Who's that?' asked Pa. 'Do I know him?'

Carrie smiled. 'He's a philosopher,' she said. 'He's brilliant and he says pretty much what you've just said. You've got to understand the past in order to stop it happening again.'

'And that is why you're heading to university just as soon as this war is over,' said Pa, squeezing her arm. 'I've never held much for philosophy myself – and this chap may be right – but what I've learnt these last few weeks is that caging someone and clipping their wings isn't the right way to keep them safe.' He paused a moment and then continued. 'Miss Arnott told me all about your efforts tonight,' he said, his voice thick with emotion. 'Miss Bateman told me what you'd been doing at St Mark's Avenue. I can't tell you how proud I am of you for all that – to say nothing of Little Poppies. There's strength and a courage in you that I haven't appreciated until now.'

Carrie stared at her father, searching his face.

How long had she waited for him to say these words?

'I didn't think you'd ever say anything like that,' she admitted, her voice catching. 'I've always felt like I wasn't good enough. I just felt like I was always *trying* to prove myself and falling short.'

Pa smiled, his expression softening further. 'My generation aren't as good as yours at saying how we feel,' he said. 'It was all "stiff upper lip" and "spare the rod and spoil the child" with ours. But let me tell you, once and for all, that you've done more than prove yourself. You've shown bravery and compassion in ways I could never have expected. I've seen you face challenges head-on, work tirelessly and give everything you have. I'm realising only now just how much you've grown.'

Carrie felt a lump form in her throat. 'Thank you, Pa. I'm just doing what I can. Like we all are.' She took a deep breath. 'Like *you* are. I do understand how much you care for the Poppy Factory, and I do know you have its best interests at heart.'

It felt good to say that out loud.

Her father grunted. 'Going forward, I need to make sure I have my family's best interests even more close to heart,' he said.

The two of them had crunched along the gravel paths away from the ruined shelter and now found themselves going into the old pet cemetery.

Carrie's breath caught in her throat.

Would they – *could* they – acknowledge what had happened the year before?

It was now or never . . .

Carrie took a deep breath, but Pa was too quick for her.

'I never thought the flowers I planted would have lasted as well as they did,' he said. 'Took some tending, the thirsty little buggers . . .'

Carrie gasped, both at the uncharacteristic bad language and at what her father was saying. She took a tentative step forward, her pulse quickening.

'It was . . . *you* who planted them?' she said. 'For some reason, I thought it was Mabel and Sarah.'

Pa glanced down at the small grave. 'I've been coming here for a while now,' he said. 'I didn't think it was something you'd want to talk about.'

Carrie felt a knot in her chest. All this time, she had hated him for destroying Marigold. He had been so cold, so unfeeling. But now, knowing he had tended to the grave with such care, she realised there'd been something she hadn't understood.

'You didn't even seem to care when we lost her,' Carrie said softly, the words out before she could stop them.

Her father's face tightened. 'I cared how upset you were, Carrie,' he said, 'much more than I let on. I thought I was doing the right thing by putting on a strong face. I didn't want you to see me upset because I thought it would just make it harder for you.'

Carrie swallowed. 'She was mine,' she said fiercely. 'I *loved* her.'

Pa nodded and his eyes glistened as he met Carrie's gaze. 'I know,' he said. 'I thought I was protecting you by making the decision, but I was wrong.'

Carrie looked at her father, *really* looked at him, for the first time in what felt like years. His shoulders seemed heavier, his face older, but the rigidness she'd always associated with him had gone. Spontaneously, she reached out and hugged him.

'She's in Devon.'

Pa's words were so quiet, they were little more than a breath.

Carrie pulled away. 'I don't understand?' she said. 'Is Devon a euphemism for heaven, or something?'

'I don't know,' said Pa. 'They rhyme – so perhaps. But I'm pretty sure that Okehampton isn't.'

Carrie wrinkled up her nose. 'I still don't understand . . .' she started.

'I couldn't do it,' whispered Pa. 'At the last moment, I ruddy couldn't do it. I sent Marigold off to Okehampton with Mrs Henderson, who used to live in the flat on the bottom floor.'

Carrie gasped.

'No, you didn't!' she said, hope – nonetheless – flaring in her chest.

'I really did,' said Pa, matter-of-factly. 'I'm an absolute hypocrite! The old lady sends me updates from time to time. I should have told you, but – fool that I was – I thought it more important to keep up appearances and let people think we'd followed government advice.'

'You could have told *me*!' Carrie burst out furiously.

'I know,' said Pa. 'But I thought you were too young, that you wouldn't be able to keep the secret. I'm sorry, Carrie. For this. For being so distant. For everything. And tonight, there was a moment when I thought I had lost you and I realised I had got everything so terribly, badly wrong.'

Carrie was laughing and crying as well. 'I forgive you, Pa,' she cried. 'Marigold's *alive*.'

'We'll have her home any time you like.'

Carrie considered. 'I never thought I would say this, but I think, on balance, Marigold would be happier where she is,' she said. 'At least whilst the bombs are falling. Anyway, what about Mrs Henderson? She's probably grown to love her, too. We can't just take her away again. The important thing is that Marigold's *alive*!'

Her father smiled. 'You're a good person, Carolyn Harper. We'll talk about all this later, but, in the meantime, there are neighbours to mourn and arrangements to be made and I must pray for the strength to lead from the front.'

'Just do it from the heart, Pa,' said Carrie. 'You can't go too far wrong, then.'

Pa nodded. 'With you and your mother beside me, I can never go too far wrong. Shall we face the music?'

Carrie nodded and took her father's arm again. The two turned their back on the gravestone and walked resolutely away from the cemetery.

'Lyn!'

Carrie had no sooner arrived back on the bowling green lawn than someone bounded up to her. With all that had been going on, it took a moment or two to realise that it was Bobby. Despite everything, Carrie glanced up at her father nervously, wondering how he might react. But Pa just squeezed Carrie's hand, nodded affably at Bobby, and disappeared off to join a nearby group of people.

Carrie turned to Bobby, suddenly realising how happy she was to see him.

'I came as soon as I could,' he said. 'Another house has been hit in St Andrew's Avenue and then, of course, we weren't allowed to stand down until the all clear sounded – and then I dashed around here as quickly as I could. And thank goodness you're all right. I know what you wrote in your letter and, of course, I respect all that and you can tell me to go away again . . . but I just had to . . .'

Despite the truly dreadful evening, joy surged through Carrie.

Bobby had been looking for her.

Worrying about her.

She flung her arms around his neck, and hugged him tightly. 'Oh, Bobby. I'm sorry,' she said. 'I've been such an awful ass.'

'Me too,' said Bobby, hugging her back. 'I'm sorry for not being more transparent. I'm particularly sorry for my ruddy scarf – that's caused no end of trouble – but I promise you there never has been and there never will be anything between me and Mabel Green.'

Carrie pulled away. 'I know, Bobby,' she said. 'I *know*.'

Bobby frowned at her. 'You *know*?' he echoed. 'What do you know, exactly?'

'Well, I don't know if I know *everything*, but I know that you and Mabel work somewhere top secret that's nothing to do with Starfish. I know about the books in the basement and that they're on their way to Wales. And I know that Mabel borrowed your scarf to cover a couple of books that she was smuggling into the estate. Is that enough, for starters?'

'Blimey.' Bobby looked completely nonplussed. 'Well, what a very surprising girl you are. I'm sure Mabel had good reasons for telling you all this?'

'She did!' said Carrie. 'I wriggled down a coal hole and found the books!'

'Well!' said Bobby. '*That's* a story for another time. Look, I'm sorry I lied to you by implying I worked at Starfish. We're told to keep work very hush-hush and I was playing it by the book. In fact, they encourage us not to form any . . . significant friendships if we can help it, and I intended to play that by the book too. No romance. No distractions. And then, I met you . . .'

He petered out and Carrie couldn't help but laugh.

'So, that's why you left me high and dry?' she said. '*Twice.*'

Bobby laughed ruefully. 'I'm sorry,' he said. 'Believe me, it was hard . . .'

Carrie smiled. 'Well, I'm sorry too,' she said. 'I jumped to conclusions and I didn't give you a chance to explain yourself. That was very wrong of me.'

'Apology accepted.'

'And I'm not even going to ask you where you do work,' said Carrie.

'Well, ask it or not, I'm going to give you the bare bones. Mabel and I are part of something called Phantom Regiment . . . a small group, working in the shadows, to mislead enemy forces about military strategies.'

'Wow!' said Carrie, full of wonder. 'So, what do you actually do?'

'Oh, lots of things,' said Bobby. 'Create fake units, make false radio transmissions, employ elaborate decoys . . .'

'Nothing serious, then?' said Carrie, pulling a face. 'And will you have to kill me, now that you've told me?'

'Not at all,' said Bobby. 'I haven't actually told you anything and, besides, I was going to tell you, anyway, because I think that you're exactly the type of person they would like to recruit. In fact, when I mentioned you to them, they seemed to very much agree. The fact that you've – presumably – single-handedly discovered our bookstore will, I'm sure, make them even keener to sign you up. Might that be something you're interested in?'

Carrie blinked in surprise. It was almost too much to take in, but working for that type of agency really would be quite something. Whatever Santayana might think, she knew now that it was up to the living to fight the good fight until the world was free. That would be the best way to honour those who had lost their lives.

She took a deep breath and turned to Bobby.

'I don't know,' she said. 'Maybe. But not tonight. Tonight is about recognising all the important things in life. Community. Family. The Poppy Factory. Love and loss and grief and sorrow . . .'

'Pulling together in the best and worst of times,' said Bobby.

'Friendship,' said Carrie, as Sarah – arm in arm with Harry – and Mabel came over to join them.

'Maybe more than friendship?' asked Bobby, arching an eyebrow at her.

Carrie smiled at him. '*Definitely* more than friendship,' she said, reaching up and kissing him on the cheek.

Then, with Bobby's arm around her shoulders, she turned and greeted the Poppy Girls.

'Look,' said Sarah, pointing straight ahead. 'It's getting light.'

And, so it was.

The first rays of the early morning sun were kissing the stark white lines of the Poppy Factory and bursting into life.

Acknowledgements

I am very lucky to have so many wonderful people in my life who have helped *The Poppy Girls* see the light of day.

Firstly, enormous thanks to my wonderful editor Madeleine Woodfield at Michael Joseph for giving me the opportunity to tell this story – and then for helping me to make it better. You're a star and here's to enormous success for both the Gooners and the Chairboys this season! Thank you to Bea McIntyre, Kay Delves and the wider MJ team for helping me to polish the manuscript and to my agent Safae El-Ouahabi at RCW for support, advice and always having my back.

A huge thank you to Dan Hodges, Communications and Marketing Director at The Poppy Factory for generously sharing information, showing me around the factory and estate, and answering my many and varied questions. Of course, any mistakes in the manuscript are mine alone.

A massive thank you to Cerrie Burnell for her enormously helpful inclusivity read and thank you to my friend John Print for his general advice on WW2. Likewise, any mistakes or inaccuracies are mine alone.

I read many books and articles whilst I researched this book, but one that I found particularly helpful was *Richmond at War 1939–1945* by Simon Fowler of the Richmond Local History Society which has proved invaluable – as well as being a cracking good read.

Writing can be a lonely old business, so thank goodness for lovely chums who are always there to support, encourage and pour the drinks. In particular, huge thanks to my writing pals in the NaNas, the Henley Writers and Writers on Thames.

A huge thank you, of course, to you the reader for choosing *The Poppy Girls*. I do hope you enjoyed it and, if so, that you will consider sharing it far and wide.

Thank you to the whole clan: Mum; Ingrid, David, Iain, Alexander, and Anna Hamilton; Tonia, Richard, Matthew, and Laura Lovell; UP; Liz, Chris, Louise, Michael, and Bex Smith; Mo, Lucy, and Gregory Harrison.

Finally, the biggest thank you to my lovely husband, John and to my fabulous children, Tom and Charlotte. I love you all xxx

On a station platform, with nothing to read,
and a four-hour train journey stretching ahead of him...

That's where the story began for Penguin founder Allen Lane.
With only 'shabby reprints of shoddy novels' on offer,
he resolved to make better books for readers everywhere.

By the time his train pulled into London, the idea was formed.
He would bring the best writing, in stylish and affordable
formats, to everyone. His books would be sold in bookstores,
stationers and tobacconists, for no more than the price
of a ten-pack of cigarettes.

And on every book would be a Penguin, a bird with a certain
'dignified flippancy', and a friendly invitation to anyone who
wished to spend their time reading.

In 1935, the first ten Penguin paperbacks were published.
Just a year later, three million Penguins had made their
way onto our shelves.

Reading was changed forever.

—

A lot has changed since 1935, including Penguin, but in the
most important ways we're still the same. We still believe that
books and reading are for everyone. And we still believe that
whether you're seeking an afternoon's escape, a vigorous debate
or a soothing bedtime story, all possibilities open with a book.

Whoever you are, whatever you're looking for,
you can find it with Penguin.